A
PLEDGE
OF
SILENCE

A PLEDGE OF SILENCE

FLORA J. SOLOMON

LAKE UNION
PUBLISHING

Text copyright © 2015 Flora J. Solomon

Published by Lake Union Publishing, Seattle

www.apub.com

Amazon, the Amazon logo, and Lake Union Publishing are trademarks of Amazon.com, Inc., or its affiliates.

ISBN-13: 9781477820865
ISBN-10: 1477820868

Cover design by Shasti O'Leary-Soudant/SOS CREATIVE LLC

Library of Congress Control Number: 2014946875

Printed in the United States of America

For those closest to my heart:
Art, Beth, Emily, and Andrew

CHAPTER 1

Little River, Michigan, May 1936

Margie Bauer hastily scanned the yard and front porch to see if anyone was watching before she kissed her boyfriend good-bye. What was supposed to be a quick peck turned into a lingering buss, but when she pulled back, Abe Carson's face followed hers, and he planted another smooch. She grinned, liking the sensations his kisses brought. "Call me later?"

"Gator," he said in return.

With schoolbooks in her arms, she jumped out of the Olds and took the porch steps two at a time, then turned to wave before opening the door and stepping into the kitchen. She heard tires squeal as Abe peeled onto the road.

"Is that you, Margie?" her mother said. "You're early. Daddy was going to pick you up at four."

She dropped her books on the kitchen table and rummaged in a drawer for a ribbon to tie up her curly red hair, which sat hot on her neck. "Abe drove me home, Mama."

"You know I don't like you riding with Abe. He's reckless. Yesterday he almost hit the Wilsons' dog."

"Abe's a good driver. The Wilsons should keep their dog out of the road."

At the kitchen table, her brother, Frank—all feet and elbows at fourteen years old—taunted, "Abe and Margie sitting in a tree. K-i-s-s-i-n-g."

"That's enough, Frank. Run out and tell your dad he doesn't have to pick up Margie. And, Margie, as long as you're here, change your clothes and dig up some new potatoes for dinner."

She drew a glass of water from the tap. "I can't. I have three costumes to finish. The dress rehearsal's tomorrow."

"Don't say *can't*. While you're in the garden, check the lettuce and onions. There might be enough for a salad. I'll help you with your sewing after dinner. There's a magazine and a letter for you on the hall table."

Margie glanced at the return address on the envelope and wrinkled her nose. She studied the model on the *Vogue* cover, then flipped through the magazine's pages, noting the slim cut of the jackets, the longer length of the skirts, and the muted colors coming for fall. With a sigh, she picked up the letter. She read the message from Grand Arbor Hospital School of Nursing congratulating her on her acceptance into their fall class. She stuck out her tongue and tossed the missive into the drawer of the table.

The phone rang. Answering it on the first ring, she listened, then said, "Hi yourself." She chatted with a smile on her face and a dance to her step. Covering the mouthpiece with her hand, she yelled, "Mama, can I go out with Abe tomorrow after dress rehearsal? I might be home a little late."

Mama's voice came from the kitchen: "Don't say *can*. Yes, you *may*."

It was the evening before Little River High School's debut of *The Pirates of Penzance*. Mangled lines and too many missed cues caused the cast and crew to be stressed. Backstage was frenzied with actors hurriedly changing costumes and throwing the worn ones aside. Margie picked up the flimsy garments and inspected them for damage. Hanging a poufy dress on a rack with a dozen others, she admired the rainbow of colors. With their bright cummerbunds and lacy bonnets, the dresses looked elegant enough for a modern Major General's bevy of daughters.

Through a space on the rack, she saw Abe approaching. His clothes hung easy on his frame like they did on the male models in *Vogue*; he had a certain flair and a cool, loose-jointed walk she liked to watch. She felt warm all over as he came near. "Boo," she said as she popped out from behind a pink dress.

He jumped, then brushed a forelock of blond hair out of his eyes. "Have you heard? Alan broke his arm."

Adding to the drama of the night, Alan, who played the Major General, had fallen into the orchestra pit during rehearsal and was taken to the hospital. Margie covered her mouth with her hand, and through her fingers she said, "That's awful."

"Yeah, well. The idiot doesn't know left from right. Are you about done? Let's get out of here." He helped her with her jacket and led her out the back door. A fine mist made the muddy parking lot slippery and transformed the streetlights to fuzzy orbs against the dark sky.

Abe revved the motor of his dad's Olds and peeled out into traffic, weaving around slower-moving vehicles. As he adjusted the wipers and opened the side vent to clear the fogged window, he missed seeing a red light and accelerated toward a car in the intersection.

"Abe!" Margie screamed as she grabbed for the dashboard.

He jerked the steering wheel to the left, causing the car to fish-tail and the tires to squeal. A horn blared, and Margie caught sight of a panicked face.

Glancing in the rearview mirror, Abe scoffed. "Aw, I missed it by a mile. You all right?"

"Yes," she said, though shaken, and thinking her mother may have been right about Abe's driving.

When they arrived at the diner, he trotted around the front of the car and opened her door. They hurried through the drizzle, their shoulders hunched up and their heads tucked in turtle-style. Inside, they snaked past occupied tables and display cases of creamy desserts to a red vinyl booth in the back. Margie hoped they wouldn't be discovered by their friends. Tonight, they were celebrating.

The waitress, a classmate who had recently dropped out of high school, provided paper place mats and cutlery. She looked tired, and a swell under her apron revealed her pregnancy. Margie glanced discreetly at the bump and wondered what it would be like to sleep with a man. She'd let Abe get to second base once, which both excited and frightened her. She said, "Hey, Candy, how y'doin'? Haven't seen you around."

Candy smiled thinly. "Hangin' in there. What can I get for you two?"

Abe ordered without looking at the menu. "Two hamburgers, no onions, two fries, and two Cokes."

When they were alone, Margie dug through her purse and retrieved a brightly wrapped gift. She placed it on the table. "Happy 'going steady' first anniversary." A whole year, and Abe was as funny and sweet as ever.

Abe reached in his coat pocket and produced his own gift, wrapped in white tissue paper and tied with blue yarn. He placed it on the table next to hers. "Bet you thought I forgot."

"Not you, fella. I have you trained." She nudged the gift toward him. "You first."

He tore the paper off and tossed it into the ashtray, then opened the box. "Peanut butter fudge! My favorite!" He offered her a piece and took one himself. "Yum. It's great, Margie. Will you give this recipe to my mom?" He smacked his lips in satisfaction and pointed to her gift. "Here, open yours."

She carefully untied the blue yarn. The tissue paper fell open, revealing a swirl of blues and greens, a touch of black, and flecks of brilliant yellow—a colorful silk scarf. She gasped at its splendor. "It's gorgeous!" Her expression changed quickly from joy to discomfort. "Abe, I can't accept this."

His smile collapsed. "Why not?"

She loved the scarf. It was beautiful, but her mother would never allow her to keep such an extravagant gift from Abe. It wasn't proper. She murmured, "This is way too expensive."

He blushed. "It's okay, Margie. It's my mom's scarf. She said the colors were perfect for you. She wants you to have it."

Margie was touched. She was fond of Mrs. Carson, who gave her piano lessons on the ebony grand in the alcove off the Carsons' living room. She treated Margie like a daughter. "Thank you. Both of you. The colors are my favorites." She folded the scarf into a triangle and draped it over her shoulders, caressing its softness. She had never owned anything so luxurious.

"Hey. Why are you two hiding?" Jim said, and Abe's tubby friend slid into the booth, scooting Margie over with his hip. She groaned inwardly, wanting Abe all to herself and knowing the conversation would turn to sports.

Jim helped himself to the fudge. "Have you heard the latest about Jesse Owens?"

The Ohio State track star had broken three world records and tied another while competing in a track meet at Michigan's stadium not long ago.

Margie slid the fudge out of Jim's reach. "Who hasn't? He's on his way to the Olympics in Berlin. I don't think he should go."

"Not go? You kidding? Why not?"

"Berlin. Hitler. Nazis. Don't you read anything but the sports page? Hitler won't even let his own Negro athletes compete. I read in the newspaper that the US might boycott."

Jim sniggered. "That won't happen. Sports is bigger than politics. Isn't that right, Abe?"

"Jesse doesn't care anything about politics. He just wants to compete. He'll leave those blue-eyes in the dust, and so much for Aryan supremacy."

The topic left a pall over the anniversary celebration. Hitler's name was often in the news. After building up the German army, his troops had entered the Rhineland, breaking the terms of the Treaty of Versailles. Meanwhile, Italy had invaded East Africa, and Japan had declared war on China. Margie had heard her dad say that the Great War he had served in was supposed to end all wars. Apparently, it wasn't so.

When the food came, Jim thankfully took that as his cue to leave. Margie and Abe wolfed down their hamburgers and fries, and then lingered over their Cokes. Stirring the ice with her straw, she asked, "When are you leaving for Chicago?"

"I'm not. My uncle lost his funding and had to close the art gallery. He can't use me this summer. He hung on as long as he could . . . This stupid economy."

"I'm sorry. You loved hobnobbing with the artsy set."

He shrugged. "Plans change. I'm not crying. I'll be taking flying lessons with Donny. His brother has a Taylorcraft monoplane."

"Where'd you get that kind of money?"

"I'll do grub work at the airfield in exchange for lessons."

She applied lipstick without looking in a mirror and blotted it on a thin paper napkin. "And this fall then?"

"Yeah. That's a bitch. Guess I'll live at home and go to the Michigan Normal College. Dad's almost happy. We're having this little altercation." Abe picked up a spoon and balanced it on his finger. It clanged to the table, and he shoved it aside. "I want to major in creative arts, and he wants me to major in anything else. He thinks I should teach, but I don't want to repeat his life."

Dr. Carson was chairman of the History Department at the college and relished a lively discussion. Margie learned more current events from animated debates over dinner with the Carsons than she ever had in a classroom. "You could do worse," she admonished him.

"Yeah, teaching's great, but why just *talk* about life when you can live it? I want to *live* life." Abe's exclamation drew the attention of the other diners. Grinning, he slouched back in his seat. "Why don't we run away and live life together? Where do you want to go?"

"New York City to study fashion design. I'd give my right arm." Fashion design had been her dream since she was a little girl making doll clothes. She loved sewing, and her teachers said she had a special talent. She pushed her unruly hair back. "But, you know Dad. He's set on me being a nurse. I've been accepted at Grand Arbor. I got the letter last night."

Abe reached across the table and took her hand. "It's not that far away."

"No, fifteen miles, but I have to live in the dorm. Dumb school rules."

The diner began filling with truckers coming in for the blue-plate special, a piece of lemon meringue pie, and a fifteen-cent shower in the shed around back. Margie watched two waitresses hustle between the tables and the long chrome-and-white counter, taking orders, delivering food, clearing dishes, and depositing dime tips into their red-checkered pockets.

"At least I'll be getting out of this town," she said.

"Nursing's not so bad."

"No, I guess not. I've been patching up sick farm animals most of my life. Can it be so different?"

"Geez, I hope so. I've seen your work."

She balled up the lipstick-stained napkin and threw it at him. "Don't show up on my doorstep in need of stitching up, fella."

Their eyes locked, and a brief look of sadness flickered in Abe's. Margie felt a sudden chill, and she folded her arms over her chest.

"Look, Margie. You'll love it in Ann Arbor. You'll be on the edge of the U of M campus. Think big university, think football games, think about all those beer parties."

"Yeah." She slumped back. "Think living in a women's dorm, think starched white uniforms, think clunky black shoes."

"You'll be cute in your white uniform."

"I'll itch underneath all that starch."

He glanced at the clock on the diner wall. "It's almost eleven. Your dad's watching the time."

"This year Daddy, next year some old biddy of a dorm mother. You guys have an easier time of it. Sometimes, I wish I'd been born male."

Abe laughed and said too loudly, "Love you any way you come, baby, with or without a dick."

Margie gasped, though she was not altogether surprised. Abe wasn't afraid to stir the pot for a reaction. His quirky irreverence made their dates fun and unpredictable. People at nearby tables whipped their heads around. A bull of a man stood and stepped toward them, his hands clenched into fists and his face skewed into an angry scowl.

Abe threw money onto the table and grabbed Margie's hand. They skittered around tables and out the back door to escape the diner's irate patrons. Jumping into the safety of the car and locking the doors, they guffawed at their boldness and careened onto the open road.

CHAPTER 2

Little River, September 1936

Conflicting emotions surged through Margie all summer, making her alternately keyed up and weepy. She sassed her mother, acted sullen with her dad, and found Frank's antics intolerable.

"Marry me, Margie," Abe pleaded. "I love you. I'll get a job. We can get by." She agreed. They could get by. But here she was, at her dad's insistence, standing in the parking lot of Grand Arbor Hospital School of Nursing saying good-bye. She leaned against Abe, not wanting him to leave.

"Be good," Mama said with a teary smile.

"You got enough pocket money?" her father asked.

She nodded, tears clouding her vision.

Frank looked as if he might cry too. "Heard this one, Margie? Nurse, nurse, I feel like a vampire. Necks please." He grinned. "Get it? Necks please?"

Margie grinned and slapped at the fedora he had taken to wearing. He had been telling nurse jokes all summer long and didn't ever seem to run out.

"Did you hear this one? Nurse, nurse—"

"That's enough, Frank," Dad said. "Get in the car."

Margie thought herself prepared for this parting, but she had misjudged how hard it would be. She blew kisses until the car and Abe's waves disappeared around the corner. Her tears turned to sobs. Looking for a place to be alone, she walked to a nearby park, where a young woman pushed a child on a swing.

"Higher, Mommy, higher!" he shouted.

Sitting on the merry-go-round, she struggled to compose herself while surveying her new surroundings. The ten-story hospital took up most of a city block on the northern edge of the University of Michigan campus. Behind her loomed the school of nursing and residence hall—twin boxlike, dark brick buildings with narrow windows. Everything looked foreign and unfriendly. Her tears continued to flow.

The little boy left the swing and ran to her. He had a smudge of dirt on his cheek and a scratch on his chin. He said, "You got a boo-boo?"

Margie sniffed. "No. No boo-boo."

"Then why you crying?"

"I'm not going to anymore." She dried her tears on her sleeve. "You like to swing?"

"Yes!" the child shouted. "Watch me, I can zoom." He ran in a circle, flapping his arms.

She took a drink from a fountain and splashed cold water on her face to wash off the salty tears. Waving good-bye to the engaging tyke, she walked back to the dorm, passing Miss Anita, the matronly clerk in the lobby who answered the phone and kept the students' time sheets that tracked their whereabouts. Margie's room was up two flights and left down the hall.

Through the slightly open door, she heard music and laughter. Through the crack, she saw a man and a woman dancing cheek-to-cheek, their bodies pressed together, the man's hand low on the woman's back. Margie said, "Knock, knock," and stepped inside.

The woman turned, revealing a flawless complexion and cornflower-blue eyes. Dark red nail polish matched what was left of her lipstick. She smiled, smoothed her blond hair, and held out her hand. "Hello, I'm Evelyn Ross. This here's Garth."

Margie shook Evelyn's outstretched hand and mumbled her name, but she couldn't take her eyes off the man. He was old. His face was a roadmap of wrinkles, his hair was gray-flecked, and his teeth were yellowed from cigarettes.

Evelyn wiped a smear of lipstick off her friend's craggy face and poked him in the chest with a manicured fingernail. "If you're playing poker tonight, you better scram. Thanks for the lift. Tell my little brother he's a marked man."

"I wouldn't want to walk in Little Brother's shoes," Garth chuckled.

Evelyn glanced at Margie, explaining, "My brother promised to drive me here today, but he stood me up." She turned the radio down. Rummaging in her purse, she took out a mother-of-pearl lighter and a pack of cigarettes. She offered one to Margie.

She had never been offered a cigarette before. Smoking was sinful, according to her minister back home, who preached about the evils of cigarettes and alcohol—steps down the slippery slope. "Uh, no thanks."

Evelyn addressed Garth: "Want me to walk you out?"

"I can find my way down the stairs."

She said, "Well, watch out for Anita Man."

He threw his head back and laughed merrily.

Evelyn chuckled while lighting her cigarette, then opened the door and nudged Garth through it. "Get a wiggle on, guy. Go see if you can cheer up the killjoy in the lobby."

He left with a wink and a wave.

Evelyn sat at her desk, her foot jiggling in time to the music. She tapped her cigarette on the rim of a silver ashtray, and smoke spiraled upward.

Margie perched on the edge of her bed, watching Evelyn smoke and wondering how she was going to live with a roommate so unlike herself. Feeling awkward, she didn't know how to sit, or what to say. When the song ended, she mumbled, "Um . . . was that your . . . um, boyfriend?"

Evelyn exhaled smoke through her nose and looked at Margie as if it were a ridiculous observation. "No. He's just a friend of my father's."

"Oh!"

A smile twitched on Evelyn's lips. "Employee, rather. He drove me over here on short notice. Least I could do was say thank you." She stubbed out her cigarette. "Would you mind helping me with this luggage?"

Annoyed by Evelyn's condescending attitude, she hesitated at first, but then thought it better not to get off on a bad foot. They hefted the heavy suitcases onto Evelyn's bed, and Margie shyly offered, "You want help unpacking?"

They shook wrinkles out of skirts, blouses, and jackets and put them on hangers. Evelyn placed purses on the top shelf, and Margie put matching shoes on the closet floor. She had never seen so many beautiful clothes. Caressing the softness of a cashmere sweater, she said, "You and your mother must have shopped all summer."

"My mother died when I was thirteen. Dad traveled a lot. My brother and I were pretty much on our own except for the housekeepers. I could tell you stories about that string of creepos."

Caught off guard for a moment, Margie was tongue-tied. Thoughts of her mother's warm embrace came to her mind, and she couldn't imagine being without it. "I-I'm sorry," she stammered.

"My mother was a nurse-midwife," Evelyn said proudly. "She taught women in the slums of Detroit about diet, hygiene, and birth control. Men gave her grief about *that*. She caught influenza from a fourteen-year-old patient who was pregnant by her brother."

Pregnant by her brother? Margie caught her breath, appalled by such open talk about an unmentionable subject. She felt warmth rising to her face, and she pretended to brush lint off her skirt so Evelyn wouldn't see her embarrassment.

Evelyn snatched two plain garments from the bottom of the suitcase. "And last but not least"—she held them at arm's length—"a *lovely* pink shirtwaist dress. And this *exquisite* white cotton apron. Notice the two-inch waistband, the four-inch hem, and the patch-pocket detail." She wrinkled her nose at the probationary uniform. "Can you believe these things? Pink?"

Margie laughed. She felt the same way about the ugly pink uniforms. "Why do you want to be a nurse?"

"It's as good as anything. I like people. I want to travel. I need adventure. My uncle is a rear admiral in the navy. He said if I got the education, he'd get me a job in a naval hospital. The navy has bases in exotic places all over the world."

Travel? Adventure? Margie had never equated nursing with anything but drudgery.

Life as a student nurse kept Margie busy from the six o'clock wake-up bell to ten thirty lights-out. She took classes in anatomy, chemistry, bacteriology, and nursing arts, and then worked long hours on the wards, where nursing instructors monitored her progress. Rules and dress codes dictated her conduct, and random room inspections stripped her of privacy. She wrote Abe long, maudlin letters complaining about domineering instructors and the endless days.

He wrote back about his own trials, living at home in a town he felt he'd outgrown. His dad continued to pressure him to give up his job at the airfield and to concentrate on his studies. The battle over his major course of study was ongoing. But all that had changed. After a big blowup with his dad, Abe had joined the army. She opened his latest letter.

Fort Sam Houston, Texas

My Dearest,
   I think I made a horrible mistake by joining the army. I feel like I'm in prison. All around me is a wire fence, and my world consists of a chow hall, a store, a head, a drill hall, and two dozen oversized doghouses called barracks, a.k.a. home. My days are all the same. Up at 5:30 a.m., to the drill field for PT (physical torment), then to breakfast, inspection, and Colors, followed by military training and lectures. I'm becoming proficient at hand grenades, bayonet drills, and saluting.
   Part of every day includes policing the grounds; cleaning the heads; washing, drying, and rolling clothes; and shining shoes. Evening is free time for letter writing and such. Then "Taps," the highlight of my day, when I can check out of this hell for a few hours. I've never been so tired and sore. The food is vile, and the water is putrid. To add more misery, I'm being inoculated against tropical diseases, and the shots make me feel sick for several hours.
   I took a series of tests for flight-training school. I have to make the cut. I'm having nightmares about being assigned to the infantry with a sadistic sergeant who finds my background in art and design offensive. There are some real bozos here, Margie. Hicks, hobos, and psychos. One good old boy won't shower, and another saves his cigarette butts in a can under his cot. The smell of those two makes me gag.

I'm sorry about this sad-sack letter. Wish me luck and please write. Your letters are the only bright spots in my days right now. Love you forever,
Abe

She kept his letters in a growing stack in her drawer to reread on nights when she was alone and listening to love songs on the radio. *Mrs. Abe Carson, Marjorie Olivia Carson*—she dreamed about their future together.

It was a bad day on the ward. Margie had slopped bathwater from the basin onto a patient's bed in the morning. It was a capital offense, according to the instructor, who was on her case for the rest of the day. Margie ambled to her dorm room, found a red pen, and then X-ed out February 28 on the calendar and flipped the page. She sighed at the realization—only six months done, twenty-eight long ones to go.

Stepping out of her uniform, she threw it on the floor, too exhausted to remove the button studs and collar and shove the cardboard-like garment down the laundry chute. She tumbled into bed, needing sleep.

A while later, Evelyn bounded in. "Hey, roomie! Wake up, kid."

Margie stirred and reluctantly opened one eye. "What?"

Evelyn danced a little jig. "I've got us dates. Two premeds I met in the lobby while I was discharging a patient."

"You picked them up while you were on duty? Are you crazy? You could be expelled." Margie pulled the pillow over her head.

Evelyn yanked it away and plopped down on the bed. "Only if I'm caught, and that won't happen. Come on! It'll be fun!"

Margie sat up. She was exasperated with this roommate who was always on the edge of trouble, even sometimes sneaking out at night and coming back reeking of alcohol. "I can't go out with anyone. I'm going steady with Abe—*remember?*"

"Margie! It's just a hamburger. I didn't see you at dinner, and you have to be hungry. Get your glad rags on." Evelyn rummaged in her closet, throwing expensive clothes on the floor.

Margie looked on with resentment as a silk blouse got kicked under the bed—if only she could afford such a luxury. Her stomach growled with hunger, and a hamburger sounded good. Remembering her bad day and the despotic instructor, she changed her mind about going out and got dressed. "Let's get out of here," she said, slamming the door behind her.

The premeds were waiting in a booth by the time the girls arrived at the diner. Evelyn scooted in next to the blond one, and Margie sat next to the one wearing glasses. He offered Margie a cigarette, which she accepted. They ordered Cokes and smoked while they chatted about classes and dorm life. The blond said, "We can get into a frat party. Are you girls interested?"

Evelyn perked up. "Of course we're interested, aren't we, Margie?"

Margie felt three pairs of eyes on her. She didn't want to go to a frat party. She heard they were wild affairs. "I can't. I have to work tomorrow."

Evelyn said, "Come on, live a little. I'll get you back before curfew."

"I've got a car," the blond said.

Feeling pressured, Margie said, "All right, but we better be back by curfew." She shot Evelyn a withering glance.

The fraternity house was jammed, a sea of bodies drinking, singing, kissing, and dancing close. Smoke from cigars and cigarettes floated to the ceiling, and the walls vibrated with sounds of shouting, laughter, and Duke Ellington booming from the Victrola.

Margie found herself enjoying the din, tapping her feet and swaying to the beat of the music. Her date walked over with two beers. She accepted the bottle and pondered what to do. Her parents wouldn't approve. Shrugging, she took a sip and found it bitter; she couldn't help her lips from screwing into a pucker. Her date laughed and nudged forward a bowl of pretzels.

Nibbling on pretzels made the beer taste better. Soon a warm, fuzzy feeling came over her that reminded her of Abe's kisses. Missing him and becoming morose about it, she sniffed back a tear. When she emptied the first bottle, her date gave her another. She snuggled into his neck and downed the second drink as they slow-danced in the crowded living room. He proved to be a good dancer, and when he held her close she pretended he was Abe. He provided a third beer, which she drank as they cuddled on a couch. Her vision was swimming and she couldn't help but giggle when he kissed her forehead and nose and put his hand on her breast.

She heard, "Hey, lover girl. We gotta split." It was Evelyn. "Get your coat on. We've got the car started."

Carrying her coat and stumbling, she followed Evelyn to a car waiting at the curb. Evelyn slid in beside a man whose hair was gray at the temples.

Margie looked around. "Where're our dates?"

"Who cares? Get in." Evelyn said to the old man, "Put the pedal to the metal, guy."

"Sure enough, babe." He put his hand on her knee, and she slapped it away.

They made it home with minutes to spare before curfew.

Standing on the sidewalk, a cold wind whipping their coats, Evelyn instructed, "Take some deep breaths. Pick a point on the front of the desk and don't take your eyes off it. Just walk. Try not to wobble. Can you do it?"

Margie took a deep breath. "I think so."

"Okay. No giggling. Here we go."

Sober-faced, they walked through the door straight to the desk where Miss Anita waited to check them in. Tonight the matron wore a striped blouse, and to Margie's eyes the stripes were moving in swirls. Her stomach lurched, and she quickly covered her mouth with her hand. Miss Anita looked sharply at her, but just then the telephone rang and diverted her attention. Evelyn signed both their names in the log and the time, 9:55 p.m. The girls tottered arm in arm through the double doors and up two flights of stairs to their room, where they fell on their beds and giggled until Margie almost peed her pants.

She spent the night with her head in the toilet. Headachy and queasy the next day, she mulled over the evening before—drunk! The things Evelyn got her into! And who was that old man?

So she asked. "Why the old guys?"

Evelyn smiled. "They're a little dangerous. Doesn't that excite you?"

A little dangerous? Margie found the response chilling.

Margie had a research paper on the benefits of massage due for her nursing arts class in the morning. She was half done typing the final copy on her portable Remington—a high school graduation gift from her parents—stopping only to consult one of the nursing journals stacked beside her.

Evelyn came into the room and sat on the edge of her bed, her shoulders slumped and brow furrowed. "Have you ever wanted to resign from the human race?" she asked.

It was an odd question from Evelyn, whom Margie considered a caring nurse who offered comfort and hope to her patients with her sympathetic ear and optimistic attitude. She liked that about Evelyn. Concerned, she said, "Are you all right?"

"I just read something that made me feel sick." She waved a *Time* magazine she was carrying. "The Japanese army invaded China's capital city, Nanking, and raped and slaughtered over three hundred thousand men, women, and children. Three hundred thousand! Even babies and pregnant women. A Japanese newspaper kept a running account of the number of heads severed by two soldiers, like it was a contest."

She opened the magazine and showed Margie a picture of a naked child sitting in the middle of the street with beheaded corpses strewn all around him. Even a quick glance was disturbing to her, and Margie quickly turned her head away. "It's foul. No one could be that vicious."

"Yes they can. My uncle has been there. He says Japanese soldiers are trained to be brutal from childhood." She held out the magazine to Margie. "You want to read about it?"

"No." She knew if she read the ghastly story it would haunt her during the day and work its way into her dreams at night. She resumed her typing, but found it harder to concentrate.

By senior year, woes over unyielding instructors and long workdays were replaced by concerns about the bad economy and the lack of available nursing jobs. Many hospitals had closed their doors, while others staffed their wards with senior-year students.

Margie sent out a dozen applications, and all were rejected or ignored. Private-duty nursing required experience and contacts, of which she had neither. Some of her friends opted to stay in school to specialize in midwifery or psychiatric nursing, but she cringed at the thought of more years as a student.

Evelyn said, "Come with me, kiddo. We'll join the navy together. My uncle will get you in."

"He'd do that for me?"

"Of course. You're my best friend."

The thought exhilarated Margie, but she had to decline. She and Abe were planning to get married as soon as he finished flight training in December.

She and her classmates attended a reception held by the American Red Cross, which was compiling a roster of nurses for the army and navy to draw upon in times of war or local disaster. After cookies, punch, and aggressive persuasion, most of the class filled out an application for a reserve nurse position.

"What was I thinking? I'm planning a wedding," Margie later said to Evelyn.

"Don't worry about it," Evelyn advised. "With more than twenty-two thousand nurses in the pool, nothing will come of it."

CHAPTER 3

Little River, June 1939

The auditorium at Grand Arbor Hospital hushed as Miss Denver stood to welcome families and guests to the graduation ceremony and introduce the speaker, Dr. Herbert P. Steele, director of medical services at the University of Michigan.

He kept his speech blessedly short. The graduates, he said, had sacrificed the freedom of their young lives to prepare to enter one of life's noblest professions. He counseled them on faithfulness, sympathy, tact, and cheerfulness, and then warned them of the undesirability of gossip. He advised them to minister to their own needs by reading good literature, taking walks in the open air, and spending a jolly evening with friends.

The auditorium was stifling hot, and Margie, struggling to stay awake, snapped alert when she heard, "May I close by wishing you Godspeed." The audience applauded. She stifled a yawn, wondering what century the old guy came from.

At the lively reception, people milled about and joyous cries rang out when families connected. Standing on tiptoes, Margie searched the crowd for her parents.

"Hey, beautiful," she heard.

Turning, she was face-to-chest with an army uniform. "Abe!" she cried as she clutched him in a bear hug. Pushing him back, she looked into his face, the best sight she had seen all day. "What are you doing here?"

"Waiting to squeeze you," he said, lifting her off her feet and whirling her around. "My leave coincided with your graduation. I thought I'd surprise you." He kissed her lightly. "Are you surprised?"

"Dumbstruck," she whispered, returning his kiss.

Her mother waved from across the room. She wore a royal-blue dress and a hat with a feather that swayed as she approached. Margie saw a loveliness in her mom she had never noticed before: her creamy skin, dark curly hair, and a slim but curvy figure. Mama glided through the crowd, smiling, her eyes crinkling at the corners.

"Where did this handsome soldier come from? You get better looking every time I see you, Abe." She bussed his cheek, leaving a smidge of red. She admired Margie's class pin and touched the brim of her nurse's cap. "It's official now, dear. You're all grown up. I'm so proud of you! I don't know where the years have gone."

Rimless glasses now framed Dad's eyes, something Margie didn't like to see, but his hug felt as hearty as always. He pecked at her forehead. "Margie, I couldn't be happier."

Frank, standing to one side, stood taller than Dad, and Margie took notice of the stubble on his chin. "Come here for a hug," she said. "When did you get so tall?"

"About the time you started shrinking," he retorted. "Bet you can't guess Dad's surprise."

"Hush up, Frank!" Dad glowered at his son. He shook Abe's hand. "How's the army treating you, young man?"

Abe's demeanor became gleeful as he related his experiences in primary flight school. "I learned basic maneuvers in an open-cockpit, two-seater biplane we called the Yellow Peril. It's a bugger on the ground. Too sharp of a turn sends it into a nose-over. That happened to a buddy. It wasn't pretty."

Dad guffawed. A generation ago he'd served as an army mechanic when all the planes were biplanes. Margie detected envy in his voice when he asked, "What's waiting for you when you get back?"

Abe revved again. "Ten weeks in Bakersfield, California, to learn flying in formation, at different altitudes, and nighttime flying. The trainer's faster, heavier, and more complex—a BT-13 Valiant, a single wing. The guys named it the Vibrator."

Dad nodded, nostalgia flickering in his smile, and Frank looked on admiringly.

The level of noise in the room continued to rise, the music too loud, and people had to shout to be heard. A contentious voice pierced the air: "Hitler, that son of a—" Heads turned, seeking the source.

Germany monopolized conversations whenever people gathered. The rogue country now occupied Austria and Czechoslovakia, and in a recent speech, President Roosevelt implied the US frontier had moved to the Rhine. The press reports were alarming.

Dad asked Abe, "Any new information?"

Abe nodded. "Hitler's Luftwaffe is getting stronger. His bombers are using a new technology; it's called an X-apparatus. By interlocking navigational beams, they can hit within three hundred yards of a target. They've almost wiped out the Polish air force using it. I heard Roosevelt has asked Congress for millions more dollars for defense."

Mama said, "Why would he need to? He promised we'd stay neutral."

Dad said, "He's asking Congress for a revision of the Neutrality Acts, Anna. Europe's a powder keg waiting to blow, and he wants to send aid to England. If England falls to Germany, we'll be in big trouble."

With Abe standing next to her in his uniform, Margie felt protective. She leaned against him, catching the smell of shaving lotion. She didn't want to lose him to a faraway war.

He leaned back against her as if to say, *Love you,* and asked, "How's the job hunt going?"

"Good! Mama worked her magic. I got hired as assistant director at the Ann Arbor chapter of the American Red Cross. I start two weeks from tomorrow."

The job offer came from Myra Walker, the director of the chapter and her mother's good friend. It was the only employment opportunity Margie had received, and she had mixed feelings about it. She would be living at home and taking the train to work.

"Look," she said to divert the attention away from herself, "they're cutting the cake. Does anyone want some?"

Evelyn stood in the crowd gathered around the cake table. She nudged Abe with her elbow. "You're a dreamboat of a man in a uniform, flyboy."

He flashed a smile of even white teeth. "You're a tease. I know all about you."

"Oh, I doubt that." Evelyn poked Margie. "Hey, kid, what rumors have you been spreading about me?"

Margie raised her eyebrows innocently. "Only the juicy ones, Evie. I promise. No others."

"All right, then. If it's only them and no others. I guess it doesn't matter anyway. I'm leaving town. Did Margie tell you, Abe? I'll be at the US Naval Hospital in Annapolis, Maryland. I wish she could come with me."

Abe said, "You'll have to stand in line. I have first dibs." He winked at Margie.

She slapped his arm. "First dibs? For all you know, I just might go with the highest bidder!"

After the festivities, Dad packed Margie's bags in the trunk of the car. As she slid into the back beside Frank, sadness settled over her. While Evelyn would be leaving for new adventures in Annapolis, and Abe would be learning to fly airplanes in sunny Bakersfield, she was returning to her childhood home. A rogue tear rolled down her cheek that she quickly wiped away. She should be happy. Her long years of education were behind her, and she had a coveted job waiting. Still, all she felt was cross.

Looks like I'm going nowhere.

CHAPTER 4

Little River, June 1939

Dad's surprise turned out to be bigger than Margie had dared expect. He handed her the keys to his Pontiac coupe and opened the driver's-side door. "I've been saving her for you, Margie. She runs as smooth as she did the day I bought her. She's yours now."

Speechless, she laughed in delight and kissed her father's beaming face. "It's wonderful. Thank you." The maroon car, with its black landau top, shone like a new penny.

Mama said, "He had it painted, and he polished all the trim by hand. Isn't it pretty?"

"I helped," Frank said, pointing out the wood-spoke wheels he had sanded smooth, the Chief Pontiac hood ornament polished to a high gloss, and the gray velour seats brushed clean and soft. "Can I borrow it sometime? I'd be careful. I'm a good driver," he insisted as he tipped his hat back.

Dad opened the hood and identified each engine part. She watched attentively as he demonstrated how to check the oil, clean the carburetor, and fill the radiator. He said, "Tomorrow, I'll show you how to change a tire. You need to know that."

They all piled in for a trip into town for ice cream, stopping to pick up Abe on the way.

That evening was warm, the sky was full of stars, and the smell of lilacs sweetened the air. Margie and Abe sat on her front porch swing, mindful only of each other. Cuddled up to him, she whispered into his ear, "I love you." Her hand ran down the front of his shirt and rested on his lap.

He fumbled with the buttons on her blouse, and she felt herself melting. "We better not. Daddy's still up." She leaned back against him. "December's getting close. We should start planning our wedding." She locked her fingers into his. "What do you think of a Christmas theme? The attendants in red satin and the church filled with poinsettias and holly? You'll need a best man and two ushers."

Abe gave the swing a push with his foot, starting it in motion, its squeak competing with the chirping of crickets. He took a deep breath, then said, "Promise you won't be mad?"

She tensed. "What?"

"December won't work."

"Why not?"

"I've been selected for advanced training. It's an honor. I can't pass it up."

"Can't we get married anyway?"

"Not as long as I'm in training. I'm sorry. Please don't look so disappointed." He tipped her chin up and kissed her lightly. "It's only six months."

"That long?" She felt her future and her face crumble.

"It's not so long, and with both of us working, we can build a nest egg. I'll open us a joint savings account and send you my paychecks."

"It's you, not your paychecks, I want, Abe. Where will you be stationed?"

"At an airbase in the desert north of Los Angeles. Muroc Bombing and Gunnery Range. It's desolate out there. I'll be living in a tent. It's no place for a woman to be, Margie."

"A bombing and gunnery range?"

"I'll be learning aerial combat. When I finish, I'll be qualified to fly fighter planes." He held her hand. "Is a June wedding okay? I promise you an extra-special honeymoon."

A year to wait. She loathed the thought of sleeping alone in her childhood bedroom while he was off learning to fly fighter planes. She tried to make light of it, but her voice sounded thin. "It better be an extra-extra-special honeymoon."

"I promise," he said, handing her a small box.

As he slid the engagement ring on her finger, the diamond sparkled like the brightest star in the sky, and her heart soared to the heavens.

Margie fussed with her hair and makeup, then slipped on a green rayon blouse and a slim-fitting skirt. She checked her image in the mirror and liked how she looked, but she felt blue. She watched for Abe's car from the front porch swing. Today was their last day together.

Mama came out and sat beside her. "Where are you and Abe going?"

"Ann Arbor. He wants to go through the art galleries and see what's new. He used to talk about owning one. Did I ever tell you that? His uncle owned a gallery in Chicago. Abe spent summers there and did odd jobs. He liked hanging out with the artists."

Abe pulled up in front of the house and waved through the car's open window. Margie slid over close to him. She hollered to Mama, "We're meeting friends for dinner. We might be home late."

As they drove, Margie considered Abe's decision to become a fighter pilot. "You love it, don't you? What's it like up there in the sky?"

"Cold mostly." He laughed, then sobered. "Flying up through the clouds and breaking into the clear—it's exhilarating. I like it all—the planning, the anticipation, the preflight procedures, waiting to hear those three little words"—he grinned—"*cleared for takeoff.*" The force of the acceleration pushes you back in the seat."

"You're never afraid?"

"No. When I'm up there I'm in total control. Free as a bird. Then during the landing approach, the wind whistles in my ears, the ground rushes toward me, and my heart races. There's nothing like it." He thought a moment. "I take it back. I was afraid once. My first inverted flight. I was at four thousand feet and dangling upside down. I couldn't see because all the dirt from the plane was flying in my face. Then I felt the harness give. You better believe I prayed like a repentant sinner! Whoo-ee! What a rush!"

"What happened?"

"Nothing. The plane righted."

"That sounds horrible."

"Nah! I wouldn't expect you to understand."

Taken aback by his tone, she gazed out the side window. Sometimes Abe seemed different from before his flight training— arrogant, and dismissive of her. Her ire up, she spit back, "Of course, you wouldn't expect little old me to understand. If I'm so dull-witted, why don't you just take me home?"

A look of confusion covered his face and he quickly said, "Come on, Margie. That's not what I meant. Look. For me, flying is the ultimate thrill. That's all. It has nothing to do with you."

"Nothing to do with me? Everything you do impacts me. We're getting married, Abe. Now you want to be a fighter pilot. Why didn't you ask me how I felt about it? Ever since you told me, I've been having trouble sleeping. What's this need of yours to push to the edge?"

He grimaced and slapped the steering wheel with the heel of his hand. "It's my life. I'll live it my way, okay?"

Margie jumped at the sharp retort and felt like she'd been stabbed through the heart. "Fine, if that's what you want. You go your way, and I'll go mine. I'll call off the wedding." The passing scenery blurred through her tears. Just saying those ugly words opened a door she didn't want to go through. She held her breath, waiting for his response.

He pulled to the side of the road and turned toward her. "I'm sorry. I didn't mean that. I love you. I need you, Margie. You keep me grounded. I don't want to live my life separate from you." He ran his fingers through tendrils of her hair. "What do I have to do to prove that to you?"

"Just be your old self. You seem to be moving away from me."

"I'm not! It only seems that way because we are apart so much. That will change. Soon we'll be married and living together. I dream about that. You'll work in a hospital, and I'll fly planes. I can't imagine my life without you in it." He gave her a lopsided grin.

Margie's defenses melted, and she kissed the grin she loved so much. He'd be leaving for California in a few hours, and she didn't want to squabble.

He turned back onto the road. "All right. No more serious talk. No more thinking about tomorrow. It's just you and me and a sunny day. Send me off with a bang, baby."

"All right, fella. If it's a bang you want, you got it."

They toured the art museum and roamed through Ann Arbor's galleries and antique shops. Abe bought a filigree brooch and pinned it on the collar of her blouse, where his hand lingered before caressing her chin. In a used-book store, she purchased *The History of Military Aviation* and wrote inside the front cover, *To my favorite flyboy. I'll love you forever.*

That evening they met Diane and Paul at the Kneebone, a jazz club where blue lights illuminated the dining room. They could barely see their booth until the silhouette of the waitress lit a tiny candle. The air was heavy with smoke and smelled of garlic and hot sauce, and Ethel Waters's "Stormy Weather" played on the jukebox. The foursome drank pitchers of beer and ate slabs of barbecued ribs.

Margie showed off her new diamond ring, and Diane and Paul chattered about their own upcoming wedding.

No one mentioned the listless economy, the war escalating in Europe, or Abe's leaving for California in the morning. They left the Kneebone and went to Charlie's, where a combo played dance tunes. Margie and Abe clung to each other on the dance floor, and she struggled not to dwell on their parting, but, nevertheless, she left tearstains on his shoulder.

As she quietly cried, he pulled her closer against him and nuzzled his nose into her hair.

And so the evening went.

"Are you sure you can drive?" she asked.

"Why not?" he said, stumbling into the driver's seat.

He drove while she dozed. Pulling into a park on the edge of town, he stopped the car behind a dense grove of trees. Sitting up, she looked around. "Where are we?"

"Davis Park. I don't want this night with you to end." He pushed the seat back and turned on the radio to a station playing Frank Sinatra crooning "The Lamp Is Low," then reached for her. She scooted closer. She didn't want this night to end either.

They shared deep kisses as he unbuttoned her blouse and released the clasp on her brassiere. He covered her face, neck, and breasts with flicking kisses.

Margie ran her fingers through his hair as she enjoyed the sensations that were coursing through her body.

Abe's kisses came back to her face, and he murmured, "Make love to me, Margie." He caressed her breasts and gently squeezed a nipple.

"We shouldn't," she managed to whisper, but as he slipped his hand under her skirt, she unzipped his trousers. He groaned in pleasure, and his fingers sought the edges of her panties.

She pulled away. "We can't do this," she said, but she was pulsing with desire. "What if I get pregnant?"

He reached in his pocket and pulled out a condom, then pressed it into her hand.

"What's this? Oh! You devil! Where did you get it?"

He flicked her earlobe with his tongue. "They give them out like candy at the base."

She recoiled, feeling herself blush. "You?"

"No. Not once. Not without you."

She nestled into him. What would it hurt? Their wedding plans had been set into motion, and he was leaving in the morning. She caressed his face.

"Make love to me, Margie. We've waited so long. We're not children anymore, and I love you so much." He pressed into her while his hands moved roughly over her breasts, down her back, and under her skirt again. His fingers tugged at her panties. "Please, Margie. I can't leave you again without making love to you."

Desire overwhelmed her, going contrary to everything she'd ever been taught. She was so in love, and they were parting. She couldn't refuse Abe. She didn't want to. Not again. Not this time. Shivering with anticipation, she whispered, "Okay."

"Okay!" he murmured. Elbows and ankles jockeyed for space in the tight confines of the car as they made love, her head at an odd angle, and him heavy on top.

Withdrawing, he threw the condom out the car window and cleaned them both up with his handkerchief. They stayed in Davis Park for a while, disheveled, panting, entwined in each other's arms, and in awe at the enormity of this new experience.

CHAPTER 5

Little River, June 1939–January 1941

Saying good-bye to Abe had been grim. In the week since he left, she constantly thought about their last night together. What had possessed her? Too much to drink? His persistence? Her love for him? Truth be told, she was glad to get the initiation out of the way. Was that normal? With Evelyn away at Annapolis, she had no one to talk to about it.

She reported for her first day of work at the Red Cross. "I'm so glad you're here," Myra said. A compact dynamo of a woman, she never seemed to stop moving. She took Margie to a small desk in a back corner and wheeled over a chair. "You'll be teaching first aid to the Health Aid Corps and supervising the Junior Red Cross. They're a fun bunch of girls. You'll enjoy them."

Myra handed her a pile of file folders. "This is the background reading on a new project. Sometime this year, we're going to become a blood-collection center, and our workload will double. I want you to become the expert . . . the go-to person. There's a weeklong seminar in Lansing next month I'd like you to attend. You need to fill out this paperwork right away and send it in." She handed Margie a sheaf of papers. "Tomorrow night our volunteers are assembling medical supply kits that we distribute overseas. I'd like you to stay and meet them. The coordinator of that project is pregnant, so when she leaves, I'll turn it over to you. Get yourself settled in. You'll find office supplies in the closet." She pointed to a closet door. "I'll be up front if you have any questions."

Margie felt out of breath just listening to Myra talk. A go-to expert? She had administered blood in the hospital, but she had no knowledge of blood usage beyond that. She found office supplies in the closet, arranged her desk to suit herself, and then opened the file folders and started reading about the chemistry of blood storage.

Mama was tickled to help Margie plan her June wedding. Evelyn had agreed to be her maid of honor. "How's Evelyn doing at Annapolis?" Mama asked.

"She's surrounded by midshipmen, so she couldn't be happier, Mama. She says the corpsmen assigned to the wards do most of the medical work under the nurses' supervision. Some of the rules are screwy, though, like the curtains at the windows have to hang just right, and casters on the beds must line up in the same direction."

"There must be a reason."

Margie couldn't think of one.

She had asked two of her girlhood friends to be bridesmaids, and a cousin's daughter to be the flower girl. She designed her wedding dress and ordered the fabric from Mitchell's Department Store.

In December, Abe graduated as an officially commissioned pilot and second lieutenant in the US Army Air Corps. Excited he

was coming home on leave, Margie styled her hair into an updo—
thinking it made her look more sophisticated—polished her nails,
and pressed her best dress. When he bounded off the train, she
flew into his arms. After they kissed, she touched the flight wings
pinned on his uniform. "Welcome home . . . sir."

He laughed again and twirled her around. "What did you do
with your hair?"

"It's a new style. Do you like it?"

"You'd be beautiful bald."

"So you don't like it?"

"You're beautiful. What more can I say? Are you ready for
some loving?" he whispered in her ear, and she leaned into him
in response.

It was joyous having him home, and Margie proudly showed
off her handsome pilot, taking him to Christmas parties and family celebrations. They made love whenever they could sneak away
and sent joint Christmas cards signed, *With love and good cheer,
Margie and Abe.*

She showed him the color palette of their wedding and the
just-completed flower girl's dress, but not her half-made wedding
gown. At Mitchell's, they selected a china pattern with light-blue
flowers and flatware embellished with a small floret. He needed
one more usher, and he contacted his friend Chuck to see if he was
available.

They met with Reverend Markel at the Little River Methodist
Church to discuss their vows. After a prayer and a blessing, they
felt their wedding plans complete.

Two weeks after Christmas, Abe left for Muroc on the 5:00
a.m. train.

Margie was bereft. Her only consolation: it would be their last
parting.

The war continued to escalate in Europe. In Germany, massive coordinated attacks threatened Jews, and thousands had been transported out of the country in boxcars, while thousands of others had been rounded up and sent to concentration camps. Britain and France declared war on Germany, and Germany invaded Poland, Norway, and Denmark. The United States remained neutral, though at the Red Cross, Margie worked overtime to keep up with demand for blood products, medicine, and bandages being sent to England and France.

In April a letter arrived from Evelyn. The navy was increasing the number of troops in the Far East, and she'd been transferred to Cañacao Naval Hospital at Cavite, a naval base near Manila in the Philippines. Though she was thrilled with the assignment, she was sad she wouldn't be able to be Margie's maid of honor. Margie was devastated by the news. She wanted her best friend to be in her wedding. She thought about who she could get to take Evelyn's place, but no one seemed right.

Three weeks later a letter from Abe arrived, and his first words caused her to hold her breath.

May 17, 1940

My Dearest Margie,
    The blots on the paper are my tears. It hurts me to write you this news. I've just received orders that all leaves have been canceled, with no exceptions. Something is going on, but nobody will tell us what. My darling, I won't be home for our June wedding. How will I ever make this up to you? I've never been so sad. Do I even dare ask you to wait awhile longer?
    How very much I love you,
    Abe

She lay curled on her bed, her pillow wet with tears. Dreams of her life with Abe seemed to be slipping away. His letter crumpled in her hand as she read it again: *I've never been so sad.*

"Me neither, my love," she whispered. Her throat tightened as a fresh round of tears threatened.

Her mother came in carrying a tray. "Honey, you've got to eat. I made you some chocolate pudding, your favorite. Sit up and eat it for me, won't you please?"

"I don't think I can."

"You've got to try. You'll feel better with a little something in your stomach. Please sit up."

She rose up into a slump and sighed deeply.

"I know you're disappointed, but it's just a postponement. As soon as Abe comes home, you two will get married. You'll have a long life together."

"He's a fighter pilot, Mama; what are his chances of coming home? I'm afraid for him."

"You're being negative. We're not at war. He'll be safe. Come, now. Eat the pudding. You'll feel better."

Margie did as she was told while thinking about canceling the church, food, and flowers and contacting the guests. She would store away her wedding dress, veil, and the tiara she had splurged on. That evening, still sad but calmer, she answered Abe's letter.

May 21, 1940

My Dearest Darling,

Your letter brought bad news, but I beg of you not to feel so sad. Fate might get in the way of our plans, but never our love for each other. The army can't keep us apart forever, and when you return home, I'll be here for you. In the meantime, I'll think of you every time I look at the sky.

Love and many kisses,
Your Margie

Abe was sent to Newfoundland to fly reconnaissance over the North Atlantic. For Margie, summer dragged on, long, hot, and lonesome. Now, with winter winds rattling the windows, she huddled around the radio with her family to listen to President Roosevelt's Fireside Chat. Dad solemnly smoked his pipe, Mama put her knitting down, and Frank sat forward to concentrate on every word the president said.

My Fellow Americans:
It is with profound consciousness of my responsibilities to my countrymen and to my country's cause, I have tonight issued a proclamation that an unlimited national emergency exists and requires the strengthening of our defense to the extreme limit of our national power and authority. The nation will expect all individuals and all groups to play their full parts, without stint, and without selfishness, and without doubt that our democracy will triumphantly survive . . .

Dad's voice broke after listening to the report. "Well, it looks like we're gearing up to get in the thick of it."

Mama looked thoughtfully at her two children, both young adults now and of military age. She wiped tears from her eyes.

That night Frank knocked on Margie's bedroom door. "You asleep?"

She put her letter aside. "No. Come on in."

Frank glanced at the letter. "How's Abe?"

"Cold. He's complaining a lot."

"Has he spotted any Germans?"

"He wouldn't tell me. It's all pretty hush-hush."

"Margie, I, um . . ."

Something in his voice made her take notice. Lanky and green-eyed, he resembled Mama's brother, Uncle Leo. Mama always said he was cocky like Leo too. And probably a heartbreaker, Margie thought. The girls had been vying for his attention for a while. He was a freshman in college already.

"I'm thinking about joining the navy. I talked to a recruiter a couple days ago."

Margie's brow furrowed. "Have you told Mama and Daddy? They'll have to give their consent."

"Not yet. I thought if you were there with me . . ."

"What about college?"

"It's their dream, not mine. I don't want to sit in a classroom. I want to get involved. I want to see more of the world. Some of my friends already are. Eugene joined the army and is training in Illinois, and Clyde's on a ship sailing around the Cape."

"Why the navy? You've never even been on a boat."

"Men are needed. You've seen the recruiting posters."

She had. *FIGHTING MEN NEEDED. Keep the world safe for democracy.*

She said, "It'll break Mama's heart."

"I know. Will you help me?"

Margie teetered between understanding his desire to escape a humdrum existence and feeling protective of the brother who wasn't yet out of his teens. "It could be dangerous. Is there anything I can say to stop you?"

"No. I can take care of myself. I've made up my mind."

She saw his determined look and heard fervor in his voice. *When did this kid grow up?* "All right then."

But it wasn't meant to be. The navy doctor detected a heart murmur, and Frank's desire to see more of the world collapsed on itself when he received a letter of rejection.

Dad often read the newspaper aloud to anyone within listening distance. "It says here Roosevelt has approved purchases of
hundreds of military aircraft and warships." He put the paper
down. "I heard the Ford plant is going on three shifts. They
have a multimillion-dollar contract from the government to
build tanks."

Margie said, "Myra's daughter, Junie, got a job there. She's an
inspector on the line."

Mama said, "In the factory? Since when do they hire women?"

"Since the men are being drafted; someone has to do the work.
They're hiring anyone who can pass the Civil Service exam. The
pay's good too. Junie's making twice as much as she did working
as a waitress."

Mama's hand went to her chest. "This awful war—our young
women working in factories. Our young men being drafted. It's a
nightmare. It's too horrible to even think about it."

Mama's worst nightmare became a reality in January 1941,
with Margie's call to active duty. As a second lieutenant in the
Army Nursing Reserve, she received orders to report to Walter
Reed Army Hospital in Washington, DC.

Mama said, "I feel so responsible." She was sitting on the edge of
the bed watching Margie pack her suitcase. Her voice sounded sad.
"I had no idea that working for the Red Cross would lead to this."

Margie saw the concerned look on her mother's face. "You're
not responsible. Working at the Red Cross has nothing to do with
it. I enrolled in the Nursing Reserve when I was still in school.
Most of the class did, along with thousands of other nurses. I knew
there was a chance the Reserves would be mobilized. I'm going to
Washington. I'm excited about it. As long as my wedding has been
postponed, I might as well see more of the world."

"The world's a dangerous place right now."

"I'll be all right. I won't be in any danger."

"That's what I keep telling myself, and you're a capable girl." She folded the nightgowns lying on the bed and put them into the suitcase. "The army could send you anywhere."

"I'll do what needs to be done, just like you taught me." She reached for her mother's hand. "Remember when I was naughty and you made me explain how I would improve my behavior? I hated doing that, you know."

They laughed together.

"You were a bit of a pistol, my dear."

"You taught me to be truthful and think critically about myself. You're a wonderful mother, and I love you. I don't want you to worry. When I come back, Abe and I will have bunches of grandbabies for you to spoil."

Margie didn't blame her mother for being worried. She was apprehensive herself of all the unknowns ahead. Her enthusiasm far outweighed her trepidation, however, and she pushed aside any misgivings. At the train depot, with hugs and kisses and a last wave good-bye, she jauntily stepped onto the train and into a new life.

CHAPTER 6

Washington, DC / Manila, January–June 1941

Margie crossed the threshold into a bigger world the moment she stepped through the doors of Walter Reed Hospital in Washington, DC. The immense 2,500-bed facility dwarfed her hometown hospital and stood five times larger than Grand Arbor. She was to train as a nurse-anesthetist.

In the nurses' residence, she met her roommate, Helen Doyle, a round faced obstetrical nurse who wore her hair in thick braids coiled around her head. With an American father and an English mother, Helen grew up traveling between the two countries, never sure which one to call home.

"It's a leap, isn't it, from obstetrics to anesthesiology?" Margie asked.

"A bit, but I heard anesthetists are in short supply, and obstetrics would be somewhat unnecessary in a field hospital, don't you think?"

A field hospital with tents and latrines? The possibility had never crossed Margie's mind. "I'm not the field-hospital type. I like a clean bed."

"Not me. I want to be where the action is. I'm looking to get into the middle of it and help our boys." Helen turned up the radio to hear what was happening in England. "It's terrible, the bombing. London's a shambles. I'm afraid for my mum and dad. They live right in the city."

A few days before Margie finished her training at Walter Reed, a letter arrived from Abe. He had been flying reconnaissance missions over the frigid North Atlantic for almost a year. He often complained about the subzero weather and the boredom of the routine. She pushed aside her textbooks and tore open the envelope.

Langley Field, Virginia
May 4, 1941

Dear Margie,
Haven't written in a while. The mind-numbing boredom of the North Atlantic doesn't lend itself to chatty letters. But I'm at Langley Field in Virginia for now. Good to be out of the bitter cold. The army brought me back as an operations officer for the Twenty-Second Pursuit Squadron. They're developing equipment to detect submarines, a.k.a. the German U-boats, those devils that harass our supply convoys. My guys will be testing the equipment for them. I hope it takes a good long time. I'm not in any hurry to return to the deep freeze.
I've written for a specific reason, Margie. I hope it doesn't hurt you too badly. I want to break off our engagement—just for now. I've met a woman here, and I want to enjoy her company

without feeling guilty. So many miles have separated you and me
for so long a time. You have to be as lonesome as I am.

Betty is a pilot. I think you'd like her. She's pretty, like you,
only she has blond hair. We talk a lot and goof around—like you
and I have always done, and I miss that so much. Please don't
be mad or sad. I don't want to lose touch with you. We have
so many good memories, and I hope we can still have a future
together. I'll keep writing. Please write back, okay? When we get
home, we can pick up again. Know that you will always be the
love of my life.

Truly yours,

Abe

Margie sat for a long while, holding the letter in her shaking
hand. So many miles separated them? How far was Virginia from
Washington—walking distance? Betty was a pilot? Margie would
like her? Most certainly not!

She ripped the engagement ring off her finger and tossed it in
the drawer where she kept his letters. Impulsively, she threw the
whole stack of them into the trash can. Creep! The love of his life?
While he's chasing around? How could he? Changing her mind,
she retrieved the letters. She cried tears of hurt and anger. An
empty spot opened in the place Abe always occupied.

Helen came into the room. "Are you okay, Margie?"

"No," she sniffed. "I just got a Dear Jane letter. Seems Abe's
found a blond tart."

"Oh, I'm so sorry."

"How could he, Helen? We've been together since we were sixteen." She blew her nose and blotted her tears. "We had all these
plans, and he just tosses them away like"—she swirled her arm in
the air—"like they mean nothing to him." She hiccupped a sob.
"Like I mean nothing to him. I never dreamed he'd do that."

"I'm sorry, Margie. Maybe you can still get back together."

"Don't count on it," she said, and the flood of tears started again with no indication they would stop anytime soon.

With the breakup heavy on her heart, Margie found it difficult to study for her final tests. She muddled through the days dejected and weepy, and broke into sobs when certain love songs played on the radio. When exams ended, Helen tried to persuade her to celebrate with their classmates, barhopping DC's hot spots. Margie declined and spent the night writing Abe a letter, but all six drafts ended up in the trash can.

The next morning, the chief nurse called the bleary-eyed graduates together. She wished them well and told them their orders were being processed. Because their transportation was on an "as available" basis, they must be ready to leave DC at a moment's notice.

"Do you know where we're being sent?" Helen asked.

"No. For security, that's kept confidential. Finish any business you have here. I suggest you keep your bags packed."

Their orders arrived soon after, and Margie and Helen hastily left Walter Reed for the DC train station. It teemed with khaki-clad men carrying oversized duffels and walking briskly in all directions. The girls grabbed coffee and a muffin from a vendor and hurried to Gate 6, where a sleek Transcontinental Limited waited. After walking through the dining car, a lounge, and then an endless number of Pullmans, Helen said, "Holy Toledo! We must be in for a long ride."

A two-day ride to San Francisco, to be exact. Upon arriving, they checked into the Armand Hotel. Over the next few days they underwent the tedious business of being processed for active duty, which included a physical exam and inoculations against tropical diseases. They stood in long lines, waiting to be issued clothing, field gear, and metal identification tags stamped with their name, rank, and other relevant information. After a free day to shop and see the highlights of San Francisco, they boarded the USS *Coolidge* with two thousand exuberant soldiers and sailors. By that evening, they were sailing the Pacific Ocean.

Accustomed to the wide-open fields of home, Margie found the warrens of tiny rooms in the ship's hold claustrophobic. When she sought fresh air on deck, the blazing sun fried her light skin to blisters. As they crossed the International Date Line, suddenly Tuesday became Wednesday. *What day is it?* she asked herself. *Where am I?*

Ryan, a sailor from Mississippi, said, "We're going to the Philippines."

"How do you know? I don't see anything but endless water and sky," Margie said.

"A gut feeling. I've got twenty bucks on it."

Margie rolled her eyes. These men placed bets on anything and everything to break the long days of monotony. However, Ryan won this bet, and Margie cheered when she learned of her assignment to Sternberg General Hospital in Manila, not far from the Cañacao Naval Hospital, where Evelyn worked.

"Lucky you," Helen said, grumbling, unhappy with her deployment to Camp John Hay, a mountainous army post and posh resort 170 miles north of Manila.

Standing on deck with Ryan, Margie watched the sights as the *Coolidge* approached Luzon, the largest island in the Philippine archipelago.

"Manila Bay is the finest harbor in the Far East," Ryan said. He pointed to a small island standing sentinel at its mouth. "That's Corregidor. It's so heavily fortified, it's called the Gibraltar of the East. The country that controls Corregidor controls the harbor. See that ship docked over there?" He waved toward the shore. "It's a mine planter; this harbor's full of mines."

Volcanic peaks rose up on both sides of the bay. They were covered with the lush, tropical trees of the Philippine rain forest, including tall mahoganies, palms, strangler figs, and mangroves, whose aerial roots made the trees appear to be growing on stilts. Wide sandy beaches connected the forests to the water's edge. As the *Coolidge* sailed farther into the harbor, Ryan pointed to a landmass on the left. "You're looking at the Bataan Peninsula. I've heard the jungle there's impenetrable." Over on the right, the compact and crowded Cavite Naval Base occupied the fingerlike projection of Sangley Point.

Ryan identified other ships cramming the immense harbor. "That's a destroyer. It's fast and maneuverable. It's used mostly as an escort ship. Over there's a battleship. It carries the big guns." He pointed out flat-decked aircraft carriers, hospital ships, and submarines. "Looks impressive, doesn't it? Truth is, this fleet's from the last war." He shook his head.

An army band played Sousa marches as Margie and Helen disembarked. A cloud opened up and delivered a deluge, soaking Margie's navy-blue slim-fitting dress and matching high-heeled shoes. The rain lasted only minutes, and then the sun came out and it became steamy. She took off her white gloves and picture hat and would have liked to take off her girdle and silk stockings.

A car waited at the end of the pier. The girls tumbled in and were chauffeured through the port area, past warehouses and fuel-storage tanks. Trolleys, bicycles, scooters, and small carts drawn by ponies no bigger than dogs jammed the narrow streets. High-wheeled wooden carts pulled by strong-backed Chinese or great lumbering oxen blocked the flow of traffic.

The crowded streets widened as they drove past Santo Tomas, the oldest university in Asia. When the avenues broadened into palm-lined boulevards, majestic high-rise apartments, huge hospitals, museums, and modern government facilities came into view. The driver pointed out the small, elegant American embassy and the mission-style Manila Hotel overlooking both the blue waters of Manila Bay and the flower-laden promenades of Luneta Park. Margie craned her neck this way and that, trying to see everything.

"I've never been so hot," she complained. She waved her hat in front of her face, trying to create a breeze, but the sodden air refused to move. They stopped at the Army and Navy Club, where another car waited to take Helen to Camp John Hay. The two women hugged, said their good-byes, and promised to get together soon. Margie, glad to have her feet back on solid ground, purchased a Coke and looked around.

The club was the center of social activity for military personnel in Manila, and its calendar of events included dates for poker, pinochle, bridge nights, and a lecture series covering Philippine history, culture, and points of interest. A dining room served meals, with a dance band playing through the dinner hour, proper dress required. Meeting rooms, game rooms, a gym, and a swimming pool were available, and the club hosted a sock hop every Friday. For families with children, an old-fashioned picnic with games and prizes was in the works.

"Marr-gee," she heard. She turned and saw Evelyn. Her blond hair was rolled back from her deeply tanned face, and the blue of her eyes dazzled. She wore a sleeveless pale blue dress that looked tailored for her tiny figure, and delicately beaded sandals graced her feet. The two women hugged as they twirled in a circle.

A tall, elegant man dressed in a white linen suit and a Panama hat tipped over one eye accompanied Evelyn. Grabbing him by the arm, she pulled him forward. "Margie, I'd like you to meet Max Renaldo."

Evelyn had written to Margie about Max, who she'd met at a charity ball at the Manila Hotel. In her most recent letters, Evelyn confessed she had fallen in love with this dream of a man. At thirty-two, he was already a captain in the army and chief surgeon at Sternberg Hospital.

Max tipped his hat, revealing black hair with a startling streak of white sweeping back from a widow's peak. Smiling, Margie offered her hand; to her surprise, he lifted it to his full lips. His eyes, deep-set and dark, bored through her. Not knowing how to respond, she foolishly murmured, "Thank you." Max looked amused. Feeling unsettled, she stepped away from his mesmerizing gaze.

Evelyn said, "We'll drive you to Sternberg, Margie. I've seen the nurses' quarters and they're really beautiful. Are you hungry? We could stop for dinner. There's a restaurant that has this delicious noodle dish. You'll probably want to freshen up a bit—your dress is kinda limp. Where's your luggage? Your trunk will be delivered to the hospital later. Let Max take these suitcases."

Margie listened to Evelyn babble, not able to get a word in edgewise. As she gathered her few pieces of luggage together and Max loaded them into the car, she felt his hand brush across her backside. She quickly stepped back and looked at Max, whose face was hidden behind the car door. Frowning, she wondered if the unwelcome touch had been an accident.

A few days later, Margie reported for her first day of work in the surgical unit at Sternberg. Lois, a nurse, scrubbed at the sink while humming along with the popular tune playing on the radio. She told Margie, "Wash up to your elbows. Clean towels and gowns are over there." Her pudgy hands and ample arms were soapy, so she nodded her head at a basket, then at a cupboard. "How long have you been in Manila?"

"Five days," Margie said. With a surgical mask covering her face and her abundant hair stuffed under a tight-fitting cap, only the twinkle in her eyes conveyed her excitement.

"Welcome to Sternberg Hospital. You'll be my shadow this week. Next week, you'll be on your own. Where'd you get your training?"

"Walter Reed."

"Super. They're sending us first-class nurse-anesthetists." They entered the operating room. "Hey, everybody," Lois called out. "This is Margie. Be nice to her; she's fresh off the boat."

"Morning," a nurse said. She was dressed head to toe in surgical garb.

"Margie, meet Eunice. She's the scrub today."

Margie stood to one side, watching as Eunice opened a package of sterile instruments: a dozen forceps, large and small scissors, scalpels, and an assortment of clamps and retractors. She arranged sterile towels on the Mayo stand and placed the instruments in perfect order, according to the surgeon's preference. She slid knife blades into handles, checked the sizes of needles, and opened suture packets, unwinding and cutting strands to the proper length. When done, she covered the tray with a sterile towel.

A corpsman wheeled the sleepy patient into the room, and Margie helped position her on the operating table, covering her with a light blanket. The woman smiled. "Thank you, dear."

The surgery door flew open, and Dr. Renaldo strode up to his patient.

Margie's eyes flickered in surprise.

He addressed his patient. "Mrs. Clark, are you comfortable?" With his head bent down, the silver streak in his dark hair fell over his right eye. "I'm going to scrub. When I come back, you'll be sound asleep. I'll see you in post-op." He patted her arm. "You'll be fine. You believe that."

Turning to leave, he bumped into Eunice and the Mayo stand. The sterile towel flipped up, and his elbow brushed over the instruments. He took no notice. "I'll be back in ten minutes. Get that drivel off the radio."

Hostile stares followed him out the door and Eunice whispered, "Arrogant SOB." Her work contaminated by the encounter, she would have to start over, keeping her gown, gloves, and instrument tray sterile according to the rules of asepsis.

When Dr. Renaldo returned, a nurse assisted him into a gown and gloves. His dark eyes swept the room. Margie looked down, not wanting to attract his attention.

He palpated the patient's abdomen to locate the mass. "Is she under, nurse?"

Lois checked the patient's responses. "Yes, doctor."

Beethoven's Symphony no. 3 played in the background, and the surgical team fell into a rhythm, their light conversation punctuated by orders.

"Anyone seen the Kate Hepburn movie? Retractor here."

"*Bringing Up Baby*? It's a good laugh. I'd take Cary Grant home with me any day."

"Have you tried the new restaurant next door to the theater?"

"Suction here, nurse. *Come on!* Hemostat. Get this bleeder!"

"Sorry, doctor."

"The food's so-so. Good desserts, though."

Dr. Renaldo stepped back from the table. He turned his head to the side, inhaled sharply, sneezed loudly, and snuffed wetly. "Get this mask off me."

A nurse untied it and threw it in the laundry.

Dr. Renaldo wrinkled his nose and snuffed again, his bloody gloved hands unusable and held up to keep them sterile. "Come over here," he said, jerking his head at Margie.

She went to him, sensing no sign of recognition.

"Turn around," he ordered.

Margie turned, and he wiped his nose on her shoulder, snot staining her white gown yellow.

The surgery became quiet as she returned to her stool. Feeling small, she sat with her shoulders hunched and her arms folded in her lap, blinking back tears of humiliation.

Margie loved most everything about her new luxurious lifestyle. Wide-open porches and deep overhangs brought ocean breezes into the nurses' quarters. A comfortable bed and thick-cushioned chairs and tables made from native bamboo and rattan, which stood up to the heat and humidity, furnished her room. Her window overlooked a well-tended garden of orchids, gardenias, and purple bougainvillea. A mahogany ceiling fan stirred the air. A houseboy greeted her each day with a glass of juice and the newspaper and, for a small fee, did her laundry and shined her shoes. Manicures, facials, and massages were readily available after a day of tennis, golf, or sunning at the beach. Evenings might mean dressing formal for dinner and gaming at the Jai Alai Club or attending an opera at the Metropolitan Theater with one of the many available doctors.

Because of the hot, muggy climate, work schedules were light, leaving time to explore the island. With a long weekend ahead, Margie hopped on a train for a four-hour trip north to the town of Baguio to shop in its open-air markets and to visit Helen at nearby Camp John Hay.

Helen met her at the station, helped her settle into one of the guest rooms kept available for visiting nurses, and then showed her around the compound.

"It's the most picturesque scenery in the world," Margie said. She and Helen gazed over the ridge of a lushly forested mountainside, which plunged steeply down to a still mountain lake. "You don't get the humidity like in Manila. It's refreshing up here."

"It's pretty; I'll give you that. But all I do is pass out quinine pills. I don't know why I'm here. I'm putting in for a transfer. I want to go to Europe where I can be useful."

"Then think of this as a well-deserved vacation."

Helen introduced her to Hattie, the only other nurse at the camp, and Dr. Robb, a rail of a man with a friendly smile. They toured the barns where the Twenty-Sixth Cavalry Regiment's horses were trained, feeding the handsome animals oats from the palm of their hands. They tried playing the hilly golf course, but gave it up after three miserable holes to go shopping in Baguio. The next day, they hiked along trails through trees filled with monkeys, gibbons, and rainbow-colored birds.

"Helen, I love it all. It's so peaceful. Can you smell the cinnamon and cloves?"

"Now that you mention it, I can."

"What's that noise?"

"Just a waterfall. They're all over the place." They rounded a bend, and sure enough, gushing water cascaded from a limestone cliff.

Margie took off her shoes and dipped her toes into the water. She peered through the dense forest. "Do we dare?" she said with a mischievous smile.

"Margie!" Helen looked around. "Well, I guess it's okay. Most people are napping this time of day."

Stripping off their clothes, they waded in, skinny-dipping in the emerald pool at the base of the cascade. Floating on her back, Margie tilted her head and let the cool water flow through her hair, thinking her life had turned into a delightful fantasy.

CHAPTER 7

Manila, July–October 1941

Evelyn delighted in showing Margie the sights of Manila, with its complicated overlays of Chinese, Arab, and Spanish influences. More recently, forty years of American intervention brought modernization to the flourishing, cosmopolitan downtown area. She pointed out the curvilinear forms of the art nouveau buildings in the business quarter, and the stylized geometric art deco architecture in the newer theater district.

Parks were plentiful and luxuriant, and the avenues wide. Off the main streets, wealthy Filipinos had built large houses with brick walls, tiled roofs, and windows made from translucent shells called *capiz*.

They explored the old walled city of Intramuros, built in 1571 while the Spaniards reigned. Its thick stone walls enclosed ancient barrios crowded with colonial houses, dungeons, baroque cathedrals, and museums, promising many lifetimes' worth of intrigue to discover.

"Chinatown is even older," Evelyn said. "It dates back to the tenth century. How about lunch there? The restaurants have everything from soups and noodles to exquisite dinners. What sounds good to you?"

Margie didn't know. The menus the waiter brought were printed with strange symbols. She finally pointed to a dish of vegetables over rice that a diner at the next table was eating.

After lunch, Evelyn purchased a pair of soft slippers and immediately put them on. Margie bought a tin of Chinese tea and a silk evening purse. Having enjoyed the day and each other's company, they planned to make the outing a monthly excursion.

In sharp contrast to the bustle and wealth of Manila, the countryside peasants lived in bamboo nipa huts perched on stilts next to mud wallows. Margie gaped at the new sights through the car window while on a day trip out of the city. Evelyn and Max occupied the front seat. Margie was friendly with Max for Evelyn's sake, but she disliked his piercing gaze and unbearable arrogance.

Royce Sherman, a surgeon and former Texas A&M quarterback, shared the backseat with Margie. Their mutual attraction had been immediate—her long gaze, his wink in return, and then her blush. She found he was friendly and outgoing and affected a bit of a swagger, which she thought amusing—but he wasn't a flirt. They had been sharing lunch hours over the past couple of days.

"People live in those shanties?" she asked.

"People and animals," Max said. "The floors are made from split bamboo so food scraps can fall through to the pigs and chickens underneath. The water buffalo over there are called carabao. They don't sweat, so they need those mud wallows to keep cool."

"Carabao pull those high-wheeled carts you see all over," Evelyn added.

A convoy of sixteen open buses approached from the opposite direction, each bus holding sixty-some Filipino men singing gaily. Conglomerations of suitcases, boxes, guitars, cooking pots, chickens in cages, and piglets in bags were stowed on top and underneath and lashed to the sides of the buses. Clanking, squawking, and squealing noisily, the convoy rattled along. The Filipino men waved and shouted as they passed by.

"Look at those jokers. It's the Philippine army," Max said. "They're training with bamboo guns."

"Bamboo guns?" Evelyn said. "They use darts dipped in poison—what is it . . . curare?"

Max scoffed. "Don't be absurd."

"It's not absurd. In South America, the Indians hunt with blowguns made from bamboo and darts dipped in curare. I read about it in the *National Geographic*."

Max said, "Stop showing your ignorance. This isn't South America."

Margie frowned, disturbed by Max's scorn, and was surprised Evelyn allowed it. This wasn't the Evelyn she knew, the one who took control of a relationship.

Royce calmly explained, "The Philippine army is short on equipment. They make guns from bamboo for practice drills."

"Just as well," Max said. "They'd shoot holes in their own feet."

"I thought the Filipinos had a well-trained army," Margie said.

"They do—the Philippine Scouts," Max said. "They're part of the US Regular Army, commanded mostly by American officers. The reserve divisions you see here are ragtags from the rice paddies. Thousands of them are in this so-called training. I wouldn't want my life depending on them."

The road took them through miles of flat farmland before skirting the southern shore of a large freshwater lake. From there, the terrain became hilly. In a little while, they reached a small town in the foothills of the Sierra Madre. Max stopped the car, and they got out.

The town itself was worth the journey. They snapped pictures of one another posed in front of its magnificent arched gate, grand ancestral homes, and panoramic views of pristine hills and crystal waters. Max retrieved a picnic basket from the trunk and carried it to a riverside dock, where he haggled with two locals. Money changed hands, and Max put the basket in what appeared to be a floating log. He waved Evelyn over.

"What's this?" she said.

"It's a *banca* and the guides are *bankeros*. Get in."

"You serious? Will it hold me?" She stepped in and squealed as the *banca* tipped. Max grabbed her arm to steady her.

Royce helped Margie into their *banca*, she in front, he behind with his legs stretched on either side of her. The boat rolled, and he grabbed her around the waist. "Whoa! If it turns turtle, you go in with me."

The *bankeros* paddled against the current, making their progress upstream lazily slow. Margie leaned back against Royce and watched the multicolored birds that fluttered in the coconut trees fringing the river's edge, and the monkeys frolicking among wild orchids. Intermittently the calm was interrupted by gushes of rapids that they traversed on foot, transporting the *bancas* on their shoulders.

The river widened as they entered a gorge where lushly vegetated cliffs soared three hundred feet straight up, and the emerald water around them reflected the clouds in the heavens. No sound disturbed this spiritual paradise. Margie felt Royce's arms tighten around her, and they shared their first kiss, cautious and inquiring.

When the *bankeros* landed the small craft on a sandy point, Royce retrieved the picnic basket, Evelyn laid out sandwiches and apples, and Max opened a bottle of wine. They ate while lounging on the sand, toasting their good luck in coming to this spectacular place. Then, stripping to the bathing suits they had worn under their clothes, they played an inventive game of water volleyball with a beach ball provided by the guides.

After lunch, the trip continued upstream. A distant rumble increased to thunder as they approached a falls. Water surged down four hundred feet from above in torrential splendor that pulsed the air and eddied the river as light danced in a rainbow mist. While the group watched in awe, the *bankeros* put down their paddles and let the *bancas* drift back in the swift downstream current.

"You shoot rapids?" a *bankero* said in stilted English, and laughed heartily.

"What'd he say?" Margie asked, but before Royce could answer, the *banca* flew like a winged horse on a mission, bucking in the turbulence and barely missing outcrops of boulders. With river water pelting her, Margie gritted her teeth and clung to Royce's legs, expecting in any second to be ejected from the boat and her life.

The trip back was short and furious. At the end, Margie wobbled out of the *banca* with Royce right behind her. He gathered her in his arms, their knees weak, their hearts thumping. Max and Evelyn joined them on the shore, and they all breathed sighs of relief before breaking into whoops of laughter.

Back in Manila, hungry and sunburned, they stopped in a bar frequented by the hospital crowd. Its thick walls, heavy beams, and dark wood bespoke Spanish influence. It was cool inside, and they found a table under a fan. Max glanced over the menu. "I recommend the house specialty, beef and vegetables cooked with garlic and vinegar and served over rice."

Evelyn said, "It's too heavy. I'd rather have a salad."

Max said, "You eat like a bird. You need some meat on those skinny bones."

Margie grimaced and glanced at Royce. He winked in return.

They ordered their meals and pitchers of cold beer. Max said, "Who's in for a hike in the mountains next week? I know a trail through a gorge. There must be a dozen waterfalls. Can you girls handle the food?"

"I wouldn't know what to bring," Margie said. "The food's different here. What I'm hungry for is potato salad with chopped eggs, green onions, and a little mustard to season the mayo."

Evelyn said, "A taste of home. I know where we can get green onions, and they might have potatoes. I don't know about the mayo, though—it could go bad in the heat. How about if we have a lunch packed for us at the cafeteria?"

"I vote for that. Will I need hiking boots?" Margie asked.

"Sturdy shoes should do. It's a trail. How about Thursday?"

They all agreed.

Evelyn finished her salad and pushed the plate aside. She turned to Margie. "At the end of November, there's a holiday dance, the biggest one of the year, and it benefits the children's wing of the hospital. Would you two like to go with Max and me? It's *mucho swanky.*"

Margie looked at Royce for an answer. He smiled and nodded.

Evelyn said, "Oh! Goody! Margie, do you have a dress?"

"Not one that fancy. There's a sewing machine in the common room. I could make one."

"Don't bother. I know this fabulous Chinese tailor. He's cheap and fast, and he can work from a magazine picture. We'll shop for material in Chinatown; the silks are gorgeous."

The meal finished and their social calendar arranged, they danced to a Billie Holiday song playing on the jukebox. As Royce and Margie swayed to the music, he asked, "Are you a golfer?"

"I'm a duffer. Does that qualify?"

"Close enough. If you're free tomorrow afternoon, I'll get us a tee time."

Delighted, she tilted her head up to look at his smiling face. The slowness of his speech and deep, rich timbre of his voice conveyed a calmness so different from Abe's cocky sureness. Though their breakup seemed long ago, some hurt still lingered, troubling her on the nights she felt lonely.

She said, "I'm free. I'd like that a lot." He pulled her in closer and she felt comfortable in his firm hold. Laying her head on his chest, she mused over his name—Royce. When the music changed to a jitterbug, they stopped for a smoke.

Cheers arose from the dance floor. Evelyn and Max were putting on a show, bopping to the boogie-woogie beat of the Andrews Sisters. Max twirled her around and reeled her in with one smooth motion, Evelyn swiveling her hips like a woman walking sexy. Other couples stopped dancing and formed a circle around them, clapping and chanting, "Get hot! Get hot!"

Margie was amazed.

"He's a pro," Royce said. "Max worked as a dance instructor when he was in medical school. That guy lives for dancing, booze, and women."

That wasn't what Margie wanted to hear. This egotistical man would hurt Evelyn. How could her best friend be so blind?

"Cock your wrists," Royce told Margie. He stood behind her, his hands over hers on the golf grip, giving her a lesson. There had been several over the last few weeks. "Swing through, shift your weight, bend your knees, and pivot. The power should come from your legs, not your arms."

She collapsed, giggling. "What about hitting the ball?"

"You have to keep your eye on the ball."

"How can I do that when I'm twisted up like a pretzel?"

He sighed. "I think it's time for a break." He put the clubs in the bag, hoisting it to his shoulder, and they strolled toward the clubhouse. He said, "Max and I signed up for a golf competition. We need cheerleaders. You up for it?"

"Cheerleaders? No way. Golf is *quiet.*"

"Yes, cheerleaders. And costumes."

"Costumes? Are you kidding? Golf is *stuffy.*"

"It's for Halloween."

"That's only a week away! What kind of costumes?" She stopped walking and turned to him.

His gaze traveled from her face to her breasts, prompting her to pose, chest out and head tipped to one side. Grinning, he said, "Surprise me."

She found she enjoyed his scrutiny as much as the intimate stroke of his hands when they were alone. She caressed his cheek and slipped her thumb into his mouth. "Naughty or nice?"

He nibbled on the tip of it. "You choose."

Margie never knew what to expect from her new crowd of friends. There was always a reason to party—picnics on the beach, cocktails around the pool, dinner out, and theater afterward. The day of the golf competition, she and Evelyn wore harem pants and midriff-baring tops made of shiny yellow satin and veils fashioned from fluttery pink chiffon.

Royce came dressed as a sultan, his headdress adorned with sequins and sparkling jewels, and Max came costumed as a thief, a dagger tucked into his belt. They played on the scenic course that skirted the ocean, with Margie and Evelyn trailing behind, buzzing kazoos, jangling tambourines, and offering the competition whiskey shots. Max smirked and Royce ogled. Everyone passed way beyond tipsy by the end of the day.

The next morning, Margie stretched languidly between the sheets. Her mouth was dry, and her head ached. She kept her eyes shut, because they hurt too. A hangover day, like too many others. She would take aspirin, then go float in the pool with her ears under the water to block out noise. While sinking back into a snooze, she heard a rustle. She opened her eyes. Royce lay in the bed, smiling down, propped on one elbow. He said, "Nothing happened."

Her gaze darted around. The room was unfamiliar. On the floor by the bed lay her billowy costume and the kazoo. The world popped sharply into focus—Royce's bed! She grabbed the sheet and tucked it under her chin. "Nothing?"

"Not a thing."

"Humph. That's not saying much for either one of us."

He chuckled, falling back on his pillow. "Well, maybe I remember just a little."

Rolling to face him, she demanded, "Gimme all the details."

"We passed out. End of story."

"Passed out? Are you sure?"

He played with her tangled hair, fanning it out on the pillow, combing it with his fingers, crushing it in his hand. Rising up, he leaned over her. "I'm sure I didn't do this," he murmured, kissing her.

She took pleasure in the feeling of his lips on hers, soft and wet, and she caressed them with the tip of her tongue. So often in the past weeks her thoughts had wandered to this moment, leaving her weak with yearning for him. Of their own accord, her fingers played with the stubble of his beard, the curve of his ear, the line of his jaw, the taut muscles of his chest.

Peeling back the sheet, he ran his fingers up her back and down again, causing her to shiver with desire. "I'm sure I didn't do this," he said as he gently squeezed her breasts, caressing them, kissing them, flicking the nipples with his tongue, hungrily squashing his face into them.

Margie whispered, "Hmm! That feels familiar. Are you sure you didn't do that?"

Chuckling, he pulled back so he could reach the flat of her stomach, softly tracing figure-eight patterns with his fingertips. "You're more beautiful than I ever imagined."

"Have you been undressing me with your eyes?"

"Every minute of the day and night."

Savoring the image of Royce lusting for her, she moved her hips to the rhythm of his caresses. Closing her eyes, she let the heat of the moment carry her away as his hand slipped lower, his finger flicking and stroking until she grabbed his hand and crushed it into her, every nerve in her body firing and every muscle contracting. She cried out, then went limp in his arms.

Rolling back, she pulled him on top of her, wanting the feel of his weight. Pulsing with pleasure, she wrapped her legs around him to hold him tight against her.

He murmured into her ear, "My darling, are you sure you want to do this?"

"There's nothing in the world I've ever wanted more."

CHAPTER 8

Manila, November 1941

Margie crawled out from under the mosquito netting tenting her bed and almost stepped on a gargantuan cockroach. Yelping, she jerked her foot back as the hard-shelled critter skittered through a gap in the wall. Despite the chemicals sprinkled in the cracks, the creepy-crawlies got in anyway, unrelenting and dangerous, carrying malaria, dengue fever, and dysentery.

She showered in the communal bathroom, then combed her hair and applied lipstick at the dressing table in her room. Opening her closet, she caught a whiff of mold, though keeping the light on supposedly prevented it from growing. The formal dress made for tonight's holiday dance crowded the space. She caressed the ivory silk of the skirt, slinky as a nightgown. The breeze from the ceiling fan offered scant relief from the oppressive heat, so she dressed and moved slowly.

Royce came to mind, often now. She found pleasure in his steady, easygoing manner. Together they explored the baroque cathedrals and museums of Intramuros, shopped in Chinatown, and sampled strange foods in restaurants. His passion for golf became hers too; under his instruction, she was getting the ball into the air. In a world of their own, they walked on the beach, or swam in the ocean, then changed into formal dress for dinner and the theater. They attended pool parties and dances, and played euchre with friends. Margie's favorite times, however, were when they were alone, sharing a bottle of wine and a crossword puzzle with music playing softly in the background.

They talked endlessly. She told him about her mother and dad, her home in Michigan, her experiences with the Red Cross, and her college days when she had met Evelyn. She confided that she had been engaged to her high school sweetheart, but it hadn't worked out.

He told her about his older sister, who still bossed him around, of his years in medical school, and his fantasy of being a golf pro. "I grew up on a ranch in Texas with horses and dogs. Someday, I'll return there. I want you there too, Margie. Would you consider it? Just hypothetically, of course."

She saw Evelyn on days when their schedules allowed, and they sometimes double-dated. These occasions were trying, though, because Margie found Max insufferable. She also had heard rumors of his conquests of Filipino girls, some of which were allegedly not consensual. Over a drink in the bar, she discussed her worries with Royce.

"There's something off about that guy. I hate how he treats Evelyn."

Royce swirled his drink. "He lives by his own rules; brilliant people often do. Maybe that's what attracts her."

"I think he's sinister. There's the Filipino nurse who was raped—"

"There's no evidence it was Max. She won't name her assailant. Don't spread rumors, Margie."

"I'm not. I'm only telling you what I heard." She emptied her glass and debated if she wanted a refill. "The woman is scared. She's afraid she'll lose her job. I think Evelyn should at least be aware of what's going on. Don't you?"

"Only if there's proof that it was Max. Even then, she would blame you for being the messenger. Are you willing to risk your friendship?"

No, she wasn't, and that only made her quandary more problematic, because the nagging thoughts persisted. Max had no regard for anyone but himself, and Evelyn could be in harm's way.

The night of the holiday dance, the residence hall lobby overflowed with fine-looking men greeting dazzling women in colorful dresses. High-heeled shoes clicked on tile floors, and perfume and shaving lotion mingled with the scent of fresh flowers.

Royce's smile widened as he watched Margie make her entrance down the staircase, a vision in ivory silk and pearls. In her fiery red hair looped and curled from the heat, she had pinned a white gardenia. Grinning like a Cheshire cat, he whispered into her ear, "You're drop-dead gorgeous."

Evelyn was equally stunning in her mint-green gown, which flaunted her ample bosom. Her blond hair, pulled back into a soft chignon, accentuated her small, even features and flawless complexion. A clear glass-bead necklace and dangling earrings sparkled multicolored in the light, and a huge orchid encircled her wrist.

"The car's waiting," Max said, ushering them toward the door. "Evelyn—stop a minute." He inspected the back of her leg. "You've got a run." He turned to Margie. "Do you have a stocking Miss Clumsy here can borrow?"

Dresses swished and heels tapped as the girls ascended the stairs. "Why do you let him talk to you that way?"

"What way? Oh that." Evelyn shrugged. "It's just the way he is. He grew up with six older sisters." In the room, Evelyn unbuckled her silver sandal and peeled off the damaged hosiery. She waggled her newly freed toes. "I have some news. Promise not to say a word."

"I promise."

Evelyn tapped a cigarette out of the pack. "Max asked me to marry him." She lit the smoke, glancing at Margie over the top of the flame.

"And what did you say?"

"Yes, of course."

Margie reached for the pack to cover her crestfallen expression. Her hand shaky, she couldn't get the lighter to flick a flame, so she banged it against the edge of the table. What could Evelyn be thinking, planning a life with this unbearable man? She tried the lighter again with success. Recovering her composure, she said, "That's wonderful. When's the big day?"

"We haven't set a date, but soon."

"What's your hurry? You don't really know much about him."

"That's not so! We've been dating for months. He's told me all about his family. His grandparents still live in Italy. His mom and dad came over to start an import business. His sisters are all married, and he has dozens of nieces and nephews. It was his mother's dream that he became a doctor."

Margie retrieved a stocking from the dresser, checked the color against Evelyn's ruined one, and handed it to her.

Evelyn scrunched it from thigh to toe into a donut shape. "When we get home, he wants to specialize in pediatric surgery. He loves kids." With her heel on the edge of the chair, she reached for her toes, the formal dress difficult to work around. "He sends his mother flowers every month. I bet you didn't know that."

Margie didn't, but the revelation didn't change her low opinion of the man. She inhaled deeply on the cigarette and said through blown-out smoke, "We're all living in a fantasy world here. It's not the best time to make a big decision. Are you sure?"

"I've never been more sure." Evelyn stopped struggling with the stocking. "Look, Margie, I know you don't like him. I can tell. But you don't know him like I do. He can be arrogant, and sometimes he says things that sound mean. He doesn't always relate well to other people. It's because he's a perfectionist. He doesn't tolerate stupidity or anything sloppy, especially when it comes to his patients. I think that's a good trait. More of the doctors should be like him." She slipped the stocking over her foot. "Underneath, he's soft and sweet. He's a romantic. He writes me love poems."

Margie observed Evelyn's beaming face. She couldn't tell her about the rumors making the rounds, so she faked a big smile. "Then I'm happy for you! Congratulations!"

Evelyn slid the stocking up her leg, clipped it to the garters dangling from her panties, and then smoothed her dress. "Max is different from other men. He's a little mysterious."

Margie's brow wrinkled with concern. Mysterious . . . or dangerous?

They entered the Manila Hotel through an atrium of waterfalls and tropical greenery lit by hundreds of twinkling lights. The pavilion teemed with men in formal dress and women dripping in diamonds. Roving waiters offered appetizers and drinks, and an orchestra played holiday songs. Margie and Royce wove through the room to a patio that overlooked the harbor. The moon had risen, and the sky winked with stars—a storybook setting.

They sipped French champagne, and Margie tapped her foot to "Jingle Bells" while watching sailboats slowly drifting by, their masts and riggings decorated for Christmas with garlands blinking red and green. Nearby a group conversed in booming voices.

"The Filipinos jump at their own shadows," a loudmouth said. "Take my cook. I'm waiting for breakfast, and he's nowhere around. When he shows up, he says"—the loudmouth slipped into a falsetto—"'Ah, sir. The streets are haunted at night. An evil spirit followed me home and flew in my window. I begged a friend to share my bed to protect my soul.'"

The group laughed at the performance.

A woman in red said, "I like the locals. They're friendly. They tell a good story."

The loudmouth lit a cigar. "Bullshit! He wanted a screw at my expense. God help us if our lives are ever in their hands. To them, every shadow's a ghost and every slanty-eye's a spy. Hell, half the Japs in the Osaka Bazaar are FBI."

"Then half the Japs in the Osaka Bazaar *are* spies," a mustached man quipped.

"You better believe it. Spies are everywhere." He lowered his voice. "I know for a fact there's a mole on the air-raid alarm staff."

The woman in red said, "My friend saw planes over Camp John Hay. The Japanese are parachuting in. They poisoned the water at Baguio, you know. My friend's cousin got so sick she went to the hospital."

The mustached man said, "Our guys found a horse slaughtered in the woods. They think the Japs are eating the meat."

"Can't be too careful. They'll slit your throat for no reason at all."

"Or for a meal. They're cannibals, you know. Human liver's a delicacy."

Royce steered Margie away from that bunch, but she could still hear the boozy drivel and tried to shut her ears to it, not wanting it to ruin the beautiful setting.

The mustached man said, "I heard they're building bomb shelters in Tokyo."

The loudmouth blustered, "Those bucktoothed monkeys will need their bomb shelters if they keep messing with us. I say, bring them on! Let them attack us! We'll wipe 'em out in a week. Let 'em come and see what they'll get."

The sound of a gong announced dinner. The partiers feasted on crab soup, mixed-greens salad, prime rib with thyme au jus, whipped potatoes, creamed peas, soft rolls with butter, chocolate truffles, coffee, and cigarettes. Wineglasses brimmed with fine Cabernet. After consuming all the food partygoers thought they could possibly hold, the waiters brought out cheese blintzes with raspberries.

As the orchestra turned up the volume and livened the beat, overstuffed people flocked to the dance floor. The bar stayed open, ensuring further imbibing, and the lights in the room dimmed. Margie and Royce box-stepped around the crowded floor, bumping others' shoulders and backsides. After a drunken dancer elbowed her, Royce led her to the less-crowded patio. He inspected her arm.

"It's nothing," she said, dismissing the bump and taking in the beauty of the scenery. A soft breeze stirred the heavily scented flowering trees, and moonlight shimmered on the bay. Music drifted from inside, the singer crooning a dreamy tune.

Royce took her in his arms, and they swayed to the slow music. He gazed at her face and hummed along softly. "You're truly beautiful. I must have dreamed you up." His lips brushed her cheek before finding hers. Enjoying his spicy scent, she found pleasure in the rhythm of the music ebbing and flowing, and she wished she could live in this moment forever. She nestled into him, laying her head against his chest to listen to the steady beat of his heart. She felt like she was floating.

The music swelled, and Royce twirled her around and dipped her back. She laughed as her hair swept the floor. Then drawing her close, he looked into her eyes. "You've touched me more deeply than I ever dreamed possible." Time and place blurred as they shared passionate kisses under the winking stars in the soft, scented breeze. He whispered, "I love you. I love us."

Margie melted in his arms, and her thoughts drifted to love-spangled years and chubby babies shared with this sexy hunk of Texas charm.

The music stopped, and the spell broke.

Breathless, they rejoined Max and Evelyn at their linen-draped table. A photographer aimed his camera at them. "Wonderful! Big smiles." Royce draped his arm over Margie's shoulder, and she leaned into him. The foursome raised their champagne flutes in a toast to the camera. The flash popped, recording the magic moment in time.

"Come dance with me, Margie," Max said. "It's the Lindy hop."

She grabbed Royce's hand under the table. "Um, thanks, but I don't know the steps."

"I'll show you. Come on," he insisted, tugging at her arm. She followed him onto the dance floor, biting her lower lip in distress.

When he turned to her, however, she smiled brightly. "When did you start dancing?"

"I was ten. I broke my ankle when my sister pushed me out of a tree. The doctor said I'd walk with a limp. My mother didn't want a gimp for a son, so she signed me up for ballet lessons. I was the only boy in a sea of tutus."

"What did your father say about *that*?"

Max shrugged and tapped his foot in rhythm. "It's eight beats; follow me." Holding her firmly, his precise movements in sync with the music, he led Margie through the steps. She found his smooth, solid style easy to follow. When he released her right hand, spinning her out and reeling her in, she danced as if she had been doing it all her life. She laughed, marveling at her newfound ability.

The Lindy hop ended, and Margie turned to leave, but Max grasped her arm. "One more," he insisted. "It's a fox-trot." She held herself stiffly as he propelled her around the floor, expertly avoiding collisions with others. While maneuvering a step, his hand stroked her breast.

She stepped away, remembering the brush of his hand on her backside her first day in Manila. Tight-lipped, she said, "Evelyn looks beautiful tonight, don't you think?"

"She's pretty enough, but I've a taste for redheads." With a thrust and a spin, he dipped her back until she was unbalanced and at his mercy. As she struggled to regain her footing, he licked the base of her throat.

She stifled a cry, and then she heard Royce's voice. "You've had Margie long enough, Max."

She buried her face in Royce's shirt and muttered, "That guy's a pervert. He gives me the creeps."

Royce held her closer. "If he's bothering you, we won't do this anymore. See Evelyn when you can, but no more double dates."

"That's fine with me," she said, but wondered what she would tell Evelyn.

The festivities continued late into the night. Though rumors of espionage and sabotage swirled around, Margie felt safe. A portly captain assured her Japan wouldn't strike the Philippines. The island was heavily fortified, he said, and more airfields were under construction. More troops, more bombers and fighter planes, and a flotilla of PT boats were scheduled to arrive soon. Additionally, the Filipino army continued to train intensively.

General MacArthur, upbeat and looking a little flushed, circulated through the crowd, proclaiming everything was coming along splendidly.

Only a few people knew the White House had issued a classified dispatch to commanders in the Pacific: *CONSIDER THIS DISPATCH A WAR WARNING . . .*

The brass in Manila disregarded the dispatch. More important things called to them, like the evening's festivities—the women, the food, and the booze.

While Royce took part in a discussion with his colleagues and Evelyn chatted with her navy friends, Margie went out to the patio for a view of the bay. Carrying her shoes, she tiptoed through the sand to the water's edge. In a reverie, she walked along the beachfront, following the pale light of the moon. The jungle soon encroached on the shore, and the lights of the pavilion disappeared behind a thick cover of vegetation. Coconut trees loomed eerily, and giant mangrove roots reached out like talons.

A voice from the dark said, "You shouldn't be out here alone."

She whirled around to see Max staggering toward her. He was rumpled and drinking from a long-necked bottle. She said, "I was just going back." She took a step, but he blocked her way. Fear prickled at the base of her neck. "Get out of my way, Max. Royce is waiting for me."

He hiccupped and burped. "Don't flatter yourself. He's talking surgery. He doesn't even know you're gone."

Beyond Max, she saw only the deserted beach. She darted sideways, but he grabbed her arm in a grip she knew would leave bruises. Twisting in his hold, she yelled, "Stop it! You're hurting me."

"Oh, come on. Where's that big smile you gave me while we were dancing?"

"You're sick! Let go of me!"

Responding swiftly, he yanked her closer.

She smelled his sour breath as his whiskered chin scraped the side of her face. "Let go of me," she hollered, pushing with her arms and jabbing at him with her knees and elbows.

He growled, "So the bitch likes it rough," and grabbed her breast in a viselike grip.

The pain made her whimper, and Max moaned. He searched for her mouth with his slobbering tongue, but she whipped her head from side to side.

He clamped down on her ear with his teeth.

In agony, she froze.

He kissed her ear and the base of her throat and started peeling back the top of her dress.

She inhaled sharply and flailed with the hand still holding her shoes, aiming for his face, her adrenaline surging. She swung hard, and the spike heel found its target.

Max staggered and fell backward, letting Margie go. He covered his face with his hand and cursed in Italian.

Margie ran through the sand toward the lights of the hotel. Shivering, she huddled in a stall in the ladies' room, counting to one hundred, and then to one thousand, while trying to catch her breath and calm herself. She knew the truth for sure now. She would tell Evelyn everything and it would be good riddance to Mr. Mysterious. Evelyn would be devastated, and Margie cried harder at the thought of hurting her friend. When she felt able, she fixed her face, ear, hair, and dress as best she could with trembling hands and damp towels.

That night, she slept fitfully, rumors of invasion mingling with vivid dreams of Helen at Camp John Hay surrounded by Japs slitting throats and eating ears. She bolted upright, her heart pounding and her stomach pitching. She threw up on the floor by the bed.

CHAPTER 9

Manila, December 8, 1941

Margie skimmed the headlines in the morning newspaper: Germany and Russia continued to battle over Moscow; President Roosevelt had appealed to the emperor of Japan for peace. Putting the paper aside, she went to the buffet for breakfast. The war seemed far away. She had other things on her mind.

She had avoided Evelyn since the night of the dance and dreaded their next meeting. She rehearsed the likely conversation a hundred times in her mind, never once finding a happy ending. Max wore an eye patch, telling everyone he'd walked into a low-hanging tree branch. *Serves him right,* she thought as she touched her ear, still tender from his bite.

Outside the window, she saw Tildy, long-legged and panting, running across the lawn. With a small head and slicked-back hair, she resembled Olive Oyl, Popeye's lanky girlfriend. She burst through the side door, screaming, "The Japs are bombing Pearl Harbor!"

FLORA J. SOLOMON 83

The women sat like statues, stunned. Gracie, doll-faced and chubby, looked out at the sky, but there was nothing to see, not even a wisp of clouds. "Do you think they'll come here?" She chewed on the tip of her thumbnail.

Margie heard whimpering, and she turned to see Karen weeping into a napkin. She rubbed Karen's back and leaned over to hug her. "We'll be okay."

Eyes glistening with tears, Karen shook her head. "My fiancé is at Pearl. He's on the *Arizona*."

Margie had friends in Honolulu, and she feared for their safety too. Wanting to believe the best scenario, she said, "He'll be all right. Honolulu's a fortress."

Three night-shift nurses arrived for breakfast and a smoke before they retired. Usually a subdued group, this morning they were edgy and talkative, telling what little they knew. The bombing had started at 2:00 a.m. Manila time. The naval station at Pearl Harbor was a disaster—fires raging and untold casualties. Sobbing, Karen fled the room. A siren wailed. Outside, people ran about in confusion. Desperate to see Royce, Margie left her breakfast uneaten and hurried to the hospital.

The corridors buzzed with unusual activity. The charge nurse answered incessantly ringing telephones. Bedridden patients jangled call bells, imploring doctors and nurses for information. Knots of ambulatory patients in gowns and slippers congregated in tight groups, conferring in hushed voices. Margie zigzagged her way through hallways jammed with anxious people, linen carts, and aides trying to deliver breakfast trays. She stepped through the surgical unit's double doors where it was quieter. She saw Royce standing at a sink, scrubbing from fingertips to elbows with a stiff, soapy brush.

She needed his hug, but checked her impulse. "Hey," she said, mimicking the Texas greeting he often used. "Trouble's brewing."

Royce spoke, his voice tight and muffled by his surgical mask. "What've you heard?"

"Just what the night nurses said. Pearl Harbor's in flames. You think the Japanese will bomb Manila?"

Worried blue eyes peered over the mask. "Let's pray not. Sure hope the air corps is ready." He rinsed his hands and arms under running water and turned the tap off with his elbow. "I'll be done here in a couple hours. Where are you going to be?"

"Room two. Hernia. Should I cancel our tee time?"

"Not yet. Business as usual until we hear otherwise." With arms held up and away from his body, he gave her a wink before backing into the surgery.

Margie rolled her gas machine into Room 2, readied an instrument tray with her anesthesia supplies, and then found a stool to sit on. A corpsman wheeled in the patient and transferred him to the surgical table. A nurse draped him with layers of sterile sheets. Groggy from the sedative given earlier, the patient grinned when he saw Margie. "Sweetheart, I'm feeling good," he slurred.

Margie lowered the gas mask. "Bye, bye, baby. You're off to dreamland."

"Tell the doc to make this quick. Nips are—"

He lost consciousness before he finished his sentence. The surgeon started the routine surgical procedure, and for the next sixty minutes Margie tried to clear her mind of what was going on outside and focus on her patient.

By the time Margie left the hospital, the beauty of her surroundings—the blue sky, the manicured lawns, and the gardens abundant with exotic flowers—could not mask the nervous energy of a tense population. People stampeded stores to stock up on food and supplies. At the post office and every bank, crowds spilled out the doors and lines wound down the streets.

Margie's plans for an afternoon golf date changed when Miss Clio Kermit called a mandatory meeting for all nurses. The kind and knowledgeable director—a short, boxy woman with salt-and-pepper hair and dark brown eyes—had earned the affection of her staff and the respect of the doctors. Margie edged her way into the room of restless women and found a chair next to Karen.

She squeezed Karen's arm. "Are you okay?"

Karen nodded, but her red-rimmed eyes and tightly held body told a different story.

"Girls!" Miss Kermit yelled out over the chatter. "Girls, quiet down. I have some important things to say."

The room quieted as they gave her their attention.

"The Japanese are bombing military installations in northern Luzon. Camp John Hay, Fort Stotsenburg, and Clark Air Base are reporting casualties."

The room hummed with agitation. Margie feared for Helen stationed at Camp John Hay. She leaned forward, straining to hear more.

"Girls, settle down, please. We must use this time to prepare for whatever lies ahead. Expect unusual activity. Workers are hanging blackout curtains inside. Outside, they're sandbagging around the hospital and digging foxholes in some areas."

"What? Sandbagging?"

"Foxholes?"

"Please settle down, girls. This work is just a precaution. At the end of this meeting, you will be issued a gas mask and shown how to use it. There is the slimmest chance the Japanese could use chemical warfare, so we must be prepared. I know it's upsetting, but again, this is just a precautionary measure."

The women fell silent. Margie's mouth went dry.

"All ambulatory patients will be discharged. Those who are confined to their beds will need extra assurance they are safe. We may get very busy later. For those nurses on duty, make sure your units are well stocked with supplies. For those not on duty, eat well and get some rest. You will need your strength. Remember, we are here to serve. Are there any questions?"

Yes, there were questions. Would the Japanese attack Manila? Would they bomb a hospital? How could they contact their loved ones back in the States to allay their fears? The director reassured her staff that they were protected. The army and navy patrolled the island, and Manila was secure. The director dismissed the group but asked the surgical nurses to stay behind.

"Gather around, girls." Miss Kermit's demeanor was grave. "We've received word from Fort Stotsenburg. They are overwhelmed with wounded. The situation is serious, and they're desperate for help. I'm asking for five volunteers to go there to assist." Two hands shot up, and a third slowly rose. "Thank you. I need two more. Anybody?" Margie furtively glanced at her coworkers, all looking ashamed of their reluctance to sign on to help. She too didn't want to leave the safety of the city. "Don't make me assign this duty, girls," the director prodded. Still, no one raised her hand.

"Why don't we draw straws?" a nurse beside Margie suggested.

"Excellent idea, thank you. Does anyone object?" Miss Kermit quickly fashioned straws from cotton-tipped applicator sticks, then arranged them in her hand. After each woman pulled one, Margie and Tildy discovered they held the short ones. Margie's jaw clenched in dismay, but she nodded her assent.

Finding Royce in the doctors' lounge later, she told him her news. "I'll be back before you miss me," she tried to quip, but a tremor in her voice betrayed her true feelings.

He hugged her with a ferocity, and she slumped into it. He whispered, "Let me talk to Miss Kermit."

"No! The selection was fair. I'll do what has to be done." She stepped back and smoothed the worry lines from his forehead, caressing his cheek and chin. "I'll be okay. I love you."

As they kissed, she cried. She hated good-byes.

Wearing her white uniform and carrying her wool cape, Margie boarded a bus with four other army nurses, fifteen Filipino nurses, two doctors, and a score of enlisted men. She took the seat next to Tildy, who was knitting a cap for her sister's new baby. Supply trucks packed with medical equipment and food followed behind. The convoy lurched, stop-and-go, through streets busy with people stacking sandbags, taping glass, and boarding up windows. Everyone anxiously watched the sky. Margie looked upward too, and saw nothing but a few fluffy clouds. After the bus left the city, the ride smoothed to a rhythmic rock, lulling her into a restless sleep.

She awoke with a headache. It was dark, and jungle trees formed a canopy over the narrow road. The bus engine whined noisily from the steepness of the terrain, and the lumbering supply trucks following behind growled like tired beasts.

"Where are we?" she asked Tildy.

"About halfway there. The going is slow."

The trip dragged on endlessly. Just when Margie thought her bladder would explode, the convoy stopped. The driver jumped up.

"Stay in your seats," he ordered, then beckoned to a group of soldiers, who put on steel helmets and bulky vests. They grabbed rifles and followed the driver out the door. Staring out the window but unable to see, Margie heard footsteps, shuffling, and muffled voices. It seemed a long time before the soldiers returned.

The driver explained, "There's a downed plane partially blocking the road. I think I can get around it."

Margie appealed for a rest break. She grabbed her cape to hold it up for privacy, and several passengers left the bus for a brief visit to the side of the road. Just ahead lay the smoldering carcass of the airplane flipped on its side with one wing pointing to the sky. The pilot's compartment gaped empty, and Margie's first thought went to Abe. She had feared for him before, but the realities of what he might face—the twisted metal, the spiral of smoke, and the smell of fuel—had never before been so stark.

The driver eased the bus through the tight passage between the downed plane and the trees. A glow colored the sky orange, and an acrid smell permeated the air. Outside the window Margie glimpsed a jeep nosed into a ditch and another thrown on its side. The bus hit a crater, jostling everyone inside. Slowing to a crawl, it continued to climb until it crested the hill. Sixty-three pairs of eyes witnessed the nightmarish scene below.

"Holy shit!"

"Christ!"

"What the fuck?"

"God help us."

Massive fires engulfed Clark Air Base. Skeletal remains of dozens of aircraft lay strewn over acres of bombed-out land. Propellers littered the road, tires hung in trees, and holes the size of swimming pools gaped all around the land ripped open by multiple strafing runs. The passengers stared in horror. Hearing wails from unknown origins, Margie shivered.

As the bus approached Fort Stotsenburg, the source of the cries became evident. Bodies in all states of distress littered the grounds. Once inside the fort's hospital, Margie saw injured people lying on gurneys, on tables, and on the blood-splattered floor. A few exhausted medical staff tended the wounded.

Margie became light-headed. Her vision dimmed and the room began to spin—the dark chaos, evil smells, eerie flickering of the fires, and pleas for help came from every direction. Overwhelmed, she squatted down and tucked her head between her knees and tried to breathe slowly and deeply.

"Move it!" She heard and felt a thump on her back. Shaking off her dizziness, she was brusquely introduced to the grim reality of trauma and triage, war's urgent and scanty medicine.

In a makeshift surgery cobbled together in a tent, Margie administered anesthesia to men riddled with bullets and torn by shrapnel. Wounds of the abdomen, head, and chest that in normal times warranted serious consideration were assessed hastily and patched, or not. She lost count of the number. At dawn, she slogged to an improvised mess for breakfast.

"I was setting up my first surgery when the bombing started," a dark-haired nurse exclaimed. "A bomb fell so close that my bones rattled. I dove under the table and almost broke my neck!"

Tildy leaned on her elbows. "At least you had a—" She covered her bloodshot eyes with her hands.

"Then the strafing started," the nurse continued. "I swore those bullets were coming right through the roof. I was sure I was going to meet my maker."

Tildy spit, "Well, you're still alive. What's your problem?"

The nurse shot Tildy a withering glance. "You weren't here when the bombs hit!" Her quivering voice rose. "Do you know how it feels to think you're going to die?"

"I know how it feels to pump morphine into one dying kid after another, and that's close enough for me." Choking, Tildy ran from the table with her hands covering her mouth.

Feeling sick, Margie forced herself to swallow food that stuck in her throat. A siren blasted. "Air raid!" someone shouted, and everyone dove under tables. Curling into a ball, every muscle taut, she wrapped her arms around her head. Whistling bombs searched for targets, and the ground thundered from the impacts, pounding once, then again, and again, and a hundred times more.

Then, a strange quiet fell, except for a distant buzz. The sound grew to a roar, and, through the tent flap, Margie saw Japanese Zeros circling and diving, their guns hammering everything in sight. The ground vibrated under her, and she scrunched herself into a tighter ball, now understanding the other nurse's fear of impending death.

When the drone of the last plane died away, the survivors crawled from under the tables to wobble outside and assess the damage. A gray haze hung in the air. In every direction charred skeletons of burned-out buildings and smoldering piles of rubble confronted them. Fires that had died overnight flared again, spewing black smoke that reeked of rubber and hot steel. The injured cried in fear and pain, "Help! Over here! Help me!" Margie hurried back to the surgery while her sisters in the field sprayed burns with tannic acid and administered sedatives and morphine.

She worked endless days, anesthetizing patients while doctors and nurses stitched and patched. She slept in one tent, ate in another, and did laundry and bathed using her steel combat helmet as a basin. She wore men's heavy boots, dog tags, and size forty-four army-issue coveralls. Working in a fog of sleeplessness and fear, she felt like a zombie and imagined she looked like one too. When asked to accompany an ambulance bus back to Manila, she jumped at the chance, anxious to get away from this horrible place and excited she'd be with Royce again. Dressed in the white uniform she arrived in, she said good-bye to Tildy, who was assigned to accompany the next busload of wounded to Manila. "Take care of yourself, kiddo. I'll see you in a few days."

Slated for additional surgery, eight sedated orthopedic patients lay restrained on cots by a variety of plaster casts, appliances, ropes, and pulleys on arms, legs, backs, and necks. Their destination was Sternberg. The passengers rested quietly as the bus pulled onto the main road. Margie checked each man's color, respiration, and dressings, then took a seat. When the road smoothed out, the gentle rocking motion made her sleepy. She couldn't doze during this important assignment, so she checked each patient again before moving up front to chat with the bus driver.

He said, "I was nineteen when I enlisted two years ago. I've been in the Philippines for six months stationed in outposts. The troops live in tents out there, you know. Being transferred to Fort Stotsenburg with its barracks and good food was sweet. Until the bombing started."

A shout came from the back of the bus, and Margie went to investigate.

The soldier who'd cried out was just a kid. He had one leg in a cast, and the other was a wrapped stump.

"Hey, tiger. What can I do for you?"

His eyes brimmed with terror. "I hear them coming! You've got to get me out of here!" He tried to sit up, but the cast extended over his hip, restricting his movement. "Get me out of here right now!" he insisted through his drug-induced haze.

"I don't hear anything, Johnny," she told him as she glanced out the window. "I can't see anything either. Nothing's out there."

"It's the Zeros! I hear them! Get me out of this coffin! Do you hear me? Get me out of here!" His panicked voice woke the men around him.

Margie hastened to assure the groggy men that things were okay, but when she looked out the window again, what she saw terrified her. Overhead flew dozens of Japanese Zeros, and two broke away to target the bus. Spotting the enemy bearing down, the driver jerked the bus onto a densely treed logging trail. Veering sharply into a small opening, he crunched the bus as far down the overgrown path as he could. They could do nothing else but wait.

Covering his head with a pillow, Johnny resigned himself to his fate. However, the men he'd awakened demanded they be released from their restraints. They clutched at Margie as she walked past them. "Jesus Christ, we're going to die in a stinking bus!" one of them yelled as the roar of the planes swelled. She grabbed the hand of the soldier nearest her, braced her body against the steel frame of his splint, and mumbled a prayer. The Zeros zoomed overhead and their gunfire rattled the windows, but their bullets were off target. The buzz of aircraft engines faded to a drone. The soldiers quieted as they listened for the devil's return. Once sure the danger had passed, the driver eased the bus back onto the road.

They drove through a small village where Filipino families warily emerged from their huts. Seeing the bus, they waved and flashed the two-fingered victory sign.

When it neared Manila, the bus slowed to a crawl in heavy traffic. A hodgepodge of vehicles blocked both north- and south-bound lanes as city people fled to the countryside and country folk sought safety in the city. The travelers had lashed as much of their household inventories as they could manage—including squealing pigs, chattering chickens, and barking dogs—onto trucks, carts, bicycles, and the backs of oxen. The bus joined this motley convoy. Despite everything they had been through, the mood of Margie's charges was surprisingly good. "Are we there yet, Mom?" one young man whined. "How much longer, huh, Mom?" another teased.

As they crept closer to the city, darkness descended early, heavy smoke covering the sun.

"It's from Cavite," the driver said. "Dirty Nips have been bombing it all week. It's where those Zeros we met on the road were headed, I'm sure."

Margie worried about Evelyn at the naval base. She suppressed her feelings by focusing on her charges instead, preparing them for the move into Sternberg. She pulled her hair back and refreshed her lipstick.

"Do it again?" Johnny asked.

"What?"

"Your lipstick. I like to watch."

Sadness squeezed her heart as she studied the broken boy. Brushing his hair with her fingers, she kissed his cheek, leaving a smidge of red.

During her absence, Manila had mutated into a city Margie hardly recognized. Camouflage-clad, big-booted soldiers carrying rifles over their shoulders marched through the streets and assembled in parks where antiaircraft guns pointed upward. Trenches snaked through ornamental greenery, sandbags lined sidewalks and blocked padlocked doorways, and strips of tape made a mosaic of black-curtained windows. Air-raid sirens wailed, though nobody took cover. The bus carrying Margie and her wounded charges crawled along streets teeming with high-wheeled wooden carts and bicycles, now joined by jeeps filled with soldiers and vehicles mounted with machine guns. Ambulance sirens blared, and fire truck horns bleated. When the bus pulled up to the entrance of Sternberg, Margie sighed with relief. Inside the hospital, however, the chaos looked sadly familiar.

Patients lay haphazardly on makeshift beds that lined hallways and filled the dining room, the porches, and the gardens out back. Frightened young women with squalling babies, wizened old people, and the sick and crippled waited for help, many gray-faced, dirty, and wrapped with bloody rags or bandages. No one was safe from the carnage. The hospital staff wore the same beleaguered look as Margie's friends at Clark.

"Hey, kid, what's happening?" she heard. Behind her, Evelyn stood with her arms full of linens.

Margie cried in surprise and relief. "Boy! Am I glad to see you!" She wanted to hug her friend, but the linens were in the way. "How'd you get here?"

"Cañacao got bombed. I have stories to tell but can't talk now. I'm in OB and don't know when I can get away." A corpsman handed Evelyn a chart for another new admission. "They just keep coming," she said, glancing at the chart. Her brow furrowed. "Christ, another burn case. Those are the worst. I have to go, Margie. See you later."

As she started to leave the room, Margie heard a small voice say, "Help me, please?" A young woman with a bloodied child lay on a cot. "I need to go to the bathroom. Will you watch my baby?"

When the woman returned, Margie tried to leave again, but a toothless old man grabbed her white skirt. "I need something for this pain." His eyes were bright with fever, and she guessed from the odor that his wounds were infected.

"Nurse, please," patients called. "Help," they pleaded, and she responded again and again before managing to escape to the nurses' residence. Relieved, she entered her room, breathing in its welcome familiarity. Margie was drained of energy and emotion; the decision to shower or to sleep seemed a big one. She stripped off her soiled uniform and put on a robe and slippers. From a phone in the hall, she paged Royce. The nurse on the surgical unit answered the page.

"He's asleep in the doctor's lounge. Do you want me to wake him?"

"No, don't do that. When he wakes up, just tell him I'm here."

The nurse heaved a tired sigh. "We're swamped. Could you possibly work tonight? Come in at eleven o'clock?"

"Sure," Margie responded, feeling disheartened. Dirty, hungry, exhausted, she needed a night off. After a shower and a light meal, she crawled into bed. Some while later, a knock on the door roused her.

Evelyn nudged the door open with her hip and put two whiskeys on the bamboo side table. She removed her surgical cap, then flung it aside and fluffed her hair. "Did I wake you?"

"It's okay," Margie said, climbing out from under the mosquito netting. When they embraced, an overwhelming feeling of despair descended—she couldn't stop tears from flowing. "What have we gotten ourselves into?"

Evelyn patted her back and let her cry. "Come on, kid. This is our chance to be noble."

Margie sniffed. "I don't know why I'm blubbering now. I've seen more horrible things than I expected to see in ten lifetimes. I've been bombed and strafed, all without a whimper. You come into my room, and I fall apart."

"So you're human. We're all due for a good cry. Here, have a drink."

Margie dabbed at her tears and accepted the drink. They sat in chairs by the window. "You been here long?"

"A week, almost. There's not much left of Cañacao."

"Did everyone get out?"

"I doubt it. The sky was black with Nip bombers. I hid with my patients behind sandbags underneath the hospital. The noise was so loud my ears are still ringing. Guess how many of our planes defended us. None!"

Margie said, "The airfields up north are gone. You can't imagine the destruction."

"Shit, I can't! The naval base is gone—the ships, the submarines, the docks, everything just gone. Now the Nips are dropping bombs on Manila. The port area is wrecked, and Chinatown is taking hits. It's just a matter of time before the whole blasted city gets obliterated."

And us with it? Margie wondered.

Evelyn said, "Were we blind or stupid? All those blackout drills we treated like a nuisance. Our mail was censored, and we were ordered to send our valuables home. What did we do? We merrily shrugged it off and looked for the next party."

"MacArthur told us Manila was safe."

They lit their cigarettes off one match and smoked in the dark, listening to rumbles and explosions in the distance.

"It's the burn cases," Evelyn said softly. "When they bombed the ships, I saw guys jumping off burning decks into fire-filled water. They flailed around awful, Margie. I can't get that picture out of my head. Now women burned in the bombings come here to have their babies." Leaning back in her chair, she sighed deeply. "I've never felt so helpless."

The intercom buzzed and Margie went to the hall phone. It was Royce. "I thought you would sleep for hours," she said.

"Sometimes I do. Sometimes dreams jerk me awake. I missed you. I'm glad you're back. Are you hungry?"

"Always for you. I'm with Evelyn right now."

"Bring her along. We'll go to Louie's."

Evelyn declined the invitation, saying she was too tired to eat. All she wanted to do, she said, was sleep for a year.

Royce hailed a taxi. Although Manila was under blackout restrictions, smoldering fires illuminated burned-out buildings. The taxi maneuvered around potholes and erratic chunks of concrete. Skinny dogs, eyes flashing red in the cab's shielded headlights, slunk about feasting on uncollected garbage. Despite all the destruction, an edgy energy filled downtown.

They found Louie's undamaged and open for business, its nervous clientele huddled in booths, murmuring in low voices. Billie Holiday's "Fine and Mellow" played on the jukebox, muting the mood even further, while slow-turning ceiling fans blended odors of ginger, garlic, and cigarettes. Sliding side by side into a booth, Royce ordered drinks from the scrawny, dark-eyed waiter. Margie leaned into Royce, needing the solid feel of his embrace. "What's going to happen to us?"

He avoided the question and held her tighter.

"There is no sign of relief," she said.

"Let's not talk about it."

"Then what?"

"I don't know. I just need to get away from it." The waiter brought their drinks. Royce downed his in one swallow and ordered another.

"You're exhausted," she said.

"No more than anyone else."

"Stay with me tonight," she said, and then remembered she was scheduled to work. "No. Can't. We've only got a couple of hours."

A group of officers came in, choosing the booth behind Margie and Royce. The men ordered a round of beers and quietly talked business. Margie's curiosity was piqued when she overheard them mention Fort Stotsenburg. She leaned back, the better to eavesdrop.

One officer said, "They're evacuating the base. I was assigned to gut the place and haul all the supplies to Bataan."

She whispered to Royce, "They'll bring the patients here. I don't know where we'll put them."

Straining to listen, they overheard—

". . . small expedition's landing . . ."

". . . secure advanced bases . . ."

". . . no resistance . . ."

". . . main invasion force . . ."

". . . War Department dependent on ground forces, no air cover, no navy . . . sitting ducks."

Fear enveloped Margie as she realized the officers were discussing a Japanese invasion. "Imminent," they said, and she stiffened.

Royce tightened his arm around her. "Do you want to leave?"

"No. You've got to eat," she said, knowing she couldn't. She thought of what happened during the occupation of Nanking. The Japanese forces were wicked, their savagery legendary. Royce and Margie clung together in sorrow and fear.

The nightmare unfolded. Four days before Christmas, invasion forces crowded the island's harbors, and forty-three thousand Japanese stormed the beaches. Casualties poured into Sternberg by the busload.

Stretched out and restrained on the operating table, a soldier whipped his head from side to side as he shouted, "No fuckin' use! Yellow buggers all over us!" He tried to sit up, but a corpsman held him down. "Duck! Duck! Fuckin' planes!"

"Steady, fella. Let's get you relaxed," Margie soothed. The corpsman held the man flat as she administered the anesthesia. "Deep breath," she coached.

"Gotta get the damn shit outta here!" the soldier yelled as his back arched. The gas kicked in, and his eyelids fluttered shut.

"Couldn't say it better myself," the corpsman snorted. "MacArthur better the hell pull these guys back before they're all plant food." Removing a sling from the kid's arm, he shook his head in dismay. "Amazing what a bullet can do, ain't it, doc?" He doused the wound with antiseptic while the nurse helped the surgeon snap on sterile gloves.

The door opened to reveal a pre-op area gridlocked with gurneys. Nurses and corpsmen buzzed like bees around them. A nurse popped her head in. "You wanted to be notified, doctor. Another busload just arrived."

"Where're you putting them?" he growled.

"We're triaging on the front porch and stacking them two deep along the hallways."

The surgeon grunted, and as he moved into the sterile area, he said, "The army's pulling out. Got orders this morning to begin evacuation." He inspected the wound, palpating it with his fingers. "Scalpel," he ordered, and the nurse slapped the knife into his hand. "They're retreating to Bataan. Anyone heard of it?"

The corpsman replied, "The Bataan Peninsula. I can describe it in three words—jungle, swamp, and malaria. Japs would never find us in there. Can't see nothing from the air."

"Is there a hospital?" Margie asked, not liking the description of her destination.

"One's built, another's getting started," the surgeon replied while probing the wound. "There's the bullet. It's lodged behind the bone. Forceps," he said, reaching out his hand, concentrating on the delicate task.

Sternberg Hospital felt ghostly, and footsteps echoed in its empty hallways. Buses loaded with patients and trucks with supplies formed convoys that departed Manila in the dark of night. Margie packed up her anesthesia equipment and watched as it was carted away. She saw Royce in the hospital dining room and nudged him in the back with her elbow. "Hey, stranger. How's it going?"

He gave her a big Texas smile. Taking her arm, he led her to a table. His body drooped with fatigue, and stubble covered his face and neck.

"Are you packed yet?" she asked. They were scheduled to leave on a bus that night for Hospital Two on Bataan. He hesitated too long, and she frowned.

"Margie, my plans have changed. I'm staying here in Manila."

"No!" she cried. She knew that volunteers were being recruited to stay and care for the soldiers too shot up or cut up to be moved to safer quarters. "Please, no!" she pleaded.

"It's something I need to do. I can't leave these men here."

"Then, I'll volunteer—"

"Don't even think of it!"

"But—"

"You're not staying here!"

Tears clouded her vision.

Royce took her hand and held it to his lips. "I'll be right behind you. A few days to get these guys stabilized." He kissed her fingertips, his gaze meeting hers. "You understand, don't you?"

She nodded, but she didn't understand. Not at all. She wanted Royce with her on that late-night bus.

He whispered, "My room? In an hour?"

She nodded again, attempting to smile. Dabbing at her tears, she said, "Then it's just us girls leaving tonight. Max left this morning on a hospital ship sailing to Australia."

Royce scoffed. "Hardly a hospital ship. Three hundred injured men on a dinky island steamer. Someone's birdbrain idea."

"Evelyn's worried."

"Me too. *If* they break through the Jap blockade, they face fifteen hundred miles of open ocean." Royce glanced at his watch and stood to leave. He let his kiss linger.

In the noisy confusion of the midnight evacuation, Margie and Royce said good-bye. They kissed fiercely as they stood on the steps of the hospital, where exhaust from idling vehicles thickened air already heavy with smoke from the burning city.

A horn blew. "Everyone in who's going!" the truck driver bellowed.

"I can't leave you here," she cried, afraid she would never see him again.

He smothered her in a last hug. "Hurry, the truck is pulling away."

"I love you!" she shouted over the commotion. Grabbing Evelyn's hand, she jumped on the back of the moving vehicle and watched Royce's image recede through a blur of tears.

They bumped along in the back of the truck, feeling concussive boom, boom, booms as demolition crews ignited great stores of ammunition. Eye-dazzling fireworks lit up the sky. In the distance, Japanese bombs detonated.

Over the din, a soldier yelled, "Be ready to dive in a ditch if they start dropping bombs or strafing! Drop and roll like you were taught!"

Drop and roll? Taught? She had never been given a minute's training on how to drop and roll out of a truck, or how to survive in a jungle. Facing a great unknown and a terrifying enemy, Margie grabbed Evelyn's hand, who then grabbed Tildy's as Tildy grabbed Gracie's.

CHAPTER 10

Bataan, December 1941–February 1942

The open-bed truck rocked one wheel at a time over the rocks and ruts in the primitive road, leaving the twenty occupants clinging to the wooden benches nauseated and bruised. *Sort of like riding a mean horse,* Margie thought. The only relief the passengers got from the hard seats and harder jolts were their dives onto the roadside when someone spotted Japanese planes in the early-morning sky.

Fleeing from the advancing Japanese army, Margie and her companions traveled south through the Bataan Peninsula, their truck one of a mishmash of vehicles carrying medical personnel, supplies, and equipment from Manila to an unknown destination deep in the tropical rain forest. No one knew much except that American and Filipino troops had retreated to the peninsula, where a hospital was under construction.

Margie rested her head on Evelyn's shoulder.

"Buck up, kid," Evelyn chided. "There has to be an end to this road somewhere. Remember, we're on an island."

Evelyn was right. There was an end to the road, but not the journey. The narrow road turned into a narrower path as the truck lumbered deeper into the lush forest. It stopped in a clearing, and the medical crew piled out. Margie looked around in wonder. She didn't see any hospital, just a conglomeration of vehicles: supply trucks, troop transports, backhoes, wide-bladed bulldozers, and a whole area full of mud-splattered buses. A crude road ran through the center of the clearing, with a cluster of tents off to one side. Hordes of US soldiers and Filipinos scurried everywhere.

An army captain greeted them. "Listen up!" he hollered over the babel of voices. "This is Field Hospital Two. In thirty-six hours, the first patients will arrive. As you see, there's a lot of work to do."

"And who do you think's going to do it?" Evelyn murmured.

The captain paced back and forth. "There's no time to lose. Everyone's help is needed." He pointed to where bulldozers bucked and roared as they cleared land. "That's the hospital site. It will be ready for setup tomorrow. In the meantime, all medical personnel are expected to pitch in and help elsewhere. There are plenty of jobs. Working in the mess. Digging latrines. Unpacking trucks. Pitching tents. Line up to volunteer or you'll be assigned to something."

Dr. Corolla, big-beaked and edgy, leaned against a truck. His arms were crossed over his chest and a cigarette smoldered between his fingers. He mumbled obscenities under his breath before shouting, "Who's responsible for these orders?"

The captain barked back, "We don't question orders. Pitch in where you're needed or take the consequences."

Margie joined a cluster of women in the mess, where tables and benches were assembled from scrap lumber and split oil drums served as sinks. Men chopped up bushels of vegetables, and huge pots of stew simmered on stoves. She felt comfortable in a kitchen, however crude, and was willing to do whatever was needed. A churlish-looking cook approached the volunteers, squinting at the group through a plume of cigar smoke. "Let's get this straight," he said in a voice raspy from too many smokes. The stogie bobbed up and down when he spoke. "I don't want no damn girls in my kitchen."

Margie backed away. "What a dud."

"Dolt," someone else contributed.

"Dipstick."

Despite late December's brutal humidity, army crews man-handled heavy equipment to dig out shallow-rooted, low-growing vegetation. Filipinos with bolos cleared underbrush. They left the jungle trees that grew two hundred feet straight to the sun, their branches meshing into a giant canopy that rustled and swayed in the breeze. Exotic ferns and orchids flourished high in the canopy, unexpected spots of beauty. Brightly colored toucans and parrots perched there too, screeching at the disruption. Monkeys, howling in some primitive language, swung from tree to tree on coiling vines.

Margie emptied trucks, assembled cots, and unpacked and inspected timeworn supplies wrapped in newspapers from 1918. She cleaned obsolete surgical instruments with ether until the fumes set her head spinning. As she worked, sweat soaked her uniform, making it cling to her body. Her revealed curves evoked snickers and insulting comments from soldiers too long away from women. Needing relief from male eyes and ears, she joined other nurses at the edge of the Real River. She sat on the rocks lining the riverbank and dangled her feet in the cool water.

Evelyn waved her hand to scatter a cloud of mosquitoes. "If this is a hospital, I'll eat my hat."

Gracie said, "Wounded arrive tomorrow. Where are they going to? There's no shelter. Supplies are in boxes. I wouldn't know where to find a dressing or even an aspirin."

"How many will be here? Does anyone know?"

"I heard someone say around a thousand."

"A thousand! Somebody's lost their marbles."

The women were in no hurry to rejoin the men, so as the sun sank below the tree line, turning the sky an exquisite pink, they gathered driftwood and grass and built a fire. The chatter of monkeys and squawking of birds quieted, replaced by the sawing of crickets, cicadas, and grasshoppers. Gracie began to sing "Silent Night," her voice like an angel's, and they all joined in. For a while, they sang the Christmas carols denied them in the hectic days of the evacuation and reminisced about holidays past.

"Bury that fire!" A male voice boomed through the dark, and the women jumped at the intrusion. "Haven't you ever heard of a blackout?"

Ruth Ann, tall and big-shouldered, stood. "Blackout? No one told us."

"That's why you women don't belong here. You're nothing but a worry. We have enough to do without babysitting you. Just stay out of the way and don't do anything else stupid like building a fire at night." The soldier doused the blaze and led the chastened women back to camp, lighting the way with a blue-filtered kerosene lamp.

The nurses slept in the buses. Margie burrowed into her pillow. Despite the steamy temperature, she wrapped herself in a blanket for protection against spiders. It seemed like a lifetime ago that she had kissed Royce good-bye, but it had been less than a day. She whispered to Evelyn, "I wonder what the guys are doing."

Evelyn murmured, "Playing poker, no doubt. Isn't that what men do when women aren't around?"

Margie wanted to believe that. She tried to picture Royce chomping on a cigar, laughing and enjoying hands of poker with his doctor buddies, but the rumble of bulldozers and the crash of falling trees kept her rooted in reality. She drifted to sleep listening to noises queer to her ears.

In the great leafy caverns, workers erected nipa huts, the largest enclosing eight surgical stations. Smaller huts held the dental clinic, records room, and housing for the officers. Generators provided power for lights over the operating tables, and a chlorinated reservoir purified water. Using oil drums for tubs, Filipinos created a laundry to boil hospital linens, with clotheslines strung along the riverbank. Craftsmen built beds, tables, stools, and shelving from the plentiful bamboo, and supply trucks arrived by the dozens. A newfangled hospital took shape while everyone worked and watched. The thirty-five nurses assigned to it were responsible for setting up the open-air wards.

"The what?" Margie asked.

"Open-air wards. Like under the stars. Like I've got a bullet in my belly, so let's go camping and really rough it," Evelyn said.

"Even the records room has a roof."

"Well, the army has its priorities."

The women arranged fifteen hundred cots in the dappled light of acacia trees. They distributed wastebaskets, urinals, ashtrays, and flyswatters and stocked storage units with linens and medical provisions. Lister bags for sterilizing water hung from tree branches. Margie saw Evelyn digging a trench with a shovel. "Why are you doing that?"

Evelyn wiped sweat from her brow. "You don't want to know." She pointed to the containers of morphine, quinine, and vitamins that needed burying to protect them from bombardment and the monkeys.

"Now I've seen everything," Margie said. She grabbed a shovel to help. While they worked, clouds of insects swarmed in the oppressive air. Snakes, spiders, rats, and iguanas slithered through the vines and thorny undergrowth on the edges of the clearing. Stinking of rotting vegetation, dirt from the forest floor covered their shoes with black slime. Margie turned in a circle, looking around. "I can't even describe this place. There's not one familiar thing here—not one sight, not one smell, not one sound, not one feeling."

That night, a convoy of Red Cross ambulances delivered the first wave of patients. Margie held the IV as medics eased a gurney from the ambulance. The occupant moaned, and she took his hand. "Welcome to Walter Reed East, soldier. You're our first customer, so you get the best bed."

Miss Clio Kermit arrived with the convoy to take charge of her staff. She inspected the open-air wards, the buses housing the nurses, the mess, and the supply huts. She talked to the women and conferred with the doctors. She ordered permanent quarters built adjacent to the river, fenced and private, with a latrine and bathing area.

Margie and Evelyn dragged their belongings from the bus to the tent they would share with Gracie and Ruth Ann. In the cramped space, their four cots took up most of the floor. Just a few hours earlier, Filipino girls had stuffed the mattresses with rice straw. Gracie lay on hers. "Try the bed. It isn't bad."

Ruth Ann fashioned a clothesline from vines. Margie hung their one luxury, a small mirror, and Evelyn pulled out a fifth of gin. "To home, be it ever so humble," she said, toasting the crude abode and passing the bottle around.

Japanese troops relentlessly pounded the front line with artillery fire. Wounded men arrived in droves, over a hundred of them the first night, with chests ripped open, head trauma, abdomens half blown away, and limbs pierced with shrapnel. They came in buses, on trucks, in horse-drawn carts, and on the backs of mules, all of them stinking of blood, grime, and sweat. Moans, screams, and questions from still-lucid soldiers competed with a cacophony of sirens, transports, barked orders, and clanking instruments.

"Take a deep breath," Margie instructed, covering a soldier's nose with ether-soaked cotton. His body went limp. Margie monitored his heartbeat and blood pressure while the surgeon and nurse assistant probed deep in the young man's gut, searching for bleeders or holes in the delicate viscera.

"I need a clamp here," Dr. Corolla called out.

The medic searched in the Lysol-filled bucket of instruments that all the surgical tables shared.

"Too late! We've got a gusher! Get me suction!" the doctor bellowed.

The nurse suctioned inside the wound until the doctor found the damaged blood vessel and clamped it off. Following the trajectory of the bullet, he checked through the abdominal cavity, looking for nicks in the bowel. "We're good here. How is he doing, Margie?"

"His vital signs are stable."

"All right. Nurse, close him up. Who's next?"

"It's a chest case," the nurse said. "Ready on table six."

"How many more are out there?"

"Fifty-four, and there's another bus coming."

Margie prepared another young man for surgery, removing field dressings from his left ear and eye. Talkative and loopy from morphine, he told her of a fanatical enemy as she cleaned mud off his face and painted it with antiseptic.

"They live by the Code of Bushido. Death in battle's the highest honor. Suicide's nobler than being captured. Nothing stops them." He winced when she got too close to the wound.

"Sorry."

"S'okay." He continued, "Once I saw them charge into an electrified fence. The troops behind just climbed over the dead bodies. I've seen a lot. That's no way even close to human. Think I'll lose my eye?"

Wounded soldiers kept coming. Margie's adrenaline-charged body kept going, whether in the heat of the day when sweat rolled down her legs and into her shoes, or at night when blackout blinds trapped rank air in the surgical hut, making breathing difficult.

When the onslaught abated, she slept like a drugged person, waking with a headache each oven-hot morning. Disoriented, she tried to count the number of days she'd been here, but they all melted together.

Snatching her towel off a vine, she trod the short path to the river to bathe. Leaving her clothes at the water's edge, she immersed her body in the tepid water, enjoying the feeling of it sloshing over her. She washed with a bar of soap she found on a rock and scrubbed her scalp, her hair dry and brittle from lack of care. Margie slipped out of her underwear and washed that too. Wrapped in her towel, she sat on the riverbank to dry in the sun.

"Hey, Boots," she said to a woman nicknamed after her red patent leathers. She wore her black hair in an attractive blunt cut, compliments of the unit's talented barber.

"How're you doing, Margie?"

"I've been so busy, I don't even know. What day is it?"

"Friday, I think. They all blur together."

"I may have slept through a day, but I'm not sure. It's a weird feeling."

"You didn't miss anything. The surgery's been quiet." Boots lay back on her towel. "The wards are crazy, though. They opened Ward Eight yesterday."

"Eight? I thought there were six wards."

"You need to get out of the surgery more, kid."

"That would be two thousand four hundred wounded men! Are you sure?"

"Sounds about right."

"Who's staffing them?"

"Medics mostly, and some nurses transferred in from the hospital on that island south of us, Corregidor."

"I hadn't heard," Margie said, wondering what other news she had missed. "Has anyone arrived from Sternberg?"

Boots spoke languidly. "Gosh, no. I hope you're not expecting someone."

A prickle of anxiety stirred. Royce had said he would be just a few days behind her, but more time than that had passed.

Boots sat up. "Is Royce still at Sternberg?"

"As far as I know. Why?" She didn't like Boots's tone.

"You need to talk to Dr. Corolla, Margie."

"What's going on?"

"Just talk to Dr. Corolla. I saw him going out to Ward Six."

Margie tightened her towel, picked up her soiled clothes, and hurried back to the tent. She dressed quickly, then hitched a ride on a jeep going to the wards. Speeding along the bumpy path, the driver pointed upward. Margie saw a limp body caught in the tree branches. The driver shouted, "A Nip sniper! Some get behind our front line. Watch out for them."

As far as she could see, a hodgepodge of cots stretched out under the trees, their lower branches laden with boots, rucksacks, helmets, gas masks, ponchos, and pajamas. Skinny men mending from an assortment of corporal abuse or sick with jungle-rot diseases slept deeply or fitfully, read numbly, paced nervously, played games with homemade cards or dice, or just sat, staring dully into space. Some of those diagnosed with battle fatigue cried as they lay in fetal position, while others howled strings of obscenities. Birds squawked loudly and continuously, and monkeys looking down offered their opinions.

Nurses quietly moved from man to man, washing off grime and sweat with water from the Real River, cleaning open wounds with green soap, and treating them with sulfa powder. They changed soiled linens, plumped pillows, and watched their charges for fever, rashes, sores, pallor, pain, or mental confusion. They offered water for thirst, food for hunger, medicine for pain, and comfort to the frightened in this primitive setting. They worked like dogs. The men called them angels.

Margie found Evelyn and Dr. Corolla at the nurses' station. Kicking a small lizard off the toe of her shoe, Evelyn greeted her with a grin. "What are you doing out here in the boonies?"

"Slumming. It looks like I came to the right place."

"I know. It's bad. These guys deserve better than they're getting."

Margie noted dark circles under Evelyn's blue eyes, her skin sallow and bug-bitten. "You're doing the best you can."

"Tell that to the guy who's lying in a pool of blood or fecal drainage." She nudged Dr. Corolla aside with her hip, opened a bamboo cabinet, and selected a twenty-cc syringe and a large needle. She carefully ran the needle over her finger to check it for barbs before sharpening it on a rock. Dropping twenty morphine tablets into the syringe with twenty milliliters of water, she tilted the syringe gently to mix the solution. "I'm making rounds to change dressings. You want to come with me?"

"Not this time. I'm here to talk to Dr. Corolla."

He looked up from his daily log. "What can I do for you, Margie?" A cigarette dangled from his lips. His hair, thin on top, had grown shaggy over his ears and down the back of his neck.

Margie hesitated. "Do you know Royce Sherman? He's a surgeon."

Dr. Corolla inhaled, and the end of the cigarette glowed red. "Of course I know Royce. Are you the pretty nurse he talks about all the time?"

Growing warm, Margie figured she was blushing. "He talks about me?"

"Incessantly. The boy is smitten," he said through an exhalation of smoke.

Margie retrieved a cigarette from her pocket, and Dr. Corolla provided a light. She liked the idea of Royce being smitten. "I expected him to be here by now. Do you know where he is?"

Dr. Corolla regarded her. "You've been so busy in the surgery, you haven't heard."

She sensed trouble and steeled herself for bad news.

In a gentle voice, he said, "General Homma marched his troops into Manila three days ago. Before we could get the medical staff out, they'd blocked the roads. Twenty-seven physicians surrendered to the Japanese."

Not taking it in, she said, "The Japanese surrendered?"

He took her arm, lowered her to a stool, and squatted beside her. "My dear, Royce was captured by the Japanese."

"No! Not captured! It can't be! Is he all right?"

"I'm afraid we don't know."

"You don't know?" She choked back a sob. "Someone must know something!"

"I'm sorry, Margie, but there's nothing more I can tell you."

She didn't remember the jeep ride back to the nurses' quarters. She paced in front of her tent, willing herself not to dwell on the stories of Japanese atrocities that wanted to crowd out any other thoughts. Royce is a surgeon, she reasoned. He has rare and valuable skills. The Japanese would recognize that, and he would be safe. She prayed to a higher power, "Please, Lord, keep him safe!"

As the Japanese infantry pounded the front line, the spate of injured resumed, this time with the more intimate wounds of hand-to-hand combat. Margie administered anesthesia to the sliced and diced men, while surgeons and nurses stitched gashes from bayonets and swords.

Japanese warships blockaded every harbor. Medicine, food, and other provisions depleted alarmingly. Rationing decreased meals to two per day.

At breakfast one morning, Margie stirred the rice in her bowl, looking for weevils and wondering if the grayish meat was monkey or horse. Spitting out a tough chunk, she saw a spot of blood. She said to those with her, "We're not getting the right vitamins from this diet. My gums are bleeding."

"I'm not complaining," Gracie said, patting the underside of her newly revealed chin. "I've wanted to lose this baby fat for years. Now it's melting away."

"It's not a healthy weight loss, Gracie."

Margie ate the gray stuff in her bowl and every grain of rice, but what she craved was an orange. She would give anything for an orange, a cold, juice-dripping-down-your-chin orange! Her mouth watered.

Ruth Ann said, "The guys aren't getting enough calories to heal. I've noticed an increase in beriberi and scurvy. Half have dysentery."

"The other half have malaria."

"What they need are oranges."

"What they need is quinine."

"What we need is a God who knows we're here," Gracie said, then covered her face with her hands. "I shouldn't have said that. I'll never get into heaven."

Tildy scoffed. "Look around you, Gracie. You think God is interested in your every thought and word? A bit arrogant of you, isn't it?"

"I'll pray for your salvation, Tildy, as well as my own."

Tildy rose to leave. "Save your prayers for the guys. I'll take care of my own salvation, whatever that is."

Margie had no wise words. This hideous environment where so much pain and death surrounded her tested her own faith. A just God wouldn't allow this carnage, would he? Or did he have no power over evil? Was he all-seeing? If so, did he not care? Did the benevolent God she prayed to even exist?

Antiaircraft fire exploded, interrupting her deliberations. The women dove into a foxhole and hunkered under a rain of dirt.

Gracie said, "I hate these foxholes. They fill up with water."

"And snakes," Ruth Ann added.

Margie said, "We should bring a shovel with us."

The ack-ack stopped. Hearing no incoming planes, they climbed out and brushed the dirt off their clothes and out of their hair. Looking up, Margie saw nothing but a dense canopy of trees.

Evelyn said, "Shrapnel went through a bed yesterday. It left a hole as big as a basketball. Luckily, no one was in it."

"Luckily," Margie said. Bone-weary, she wobbled on her feet. "I have to get to the surgery."

Evelyn said, "I heard the gloves are gone. What're you doing?"

"Repairing as many as we can. Sometimes the docs go in bare-handed. Pentothal and ether are low too. We're using more locals."

Gracie added, "We're dispensing quinine on an as-needed basis. That's just criminal! What happened to those supply ships MacArthur promised?"

Evelyn scoffed. "Promises, promises. That was just a tease."

"Some tease," Ruth Ann said, pulling up her pant leg to reveal an ugly abrasion. "That's from shimmying up a tree to watch for those damn ghost ships."

"Where did you get the energy to do that?"

"It was a while ago. Back when I still had some."

Spending as much time as she did in the confines of the surgical hut spared Margie from some harsher aspects of patient care. Her patients arrived drowsy from drugs and with the worst grit of battle scraped off. When they left, they were asleep and swaddled in clean surgical dressings. She seldom visited the wards, where men, too weak to heal, lingered on cots under mosquito-laden trees.

She hurried to the soldier lying on the surgical table. Tildy prepared a tray of sterile instruments. Careful not to contaminate the field, Margie began her presurgical routine. Finding the soldier's blood pressure low, his pulse fast, and respirations shallow, she consulted with the doctor before adjusting the drip on his IV and starting the anesthesia. "He looks a little yellow."

Tildy said, "Poor guy. He crawled through the jungle for two days before someone found him."

Dr. Corolla inspected the wound on the soldier's thigh, swollen and oozing bloody fluid. He mumbled it didn't look good and ordered the medic to ready an amputation tray, just in case. "Is he under, Margie?"

She checked the sedated soldier's responses. "Yes, all set."

Tildy slapped a scalpel into his outstretched hand and stood ready with sponges and suction.

Dr. Corolla quickly removed necrotic tissue and shredded muscle. When he probed deeper to search for shrapnel, an overpowering stink exploded. "God!" he shouted. Bubbles oozed from the wound.

"Gas!" Tildy gagged.

The medic whipped the curtain around the surgical station in a futile attempt to contain gangrenous spores.

Margie choked, then deepened the soldier's sedation.

Dr. Corolla applied a tourniquet, then located and ligated major arteries, veins, and nerves. He amputated the beyond-repair limb in hopes of controlling the spread of the gangrene. He passed the severed leg to the medic, who took it to the dump to be burned along with the bloody dressings.

A sickly-sweet stench hung in the air as Dr. Corolla finished the surgery. When done, the surgical hut had to close for scouring, all instruments gathered up for resterilization. As the nurses and medics started the dreary cleaning task, Margie accompanied the patient to the gangrene ward.

Gracie was there, the only nurse who willingly worked on this fetid ward. Row after row of men lay on cots, most with stumps of arms and legs wrapped in mummy-like dressings. The odor forced Margie to breathe through her mouth. She handed Gracie the soldier's chart. "He's had a rough go."

Gracie glanced through the chart, then adjusted the drip on the IV and checked his vital signs. "I'll keep a close eye on him. What's his name?" She looked at his wristband and then jiggled his shoulder. "Arnie, can you wake up? Your surgery's over. You're in recovery now. Can you open your eyes?"

"It might take a while. He's under pretty deep," Margie said. She nodded to a group of men lying in the sun with their grotesquely swollen and putrid-smelling limbs exposed. "What's going on with them?"

"It's a new treatment. It's amazing. We debride the wounds, then douse them with hydrogen peroxide. They're tented with mosquito netting and left open to the air and the sun. Some of them heal up real nice."

Real nice? Margie had her doubts. As she left the ward, she heard a delirious soldier pleading, "Just get the leg off me, doc! Take it off! I want it off!"

CHAPTER 11

Bataan, February–April 1942

Mid-February brought a reprieve. While the Japanese reprovisioned their forces, the numbers of wounded soldiers delivered to the field hospital decreased to a trickle. Medical care fell into a routine of patient baths in the river or sponge baths in the bed; meals, though never enough to eat; medications, when available; cigarettes for comfort; gossip for boredom; and chitchat to chase away the blues. Proliferating rumors raised hopes or festered fears. Everyone battled rats that ate their clothes, monkeys that stole their food, and iguanas that crawled into their beds. For the first time in a long while, the medical staff had some free time.

So they slept. After restoring their tired bodies, they searched for diversions. In Miss Kermit's shack, the nurses listened to the Voice of Freedom, which broadcast radio programs three times a day from Corregidor, or news broadcasts from KEGI in San Francisco, or programs on random frequencies picked up by their receiver depending on the weather. They heard how superbly the Philippine Islands were holding up against the Japanese.

"Are they ignorant or what?" Margie spat.

"It's just hooey for the Japanese. Don't get tied in a knot." Ruth Ann rotated the dial, trying to pick up another signal. After much hissing and squawking, the song "I'm Waiting for Ships That Never Came In" played. She looked at the tuner. "I've got Tokyo. Anyone want to listen to their propaganda?"

"It's no worse than the real news," Evelyn said.

Margie didn't want to dwell on the real news. The Japanese got stronger every day, capturing one island after another in their quest to imperialize the Far East. Now they had Australia in their sights. "Shut it off!" she said. A pall hung in the air.

"I want to go to a movie," Ruth Ann said. "A comedy. I want to laugh. And I want a bucket of popcorn, dripping in butter. Did anybody see *Moon Over Miami* with those two carhops?"

"Betty Grable and Carole Landis," Gracie said. "Two gold diggers with big hearts. They have to choose between love and money. Which one would you choose, Ruth Ann, love or money?"

"Neither." Ruth Ann didn't give it a thought. "I'd choose a cheeseburger. I'd give my back tooth right now for a cheeseburger, medium rare, with American cheese, lettuce, tomato, a big salty dill pickle, and a pile of hot french fries. I like my fries really hot—with ketchup."

"I'm with you, Ruth Ann," Evelyn said. "Come on, guys, let's go to the beach. We'll take sandwiches. Unfortunately, our choices are carabao or carabao."

When alone, Margie brooded. She ached for Royce. He had to be safe at Sternberg . . . didn't he? The Japanese would be mindful of his status . . . wouldn't they? She yearned for his touch, the smell of his skin, and the blue of his eyes. She replayed their conversations, whispering his words aloud. In dreams, she felt the scrape of his beard on her breast, the weight of his body crushing hers into the bed, and she woke writhing with ecstasy. *I love you; I love us* played like music in her head. As always, the tears came.

In letters, she reassured her parents that she was okay. Though she lived in a tent, she told them, she slept in a comfortable bed, and was healthy. Caring for the soldiers gratified her and kept her busy from morning until night. She mentioned that several of the doctors and nurses came from the Ann Arbor area; one of the doctors even knew Myra from the Red Cross. Wasn't it a small world? She wrote about the beautiful, brightly colored parrots in the trees that squawked so loudly it hurt her ears. A monkey in the camp kept stealing the food. Ha, ha.

An American pilot arrived at the field hospital with a bullet in his foot. Flying through the Japanese blockade with a plane so loaded it hardly stayed aloft, he brought medical supplies and bags full of mail, including two letters for Margie. The one from her parents was postmarked early December.

Little River, Michigan
December 5, 1941

Dear Margie,

I can't believe that Christmas is just around the corner. Two letters and a package arrived from you this week. We opened the letters right away and put the package under the Christmas tree. It is sad that you won't be here when we open it. We are so concerned about you. The news we hear is frightening. We are relieved to know it is mostly rumor, and you feel safe at Sternberg.

*Your dad is buying seed for next year's crops. He will be put-
ting wheat and corn in the back twenty acres. It's hard to find
laborers. He spent all day today repairing the tractor. It needs a
part, and he's having trouble finding one. He sends you his love.*

*Frank is studying for final exams. He is doing well in his
classes, but is looking forward to a break. He's still disappointed
he's not in the navy, but I'm glad he is home. He's a volunteer
fireman and is putting in many hours at the fire hall. It is honorable work and very much needed. Our fire and police forces are
depleted with so many men gone.*

*I put two Christmas packages in the mail for you the first
week of October, and I hope they arrive in time for the holidays.
If they are held up, know that they are on the way, and that
they are full of love for you. You can expect a package from the
church, also. The Women's League assembled boxes for all the
young people who are on active duty. Prayers are sent your way
every day.*

*We think of you constantly and miss you terribly. The only
present we pray for this Christmas is your safe return home.*
With love always,
Mama and Daddy

She checked the date on the letter again: December 5, 1941,
three days before the Japanese bombed Clark Airfield. It had been
sitting somewhere in a mailbag for over three months! A lump
rose in her throat, and she wept, feeling cut off from everyone she
loved and so alone. Drying her tears on the sleeve of her shirt, she
opened the second letter, from Abe. This one didn't have the usual
government stamps on it.

Darwin, Australia
February 24, 1942

Dear Margie,

Hope this letter finds its way to you. A pal of mine is flying missions over Manila, and he's tucking it in his front pocket. He said it would bring him good luck. Flying through the Japanese blockade is always a bit dicey.

I'm now stationed in Australia, just fifteen hundred miles from the Philippines, a stone's throw from you, considering. The army needed a seasoned flier to head up a new squadron here. I was promoted to captain and joined the Forty-Ninth Pursuit Squadron on February 1. Got into trouble with the Japanese right away. Just a bullet in the leg, but it's healing well. Can't fly for another week, and I have too much time on my hands.

I heard about the hell you're living through. Sad thing is, a convoy of ships with food and medicines are in Australia but can't get out of the harbor. I was on escort to that convoy when it left for Luzon. Two days out, the Nips found us. I managed a couple of kills before my Kittyhawk was hit. I fared better than my plane. Both of us went into the drink, but I got plucked out. We were ordered to return to Australia. I was sick about it, Margie. I would have moved sea and earth to deliver those goods. MacArthur is negotiating for more escort ships and planes to help the convoys break through the blockade. Hang in there awhile longer.

I have my hands full here. Most of my guys are new graduates. They're a competitive bunch, cocky and full of bravado, like I was once. I hate to see them change, but they will. With each mission, I experience greater dread of losing another man—there have been too many. Got so tied up by it, I had to talk to the shrink. He said it is survivor's guilt, and it is normal. It doesn't feel normal. This war is hell.

Been thinking a lot about you lately. Remember The Pirates of Penzance *and how much fun that was? It seems like a lifetime ago, and it was, what, six years?*

Did I tell you I painted your picture on the nose of my plane? I gave you this really wild red hair. You led me on many successful missions. Love you and hope to see you at home sooner rather than later.
Forever,
Abe

So they weren't completely forgotten. Ships not so far away carried the supplies they so desperately needed. Somehow, they had to get through the blockade, because life couldn't go on under these increasingly wretched conditions. The open-air hospital now stretched over two and a half square miles, with cots stacked three high under the trees. The injured and sick filled seven thousand beds, and still more men slept on the ground with the snakes and lizards. Common graveyards swelled with sons, husbands, and brothers buried without so much as a sheet to cover them.

Putting Abe's letter in her pocket, she hurried to the records shack. She wanted to find the pilot; maybe he knew more about the convoy. Maybe he knew Abe. The clerk rifled through papers. "That's Lieutenant Gilbert Zybecki. He's in Ward Six. Took a bullet in his foot and had surgery yesterday."

She found Lieutenant Zybecki lying on a cot with his foot elevated in a sling. From what she could tell, he was a little shorter than the average pilot, but well muscled, like a wrestler. He looked better fed than most of the men who showed up at the hospital. He was staring into the trees as Margie approached. She said, "Lieutenant Zybecki?"

He looked her way. "Hi. Call me Gil."

"I'm Margie Bauer. I was the anesthetist when you had your surgery."

Gil cracked a wide smile. "My sleepy-time gal. Hey, sweetheart, you know where I can get some jungle juice?"

"Some what?"

"Raisin jack. Booze. The docs make it out of raisins and prunes."

She knew exactly what he meant. She had downed a slug of the burning liquid herself on occasion but didn't care to admit it. "I don't know. I can ask. Mind if I sit down?"

He gestured. "Pull up the golden throne."

She perched on a bamboo stool. "Thanks for bringing the mail. I got two letters."

"My pleasure."

"How'd you get shot? I mean, if you don't mind talking about it."

"I don't mind at all. It's not the first bullet I've taken. It's a hazard of the job. I was patrolling the forward areas. Windy that day. So rough the air shot me up nine hundred feet, then dropped me down eight hundred. Ever been on a roller coaster? You know that stomach feeling? Then, I ran into this hive of Zeros. I counted six. Shit! Pardon my French. They dart around like hummingbirds. All you can do is loop and try to stay out of their sights."

Margie nodded. "I've seen them in action."

"I peeled away to the right at 190 knots—uh, that's 220 miles per hour. I was descending five thousand feet per minute. You can't keep that up for more than a few seconds. The plane starts vibrating. Those Zeros couldn't keep up. See, their controls get heavy at high speeds. They don't roll well to the right. I know. I've watched enough of them. I got one in my sights—just long enough. Bam! I saw smoke. I'm pretty sure that bastard's history." Gil paused, reliving the moment. "Then something knocked out my rudder and got me in the foot. I think it was our AA. It probably saved my life."

"Getting hit by antiaircraft fire saved your life? Is that ironic, or what?" Margie said.

"Yeah. A real knee-slapper."

She inspected the wrapped appendage for bleeding and felt his uncovered toes, checking for warmth. "Looks like your foot's going to be all right."

"It has to. I have to get back to my unit."

"Are many of you here? Pilots, I mean. I thought most of the planes were destroyed."

"Right. F-U-B-A-R." He pronounced each letter slowly and with disgust. "Now we're the Bamboo Fleet. Mostly reconnaissance. All fifteen of us."

"Fifteen is all? Not great odds."

"No, but we're cunning fools."

She had no doubts about that. Pilots had nerves of steel, or at least pretended they did. "I have a friend who's a pilot. He's in Australia right now. I was wondering if you might know him. His name's Abe Carson."

"Abe Carson. Never heard of him. Sorry, can't help you."

"You did, though. You brought me his letter. He got shot down while escorting a convoy from Australia. He lost his plane, but he's okay. By the way, do you know anything about a supply convoy?"

"I heard about it."

"Do you think they'll get through?"

"Not a chance in a thousand. It doesn't have the backup, and we're pretty low priority over here. The big guns are going after Hitler. Hey! Find me some of that jungle juice, will you?"

Margie stood to leave. "I'll do that."

"You're a doll. Margie, is it? Soon as I get back in the air, I'll bring you a treat. What do you want? A lipstick?"

She laughed. "I'd kill for a bottle of shampoo."

"Shampoo. You got it."

Margie never got her shampoo, nor did she ever see Gil again, but the message he left her with played in her head: *We're pretty low priority over here.*

Gathered together in Miss Kermit's shack, Margie and her friends listened to President Roosevelt's Fireside Chat, straining to hear his words through the static. He spoke of aid provided to China and the importance of Australia, New Zealand, and the Dutch Indies. He talked about munitions sent to the British, the Russians, and the Mediterranean countries to help them fight off the Nazis.

Speaking of the Philippines, Roosevelt restated his long-held strategy of winning by attrition—how, with the United States' greater resources, it could ultimately out-build and overwhelm Japan on sea, on land, and in the air. He pointed out the difficulty of defending the Philippines since the enemy had the islands surrounded with its superior air and naval power. He mentioned the vast Pacific Ocean that complicated sending substantial reinforcements.

Just days after the broadcast—with soldiers dressed in rags and barely holding their positions; with rations down to one meal per day; with malaria, dysentery, and nutritional edema reaching epidemic proportions; and with medical supplies depleted—General MacArthur fled the dangerous battleground of the Philippines to the relative safety of Australia.

Feeling abandoned by their country as well as their supreme commander, the troops fought on, because there was nothing else they could do. A journalist caught their mood in a ditty:

We're the Battling Bastards of Bataan,
No mama, no papa, no Uncle Sam,
No aunts, no uncles, no cousins, no nieces,
No pills, no planes, no artillery pieces,
And nobody gives a damn!

By the end of March, General Homma's reinforced and well-fed army slammed through the country with renewed vengeance, reopening the floodgates of wounded. Bombs pelted the hospital, killing scores of injured men, as they lay incapacitated on their cots, as well as the workers attending them. Fear and anger levels rose. Margie remained stoic, working to calm her patients' nightmares while struggling to come to terms with her own.

The soldier occupying the operating table resembled a kid she'd known in high school. *What was his name? He was a whiz at math.*

Miss Kermit approached her. "Miss Bauer, the medics will take over here. Go to your quarters and pack what you can carry in your hands. Meet me in front of the records shack in thirty minutes."

Margie balked. She cradled the man's chin to keep his airway open. "Thirty minutes? I can't leave him like this."

"Thirty minutes, Miss Bauer. I kept you here as long as I could." Miss Kermit continued through the room, gathering her girls.

Margie transferred her sedated patient to a medic, giving him a five-minute tutorial on anesthesiology. Fighting tears, she apologized to the surgeon. She removed her gown and pitched it in the laundry hamper, then dashed to the nurses' quarters. It rumbled with confusion as the women stuffed their belongings in duffels or pillowcases. "Does anybody know what's going on?" she asked.

Evelyn said, "The Nips broke through the front line this morning. They're evacuating the women."

"Just the women? What about the men? I left one on the table!" Margie protested. She grabbed her stomach and bent over with a cramp, her dysentery a constant plague.

In a high-pitched voice, Gracie protested, "We can't abandon them! We can't leave them on the ground! I'm not going!"

Evelyn retrieved Gracie's duffel. "Pack, Gracie! On the double! There's no choice."

Gracie sat on her cot, her arms crossed defiantly across her chest, her expression determined.

"Come *on*, Gracie," Margie said, tugging at her arm, but Gracie resisted. Giving up, Margie hefted her own duffel and sprinted out the door, with Evelyn at her heels.

"I feel like a dirty dog leaving like this," Evelyn mumbled, and Margie agreed.

A bus was parked in front of the records shack, its engine running and tailpipe spewing exhaust. Margie tossed her bag in the back, then climbed aboard.

Miss Kermit said, "Girls, we're going to Mariveles. A boat is waiting to take us to Corregidor, where it's safer." She took count. "Thirty-four. Who's missing?"

"Gracie Hall," Margie said, and Miss Kermit sent soldiers to fetch her.

While they waited, an explosion shook the ground, filling the sky with white lights and curls of black smoke. Margie peered through the mud-plastered window, looking for Nip bombers. She couldn't see any.

After Gracie got hustled onto the bus, the driver jumped into his seat. "We're out of here!" he yelled as he cranked the gears and got up to speed.

The bus made its way down a road jammed with dazed soldiers retreating from the front and with local men and women sitting on oxen, riding bicycles, and pulling cumbersome carts filled with old folks and children. Everyone sought escape from the oncoming enemy. The going was achingly slow, and soon forward movement stopped altogether. The bus driver stepped out of the vehicle to confer with a soldier. He came back with the news. The army was destroying ammunition dumps and had closed the road until the job was done. The bus sat idle while the hours ticked away. Periodically, a blast filled the sky with the most amazing fireworks that turned the atmosphere purple green.

The constant rumble from the north heightened the refugees' fear. Filipino men banged on the bus, demanding rides for their wives, children, and aging parents. Hunkering down in her seat, feeling guilt and pity, Margie avoided looking at the panicked faces with their open, yelling mouths. *How secure was the bus door?*

The door buckled. Ruth Ann leaped up and shouldered the driver's Springfield bolt-action rifle. Aiming it at the intruders, she hollered, "One more step and you're dog meat!"

Reluctantly the men backed away.

Shortly after that incident, the bus pulled forward.

The women arrived at Mariveles in the inky early-morning hours. Nearing the waterfront, the bus sputtered to a stop, out of gas. The driver kicked the tire and looked as if he might break down and cry. "The docks are two miles ahead," he said.

"All right, girls, get your things. Let's get walking." Miss Kermit wobbled when she tried to stand, and Evelyn took her arm.

Tildy found a lantern in the back of the bus.

"Follow the light," Miss Kermit ordered, and the women joined the crowd of pedestrians on the winding mountain road. The two-mile trek felt more like ten to the careworn band of women.

Gracie started a hymn, *"I come to the garden alone . . . ,"* and they all sang along softly.

Down at the docks, chaos reigned as masses of people crowded the shore, desperately seeking transport to safer islands. The brown, oil-slicked water churned with debris. Everything that floated got used as a conveyance. The nurses pushed their way down to the water's edge to look for their boat.

"The boat's gone," Tildy said.

"It can't be. They wouldn't leave us here."

Tildy's voice turned sharp. "Then show me the damn boat! What does the army care about a handful of women? They just sacrificed thousands of men to the Japanese!"

Her words hung unchallenged in the air.

They found shelter in a copse of trees. Suffering from malaria and exhaustion, Miss Kermit lay in the sand. The others, keyed up and afraid, held quiet conversations.

"It smells like someone's broiling a steak."

"I smell cheese. What I'd give for a chunk of sharp cheddar."

"Please don't talk about food," Margie said. "It makes my stomach cramp."

Evelyn appraised Margie, then reached over and slapped Ruth Ann on the knee. "Ruth Annie Oakley, where'd you learn to shoot a rifle?"

"My daddy had me shooting those old Springfields before I lost my first baby tooth. I grew up on a ranch in Wyoming."

"Are you good?"

"Snakes are my specialty, but let's just say no one was going to get through that bus door."

Gracie sat apart from the other women. Margie went to her. "You okay?"

She shrugged and looked away.

"We all feel guilty about leaving the men. Don't be so hard on yourself."

"That's only part of it. What I did was so stupid. We might have gotten past the roadblock if it hadn't been for me delaying us. Now—" She waved her hand in the air.

"Come on, Gracie. No one's blaming you."

The sky lightened from black to pale gray. Hearing a roar in the distance, the crowd on the beach panicked and scattered. Margie watched a Zero approach like a ghost in the sky, and knew a slaughter of innocent people loomed. Leaves whipped off the trees, and water swirled in great arcs as the yellow devil strafed the shoreline. The staccato rat-a-tat of discharging guns battered their ears and bullets sought out their bodies. Everyone cowered by the piers, mothers hovering over children, husbands shielding wives. After the roar faded to a drone, Margie lifted her head. Gracie lay crumpled in a heap, her blood seeping into the sand.

"Gracie," she whispered. Carefully rolling her over, Margie opened her blouse. A messy hole showed near her left shoulder. "Oh, Gracie!"

Evelyn appeared with a medical kit. "Hey, kid," she rasped, tears in her throat. "You got in the way of a bullet." She inspected the wound and opened a morphine syrette. "I'm giving you morphine. I don't want you going into shock on me. You hear me, kid? Okay?"

Gracie nodded, and her eyelids fluttered shut.

Frenzied by the attack, the crowd keened, women wailing and children howling. Men shook angry fists at the sky. "Bastards!" they shouted. "You dirty bastards!"

Out of the confusion, a boat appeared, tumbling and pitching in the waves. Its engine slowed to a putter as it eased its way to the shore. The captain yelled, "I'm looking for the nurses!"

The women scrambled aboard, four of them carrying Gracie. Ruth Ann assisted Miss Kermit, who was so dizzy she tumbled onto the deck. The captain fended off aggressive Filipinos clambering to board. He glanced upward. "Anchor yourselves, company's coming!" he shouted over the blub-blub-blub of the idling motor. Rapidly maneuvering away from the dock, he pressed the throttle to full, and the engine roared to life. The Japanese plane closed in overhead. Just as the pilot released his load, the boat sped away. On the shore behind them, the dock disappeared in a geyser of fire and water.

The boat pitched violently to starboard, choking and stuttering, waves dousing Margie and the others. The captain adjusted the throttle, and the craft leaped forward again. With seawater sloshing around her ankles and winds lashing so strong at her face she couldn't catch a breath, Margie clung to the boat like a barnacle.

The Zero reemerged from the clouds, and the captain zigzagged the boat through the water. The plane swooped low and trained its guns on it. Hearing a blast of gunfire, Margie squatted down and waited for a hissing bullet to find her. Instead, the Japanese fighter exploded in midair. A fireball, it crashed into the churning water.

"Score one for the United States!" screamed Miss Kermit in a moment of recovered energy, and all the women cheered. The boat nosed into shore under the protection of Corregidor's formidable antiaircraft artillery.

CHAPTER 12

Corregidor, April–May 1942

The downed Japanese plane hit the water with a thud and a sizzle, and Margie first saw Corregidor through a rain of burning debris. "Impregnable!" the captain shouted over the roar of the boat's engine. He pointed to the forested island. "It's called the Gibraltar of the East. Artillery batteries rim the perimeter. The Japs will never take it."

A truck picked up the nurses at the dock and rushed them to a heavily treed hill, then through a massive iron gate and into a vast tunnel. Clusters of people clapped and cheered as they climbed out. A kind-faced woman waved. "Girls, come in where it's safe."

An arched tunnel soared eighteen feet overhead with concrete-lined floors and walls. Lamps hanging from cables provided flickering blue-mercury light, and trolley tracks running through the center disappeared into the distance. Noise bounced off the hard surfaces, creating a constant din. Even near the entrance, the air felt clammy and smelled dank.

The woman who'd welcomed them introduced herself as Lieutenant Alice Riley, director of nursing. She ordered medics to transport Gracie and Miss Kermit to the hospital, then addressed the others. "You are standing in the Malinta Tunnel," she told them, and expressed her relief at their safe arrival.

They followed Miss Riley through the wide main tunnel, then through a maze of smaller ones to the women's quarters. Dozens of narrow beds sat perpendicular to the long wall. The communal bathroom had a sink, flush toilet, and a shower.

Miss Riley smiled apologetically. "It's pretty Spartan, I'm afraid. You'll sleep two to a bed until we get more cots in here." She opened cupboards filled with towels, soap, shampoo, and personal items and pointed out a stack of clothing. "Use what you need. You'll have to take turns in the shower. I've ordered food. After you eat, a doctor will examine each of you, and then you can sleep until orientation. It's at 1800 hours."

The women's quarters looked like a luxurious hotel to Margie. In the shower, she slathered her body with soap and reveled in the lather of shampoo. She dried off using a clean towel. Combing out her hair in front of the mirror, she saw how thin she had grown. Her eyes seemed huge in her face, and bug bites, some welted up as big as her thumb, covered her sallow skin. She picked through the clothing pile to find something wearable, then went to find the promised banquet of eggs, bacon, bananas, pineapple, toast with butter and jelly, and milk, tea, or coffee.

"I've found heaven," Evelyn said, diving in.

Margie felt starved too, but when she tried to eat, the smell of the food made her stomach cramp. She nibbled on some dry toast and managed to swallow a few bites of banana. Later on, a doctor gave her calamine lotion for the bites and sulfadiazine to treat her dysentery. Achingly tired, she dropped into bed, and despite the strange surroundings she sank immediately into a deep sleep.

Margie woke hours later, feeling sheltered. Sitting up, she faced a concrete wall. She squinted at her watch in the flickering light. It read three o'clock, but in the depths of this man-made cavern, she couldn't tell if it was morning or afternoon. Evelyn, who shared the bed with Margie, stretched and yawned.

"What do you make of this?" Margie asked, hearing her voice echo.

Evelyn glanced up. "There's a ceiling over my head. Well, hallelujah." She massaged a kink in her neck. "Did I have a nightmare, or did we have a wild ride in a boat?"

"We had a wild ride. Let's look around."

The tunnel led to a passageway crowded with uniformed nurses and soldiers mingling with Filipinos of all ages in rumpled suits or dresses, many with children in tow. Some people were injured, hobbling on crutches or sitting in wheelchairs, and a few lay on gurneys. Margie and Evelyn joined the crowd and got pushed to an exit.

More hordes of humanity—smoking, chatting, praying—clustered outside near the tunnel entrance. As a guitarist softly strummed "To You Sweetheart, Aloha, from the Bottom of My Heart," the people around him sang along. Everyone lifted light-deprived faces toward the life-giving sun. Margie walked toward the shoreline with its crater-pocked beaches and great twisted coils of barbed wire.

"Don't go wandering out there," a voice behind her said.

She turned around.

"Hi! Welcome!" A nurse smiled at Margie. She was dressed in khaki, her brown hair cut in a short, off-the-collar style. "The marines have been laying barbed wire and burying land mines for weeks," she explained. She pointed across the three-mile-wide body of water to the Bataan Peninsula. "That's where you came from early this morning. I watched your boat from here. It was a terrific show, given the happy ending."

"Where's here?" Margie asked, still disoriented.

"The north entrance to the Malinta Tunnel. You slept in the women's quarters. It's mostly nurses, but there are some wives and daughters of government muckety-mucks. Two women journalists were here last week, but they left. Amazing, isn't it, how journalists get around? Even through the blockades? I'm Glenda, by the way."

They shook hands. "Margie."

Glenda pointed to an airplane overhead. "It's a Jap reconnaissance plane. We call him Photo Joe."

Squinting at the sky, Margie watched the plane circle. She recognized the sound, though she had never been able to see him through Bataan's dense trees. Surveying the area around her, she saw patches of denuded land and evidence of recent fires. "This from the bombing?"

"Yeah. It's almost continuous. Our gun crews keep the Nips too high up for them to hit the batteries or powerhouse. Those are their real targets. When they get positioned on Bataan, we'll be in range of their artillery. We'll be in more trouble then." She glanced at Margie. "I don't mean to scare you, but—"

Margie shrugged, numb to the threat of more Japanese guns. "How long have you been here?"

"Almost six months. When I first came, I stayed at the barracks at Fort Mills on the other side of the island. It was like a beautiful garden. An army regiment was stationed there. Now it's nothing but a pile of dirt. Marines came about three months ago."

"Do they stay in the tunnel?"

"Only the ones on duty in there. Most live in bunkers near their stations. They man the batteries, the big guns all over the island. They have their own kitchens and medical units for the small stuff. You won't see much of them. They're a bunch of cocky kids, really."

Margie beckoned Evelyn over and introduced her to Glenda.

Evelyn asked, "Have you seen Gracie Hall? She came in wounded."

"Yes. The bullet missed everything vital. You can go see her if you want." She pointed to the gate they had just come through. "If you go back down that lateral—that's what these side tunnels are called—you'll find the hospital. If you keep going, it will eventually dead-end. Turn left and you'll run into the main tunnel. It's pretty packed. The Japs are letting Filipinos through their front lines to crowd us and deplete our supplies. When's your orientation?"

"After dinner."

"Miss Edwards will show you the layout. She's the big cheese here, a real witch. Best to stay out of her way. Miss Riley, on the other hand, she's a sweetheart. Tough, but in a nice way." She glanced at her watch. "I have to get back. Nice talking to both of you."

Narrowing her eyes against the sun, Margie watched Photo Joe make another pass. Antiaircraft artillery blasted, shaking the ground. Her gaze went beyond the retreating plane to Bataan, just a speck of land on the horizon. From there came the grumble of gunfire, a constant clapping of booms and bangs. Seventy thousand men were trapped on the peninsula between the Japanese army and the South China Sea. "What will happen to them?" she mumbled.

"Max?" Evelyn said, misunderstanding. "He's drinking good scotch and teaching the Aussies the Lindy hop. And Royce? He's charming those yellow boys into a first-class ticket home. You'll see."

They heard a rumble like rolling thunder. "Bombers!" someone shouted. The crowd stampeded toward the entrance, their progress impeded by wheelchairs and gurneys. Margie and Evelyn picked up a man struggling with his crutches. They propelled him along, one on each arm, pushing their way inside the tunnel just as a bomb landed nearby, its shock wave slamming the iron gate shut.

Captain Hazel Edwards, a battle-hardened chief nurse, had a dow-ager's hump and an old-lady bun of white hair. She was elflike in size and peered at the new arrivals from Bataan through thick glasses. "Good evening. I trust that you are fed, rested, and ready to get to work."

The women murmured their assent.

Miss Edwards coughed into a hankie and took a sip of water, then became all business. "You're in the Malinta Tunnel. It's bomb-proof. Nothing can penetrate the rock. You're safe as long as you stay inside."

She picked up a dowel and turned to a map perched on an easel beside her, pointing to it as she spoke. "American engineers bored the tunnels through the rock in the 1920s. The main tunnel is 834 feet long and twenty-four feet wide, and an electric trolley runs down the center. Twenty-four smaller lateral tunnels branch like fish bones off the main one. Four gates, one at each compass point, lead to the outside. The hospital wing is near the north gate. Its fourteen laterals hold operating rooms, a dental clinic, labora-tory, dispensary, kitchen, dining room, and sleeping quarters for the nurses. Ten of the laterals are set up as recovery and convales-cent wards, each holding one hundred beds.

"General Wainwright commands his troops from his offices in the north laterals. You'll be meeting him and some of his staff later. Altogether, about four thousand people live inside the tun-nel, including the Philippine Commonwealth government offi-cials, their staff and families, US marines, and hundreds of Filipino refugees from Luzon. Outside are about seven thousand American and Filipino combat troops and their support units."

Miss Edwards put the pointer down. "Casualties have been light, thanks to our gunners. However, with Bataan in the hands of the Japanese, we expect numbers to increase. You must help pre-pare the hospital for the anticipated need. Miss Riley is drawing up a work schedule. Before we tour the hospital, are there any questions?"

A hand in the back went up. "How many nurses are here?"

"I have eighty-six American and twenty-six Filipino nurses under my command, along with several dozen civilian women working as aides."

Evelyn raised her hand. "What's happening to the men in the field hospitals?"

Margie leaned forward to catch Miss Edwards's answer.

"Conditions on Bataan are uncertain. The Americans surrendered to the Japanese this morning. As far as we know, the men in the hospitals are still there with the doctors and medics."

So, chances are good that Royce is still with his patients at Sternberg. He'll be okay as long as he's at Sternberg . . . won't he?

Tildy asked, "Can we get mail out?"

"We try. There's a letterbox in the front of the dining lateral. If a submarine or seaplane makes it through the blockade and has a chance to get out again, we always send mail out with them, but it's sporadic."

Ruth Ann asked, "How long do you think we'll be here?"

"Nobody knows. Corregidor is the key to controlling Manila Bay, and General Wainwright has pledged to hold the position until help arrives."

Miss Edwards introduced Miss Riley, who led a tour of the hospital wing. The fourteen narrow hospital laterals were connected honeycomb-style, and Margie doubted she would ever learn her way around.

During her first week in the Malinta Tunnel, Margie welcomed her improved living conditions. Despite the constant bombing, the assurance that nothing could penetrate the thick walls made her feel safe. She was issued khaki skirts and blouses, white anklets,

oxford shoes, and a Red Cross armband. Strictly enforced schedules gave her life structure, and the hospital's iron beds, white
enamel tables, refrigerators, flush toilets, and showers lent an air
of familiarity. A barber trimmed her hair and gave her bangs that
curled on her forehead.

"That style's adorable on you, Margie." Evelyn plucked at one
of Margie's red curls. "When I was little, I would have died for red
hair. I wanted to look like Clara Bow."

"You're prettier than she was. She had those cupid's-bow lips,
but you have good bones. Personally, I always wanted blond hair,
like yours."

They linked arms and made their way through the dimly lit
corridors to the dining lateral, food still a high priority for them.

As the second week in the shadowy labyrinths turned into
a third, life devolved into a tedious sameness. Margie couldn't
orient to time and space as day and night melted together. The
low-ceilinged laterals seemed to close in around her. Once the
Japanese moved their artillery into the mountains of Bataan,
dawn-to-midnight shelling kept people inside. They suffered
from headaches, nosebleeds, and earaches caused by the concussive blasts. The dank, dust-laden air left everybody coughing.
Government officials and soldiers, nurses and society women,
no matter what their station in life outside the tunnels, they
all walked aimlessly, chatted idly, or played marathon games of
bridge or poker as the hours dragged.

"Come on, nurse, let's boogie," a soldier said, pulling Margie
away from the wall. Three bandsmen from the officers' club had
formed an unlikely trio—trombone, harmonica, and guitar—but
they could swing, so a party started.

"Thanks, but no," Margie replied. "I'm not in the mood." He
insisted, however, so she shuffled her feet in time to the music
while he spun and stomped, having a good time. She bumped into
the woman behind her.

"Watch where you're going," the woman snapped.

Margie's dance partner flapped his arms, catching Margie in the ribs on a cluster of dankness-induced boils that had plagued her for days. The intense pain sickened her stomach, and she slumped with her back against the wall.

Evelyn came to her. "Are you hurt?"

"A little," she replied, bending to hold her side. "Help me get away from this suffocating crowd."

As the Japanese moved more guns onto the peninsula, their attacks intensified, and the post-battle parade of wounded soldiers grew longer. Men covered with grime arrived at the hospital by ambulance, or in canvas slings carried by stretcher-bearers. Caught in the path of shrapnel and flying debris, their bodies were broken, lacerated, and gashed. When they were hefted onto the surgical table, their blood trickled onto the shoes of the doctors and nurses who cleaned, stitched, and cauterized the injuries.

Miss Edwards ordered additional wards opened, and mechanics welded cots together to form two-tiered bunks, and then returned to add a third. Slow to heal due to malnutrition, patients were discharged prematurely to free up beds for the newly injured. Supplies and medicines depleted at an alarming rate, and with Japanese warships blocking the harbors, hope of restocking perished.

Second verse, same as the first played in Margie's head as she prepared another injured man for surgery.

"Just a little pinch, Roger," she said, inserting the needle into his vein. She couldn't keep her hands steady. She felt anxious most days; an uncomfortable nagging worry caused her hands to shake and her voice to tremble. A red light over the door blinked to signal an oncoming attack. In a second, explosions boomed, and the tunnel vibrated, causing rock silt to drift down from above like flour from a sieve, covering every surface, settling under her collar. The world went black as the lights blinked out. Unable to reach her flashlight, she called, "Medic! I need a light!"

She received no response.

"Lay real still, Roger," she said, holding the needle in place. "It happens all the time. It'll just be a few seconds."

At least, she hoped so. If shells knocked out the powerhouse, it could be hours before mechanics repaired the generators. Those stuck inside the tunnels would bake in the heat. Flashlights winked on, giving Margie enough light to finish the procedure. "There, done," she said to Roger, patting his arm.

At the sink, she wet a mask and tied it over her nose and mouth to help her breathe through the dusty air. A medic stood nearby.

She said, "Where were you? I needed a flashlight!"

"Bug off! I have my own patients to worry about."

"You pass bedpans. Your duty is to come when I call!"

"Go soak your head, sister."

"You're out of line, medic!"

"Yeah! And what're you going to do about it? We're dead here already. Just keeping the Japs busy. We're mouse to their cat! Don't bellyache to me about a flashlight!" He stomped away.

The tunnel lights came on as the generators roared to life.

Margie moistened gauze under the tap and went back to her patient. She too had heard the fearmongers' rumors that Corregidor was a diversion to keep the Japanese from attacking Australia, and would be sacrificed when no longer needed. Her country wouldn't be so cruel . . . would it?

Waving the ever-present blue flies away from Roger's face, she placed the moistened gauze over his mouth. "This'll make it easier to breathe." She checked his IV again.

"No surgery. Not during the shelling," he mumbled through the gauze.

"It's okay. We do it all the time. We have lots of flashlights and backup generators. You'll be fine, I promise," she said, administering more sedative to extinguish the fear in his eyes.

Margie felt neither clean nor refreshed after washing up in the sink. Salt scale covered her skin, and she itched. She slathered her body with lotion and dressed in stiff clothes. In the kitchen, she searched through the refrigerator for fruit juice. Finding none, she made a cup of tea. It tasted salty, so she dumped it down the drain. "Jesus, criminy," she mumbled under her breath. Japanese shelling had knocked out the fresh-water supply four days ago.

She pushed through the crowds to the exit. Outside, the air was heavy with grit and smelled of fuel. A tense crowd gathered close to the entrance, watching the sky for incoming shells. Lighting a cigarette, she inhaled deeply to smooth the edges of her discomfort. Nearby, silhouetted by the low-hanging moon, Ruth Ann tilted her head sideways, cupping her ear with her hand. Margie joined her.

"Earache?"

"Yeah. From the blasts. I used to get them a lot when I was a kid. I thought I'd outgrown it." She swallowed and winced. "Something's going on. Have you heard anything?"

"No. What?"

"Miss Edwards is meeting with some of the nurses."

"About what?"

"Nobody's talking. I have to get back. Let me know if you find out."

Ruth Ann wove her way through the crowd as Margie watched. She drew another mouthful of smoke while contemplating the moon's meager light, eerily illuminating the barbed-wired beachfront. It had been five months since she had slept alone in a room, lingered in a library, shopped in a store, or licked an ice-cream cone—double dip, butter pecan. Suddenly, she craved the cold confection and her mouth watered. *Is civilization still out there?* In a quiet reprieve from the booming guns, she overheard a whispered conversation.

"How many planes are there?"

"I heard two."

"Who all is going?"

"Nobody knows for sure. Probably civilians and government officials. I heard some nurses are going."

"Lucky ducks."

The conversation ended, and Margie went back inside, not knowing what to make of what she'd heard. She retired to the women's quarters, planning a couple of hours with a book. As she entered the lateral, she saw Evelyn stuffing clothes into a duffel. She asked, "Are you going someplace?"

Evelyn's eyes didn't meet Margie's. "I was ordered not to talk to anyone."

Margie stepped closer and whispered, "You can talk to me."

Glancing around, Evelyn said, "Two seaplanes broke through the Japanese blockade. They brought in supplies and mail, and they're taking out as many people as the planes will hold."

"Who else is going?"

"Shh! I don't know. They just told me to pack one bag and report to the dining lateral. I don't know why me. Maybe Max. He said a general owed him a favor. He saved a baby or something. It has to be him." She zipped the duffel. "No one else knows I'm here."

Margie sank onto the bed. "Where are they taking you?"

"I haven't been told."

"I'm glad for you," Margie tried to say, but it stuck in her throat. She stood up stiffly, conflicting emotions surging through her. Already cut off from family, she didn't want her best friend to go too. Finding her voice, she appealed to Evelyn's sense of duty. "What about the wounded soldiers? You can't leave like this."

"I can't *live* like this! I feel like enough of a rat! Don't make this any harder on me!"

Margie flushed. "What do you mean, harder on *you*?"

Evelyn slung the bag over her shoulder. "I'm sorry, Margie, but I'm not going to pass up this chance. I'll phone your parents. I'll visit if I can. I wish you were coming too." Wiping tears off her cheeks, she squeezed Margie in a hug. "I love you, kid." Abruptly, she turned and hurried out.

Saddened and feeling abandoned, Margie cried to her friend's vanishing back, "Please—don't leave me alone here!"

Who were the lucky ducks, and how did they get chosen? Miss Edwards would only say she picked the names out of a hat, but it was obvious to everyone the selection had been anything but random. Limited space on the two seaplanes meant only twenty seats allotted to the nurses. The older, sick, or injured women left, along with a few of the young, pretty ones, known to have romantic connections with military brass.

Margie stewed. She found Gracie in the wards, struggling to change the soiled linen on a third-tier bunk. She grunted as the soldier in the bunk moaned.

"Let me help," Margie said, stepping on the lower bunk and holding the man on his side while Gracie replaced the dirty sheet with a clean one. These days, Gracie had trouble making any bunk. Her shoulder still caused her pain and made lifting out of the question.

"Clean linens are almost gone," Gracie fretted. "There's no water to wash them. Even if there was, who'd risk taking them outside to dry?" She balled up the sheet and added it to the heap of laundry piling up in a corner.

Margie said, "Why are you still here? You could have left on the plane."

Gracie went to the next bunk, checked the soldier's temperature with the back of her hand, and offered him a drink of juice. "Why would I do that? I belong here, taking care of these guys."

"You were shot. Your shoulder's not fully healed. You could have gone home."

"This is my home. I told Miss Edwards I'm staying for the duration. She gave my seat to someone else. Excuse me, Margie. I have work to do."

Not everyone felt as altruistic as Gracie. Grumbling broke out about which nurses got to leave the island. Everyone prayed for another plane to break through the blockade. No plane arrived, but a submarine did, whisking away another twenty nurses. Again Margie wasn't chosen and Gracie refused to go.

Miss Kermit sent for Margie. The director had aged considerably in the months Margie had known her. Given her age and health problems, she too could have left Corregidor, but like Gracie, she had chosen to stay. When Margie reported to her, Miss Kermit chatted nervously about the deteriorating living conditions, the importance of their work, the latest shortages, and her fear of running out of water—at the moment they had a thirty-day supply at best. Margie began to wonder why she had been summoned, when Miss Kermit handed her a letter delivered by the submarine.

She recognized her mother's handwriting, and the stamped date showed it was less than a month old. She pressed the treasure to her chest, but the tears in Miss Kermit's eyes tempered her joy.

"Just a blocked tear duct," Miss Kermit said, dabbing away tears with a hankie. "A nuisance, is all." She sighed so deeply that Margie could see her chest rise and fall. Finally, she said, "Miss Bauer, we've received some news. I wanted to be the one to tell you."

A single light dangled overhead, casting shadows on the older woman's face, highlighting deep furrows of sadness around her eyes and mouth. From the tone of her voice and her dour expression, Margie knew she did not want to hear what Miss Kermit had to say.

"It's about the captured troops. The Japanese relocated over seventy thousand American forces to a prisoner-of-war camp sixty miles north of Manila." She clenched her hands tightly together. "We've just confirmed that our doctors from Sternberg Hospital were part of that relocation. So many rumors have circulated about what happened, nobody knows what's true and what's not at this point." She unfolded her hands and put one over her mouth, drawing another ragged breath, then let it out slowly. "Your young man, Dr. Sherman. Royce, isn't it?"

"Yes, Royce," Margie said. Her mouth went dry, and she couldn't swallow.

Miss Kermit plunged on. "He was on the march north, according to a good source. When Dr. Sherman stopped to give medical assistance to a fallen soldier, he was shot by a Japanese guard."

Margie heard a whooshing sound inside her head. "He's wounded? He's going to be all right, isn't he?"

Miss Kermit's voice came from far away. "No, dear. I'm afraid not. I'm so sorry."

No—it's a horrible error, a cruel case of mistaken identity. Royce was at Sternberg Hospital in Manila. "Even the Japanese wouldn't take a physician away from his dying patients, Miss Kermit; it can't possibly be true."

Miss Kermit bit her lower lip, tears running freely down her lined face.

Margie tried to stand, but the whooshing in her head grew to a roar. Her knees buckled, and the shadowy cave-world went black.

"Margie," she heard as if from a great distance.

She curled into a fetal position on the bed and covered her ear with her arm to block out her surroundings.

. . . feeling Royce standing behind her, his arms encircling her, and their four hands gripping the golf club. "Arms back, like this," he says, swinging the club to the right and over her shoulder. "Cock your wrists," he instructs, pushing his body into hers.

She collapses, giggling. "Is this a golf lesson or an excuse to get fresh?"

"Me? Fresh?" he says, looking innocent. "The backswing's the key to the game."

"So you maul all your female students then," she accuses.

He kisses the back of her neck. "Only the redheaded ones named Margie."

The woman's voice intruded again. "Margie."

She pulled her knees tighter into her chest . . .

. . . feeling Royce's arm around her as they sit on the beach and marvel at the vastness of the ocean, the endless blue sky, and their infinite love for each other. He whispers, "Bury me in the sand?"

"No! Not here. Not now."

"It has to be done."

Her hands tremble and tears well as she sweeps the sand clean of seashells. When the plot is prepared, he stretches out with his arms by his sides.

She lies beside him, petting his chest, and kissing his chin. "I want to go with you."

"You can't. Not yet."

She weeps quietly as she covers his body with sand. Sweat trickles from under her hat into her ears. She stops. "Do I have to go on?" she asks.

He gazes up at her. "Yes, you must," he says matter-of-factly.

She nods, knowing it is true, but before she can resume her task, his body begins sinking, the sand sucking him under, covering his shoulders and neck, then his face, and finally, his blue eyes.

Margie's own eyes popped open, and her fingers dug at the bedsheets. Feeling suffocated, she gasped for air. Remembering, she began screaming, her shrieks echoing off the rock walls.

By the end of April, the merciless Japanese bombardment of Corregidor stripped the once lushly gardened island of the last of its protective cover. Observation balloons, called Peeping Toms, hovered like vultures over the barren landscape, pinpointing strategic targets for Japanese bombers to obliterate.

With a gas mask belted to her waist and a lethal dose of morphine pinned in a tangle of her hair, Margie worked quickly to label morphine as aspirin and quinine as bicarbonate of soda; then she hid as many of the medicines as possible in cave-like niches behind the walls.

The din of the final assault was terrific, with booming artillery from both sides firing as rapidly as machine guns. The Japanese continued their relentless barrage from land and air until all response from Corregidor ceased. They had demolished the island's gun emplacements, flattened the powerhouse, polluted the water supply, and severed all wire communications. Blasted to smithereens, ammunition dumps blazed like kingdom come. The Gibraltar of the East—impregnable—had become a pile of gray smoldering wreckage. US Army sound detectors picked up the rumbling engine noises of Japanese landing barges crossing the North Channel.

In the aftermath's eerie quiet, a woeful tune drifted—a bugler playing "Taps."

Margie thought, *Our boys lowering and burning the flag.*

Fear prevailed in the tunnel—fear of death, fear of assault, fear of being forgotten. Tildy wrote across the top of a bedsheet, "Members of the Army Nurse Corps and Civilian Women Who Were in the Malinta Tunnel When Corregidor Fell," and the fifty-four women remaining in the tunnel signed their names. As Margie wrote her name in bold letters—"Marjorie Olivia Bauer"—she thought about her parents and their heartbreak if she didn't survive this ordeal. Her yearning for home was so overpowering, she felt crushed by it. She sank to her knees in despair.

CHAPTER 13

Corregidor / Santo Tomas, June 1942–January 1943

As soldiers carried General Wainwright's white flag of surrender to the Japanese, thousands of American and Filipino troops destroyed their large-caliber weapons and flooded into the Malinta Tunnel. With tears streaming down their blackened faces, they carried the wounded on their backs, or in slings, or flipped over their shoulders, and the already-overfull hospital swelled. One man laid his blood-soaked buddy at Margie's feet. "Think he'll make it?" he asked, his voice grave and eyelids batting.

Margie inspected the wound. "The docs will do what they can." She tagged the man for surgery and ordered a medic to carry him to the front of the line.

Updated information came with each wave of arriving soldiers—choppy waters in the channel thwarted the Japs' landing; the enemy still met resistance due to severed communications. But then—thousands of Japanese troops landed on the north shore of Corregidor, bringing with them tanks and flamethrowers.

As Margie attended to the injured men, some lying too still and others writhing in a hodgepodge around her, an image of a howitzer nosing into the tunnels glued itself into her mind. She blanked out the ugly vision and the mayhem a weapon that size would render by doggedly focusing on her patients, leaving no room in her awareness for fear. She heard a thud and then felt a shock wave so forceful her uniform skirt wrapped around her legs like a whip. She screamed in surprise and panic as the Japanese shell exploded inches from the hospital entrance. The tears of fear she'd been holding back gushed forth.

Gracie, working beside her, grabbed her arm. "You all right?"

Margie sniffed and took a deep breath. "Yeah. I think so." Recovered, but shaky, she returned to her work, assessing, triaging, and relieving her patients' pain and terror with encouraging words and the often-refilled syringe of morphine.

The hours passed by unnoticed.

While concentrating on removing a sliver of shrapnel from a soldier's eye, she felt a presence beside her and saw a brown hand. Looking up, she stood face-to-face with a Japanese officer. He wore rumpled khaki and a funny hat with a flap that covered the back of his neck. A long sword hung from his belt, and even in his big boots he was shorter than she.

"Bow," he demanded.

"What?"

"Bow to a Japanese soldier." He stiffly bent forward to demonstrate.

Margie put down her instruments and imitated his action. He nodded. "You go over there," he said, pointing to where the other nurses had lined up against a wall.

Margie picked up a gauze square to cover her patient's injured eye.

"You go! Now!" the Japanese officer shouted.

She jumped, dropped the gauze, and scurried to join the others, whose faces were pinched with fear and their arms wrapped around themselves protectively.

Japanese officers paraded back and forth in front of them, inspecting their uniforms, the Red Cross armbands that identified them as noncombatants, and the nurse insignia pinned to their collars. Margie began to tremble under the scrutiny, and she hugged herself even tighter.

"What are you women doing here?" one of the officers asked Miss Edwards.

The captain pulled herself up as tall as her elfin size allowed. "We're nurses in the United States Army."

"Impossible." He shook his head in puzzlement. "Army's for men. There's no place for women in the army."

While he conferred with his officers, Margie watched others hang a sign: "THIS IS THE PROPERTY OF THE IMPERIAL JAPANESE GOVERNMENT."

The officer returned. "You, you, you . . . ," he said as he pointed to the first ten nurses in line. "Go outside. We get your picture."

Margie, Gracie, and the others marched outside at the point of a bayonet. Gracie grabbed Margie's hand.

"No touching. No talking," a guard admonished them.

As they lined up in front of a camera, a Japanese officer said in perfect English, "Don't be afraid. We're going to take your picture and send it to MacArthur so he'll see you're okay. I know how you Americans feel. I graduated from one of your universities."

Margie's vision focused beyond the camera to the blackened, wasted landscape littered with bloated American bodies now covered with green flies. A hate welled up inside her that she didn't know existed, and she struggled to hold down bitter bile.

The Japanese allowed the American doctors and nurses to continue their work in the tunnel hospital, though under strict rules and close observation. With ventilators turned off and conversation forbidden, the laterals took on an eerie aura—the little air left to breathe as hot as an oven and noises like the tick of the clock and the clank of instruments magnified.

The stomp of heavy boots announced the arrival of a cadre of Japanese physicians. Margie and Dr. Corolla, working together to debride a patient's burned leg, stopped their task and stood at attention. Margie stiffened and prayed the Japs would pass by. The patient cowered to make himself smaller.

A Japanese physician took a cursory look at the wound and declared the soldier well. Two guards yanked him from his bed and marched him outside to join the 7,500 soldiers penned on a fenced slab with no food or cover and very little water.

Dr. Corolla yelled out in frustration at seeing another one of his patients prematurely discharged: "If the burns become infected, it's certain death! The Hippocratic oath—"

Margie watched as the flat side of a bayonet walloped the doctor's skinny back and sent him sprawling to the floor. She turned aside and wiped tears from her eyes.

In the nurses' quarters, Miss Edwards urged the women to stick close together and sleep in their clothes. "They're dangerous," she cautioned. The elderly lady took the bed nearest the door to deter Japanese soldiers from roaming through, but shifty-eyed guards still woke the women at odd hours of the night with their constant looting and endless damn inspections. Margie stood at attention beside her cot and stoically endured the sight of a guard pawing through her meager belongings.

"He took my watch," she later hissed at Ruth Ann. "My watch! How am I going to count my patients' pulse and respirations?"

"You can borrow mine, Margie. It's a little hard to read. I scratched the face so the yellow bees wouldn't take it."

The Japanese held the troops captive on Corregidor for more than two months, during which time Margie endured their petty cruelties during the day and faked sleep at night when they fondled her red hair. She craved a good night's sleep.

Today, the ventilation system was off—again—and she could barely tolerate the overwhelming heat. She thought about shedding her uniform. Let the bastards get an eyeful of her in her slip—what did she care anymore?

Gracie returned wide-eyed and out of breath from her allocated hour outside the confines of the drab tunnels. She hurried to Margie and glanced around before speaking in a furtive whisper. "I heard we're leaving. I think it's true this time, not just a rumor."

Margie had heard the rumors too. A new one sprouted every day, of ships spotted on the horizon, planes heard in the distance, their imminent rescue, their certain demise. She shrugged dismissively.

"There really are ships in the harbor this time. Several, Margie."

At that news, she sat up and took notice.

Days later, weakened by hunger and stress, Margie stood in a small wobbly boat, waiting to board the *Lima Maru*, a Japanese ship taking the evacuees to Manila. There was a hospital there where the nurses could care for the wounded US soldiers. Margie was dubious. She didn't know a single Jap bastard who had a kind bone in his body. A guard shoved her forward. Stumbling, she grabbed the bottom rung of the rope ladder hanging over the ship's side and began the long ascent to the top. Brawny hands hoisted her onto the deck, where she landed near Miss Kermit, who was on her knees retching. Margie helped the older woman move out of the way and rubbed her back until she calmed and got her bearings.

As the ship chugged away from the shore, Margie watched the scenery pass by. Less than a year ago, she'd made this same trip through Manila Bay in the company of exuberant soldiers and sailors. Then, bright sunlight danced off pristine water, and lush tropical foliage glowed a brilliant green against a cloudless blue sky. Manila had dazzled her with its beauty—the Pearl of the Orient. Today, however, the bay offered a dismal view, with oil-slicked water, denuded beaches, and the black, bombed-out city just ahead.

The men crammed in the ship's hold were off-loaded first. They stumbled into the light after days in the dark without food or water. A sad-looking bunch, emaciated, dehydrated, and dirty, they clutched their few belongings to their chests. Some had open, oozing wounds; others could hardly walk and leaned heavily on their buddies. Once queued up, Japanese guards prodded them to march north, jabbing at stragglers with fixed bayonets.

Watching from the deck of the ship, Margie realized how cruelly Royce must have suffered. Her heart squeezed in her chest, unbidden tears streaming.

Seeing her sorrow, Gracie materialized at Margie's side and took her hand. "It wasn't like this for him, honey. He cared for his men up to the very end. It was just one sick guard—that's all."

Margie felt the comfort of Gracie's touch. "You really think so?"

"I do. And you should too, or you're going to go crazy with this grief."

Margie sniffed and nodded.

Japanese soldiers herded the women onto flatbed trucks that transported them through the dock area before turning south.

"Wait!" Tildy said, standing up. "You're going the wrong way. Our soldiers went that way." She pointed north.

A guard stepped up and slapped her on the face with his small, hard hand. She sat down again and kept quiet, hate showing in the grim set of her mouth.

It was a short ride to the University of Santo Tomas, a sixty-acre campus not far from the docks and Manila's busy city center. An idyllic setting of landscaped gardens, tree-lined walkways, and large limestone buildings greeted Margie's eyes. As the truck drove along the winding campus road, she spotted a chapel, an athletic field, a gymnasium, and several shops. *Maybe it won't be so bad here.*

The truck stopped at the main building, an imposing three-story structure occupying almost two acres of land. An over-sized crucifix perched high atop a giant cupola marked the main entrance. Internees swarmed around the nurses, and Margie felt an orange being pressed into her hand.

A woman asked anxiously, "Have you seen my husband? Eddie Bailey? He was on Corregidor. He has dark hair and a small scar right here." She pointed to a spot above her eyebrow.

He could have been any of the thousands of men Margie had attended. She gave the offered gift back, shook her head, and watched the woman's face crumple.

Guards shoved the crowd back and hustled the nurses inside, where staircases and hallways teemed with men, women carrying babies, young children, teenagers, and gray-haired grandmas and grandpas. Margie peeked inside a classroom and saw more of the same. Their chattering voices echoed off yellowed walls, and the whole place reeked of unwashed bodies and overused toilets.

"Margie! Margie!" she heard. Whirling around, she saw her friend Helen. So she had survived the bombing of Camp John Hay! Wanting to give her a hug, Margie tried to break away from the group, but a guard pushed her back in line.

When questioned by Japanese officers about her family, her life in the army, and her experience since coming to the Philippines, Margie stood stiffly and answered minimally. Chattering soldiers searched her belongings while she watched with disgust as their quick hands pawed through her letters from home and her few tattered clothes.

"What were they saying?" she asked Tildy afterward.

The daughter of American missionaries, Tildy had grown up in rural Japan. She whispered, "I could only catch a few words. Something about candy."

Housed in an annex outside Santo Tomas's high stone and iron fences, the nurses had no contact with the other internees. Fatigued, underfed, and ill with tropical diseases, they rested and regained strength sapped during the violent months on Corregidor. During their six weeks in isolation, a chaplain was twice allowed to visit and conduct a Sunday service.

"Being interned here is different," he told the new arrivals. "Unlike the POW camps so brutally administered by the Japanese military, Santo Tomas Internment Camp, or STIC, as we scornfully call it—don't tell anyone I told you that—comes under the governance of the Civilian Department of External Affairs." He looked at the faces focused on him, his kind eyes gazing from behind round, rimless glasses. "The Japanese military regard us with apathy. That's a good thing."

Apathy might be good, Margie thought.

"We internees run the camp ourselves. We have elected executive and advisory committees and appointed subcommittees: the Philippine Red Cross is in charge of the kitchens and the food; Social Services oversees education, recreation, religion, welfare, and the library; Administration handles discipline and work assignments; Essential Services supervises sanitation, hospitals, and fire prevention. The Japanese allow the Executive Committee thirty-five cents per internee a day to administer the camp."

"Thirty-five cents?" Miss Kermit scoffed. "That won't feed us, much less provide anything else."

The chaplain nodded. "It's barely a subsistence amount. For anything extra, we have a camp store, and Filipino vendors can sell food and wares inside the gate. Some enterprising souls have started their own businesses, such as a coffee bar, shoe repair, laundry, and beauty salon, to name a few. We're like a small city here."

"These girls have been living in the jungle and in tunnels. They don't have any money. How are they going to live?"

"They have an income?"

"Yes, but it's tied up in the States."

"Many people in here have contacts to friends and servants in Manila who help them. Clothing, food, almost anything can be delivered through the package line at the front gate. Inspected by the guards, of course. Do you know anyone who lives in Manila who could help you?"

"No. We're alone here."

The chaplain paced as he spoke. "That's a problem. Let me look into it. There are some ways to get around it."

"How many people live here?" Miss Kermit asked.

"Thirty-five hundred, give or take. They're mostly American, British, and Australian civilians and their families who worked or lived in the Philippines when the Japanese arrived—'enemy nationals,' the Japanese call us. About six hundred children live here. We have a varied and talented group of engineers, journalists, businessmen, missionaries, doctors, bankers, several teachers, and university professors. There's even a golf pro." He smiled at his attempt at frivolity. "Everyone is required to work two hours a day."

"These girls should be working," Miss Kermit said. "They've been locked in this building for weeks reading and playing bridge. Their time could be put to better use. The days are long and boring."

The chaplain shrugged. "Boredom is a big problem, as is sanitation. Maybe the influence of your young nurses will help keep this place from becoming a swamp."

Before the chaplain left, Miss Kermit asked, "What advice can you give to help us survive this?"

His manner grew somber as he addressed the young women, all riveted on his every word. "You must stick together. You'll need each other for support. Keep a low profile, follow the rules, and pull your own weight. Always, always be mindful of the Japanese presence." He paused before adding, "And don't forget to pray."

Old and fearless, Captain Hazel Edwards met with the Japanese commandant and negotiated for the nurses to work four-hour shifts in the hospital and the clinics scattered around campus. The sixty-four nurses moved from the annex into four classrooms on the top floor of the main building. Their presence further crowded the other 250 women assigned to live on that floor and who shared the one available bathroom. The camp administrators issued each nurse a metal cup, a spoon, an enamel plate, one thin towel, and a blanket, all of which they stored under their palm-fiber cots.

Every day began with music blasting over loudspeakers.

Margie yawned, scratched at bug bites all over her body, and took her place in line for the shower. Standing behind her, Helen brushed her back.

"Sorry, Margie. It was just a bedbug."

"Did you get it off me?"

"It's gone, but your back's really bit up. You want me to dab you with calamine lotion?"

"After my shower. Anything to stop the itching." She sawed her towel across her back, then stepped into the shower and circulated under the spigot with four other women—one smoking, her lower lip thrust out and the fag tilted up, two wearing their underwear, and one with her eyes closed, as suggested by the hand-scrawled sign on the wall: "Want Privacy? Close Your Eyes!"

Margie dressed in a cotton uniform, careful not to bump the other women trying to dress in the tight confines of a room too small for the number of occupants. She packed a tote with her eating utensils and personal items; then she and Helen left for the food-service station, a walk across campus that took them through the shantytowns.

In these cobbled-together communities, internees built clusters of topsy-turvy huts and gave the neighborhoods exotic names, like Foggy Bottom and Glamourville. Construction of the huts was as creative as their resourceful owners, who scrounged for bamboo, scrap wood, palm leaves, and reeds. Streets named MacArthur Boulevard and Fifth Avenue meandered in and around these hovels that offered the occupants a few square feet of shade and a semblance of privacy during the day. At night, all internees returned to the campus buildings to sleep dormitory-style with the men separated from the women and children.

Helen walked slowly with her hand pressed against her side.

"Are you all right?" Margie asked.

"Just a little stomachache. This diet is too starchy for me. My system is all messed up. Let's walk along Hollywood Boulevard. I like to watch the kids play. I miss my nieces and nephews."

At that moment, a general service announcement crackled over the camp's loudspeakers, reminding the citizens of Santo Tomas to mind their fires, that the okra ripening in the community gardens needed volunteer harvesters, and that all trash must be deposited in the dump area.

A disc jockey shouted, "Good morning, folks! It's a splendid day in Santo Tomas! For the next two hours, I'll be spinning your favorite tunes. Let's start with one we all like to hear, 'Pennies from Heaven.'"

"Praise the Lord," Margie whispered.

"God bless," Helen answered, for the song was code for a successful Allied bombing raid.

Margie and Helen stood in one line to have their meal tickets verified, then queued up in another for a bowl of rice gruel, pineapple, and a cup of weak coffee. They joined Gracie, Ruth Ann, and Tildy at a table. Along with Boots, they considered themselves a family now, bound together by experiences few others would understand. They shared secrets, fears, food, books, and birthdays.

Gracie said, "Wednesday is Boots's twenty-sixth. Where's she been?"

"Working nights on the TB ward," Margie said. "It spreads like wildfire in this heat. How about a party on Friday? Can everyone chip in fifty cents for a gift? I hate to ask you, Tildy."

"It's all right," Tildy said through a mouthful of food. "I can't always be a mooch. I broke down and took out a loan like you said."

The chaplain had introduced Miss Kermit to American businessmen, residents of Santo Tomas but still powerful, their corporations secretly backing no-interest loans to internees through their Chinese and Swiss bank affiliations. Margie explained to Tildy that her government checks deposited in the States were safe and would continue to accumulate interest even though she borrowed against it.

Tildy swallowed her mouthful before saying, "You should go into business, Margie. You understand all that stuff."

"I helped my dad keep the books for the farm. He taught me all about debits, credits, loans, and interest payments. You'll be all right. Borrow what you need to live and don't worry about it."

Gracie said, "There's a vendor selling hand-carved combs. It'd be a nice gift for Boots, don't you think? You know how she is about her hair. I'll pick it up."

"I'll come too," Margie said. "I need cold cream and soap from the camp store."

Ruth Ann ate her last bit of pineapple and pushed the bowl aside. "I'm doing laundry later. Anyone want to join me?"

Helen said, "I will. I get off work first so I'll get in line, but I need a favor, Ruth Ann." She lowered her voice. "Um, I had a visitor. When we lay our clothes on the grass to dry, would you help me . . . um, hide . . . you know."

"Christ, Helen. Nothing's private here. When are you going to get over it?"

Margie looked at her watch. "Hup to, girls."

They scraped up the last bits of breakfast, then put the bowls in their totes before dispersing to various hospital wards and clinics for their daily four hours of duty.

Margie worked on a medical ward where she treated the internees' tropical rashes, festering bug bites, painful boils, and fungal diseases. Inadequate toilet and hand-washing facilities made dysentery a perpetual problem. Some of her patients had no awareness of the link between dirt and disease; others, accustomed to servants, had no intention of cleaning up after themselves, much less anyone else.

The Sanitation Committee launched a campaign on the importance of cleanliness, conducting mandatory classes and posting monitors in the washrooms to enforce hand-washing rules. It organized fly-swatting details and fly-killing contests, engaging even the children in the activity to control the ubiquitous blue flies that spread disease.

Margie rummaged through a cupboard, looking for something to treat a rash. She found bicarbonate of soda and added water to make a paste. They had precious few medications to treat tropical maladies. Physicians and pharmacists with access to Red Cross supplies scrounged to provide what they could. Chemists concocted teas and ointments from local herbs, barks, and flowers that helped relieve symptoms with varying degrees of effectiveness.

This morning, dozens of unlabeled boxes were stacked on the floor. "What's all this?" she asked Tildy.

"Vaccines for cholera, typhoid, and diphtheria. Compliments of the Japs."

"There are no labels. It could be anything."

Tildy sadly shook her head. "The Japanese I knew when I was a kid weren't like this, Margie. They were my friends and I trusted them. Now . . ." She shrugged. "Guess ours is not to reason why—"

Ours is but to do or die, Margie thought, finishing the line in her head.

Helen entered the room doubled over in pain and her body dripping cold sweat.

Tildy helped her onto a gurney. "You don't look so good, honey." She beckoned a doctor over, and when he palpated the lower-right quadrant of Helen's abdomen, she screamed in pain.

"It's acute appendicitis. I'm going to order an ambulance to take you to Philippine General. If the doctors there confirm my diagnosis, you may need surgery."

Hours later, Margie heard the news. Helen had an appendectomy, and she was resting comfortably. She stayed at Philippine General for five days.

After Helen returned to Santo Tomas, Margie noticed she took long walks more often, bought useless trinkets from vendors, and hung around the package line, where guards inspected everything going into and out of the camp. Curious about Helen's comings and goings, Margie asked her about it. Helen denied her actions were unusual, saying she needed the exercise to regain her strength after the surgery.

"But, why are you wasting your money on those trinkets?"

"I'll spend my money any way I want. It's no concern of yours."

Margie's curiosity grew when she saw Helen throwing the trinkets in the trash.

Margie volunteered to work in the large gardens that supplied the camp's two kitchens. On her hands and knees among the rows of fruits and vegetables, she transported herself to another world. She held long conversations with her mother and father, confiding her fears, asking advice, and listening for their sage guidance. She told them how dearly she loved them, how sorely she missed them, and how desperately she yearned to come home. She dreamed of Royce, feeling his caress on her cheek, the brush of his lips. She heard him say, *You've touched me more deeply than I ever dreamed possible.* Rivers of tears dripped off her chin, salting the soil.

Helen often joined her in the garden. As they dug and nurtured young plants to maturity, they talked. Margie told Helen about growing up in a small Michigan town, her dreams of designing clothes, her years at Grand Arbor Hospital, and the crazy things she and Evelyn had done. She told stories about Abe, now flying missions out of Australia. At first, she couldn't talk about Royce, her throat constricting whenever she said his name. Later, she babbled incessantly, describing his relaxed manner, his confident way of speaking, his skill as a surgeon, his kindness to everyone, and his tender love for her.

Helen shared her stories and dreams too, about her English mother, her American father, and her brother, Ian, who was somewhere in North Africa the last she'd heard. She had a large extended family in England and hoped to return there when the war ended. "You'll come and visit me, won't you, Margie? You'll love my cousin Mabel. She's a real stitch."

Months passed before Helen confided about her capture at Camp John Hay. "It all happened so fast," she said. "The Japanese started bombing right out of the clear blue sky. Nobody knew what was going on. We were told to evacuate, and me and Hattie—you met Hattie, the other nurse—"

"I remember Hattie."

"Me and Hattie and Dr. Robb left with the cavalry, the only military unit up there. We heard that guerrillas in the mountains would hide us. We got only a short way before the Japanese came along with their tanks and killed all the cavalry guys. Tanks against horses." Helen shook her head sadly. "We holed up like scared rabbits, sleeping in old sawmills. The Nips were everywhere, and after four days, one found us." Helen squatted down and tugged hard at some weeds. The pitch of her voice rose. "Hattie tried to run, and he shot her! He shot her in the back! Then, he stood me up against a tree and aimed his gun at my head. I saw evil in his eyes, and I felt it all around me." She sank back into the dirt, hiding her face, sobbing into her soil-covered hands.

Margie embraced her friend, patting her back. "I am so sorry," she whispered.

"Only my faith in the dear Lord saved me." Helen sniffed and dried her tears on the hem of her skirt. "They stuffed all us prisoners into one room in an old barracks. I got sent here. I don't know what happened to Dr. Robb."

Through the Executive Committee, the citizens of Santo Tomas formed education, religion, recreation, and entertainment subcommittees to organize activities. College professors and teachers established a school for the children, grades one through twelve, and classes for adults in languages, math, art, music, and history up to the turn of the twentieth century. Astronomy was a popular course—internees lying on their backs, gazing upward, following the movements of heavenly bodies and dreaming of faraway places. The Japanese forbade geography classes and confiscated all maps.

Chaplains held religious services and offered scripture classes. Sports teams sprouted up, along with choirs, an orchestra, and a drama club. Vaudeville shows, sing-alongs, and plays were

presented at the Little Theater Under the Stars, an open-air stage
built by the internees.

Margie offered to make costumes for the drama club. While
watching auditions one afternoon, she saw a man she thought
she knew. His strong jaw, distinctive profile, gangly build, and
Midwestern accent all came together to form a familiar image.
After the session ended, she approached him. "Excuse me, do I
know you?"

Brown eyes blinked from behind thick glasses. "Isn't that supposed to be my line?"

She blushed. "No. I'm serious. You look familiar."

"Wade Porter," he said, offering his hand.

Even his name rang a bell. "Hi. Margie Bauer. Where are you
from?"

"I'm a man of the world."

"What does that mean?"

"I travel around a lot. I'm a journalist. Best I could do to be
part of the action. Bad eyes, fallen arches." He pointed first to his
face, then his feet. "Originally, I'm from a little burg in Michigan.
Little River. You wouldn't know of it."

"Are you kidding? I'm from Little River!" She jumped for joy,
clapping her hands. "Oh my gosh! I don't believe it! How did you
end up here?"

He leaned against the wall and folded his arms. "By lingering
too long in Manila. It's the way of a journalist—the story and the
glory. I wanted to witness the Japanese coming. It turned into quite
a parade."

They spent the next hour roaming the compound, exploring
their common roots. Wade had grown up on a farm less than three
miles from Margie's house. He was eight years her senior and their
paths hadn't crossed in any significant way, though he knew the
farm where she lived, the stores where she shopped, and the teachers she'd had in school.

"When's the last time you were home?" she asked.

"About four years ago. Not much there for me anymore. Mom died the year I graduated from high school, and Dad remarried. It's not the same. I have a sister, Carol Hanson. She's five years older than me."

"Carol Hanson? I remember her. She worked in the library and helped me find reference material for my school reports. She was always nice."

"That's Carol. She married Greg Hanson and has a little girl, Julia." Wade grinned, and Margie noticed a scar on his lip and a chipped front tooth. "I have a shack in Broadway. Would you like to see it?"

Broadway was a shanty neighborhood on the far edge of the campus, next to the stone and barbed-wire fence. Wade's place fronted a path aptly named Back Alley. A palm-leaf roof topped the eight-by-eight hut, and woven reeds made the walls. To the right of the door sat a charcoal stove. Before entering, Wade waved to his neighbor just steps away. "Yo, Tim," he said. "My shift." He explained to Margie, "We guard each other's shanties."

Margie ducked under the thatched awning. Inside housed a cot, a bamboo table holding a typewriter, two bamboo chairs, and shelves stocked with dishes, toilet paper, books, and other items. The floor was split bamboo.

"Welcome to my humble home," he said as he propped open a window and pulled out a chair. He took two metal cups off a shelf and filled them with tea from a jar on the floor.

Margie glanced around, envious of the elbow room, the privacy, and his little stash of belongings. "Where'd you get the furniture?"

"A guy over the way makes it. I gave him a couple of guitar lessons." Wade retrieved the instrument from the corner. He strummed the strings and adjusted the tuning before launching into a spirited version of "Frankie and Johnny," slapping the guitar and stomping his foot for rhythm.

She clapped. "Bravo! You're very good."

He nodded, strummed a few minor chords, and began a song she didn't recognize:

"I'm a rambling man for many years
On my own learned to face my fears
Thoughts of home fill my heart with tears
And I yearn to hear kith and kin news
Got these soul-depressing, longing-to-go-home-again blues."

He sang in a soulful voice, the music drawing Margie in. When he finished, she remained transfixed. "Did you write that?"

"No, I wish. It's a Pearly Carl song. He's a bluesman from Mississippi. I heard about him when I studied at Wayne University. Then I got a chance to see him when I traveled through the South." He put the guitar aside. "I played that song in the bars around Ann Arbor and Detroit, never realizing someday I'd be living it."

Intrigued by this revelation, Margie asked, "You play professionally?"

"Just say it's my alter ego."

She picked up the camp weekly newsletter, the *Internews*, off the table. "Of course. Wade Porter. That's where I've seen your name. You're the editor."

"Yup. That's the morning edition."

Margie glanced through the announcements:

Rationing of milk continues. It is estimated that supplies will last approximately three months at the current rate of consumption. Outside sources for milk are scarce.

Construction of the new stage is complete, and, after a one-month hiatus, the Entertainment Committee will present the third internee floor show on Thursday at 6:00 p.m. The program includes Jerry and Phyllis Newcomb, acrobatic dance; Nick Brownell and Art Handy, guitar duet; and Frank Capella, magician.

A blanket challenge to play any baseball team has been issued by Room 42. Those accepting the challenge can sign up with Jerry Monroe in Room 42.

The semifinal round in the bridge tournament will begin Monday with sixteen teams of the original 116 competing.

Father Dennis Murphy will hear confessions beginning at 7:00 a.m. Sunday, near the outdoor altar.

For sale: All types of woodwork, boxes, tables, shelves. Your design or ours. Wooden shoes available.

From the Executive Committee: A radio message asking the American Red Cross for help in securing permission to release internees' names and addresses to a source in Washington, DC, has been delivered to Japanese authorities by the Philippine Red Cross . . .

Margie wondered if her parents knew where she was. Did they even know if she was alive? She pondered the cruelty of their praying and hopeful watching—their fear of the day that would bring bad news. "Do you think it will happen? Do you think the Japanese will release our names?"

Wade refreshed her tea. "I wouldn't count on it. We're nothing but a nuisance to them."

CHAPTER 14

Santo Tomas, February 1943–December 1944

Margie had been a captive of the Japanese for seven months and an internee at Santo Tomas for five. She hadn't seen her parents in over two years. As Japanese strength in the Philippines intensified, hope of immediate release vanished. She and Helen pooled their money and bought a bamboo shack, a daytime retreat. It was near Wade's shack and under the shade of a cypress tree. Two cots and a table and chairs crowded the inside. Outside, vegetables grew in a minuscule garden. When they moved in, the little hut felt as big as a palace.

Coming home unexpectedly one afternoon, Margie found Helen writing messages on tiny pieces of paper. Cigarettes were sliced open and tobacco sat in a little pile on the table. Helen jumped when she came in and hurriedly swept the cigarettes and papers into a bag.

Margie said, "I'm sorry. Did I frighten you? What's all this?"

"It's none of your business, Margie. I don't ask you about every little thing you do. Just because we live together doesn't mean I can't have some privacy."

Helen's venom made Margie suspicious. "If you're hiding something, it's not a little thing, and I have a right to know."

"I don't want to put you in danger."

"Helen, if you're doing something you shouldn't, I *am* in danger. Isn't it better I know what it is?"

Helen hesitated. "I hadn't thought of it that way." She brushed tobacco off the table. "When I was in the hospital, a Filipino doctor asked if I would send him information from inside Santo Tomas. He's part of the underground who fight the Japanese in any way they can. There are hundreds of them in Manila and thousands of them hiding in the mountains. He wants any information I can get him about the guards: how many officers there are, how many guards they have, what kind of weapons they carry, and what their habits are. He's especially interested in the package line. He said a lot of contraband comes through it, and he needs to know which guards can be bribed."

"How would you know that?"

"I keep my eyes open when I'm walking. I watch for the ones that are bullied or seem weak; then I look for some way to identify them. That was the hard part at first. But then I noticed a lot of them had scars, or birthmarks, or missing teeth. One had only half an ear. I send the doctor what information I can, Margie, but I don't know if he gets it, or what he does with it. It's all pretty patchy."

Margie pointed to the bag of paper and cigarettes. "Is that what this is all about?"

"Yes. I write what I find on tiny bits of paper and hide it inside a cigarette. I've gotten good at it. You can't tell my cigarettes aren't anything but . . . cigarettes. I leave the pack in a vendor's stall. There's no way for the Japs to trace it back to me. That's all I do."

"That's all? You could be shot, or worse."

"I'll take that chance. At least I'm doing something useful. I was almost shot once for doing absolutely nothing at all."

Sitting cross-legged on her cot, Margie stitched a monogram on a napkin. It was a Christmas gift for Gracie. She heard a rustle outside and quickly hid the napkin under her butt, hoping she had secured the needle.

"Knock, knock," Ruth Ann called, ducking through the doorway. She glanced around the small space. "Aren't you a Lucky Lou!" She admired the curtains Margie made for the window, the picture Helen drew and tacked to the wall, and the shelves Wade hung to store supplies.

"Shit! I need a shanty," Ruth Ann added. "If I don't get some space to call my own soon, I'm going to go crazy." She pulled a rag doll out of her tote bag. "I need some help. Some poor little girl's going to get this monster for Christmas, and it's going to scare the pants off her."

Margie took the half-stitched doll from Ruth Ann and laughed, because it did indeed have an evil leer. "What did you do to her face?"

"It's supposed to be a smile, but it came out more like a grimace. I'm hopeless at this kind of stuff. My hands are too big. I should be making trucks for the little boys."

Margie snipped a few stitches. "Leave it here. I'll work on it."

"You sure? You're pretty busy with the Christmas play."

"I'm almost finished with that." She showed Ruth Ann Wade's costume, a waistcoat and top hat pieced together from various fabrics.

"Wow! That looks professional."

"Hardly, but from the audience it won't look too bad." Standing up, she dropped the hat on Gracie's Christmas napkin. "I wanted to study fashion design at one time. You want some tea?" Without waiting for a reply, she poured two cups. "I heard Adele Ernst is sending over Christmas turkeys and all the trimmings." Just saying the words made her mouth water.

Adele—an American nurse and colleague of Miss Edwards—had married a German citizen, and through him she had Axis ally status and freely moved around Manila. Her limousine regularly arrived at Santo Tomas's gate loaded with baskets of clothing, food, necessities, and niceties for the nurses.

Ruth Ann lounged back, her long legs outstretched. "Good old Adele. You ever seen her? She wears a hat as big as the Grand Canyon. She carries a black lace parasol, Margie. When's the last time you've seen anybody carrying a parasol? She looks like Mary Poppins."

"So she's eccentric. She has a huge heart." Margie suppressed a grin and said teasingly, "Did you like the pocketbooks she sent to each of us?"

"Never carried one," Ruth Ann said, tapping her foot.

"If you see her at Christmas, you'll be nice, won't you, Ruth Ann?"

"Of course. I'm always nice."

When a fleet of British relief ships arrived in Manila Harbor, a group of internees were dispatched to the docks to load trucks with food, medical supplies, and clothing for the kitchens, clinics, and dormitories of Santo Tomas. Margie saw the trucks lined up for inspection outside the gates. Later that day, each internee received a shoebox-sized personal kit.

"I'll trade you my razor for your sewing kit," Margie offered as she and Wade nibbled on candy bars. As their friendship took root, they often met to share meals and memories of home.

"Deal. Let's eat the corned beef today. I bought four duck eggs."

Margie's mouth watered at the thought of corned beef and eggs. "Let's eat my corned beef and save yours for later."

"Okay. I'll save an egg, then. I know where I can get flour, so we can make pancakes." He reached for her hand. "I enjoy cooking for you."

Not ready to begin another relationship, she avoided his touch by rummaging through her kit. "Soap!" she exclaimed. "Who'd have ever thought I'd get excited about a bar of soap?"

On Christmas Day, the seventy-five military nurses interned at Santo Tomas gathered on the lawn outside the main building for their holiday dinner. Margie and her friends all sat together at one table. At each place was a poem written by Tildy, a monogrammed napkin from Margie, a small wooden cross whittled by Ruth Ann, a string angel crocheted by Boots, and flowers picked, dried, and bound into nosegays by Gracie. The serving table bent under the weight of several turkeys, sweet potatoes, dressing, cranberries, creamed peas, and fruitcake for dessert.

Miss Riley rose to speak. "Girls, isn't it a fine Christmas Day! Here we are surrounded by good friends, about to share a wonderful meal provided by our generous benefactor, Adele Ernst. She sends us her best wishes and knows how grateful we are. Let's each of us remember her in our prayers of thanks."

The women murmured in agreement and applauded.

"Last Christmas we traveled a dangerous road, dodging Japanese bombs," Miss Riley continued. "We've made it through a year of great peril. Today, we must be thankful for what we have— our lives, our friends, and, as nurses, the privilege of helping those less fortunate than ourselves. Let's pray for the safety of our men on the battlefield, for our country's freedom, and for our safe return home."

The Japanese allowed visitors through the gates on Christmas Day, 1942. Family, friends, former coworkers, and servants arrived laden with boxes of food and the small sundries of living. Many groups feasted at picnics spread on the lawn. Margie and Wade stood together in the shadows and watched Japanese photographers snap propaganda pictures.

One Filipino caught Margie's attention. Although his peasant clothes and large straw hat tied under his chin made him unremarkable, he kept dodging the photographers and glancing toward Wade. She nudged him, saying, "Is that someone you know?"

"I'll be damned!" Wade whispered.

The Filipino cocked his head, then melted away into the crowd.

"Let's go," Wade said, and led Margie back to his shanty. A few minutes later, the strange man slipped through the door.

"Charles! Didn't think I'd ever see you again!" Wade embraced his friend and introduced him to Margie as an American-born Filipino, and the best damn photographer at the *Ann Arbor Tribune*. Charles and Wade had worked together, first in Europe, then the Philippines.

The photographer looked around the shack. "How you holding up in this stink hole?"

"Beats the alternative. I see you're keeping a low profile."

"You like these duds? My uncle even found me a cart and ox, man. When I go underground, I go all the way." He flashed a smile, and Margie noticed a missing front tooth.

Wade said, "You fit in good enough. What can you tell me?"

"Probably nothing you don't already know. I'm assuming you've got a radio hidden in one shithouse or another." He reached in his pocket for cigarettes and the three of them lit up. As the shanty filled with smoke, Charles said, "We ambushed the yellow buggers on Midway—credit to our code breakers—and trapped and sank four Nip carriers and a fuckin' heavy cruiser."

"We heard about that. We had a little celebration."

"It gets better. MacArthur's playing offense, hitting hard on Guadalcanal. We kicked the shit out of their air power, and our guys captured the airfield. Their navy's another matter, though. The good news is they're running out of resources. We're destroying ships and planes faster than they can replace them. Soon as we cripple the navy, we'll shove their fuckin' ground forces into the sea. Locals hate the Japs and help all they can. It's just a matter of time."

Margie's voice filled with hope. "How much time?"

"Hard to say." Charles dragged deep on his cigarette, exhaling a long plume of smoke. "Those Nips will fight for their goddamn emperor until every last one of them's dead. Long live the goddamn emperor. Tell me, bro, how does anyone get that much power?" He took off his hat, revealing a shock of black hair and a wad of cash tucked in the hatband. He handed the cash to Wade. "You know how to use this. Don't know if I can get back in here, but there's a vegetable vendor with a birthmark that looks like a bird right here," he said, pointing to a spot below his right ear.

"I've seen him," Wade said.

"You can trust him. When his hatband's yellow, tell him you're making soup and ask for okra. There'll be a message inside. He'll tell you which guards are approachable."

Wade stuffed the money down his pants. "Have you heard from Henry?"

In one motion, Charles stubbed out his cigarette and lit another. "He recovered from his wounds okay. The last I heard, he was at Cabanatuan. He may not recover from *that*. Count your lucky stars—this pisshole's a walk in the park compared to what's up north."

"Tell me what I can do," Wade said.

"For Henry? Not a goddamn thing. For us? Keep the messages moving. Those wealthy guys at the top are opening their corporate wallets. The prisoners up north are grateful."

"I'm not doing much."

"It's enough. The resistance is growing. And we've got God on our side. The priests are doing more than saying prayers."

"And Mary Poppins?"

"She's got a nice operation going, but she's pushing her luck. Too many girls, you know what I mean?" Charles got up. "Keep your chin up, bro. You too, Margie. Wish I could stay longer, but I have other stops to make. You remember my name?"

"Kodak."

"Good. You need me, you let the okra man know." He hugged Wade and saluted Margie, then stepped to the door.

Wade stopped him. "The last dispatch. Did you get it out?"

"Yeah, man. Just under the wire. Good article. Great pictures of the docs at Sternberg too."

Margie's ears perked up.

After Charles left, she watched until his shadow disappeared before addressing Wade. "Kodak? The okra man?"

"I shouldn't have let you come. You shouldn't be involved."

"I am involved. I have been for a while." She told him how Helen had been recruited by a doctor from Philippine General to spy on the guards and report the ones likely to accept bribes. "She doesn't want me to, but I watch the guards too and tell her what I see. That's all."

Wade's manner became grave. "You shouldn't! You don't know . . ."

"I do know! And it's my choice. It's the least I can do. I can't just turn a blind eye."

"But the guards are dangerous. They're the dregs of the Jap army, Margie. The officers treat them like animals. They have no regard for human life. Do I have to get down on my knees and beg?" He pulled her close into a protective hug.

Her head against his chest, she could feel the beating of his heart. She said, "Tell me about Mary Poppins. I know someone who fits that description, but I can't believe she would . . . You've seen her outside the gate carrying a parasol or sitting in a limo. How do you know her?"

He checked for unwanted listeners from the window before they sat down at the table. "She hid me after the Japs entered Manila. She runs a call-girl ring catering to Japanese officers. While I was there, she had just a few Filipino girls. They were gorgeous, flawlessly dressed, multilingual, skilled at wheedling out information, and they hated the Japanese. Adele—Mary Poppins—has runners who pass information to the guerillas on Bataan."

Margie felt her jaw drop.

"She's shrewd," Wade went on. "The big bucks the Jap officers fork over for her girls' company get smuggled into the POW camps. As Kodak said, it's a nice operation."

From outside came the sounds of cheering and children's excited voices. Margie looked out the window. "Santa's coming in a truck. Those babies don't even realize . . ." She turned back to Wade. "That last dispatch of yours from Sternberg. Did you interview Royce Sherman?"

"Dr. Sherman. Big guy? Texas accent? I remember him. The Japanese were two steps from Manila and he was spreading sunshine."

"What did he say?" she prodded, fishing for any tidbit of information.

"He said he was shipping wounded soldiers out as fast as he could. Most of them were immobile, some unconscious. There was no way he'd get them all out. He didn't say that, but I knew it. Was he a friend?"

A friend? She felt the urgency of Royce's last kiss. "Yes," she whispered, "a friend." A lump rose in her throat, and she swallowed it down. "Who's Henry?"

"Another correspondent. He got between me and a bullet."

She touched his arm. "Do you want to tell me about it?"

"Maybe someday." He picked up his guitar and strummed a few minor chords.

New Year's Day dawned with the cheerless wail of a distant siren, foreshadowing a sad year of steady decline. Prices soared when extra food became scarce: sugar and other foods the internees craved became unobtainable. Babies cried, young children begged, wily teens risked being caught stealing rice from the kitchens. Their clothing, difficult to repair and impossible to replace, soon wore out. The odds and ends of everyday life—soap, toothbrushes, toilet paper—remained in short supply. Many people hoarded, traded, or stole what little was available.

Those who stayed busy fared best. Although always lethargic, Margie and Wade encouraged each other to attend classes and concerts, participate in plays and sports, and work in the gardens. They read and discussed books obtained from the internee library. Gracie and Kenneth, a professor of ancient history from Chicago, became a couple. The foursome played endless card games, shared meals, argued the finer points of baseball, and analyzed the plots of movies seen before the war—rating the actors, directors, and special effects. They sang every song any of them had ever learned, from childhood to the present. Wade provided the melodies with his guitar while the others banged and tootled an assortment of improvised instruments.

Gracie sniffed. She had been angry all afternoon, and the poker hand she held wasn't mollifying her ire. She threw down her cards, announcing, "I'd rather bow to an ape!"

"Is that a fold?" Margie asked.

Gracie scowled. "S'not funny. That dog-breath guard slapped my face because my bow wasn't up to his standard!"

Mocking his captors, Kenneth grinned and composed a haiku.

"The Japanese guard,
A louse in the bowel of man
Farts out with a bow."

Wade returned,

"The Japanese bow,
Sniff as if at a dog's ass,
Only wanting more."

Margie whispered,

"Retaliation,
The craved sugar of freedom
Must be provided."

Retaliation was the intent and was communicated by a wink or a worried look when twenty-three nurses gathered at the top of the main building's stairwell. Dressed for work, they wore handmade uniforms—wrinkled, tattered, and splattered with old blood. Many carried five-pound coffee cans with braided handles, the latest fashion in totes.

"All right," Margie whispered. "One at a time. Shh . . . no giggling."

Helen left first, trading a bow with the guard at the door.

A few minutes later, he and Gracie exchanged an obeisance.

With Sally, he bowed long and low.

Soon Boots followed.

Ruth Ann kept the guard bobbing . . .

Then Tildy . . .

And Rosie . . .

And Louise . . .

And fourteen others . . .

And finally Margie.

Not seeing an end to the line of women coming, the guard walked away.

Discreetly observing the guards, Margie had noticed most fit into types: the callow young, the dull-witted, and the older men who had been put out to pasture. Quick to detect their weaknesses, the internees assigned them names like Mighty Mouse, the Bully, Nobody's Home, the Dullard, and Quacker, whose frequent rants sounded like Donald Duck. Slap-Slap relished slapping faces. Beetle Bailey played kindly with the children, scratching tic-tac-toe in the dirt and giving the winner a banana or biscuit. Some guards liked to flirt, so Margie played what she knew was a dangerous game, engaging them in pidgin banter to study their attitudes and learn their habits. She told Helen about the lonely guard who cautiously shared with her a picture of his wife and baby son, thinking the information might be useful to the Filipino doctor at Philippine General.

Wade warned her, "Don't engage with the guards, Margie. You and Helen are too visible. If you're caught spying on them, death won't be the worst of it."

The resourceful residents of Santo Tomas whittled crochet hooks and knitting needles from bamboo. With them, they made their own socks and underwear from twine scrounged from the kitchens and supply docks. Both sexes preferred G-strings, which kept them cool and were easy to make. After curfew, sitting cross-legged on their cots in the evening half-light, the women talked as they stitched.

"What are you making, Margie? It looks like it's getting kind of big," Boots said.

"It's socks for Wade. He's been a good sport making all these crochet hooks."

"I think he's smitten, Margie."

Margie sniffed to stem the tears that had lurked beneath the surface all afternoon. Smitten. That's what Dr. Corolla had said about Royce. Hearing "the boy is smitten" had made her so happy not so long ago. Now she had trouble remembering his face.

"Did you hear me, Margie? I think Wade has a thing for you."

"I don't know. We're good friends. He reminds me of home, is all."

Tildy called out, "Has anyone worn these socks yet? I wore a pair today, and they killed my feet."

"Let me see them," Margie said.

Tildy tossed the offending footwear to her.

"Well, there's your problem. The twine's too thick. Unravel the sock and split the twine. They'll come out softer, and you'll have two for one."

As she tossed the sock back, a piercing scream ripped through the air, making Margie cower on her cot. The tortured shrieks of three captured escapees had tormented the internees all afternoon and now into the night. Dropping her crochet hook and covering her ears, Margie tried to block out the agonized wails. "All this hell," she said in despair.

Time wore on and Margie drifted through the days in a mental stupor she found impossible to shake. Listless, she willed herself to get off her cot when she heard a commotion outside. To her horror, she saw a company of guards fanning through Broadway. Before she could react, two burst into her shanty and propelled her out the door where she stood with other internees while the guards searched the shanties for contraband. She heard her cot squeak, then the mattress ripping. Pots banged and dishes rattled, followed by an outburst of creepy giggling. Her mouth went dry, and she couldn't swallow as she imagined the horrors they would suffer if the guards found Helen's jerry-rigged cigarettes.

The men came out of her shanty, one with her G-string protruding from his uniform pocket. He patted her down, his hands lingering over her breasts and buttocks. The lump in his pants proved his lurid pleasure. The other scrunched her red curls, then unsheathed his knife. She screamed and tried to twist away, but he kept her hair in his grasp. Laughing, he hacked off a lock, then held up his treasure for all to see.

Wade emerged from his shanty with a guard on each arm just as Margie screamed. He lurched, broke their grip, and ran a few steps toward her before they caught up and hit him with the butt of a rifle.

Horrified, Margie could only watch.

By the time the guards left, Broadway looked like a tornado had hit it, with shanties knocked cockeyed and their contents strewn in the dirt. Her neighbor Harry helped Wade into Margie's shack. A cut on his forehead bled freely, and his eye was swelling shut. He tried to speak, but Harry whispered, "Shh, it's all right. We moved it last night." He took a bottle from under his shirt and they all gulped a slug of burning liquid.

Harry left and Margie cleaned and bandaged Wade's wounds, then checked under the floorboard where Helen hid her supplies. They were intact. Righting a chair, she sat down to catch her breath. "Creeps," she said aloud. Remembering the G-string hanging from the guard's pocket, she snorted, "Stupid idiots."

She lit a cigarette to calm herself and pondered the value of the frantic espionage activity in this buttoned-down camp that had taken on epic proportions in the internees' minds. What worth were the smugglings of fragmentary information, the bribes to unprincipled guards, the procuring and moving around of useless radios—what cost to their welfare? She asked Wade.

"Worth has nothing to do with it," he said. "Pushing back, denying, subverting is a need, a requisite for an impotent population to stay sane."

The spring monsoon arrived. Rain poured for days and high winds ripped a hole in Margie's thatched roof. Wade tried to repair it, but water still plinked into a bucket as regularly as a metronome. Outside, ankle-deep mud made walking even a short distance difficult and dangerous.

The Philippines had only two seasons, it seemed—wet hot and dry hot. Margie yearned for the cooler temperatures of home, where strawberries would be budding and early green onions and lettuce would be ready for picking. She asked her friends, "Do you still dream about home like I do? We've been a year without mail."

Tildy said, "I do. There's not a day I don't think about my sister. She was pregnant when I left."

Gracie said, "My mama was ill. I didn't know it until it was too late for me to back out. I always wonder . . ."

Ruth Ann said, "A year's a long time. Maybe we've been forgotten."

"No!" the others chorused.

Helen added, "Don't ever think that! I think that somewhere there's a warehouse stuffed with letters from home, boxes of cookies, and new pajamas."

Tildy scoffed. "I think some Nip bugger burned our letters, ate our cookies, and is wearing our pajamas."

Margie sighed. "Probably so, but I'd give my right arm for a letter."

As it turned out, she didn't have to sacrifice a limb, because soon afterward bags of mail were delivered. The letters had been opened and censored, but no one cared. Margie and Helen

squished through the mud to their shanty, each clutching two precious missives close to her chest.

Helen said, "Wait! This calls for a celebration." She poured tea
into two cups and burrowed under her mattress to retrieve a pep-
permint stick she had saved. "Cheers!" she said as they clinked
cups.

With tea, candy, and their prized letters, they anticipated an
afternoon of pure pleasure. They would read, reread, share, savor,
and discuss the letters ad infinitum with their friends, opening a
whole cherished world through them.

Margie opened the one from her parents. Her mother wrote
that she didn't think Margie was receiving her letters even though
she wrote one every week. She and Daddy had contacted the Red
Cross, but it offered little information except to say the Japanese
had blocked all correspondence from the Philippines. She hoped
Margie was safe and well, and prayed every night for her to return
home.

"Oh my!" Margie said.

Helen looked up.

Margie waved the letter. "Frank. My kid brother. He's in the
army, and he's *married*."

"I thought you said he had a heart murmur."

"He does. He did. I don't know."

Margie continued reading. Frank had been drafted. The army
needed men and its minimum requirements were not as strict as
the navy's. He trained as a medic, then shipped out to join a rifle
platoon. His letters were censored, of course, but they thought he
was in Sicily. Before deploying, he married Irene, a young woman
he met at the university. She lived with them now, and worked as
a bookkeeper at the Ford plant. The house had felt lonely with just
her and Daddy there, and Irene was good company.

"Wow," Margie murmured. Her wisecracking little brother—a medic in the army, and a husband? It didn't fit into her frame of reference for him. She heard Helen chuckling.

"It's my cousin Mabel," Helen said, containing her laughter with considerable effort. "Mum says she has a new beau. They sent away for a dancing course, the one with brown paper templates of feet labeled 'Ladies' and 'Gents'? Mum says it's hilarious watching them practice. They get all tangled up."

Margie chortled.

"Here's the kicker, Margie. They entered a dance contest and won first prize for the fox-trot! They won a lamp!" Helen's laughter cackled, her whole body jiggling with glee. "A lamp!" Her tears of amusement suddenly turned into a sob, and she slumped back. "What I'd give to see that stupid lamp!"

Margie felt Helen's sadness; her own tears always stayed close to the surface. She asked, "How's the rest of your family?"

Helen sniffed. "Ian's in Sicily or Italy, they think. They never know for sure, but they get letters. Mum's been spiffing up the house. She had Pop whitewash the walls and stipple them with green. She made a new rag rug for the bedroom. I'll bet it's really pretty." Helen went back to reading silently.

Margie examined her other letter. Postmarked Australia, she recognized neither the handwriting nor the return address. Curious, she opened it carefully.

April 14, 1943
Darwin, Australia

Dear Margie,
I am Captain Mark Davies, and I was a good friend of Abe Carson. He asked me to contact you if anything should happen to him. It is with deepest regret that I keep my promise. Abe's plane was shot down by a squadron of Japanese Zeros on April

10, 1943, on a mission over the Indian Ocean. Before he went down, he put up one hell of a fight, taking two Nips down with him. He was a real fighter and a real hero.

Abe was looking forward to the end of the war, when he could go back to Michigan and open a flying school. That was his dream. He was a good leader and a first-rate teacher. He enjoyed working with the newer pilots, and had many friends here. We are all sad that he is gone.

He talked about you a lot, saying there was nobody who could measure up to his Margie. You must be one wonderful gal. He wanted you to have his pilot's ring. It will be sent back to Michigan with his other things.

Please accept my heartfelt condolences.

With sympathy,

Mark

Margie cast the letter away, an eerie bawl erupting from her like the howl of a dying animal.

"Margie, what's wrong?" Helen reached over and thumped her on her back. "Margie? Margie? Oh, honey, it's bad, isn't it?"

She could barely gasp, "Abe!"

Helen wrapped her in her arms while Margie rode waves of grief. Her voice thick, she muttered through her tears, "He just wanted to live his own life."

For weeks, Margie's thoughts went to Abe, and images emerged from the recesses of her memory like ghosts—she saw Abe's face morphing in the clouds, heard his voice above the din of a crowded room, or recalled his cocky attitude when she glimpsed little boys playing. During those times, she stopped what she was doing and gave full attention to the memory. Always, she felt the overwhelming ache of the forced and permanent disconnection. "Abe," she would whisper, hoping he could hear her and know her love for him still lingered.

Miss Kermit gathered her nurses together. Her face haggard, she spoke in a monotone. "My friends, you need to know about the coming changes."

The gray-skinned women stood around her, their eyes sad, mouths hard, and arms crossed over their sunken chests. Shapeless dresses hung on their bodies, wooden sandals protected their feet, and cotton turbans covered their thinning hair. They had been prisoners at Santo Tomas for eighteen months.

The War Prisoners Department of the Imperial Japanese Army had assumed administration of the camp, and this had set rumors flying. Margie didn't expect anything good to come from the meeting.

Miss Clio Kermit stoically delivered the news. The new commandant had disbanded the Executive Committee and discontinued funds to support the camp. He planned to isolate the internees from any outside contact, so he had closed the stores and shops, and evicted the Filipino vendors.

She warned her staff to mind the new curfew scrupulously. The number of guards had increased, and they all carried bayonets. She read off a list of mandates: roll calls would be held twice a day; monitors would be selected to supervise food distribution and report illnesses to the guards; and all activities, social events, and gatherings required prior approval by the commandant. "Girls," Miss Kermit said softly, "we must find ways to keep our spirits up, but we have to be very careful."

Margie found herself slipping away to the place inside her head where an orderly vegetable garden grew, now abundant with the fall harvest. She filled a basket with tomatoes, and as she bit into one of the warm red orbs, juice dribbled down her chin. She reached up and wiped it away. She spent more and more time now living in these worlds her imagination created, where she was safe and surrounded by family, and where there was always enough food to eat.

As the meeting adjourned, Margie saw Wade and Kenneth in a group of bone-skinny men carrying lumber and tools. "What are they building?" she asked Gracie.

"More guard sheds and sentry houses. Other men are stringing more barbed wire around the perimeter of the camp."

"What's the sense of it? There's no way out as it is."

"There is no sense. The commandant's insane."

Within a few days, the increased bowing, roll calls, curfews, harassment, looting, inspections, and restriction of their movements paled in importance as food became the major concern— there simply wasn't enough of it. What the Japanese supplied was often rotten, wormy, and only half the amount needed to feed four thousand people. The signs of starvation set in—lumps under the skin, swollen hands and feet, tingling and numbness, sore tongue, lost teeth, thinning hair, dimming vision, mental confusion, and extreme fatigue.

One morning Wade slipped into the shanty, where Margie and Helen lay motionless on their cots. The chess set he carried hid a bulge under his shirt that proved to be three bananas. He held them out and Margie grabbed one gratefully.

Margie smelled the banana, taking long breaths, letting its essence fill her senses before she peeled off the skin and took a tiny bite, allowing it to melt on her tongue and fill her mouth with flavor. She swallowed, feeling it slide down her throat, and then nibbled again, making that precious banana last a long time. After finishing the last bit, she wrapped the peel in a scrap of cloth and hid it under her mattress to savor the smell and chewy texture later.

"I'm scheduled to work." Helen sighed tiredly. "It takes me forever to get there. My legs don't want to move." Making a great effort, she got up and straightened her clothes. "Have you noticed how quiet it is? I heard that some mothers give their kids rock salt to suck. When they drink water, it fills their stomachs." With that, she limped out.

Margie whispered, "They could at least feed the children. I saw a Red Cross truck at the gate piled with milk and boxes of bananas. The guards turned it away. What would it hurt them to give milk and bananas to the children?" She and Wade sat on her bed staring at the chessboard he had set up, but they didn't have enough energy to play. They lay down together, sharing a pillow.

Wade said, "My mother made the best banana cream pie. Real cream, fresh eggs, and vanilla. She whipped the cream up with powdered sugar and spread it on top."

"My mother made chocolate pie. It took a special kind of chocolate that she shaved into hot sugar and cream. I'll make you both pies. We'll have a picnic. Fried chicken, of course. And potato salad. You'd love my potato salad with sliced tomatoes and green onions on the side."

"Don't forget the baked beans. My mother cooked them all day with molasses and brown sugar."

"Molasses—I forgot about molasses. I could drink a bottle right now. It's full of iron, you know." She snuggled into Wade and kissed him lightly.

His arms around her, he gently massaged her back. "I've fallen in love with you. You must know."

"I do." Enjoying the comfort of his touch, she ran her fingers over his skinny arms and skeletal ribs. They lay together cuddling, petting, and soon they were entwined. He pressed into her, and she wiggled out of her G-string. They made love for the simple pleasure of it.

While still in the afterglow, he soberly whispered, "I'm sorry. We shouldn't have done that."

"It's okay. I wanted to."

"It's dangerous if you get pregnant. What are the chances?"

"Slim, I'd guess. I doubt if I'm ovulating. My periods are scanty and irregular. I wish they'd stop. They're a nuisance in the best of times, but they're life-sapping now."

Over the following months, they continued to make love for its comfort, and she came to rely on his emotional support to sustain her through times when her spirits were low. Wade regularly shared his black-market booty—a piece of fruit, a loaf of bread, an egg or two. Occasionally, he brought a hunk of gray meat, and Margie thankfully ate it with no thought of questioning its origin. Anything edible was a godsend in this desolate place where a day's meal was sometimes nothing more than a bowl of grass soup, or a handful of weeds fried in her last dabs of face cream.

CHAPTER 15

Santo Tomas, December 1944–February 1945

Twenty-six months had come and gone since Margie arrived at Santo Tomas Internment Camp. While struggling to carry a bucket of water to the garden outside her Broadway shanty, she stumbled in a rut and dropped it. The water spilled out and seeped into the soil. Short of breath, she turned the empty bucket upside down and sat on it.

Not much was going on in Broadway this afternoon, or anywhere else in the camp either. Stringent new regulations confined prisoners to their assigned rooms in the overcrowded campus buildings from six in the evening until seven in the morning. The daily routine had narrowed to lining up for roll calls, enduring endless inspections, and gathering for twice-daily watery meals. Nonetheless, Margie persisted in tending her tiny garden.

An airplane roared out of the clouds, the noise hurting her ears. Since the Japanese stepped up aerial surveillance of the camp some weeks ago, such annoyances were common. Squinting against the light, she could make out white stars in circles of blue on the plane's fuselage and wings. Riotous shouting and whistling erupted as people realized the plane was American. Overjoyed by the sight, Margie jumped up and waved her arms. "We're here! We're here!"

Throngs of guards roughly herded internees into the campus buildings, but the ruthless treatment couldn't quell Margie's elation. In her room, she elbowed her way past her twenty roommates to the window and anxiously scanned the sky.

"It was an American plane! I'm positive!"

"It dipped its wings!"

"They know we're here!"

"We're going to be rescued!"

The B-24 didn't return, but Margie heard explosions in the distance and saw fires in the sky. In retribution, the guards lashed three men to posts, forcing them to stare at the sun for hours. Despondency settled back on the camp like a shroud.

The vegetables Margie grew in her garden improved her scanty diet of rice and sap-sap, the finger-sized, foul-smelling fish supplied by the Japanese. Pulling weeds that had grown around the leafy swamp spinach, sweet potatoes, and tomato plants, she separated the edible weeds from those that weren't. Looking closely at her crops, she saw a promising sight. Something had nibbled the tops of the spinach, maybe a rabbit. She would borrow the trap Wade had made from braided vines and set it. With any luck, rabbit stew would soon top the menu, followed by soups and sausages until every edible morsel of the rabbit had augmented a meal.

Her knees creaked as she stood up, causing her to limp a few steps before the soreness eased. She went to wash up but found the water bucket kept by the shanty door empty, and the sliver of soap missing. Annoyed, she asked Helen, "Have you seen the soap?"

"It's just inside the door, where it always is."

"No, it's not!" Margie snapped. "I can't find the soap, and there's no water. Criminy! Why can't *you* fill up this bucket sometimes?"

"I *did* fill the bucket and I *don't* know where the soap is. Tildy was here earlier. Maybe she took it."

"Tildy wouldn't take our soap."

"Yes, she would. She took my hairpin last time she was here. It was my last one too."

Margie snatched up the bucket to refill it at the tap. She stopped at Wade's for the rabbit trap on the way. She found him asleep, wearing only a thong, his body stretched out in full view. It pained her to see this kind and generous man at age thirty-four looking more like seventy. His hands were leathery, the skin pulled taut over swollen knuckles. He sometimes said his feet had gone numb, and he heard a constant ringing in his ears. His hair had thinned, and his beard grew in patches. Vitamin-deficient, dehydrated, and slowly starving, he grew physically weaker and mentally vaguer each day. Just like all of them. It seemed the easy out for the Japanese. What to do with the prisoners: don't feed them and let nature take its course.

Wade stirred, then turned toward her.

"I'm sorry. I didn't mean to wake you. I came for the trap. There might be a rabbit in the garden."

He sat up slowly, his expression dull.

"If we catch him, we could make stew."

"Oh? How so?"

She patted his face, her touch more hard than it was tender. "Wade, perk up."

He shook his head. "Sorry, I fade out sometimes."

She worried about this once-vital man, whom she was growing to care for so much. She didn't want him to lose his fortitude; he simply couldn't give up and die. She had seen that happen on the wards—a patient's will to live ebbing, his spirit slipping away.

Stored in the hospital morgue, dead bodies bloated in the heat and attracted rats that feasted on the fingers and toes. The corpses got carted away in filthy coffins too short for most American bodies. There was no dignity in death here.

"Come with me," Ruth Ann said. She led Margie down a long hallway and showed her the unlocked door and staircase that led to the cupola that sat high over the main entrance of Santo Tomas. "Do we dare?" she said, pointing up the stairs and speaking loudly over the noise of the war raging outside the confines of the camp.

"I don't know," Margie said. "This door's always locked. It's dangerous. Where's the guard?"

"Beats me. Don't you want to see what's going on?"

Margie's curiosity won over her fear. Closing the door behind them, she followed Ruth Ann up the stairs that were steeper than she thought.

"Ten more steps. Can you do it?" Ruth Ann asked.

"Think so," Margie shouted over the growl of aircraft engines. She scooted up the last few stairs backward and found the view from the top made the effort worth it. They joined Tildy and other internees watching the show. The bay area to the south roiled as American planes crisscrossing the sky dropped bombs on Japanese ships. Gray and gritty, the air smelled of burning fuel. Wherever Margie looked, fires roared and columns of black smoke spewed upward. Tremendous explosions rocked the building.

Over the constant drone of planes and shrill whistles of the antiaircraft artillery, Tildy shouted, "I counted eighty-four Allied planes this pass, and each dumped a full load. They just keep coming. Can't be much left out there."

Margie pointed to a dogfight just to the east between a Nip Zero and an American Hellcat. "Take the bastard out!" she screamed as the planes looped and rolled around the dreary sky. When an engine sputtered, she crossed her fingers. The Zero spiraled down, trailing fire, and she had to refrain from dancing a jig.

"Feels like I'm watching a newsreel!" she shouted.

"You *are* the newsreel!" Tildy said, laughing.

Every day Margie listened to and watched the sounds and sights of the war, but as January turned into February, liberation seemed as far off as ever. Fear for the lives of her and her friends intensified as each Allied victory brought more restrictions and humiliations, less food, and sometimes death to the beaten-down citizens of Santo Tomas.

Hope stirred again in February as the sky swelled with a tremendous reverberation. Margie counted seven B-24s flying in formation low over the camp. Just the sight of all that friendly power gave her goose bumps. The internees craned their necks to watch the lead plane circle. When directly overhead, the pilot tossed an object out of the cockpit. A hundred starving souls dove for it as a swarm of Japanese guards attacked. One of the prisoners prevailed. He waved goggles and a note.

"Roll out the barrel! We'll be back today or tomorrow!" he shouted to the excited crowd just before the guards beat him down and dragged him away.

Margie felt the point of a bayonet on her back. She stumbled forward with the rest of the crowd, which was crazed with joy and fear as they were herded back into the campus buildings. "Stay away from the windows or I'll shoot you," a guard growled as he locked the door.

The prisoners listened at doors and cautiously peeked out windows the rest of the day, praying for the return of the American planes. The only activity they could see, however, took place inside the camp. Skittish Japanese soldiers burned reams of records in massive bonfires and loaded trucks with guns and equipment.

Acrid smoke from the fires and quarrelsome enemy voices filtered into the rooms.

Ruth Ann nudged Tildy. "What're they saying?"

"Shh!" Tildy whispered, straining to hear the words. "They're talking too fast. Wait—something about trucks and gasoline. They sound scared."

"I hope they're so scared they're choking on it," Gracie said, sitting on her cot and hugging a pillow.

Ruth Ann snuck a quick peek outside. "Holy Mother of God! Those shit-faced devils! Look!"

Margie edged forward. She saw trucks filled with Japanese officers and their armed guards speeding out of the camp. A guard standing on the ground below her looked up, and she quickly ducked back. "So the rats are leaving the sinking ship, the yellow-bellied bastards."

"Christ, no! Not that. Stand here and look again." Ruth Ann pointed to the right. "That truck over there."

After trading places with Ruth Ann, Margie could see Japanese soldiers not far from her window unloading a truck full of red barrels. They rolled each barrel cautiously down a ramp and stacked it with the others into a niche under the building's main staircase. "What is it?"

"Gasoline storage barrels," Ruth Ann said. "I bet those fucking turds plan on torching this place before our guys arrive."

Thunderstruck, Margie watched the preparations for her demise. "They wouldn't do that, would they?"

"What's to stop them?"

As day turned to night, the flurry of Japanese activity ceased. The last truckload of officers disappeared through the gate, leaving behind a company of guards to keep the internees caged in their rooms. During the long hours without food or news, all they could do in the stifling darkness was wait and listen to the muffled sobs and whispered prayers of their fellow prisoners. Helen, who had slept through the day, struggled to breathe, and Margie pushed a thin pillow under her shoulders to ease her discomfort. She didn't like what she felt when she lifted her friend. Helen's body was swelling.

"Use this too," Tildy whispered, offering her own ragged pillow. "She doesn't sound good at all."

"She's not. She can't wait much longer." Margie stifled a sob and prayed. *Please give Helen the will to live and the strength to survive.*

From beyond the walls of the campus came the unremitting blasts of a raging war.

"There's machine-gun fire out there tonight," Ruth Ann said.

Margie listened to the staccato reports. There were other new sounds too—the rumblings and grindings of heavy machinery. "Sounds like there's fighting on the ground."

They felt a resonating thud, followed by a clunk.

"That sounded close." Ruth Ann climbed over several beds to return to the window.

They heard another thud, another clunk, and then a screech. A great resounding crash shook the building, drawing every woman in the room to the window. A light suddenly shone so brightly that Margie shielded her eyes. She rasped, "Oh Jesus, Mother of God! This is it!"

A few women returned to their cots, curling into fetal positions, heads buried under their pillows. Some dropped to their knees to pray, while others huddled tightly together for comfort. Despite the fear and horror, the room stayed as silent as a graveyard. Margie stayed at the window, mesmerized.

The bright light slowly advanced from the front gate to the main building. As it drew closer, Margie made out the long barrel of a howitzer mounted on a tank. She grabbed Tildy's hand, and Tildy reached for Ruth Ann, each needing a human touch. So this was the end. After all she had endured, this was how she would die—blown away in the middle of the night by a blast from a Japanese tank, then cremated in a gasoline firestorm. Margie hoped it would be quick.

The tank clanked to a stop in front of the main building, a time bomb ticking off their last minutes. No one dared breathe. The hatch on the tank creaked open, and two figures jumped nimbly to the ground. They peered around. Margie cringed, waiting for the detonation, but instead she heard a voice call out in English, "Hey, folks, are there any Americans inside?"

Ruth Ann flung the window open wide and screamed, "You better friggin' believe there're Americans in here!" The roomful of women stormed the window to get a look at their saviors. Then they kicked down the locked door and stampeded down the stairs.

Word spread like lightning and pandemonium reigned on the front lawn as prisoners poured out of buildings. More tanks lumbered through the shattered front gate, their lights illuminating thousands of bawling faces as the captives collectively roared out their relief and elation. A soldier unfurled an American flag over the entrance of the main building, and for a moment the throng fell silent. Gracie began to sing "God Bless America" in her clear voice, and everyone joined in. The air was electrified by the pulse of four thousand joyous hearts.

Truckloads of well-muscled American soldiers followed the tanks. GIs, they said they were called.

"What's a GI?" Margie asked the soldier standing beside her.

"Government issue. We're just regular army."

"I beg to differ," she laughed. "There's nothing *regular* about you guys." She reached out and touched his arm—no, this wasn't a cruel dream.

Margie pressed through the crowd, inebriated with joy. As she neared the front gate, she saw wounded soldiers lying on the ground and more being carried from trucks. Gracie tended to one, applying a field dressing. Margie hurried to help.

Gracie whispered, "What I'm hearing from these soldiers is pretty scary."

A medic gave Margie a bag of plasma, and she started the IV.

Gracie said, "General MacArthur sent these guys in without securing the area first. He told them to blast their way through enemy lines and get us out of here."

"General MacArthur? He came back?"

"Yes, with the big guns. They're saying the Japanese were about to annihilate the prisoners of war. Not just us—in all the camps."

As they went from soldier to soldier, they heard more of the story. Guerrillas had helped, meeting the American troops at the city line and escorting them through the streets, past nests of Japanese resistance, and all the way to Santo Tomas.

"That's the machine-gun fire we heard," Gracie said.

One wounded soldier proudly announced, "We call ourselves the Flying Columns. We barreled right through that Jap fuckin' line . . ." His gaze became unfocused, and he passed out. Gracie applied a pressure bandage to stem his bleeding, then moved him to the front of the line for surgery.

Trucks kept rolling through the front gate. Amid the noisy disorder, Margie thought she heard a voice from the past. Glancing up from what she was doing, she saw Max Renaldo. He looked impeccable, muscled and tan, his hair flowing, and his dancer's body moving with grace. She felt first fear and then revulsion for this man who had assaulted her years ago: her ear still carried the scar from his bite. When their eyes met, confusion flickered across his face, then recognition, and finally—hatred.

A shiver crawled up the back of her neck. She said to Gracie, "I need to check on Helen."

The dark passageways of the main building felt eerily deserted, and Margie feared lurking guards as she hurried past open doors. The clamor of celebration combined with the more distant sounds of battle filtered through the open window of her room, coalescing into disharmonic noise. She wondered how Helen managed to sleep through it, but a quick check confirmed her condition had worsened—her body more swollen, her skin taut and too pink. Margie patted her shoulder lightly.

"Helen, wake up. We've been rescued, Helen. Wake up. We're going to go home." Margie caressed her cheek. "Helen, honey, wake up. You have to wake up now. I have something important to tell you."

Helen's eyelids fluttered. "Margie," she whispered. "What's all the noise?"

"It's a celebration. We've been rescued. American soldiers broke through. Can you hear them? The singing? The cheering? More are coming, and they're going to take us home. You're going to see your mum and pop again, and your cousin Mabel. Remember, Helen? You want me to meet Mabel. You can't go back on your word, now."

Helen smiled. "You'll like Mabel. She's a real stitch." She shivered. "I'm so cold."

Margie gathered thin blankets from the other beds and piled them on Helen, checking her slowing pulse before tucking her arms under the covers. She stroked Helen's brow, crying inside her head, *Don't die. Please don't die.* She needed an infusion of plasma. *Plasma!* The soldiers had plasma!

She jiggled Helen's shoulder again, excited this time. "Helen, listen. I'm going downstairs to get you some plasma. I'll be right back. It will make you feel better, I promise, honey! Hang on for me!" She adjusted the pillows under Helen's head and ran out of the room.

Moving as fast as her weakened condition allowed, she sped through the empty corridors, where the smell of smoke mingled with musk, dirt, and urine. Nearing the stairwell, she sensed someone else moving and flattened herself against the wall.

A familiar voice came from the shadows. "So we meet again, Margie. I must say, you're not the pretty little thing you were when I last saw you."

Acutely aware of her jutting bones, Margie crossed her arms over her chest. Her mouth went sticky dry. "What are you doing here, Max?"

"Are you addle-brained? I came in with the troops. Where's your little blond friend?"

"Evelyn? She went home three years ago. You know that. She said you arranged it."

He belched and took a long swig from a flask. "Now, why would I do that?"

Margie slid her foot sideways, a step closer to the stairwell. "Why? Weren't you two getting married?"

"Ha!" He swayed on his feet. "I guess I said a few things. She could've taken it that way. You see—" He hiccupped. "You see, I wanted to keep her around for a while. She was a cute little cunt. She'd do anything for me. You two talked a lot. Did she tell you that? Anything for me. I have a particular appetite."

Margie took another step sideways, hoping Max wouldn't notice, but he followed her movement with his head.

He said, "Royce and I talked too. He told me all these, um . . . intimate things. What he did . . . what you did."

Margie forced herself not to listen.

"Wonder what he'd think of you now? Scrawny. Gray-faced. Hollow-eyed." Max snickered. "But then, he's no prize himself by now." He stepped closer, waving the flask in front of her face. "When's the last time you ate anything but weevils?"

She smelled the liquor. She willed herself to remain detached, but her mouth watered, and she gaped at it hungrily.

He laughed with gurgling contempt, then drank the remaining contents of the flask and tossed it aside. It clattered on the floor.

"You always were a mean drunk, Max."

"So the gray ghost's still got fight!" He grabbed her arm, and she writhed in his grasp. From down the stairs came a grinding of machinery, a thump, and a wild hurrah.

"You should be with your troops." She fought against him.

"They'll keep," he growled. "You're unfinished business." Gripping her arm, he propelled her, stumbling, from the dark hallway into an empty room. She twisted away, but he grabbed her by the hair, yanking her back and spinning her around. She gasped at seeing his one milky, sightless eye. She lowered her gaze to the cleft in his chin.

He jerked her head back, forcing her gaze upward. "Look at me, you bitch! You did this!" Spittle sprayed her face. "You ruined my life. You owe me, and I've come for payment."

She thrashed, trying to free herself, but she couldn't match his weight, strength, and thirst for revenge. He pinned her to the floor, one hand so tight to her throat it cut off her breathing. He ripped off her cotton dress, laughing at the crocheted G-string as he tossed it aside. Lowering his pants, he drove into her, each thrust like a knife slicing into her—brutal, hard, deep, again and again. He convulsed, spent but not done. He flipped her over, forcing her legs apart. Choking, she screamed as he thrust his penis painfully into her rectum while pinching her nonexistent breasts and fondling her burning vagina. Frenzied, he pounded away at her, while her chin and jutting hip bones bounced on the floor. Licking her ear, he whispered, "When you see your friend, tell her I miss that flicky little thing she did with her tongue." He rolled away. Straightening his clothes, he nudged her with his foot before he left to join the festivities outside.

Dizzy from pain and terror, Margie pulled on her torn dress and found her G-string in a corner, then limped back to her room. Sitting on her cot, she tried to sip some water, but each tiny swallow hurt her crushed throat. Blood seeped from between her legs; she couldn't tell from where, because everything down there burned. Then she saw Helen lying immobile on her cot and remembered the plasma. *Oh my God!* She had been on her way to get plasma for Helen when Max attacked her. She hobbled over to her friend.

"Helen, honey," she croaked painfully. "I was delayed a bit. I'll be right back with the plasma. I won't be but a minute." She touched her friend's cheek, but she was too late. Helen had neither breath in her body nor life in her eyes.

Margie collapsed onto Helen's chest, feeling herself shrivel inside, the howling void filling with numbness, desolation, and darkness.

That was how Gracie found her some time later, battered and weak, blood and urine soaking her dress. "Who did this? A guard?" Her gaze raked the room. She closed the door, shoved a cot in front of it, and helped Margie stumble onto it. She assessed Margie all over, muttering obscenities when seeing the bloodied perineum. Gracie placed a folded blanket under Margie's feet and wrapped her in another. "You're in shock. Keep your head down, okay?"

Margie nodded, dull and dry-eyed, her skin clammy.

Gracie went to Helen's cot. Seeing Gracie on her knees, Margie crawled off her cot to join her. They prayed together, their voices quivering. "The Lord is my shepherd; I shall not want . . ."

Margie's eyes refused to focus, and her injured throat constricted. She became mute with grief, but Gracie's voice strengthened.

"I will fear no evil: for thou art with me . . ."

Her vision dimming, Margie clutched at Gracie before crumpling against her. She awoke a few moments later in Gracie's embrace, and they clung together, trying to absorb this one more horror, while Santo Tomas's church bells clanged in good cheer.

Amid the chaos of liberation, burials were haphazard in Santo Tomas. A subdued group gathered to lay Helen to rest in the small garden outside the shack in Broadway. Through incessant gunfire from outside the walls, and bombers and fighter planes roaring and sputtering smoke into the blue sky, Margie spoke of how she'd met Helen while studying anesthesiology at Walter Reed Hospital, of her loyal friendship, her large family in England, and her unselfish desire to work at the front, where she would be most useful. The chaplain led them in prayer, and Gracie sang Helen's favorite hymn, "In the Garden." They all joined in at the refrain:

And He walks with me, and He talks with me,
And He tells me I am His own . . .

Wade and Kenneth filled in the grave, and Ruth Ann marked the sacred spot with a wooden cross. Margie returned alone to the empty shack to grieve.

Japanese guards remaining in Santo Tomas holed up on the top floor of the Education Building with two dozen internees held captive. After negotiations ensuring their safe retreat, they surrendered their weapons and left through a gauntlet of internees yelling, "Kill 'em! Kill 'em!" and children chanting, "Make 'em bow!"
    Shortly, from down the road, Margie heard a chattering of rifle fire.
    "Guerillas," Wade said. "God bless 'em."

Fierce fighting between Allied and Japanese forces continued out-side Santo Tomas. Inside the gates, however, the inhabitants experienced a reprieve. Margie, Wade, Gracie, and Kenneth relaxed on a blanket under a tree near the main building. Each had a bag of food and a container of juice. They watched trucks arrive through the front gate.

"Those eight are food trucks. That makes sixteen of them already this morning," Wade said.

With the mention of food, Gracie reached into her bag and selected a banana. Wade followed suit, but he chose a peanut butter sandwich instead, as did Kenneth.

"Eat slowly. Don't make yourself sick," Margie said as she lay back against the tree trunk. Still reeling from the rape and mourning Helen's death, she felt detached from the rest of the world. She had no desire to sit here with her friends, but Gracie had dragged her out of bed, insisting she come, and in the end it was easier to obey than resist.

Kenneth said, "I think I'm past that. The cereal this morning stayed down."

Wade ate half his sandwich and put the rest back in the bag. "One bite and I feel full."

Gracie peeled her banana and nibbled at it. "I'll never complain about being plump again."

Kenneth caressed her bony arm. "I'd like to see you plump."

Another convoy arrived at the gate with a rumble of engines and the squeal of brakes. Since liberation, traffic flowed in and out of the camp almost nonstop. Some trucks arrived with companies of burly American soldiers, while others were filled with weapons, from sidearms to howitzers, and enough ammunition to blow up the whole wretched island. Cannons perched on roofs of buildings, and tanks lined the perimeter of Santo Tomas.

"We're an armed camp," Kenneth said, "which just gives the Japs one more reason to attack us."

In response, Gracie ragged on her fiancé. "Kenneth Dowling, you are so blessedly pessimistic. I swear—"

"Well, what do we have here?" Wade murmured. Buses filled with people stopped in front of the main building. The drivers coaxed the reluctant passengers to exit. The men were no more than skeletons—some wore nothing but thongs, and all of them crouched like beaten dogs.

"Lord, do we look like that?" Wade said.

Margie sat up, but she had to turn her head away, not wanting to identify with the miserable bunch.

"It's POWs from other camps. I heard more are coming," Gracie said.

"There's no room here. Where are they going to put them?"

"By their looks, in the hospital."

Wade rubbed Margie's back. He had hovered over her since liberation, witnessing her mute despair. In a low voice he asked, "Have I done something to make you angry?"

She shook her head. "I'm exhausted, is all." The clock on the bell tower announced the quarter hour. "Time for work," she said.

"You had to say that, didn't you?" Gracie made a face and leaned against Kenneth.

The nurses worked six hours a day attending POWs suffering from the effects of starvation and soldiers wounded in the battles raging in Manila. Now buses full of prisoners from other internment camps kept rolling into Santo Tomas. Margie longed to escape into a deadening sleep. "I don't think I can do this anymore."

Wade held her in his arms and whispered, "Don't give up, Margie. All we've been through—it's almost over. I love you. I'll take care of you." His lips brushed hers.

She slumped against his frail frame, drawing strength from his words, his firm hold, and light kiss, but foreboding haunted her. She would never be free of this cruel place and all that had happened here. She felt it in her bones.

The hospital overflowed, but now the staff had enough food, soap, IV solutions, sharp needles, drugs, vitamins, plasma, linens, and bandages—everything they had done without for so long. Doctors arrived with the troops, and they brought with them a new drug called penicillin.

"It's an antibiotic made from mold," one doctor said.

Curious, Margie held a vial up to the light. "What does it do?"

"It saves lives. Infections start clearing in twenty-four hours. It's a miracle drug."

"From mold, huh? If only we'd known. What other changes have I missed?"

"You're going to be surprised. It's a whole new world out there."

Yes, a new world, she thought. One that had left her behind with worthless knowledge, outdated skills, and no strength or desire left for catching up. She cared for patients too weak to eat, going from bed to bed offering encouraging words and bits of mashed banana. She checked their IVs, cleaned and medicated their broken-down skin, and made their beds with clean linens. Still, the hours dragged; when the next shift of nurses arrived, she felt relieved.

She found Wade in her shanty, disposing of Helen's ragged clothes and dried food he found hidden under her cot. He had put aside an address book, letters from her family, an unfilled journal, and an empty fountain pen with the inscription *To Helen. Happy Birthday. Love, Mabel.*

"That's all she had," he said.

As Margie slipped the fountain pen into her pocket, sadness descended again like a wall of clouds. Together they read the letters. "She wanted to go back to England," she said. "That was her home."

"Would you like to write to her parents?"

"Yes, and her cousin Mabel." Margie's eyes filled with tears.

They composed the letters. The one to Helen's parents told them how Helen was loved and cared for until the end, the other to Mabel to let her know how much Helen admired her. Wade addressed the envelopes and put them in his pocket.

Huge explosions vibrated the ground and lit the sky like the Fourth of July. Margie and Wade dropped to the floor; they were vulnerable to Japanese shells lobbed into the tinder-dry shanty-towns. Palm-leaf roofs crackled and bamboo hissed as wind-whipped embers flared to flames. People swarmed out of their huts, children crying for their mothers and fathers, parents assembling their broods. Sirens wailed.

All medical personnel reported for duty. At the hospital, Margie stuffed her pockets with dressings, tannic acid for burns, and a twenty-cc syringe of morphine for those in pain and shock. Outside, with shells popping and fires burning around her, she ministered to the wounded, the burned, and the lost and crying children. Her mind numbed with fear again, and she practiced her skills automatically. A pair of soldiers placed a stretcher at her feet. "Head injury, lots of blood," one of them barked before running off.

Lifting the dressing covering the man's face, she jerked away from the stare of a blind, milky eye. Revulsion speared through her like an icicle. "Well, well, Max, isn't this a twist of fate?"

Laboring to speak, he stammered, "G-get m-me a d-doctor."

Her vision narrowed, and the clamor around her faded. She whispered into his blood-streaked face, "Give me one reason why I should."

He struggled to sit up. "I demand a doctor!"

She pinned him down with her body. The feel of him against her, the smell of him so close to her face, and his piercing gaze of distain all focused her loathing for him. A plan welled up from a dark place. She waved the syringe of morphine in front of his good eye. "It's full, Max."

He tried to call out, but she covered his mouth with her hand and watched his eyes grow wide as she uncapped the syringe with her teeth. *Too bad it's such an easy death—a surge of warmth, then the slide into unconsciousness.*

With the quickness of desperation, Max gripped her wrist and pushed the syringe toward her face. Morphine leaking from the needle's point trickled onto her white knuckles. She wrestled against him: this time her strength equaled his, but Max grabbed her throat with his free hand and squeezed off her airflow. She gagged, then rammed her knee hard into his crotch. As he convulsed, she collapsed on top of him and sank the needle into his neck, depressing the plunger. She felt him go limp.

She sat back on her knees, hands covering her mouth, eyes bulging in horror at what she'd done. Max's lifeless eyes stared accusingly at her. She retched, then vomited a bitter green bile.

Gracie dropped down beside her. "Margie, a wall fell." Then she saw Max and gasped. Looking furtively around, she removed the syringe from his neck, capped it, and put it in her pocket. Her eyes asked, *Was it him?*

Margie nodded.

Gracie summoned a medic. "Head wound!" she shouted. "Died on impact. Margie, come with me."

Margie rose, weak-kneed and dazed. She wobbled through the bedlam of the injured, the screaming, the moaning, the mangled, the dead, and the dying—the memory of her evil deed already buried deep in her psyche.

Soon after the horrific days of the Japanese shelling of Santo Tomas, a hundred relief nurses arrived, and the internee nurses gladly relinquished their duties. They were going home, the first in the camp to be evacuated. As they packed their few possessions into duffels, they chattered about the trip.

"I'm going to kiss the ground, first thing. American ground."

"If we can get past the Japs. Bombs are still dropping."

"Uncle Sam got troops in here; he sure as shootin' can get us out."

"Praise Uncle Sam!"

Gracie came into the room and jumped up on her bed, waving her arms. "I have an announcement to make. Kenneth and I are getting married." She did a little dance.

Ruth Ann said, "So, what's new? We've known that for months."

"We're getting married tonight! We want you all to come."

The women surrounded Gracie and began planning a festive event. Boots had made friends with one of the cooks and could get a cake, and Ruth Ann knew someone who had a Victrola and records. Tildy offered to lend Gracie her grandmother's wedding ring.

Margie watched the revelry from the edge of the room. She sat at the window, looking over the camp that for almost three years had been a perverse sort of home. How many times had she stood here aching to leave? But now that leaving was a reality, she was scared. No one could ever fathom what she'd seen and done, or comprehend the suffering. Who would believe what a person would eat if they had never faced starvation themselves? Or what a terrified person would do to stay alive for just one more day? Or what a broken person would stoop to? Deep in her thoughts, she didn't hear Gracie come up behind her.

"Margie."

She jumped, and for a second she couldn't imagine why Gracie was there. Coming back to the present, she said, "Congratulations!" and gave her friend a hug.

Gracie bubbled, "You're my best friend, Margie. Will you stand up for me?"

"Of course, I'd be happy to." Margie embraced Gracie again.

"The wedding's at five o'clock in the chapel. I need some help already." Gracie nodded toward the crowd making plans. "I don't want a party afterward. Help me get away."

"You got it," Margie conspired. "Cut the cake, give them thirty minutes, and I'll get you out somehow. You only have one night with Kenneth."

"One splendid, spectacular, glorious, fantastic night." Gracie's eyes twinkled.

With her few belongings packed, Margie felt ready to abandon her shanty; she was scheduled to leave Santo Tomas in the morning. The war still raged furiously in and around Manila, making both leaving and staying equally perilous. She and Wade discussed their fears while sitting together on the main building's front steps.

"I won't know how to act. I don't even know how to use a knife and fork anymore. I'm sure to do something odd," she said.

"You'll be with your family, and they'll help you adjust. It'll take a little time. You'll be okay."

"But I look like a scarecrow. Seeing me like this will frighten my parents."

"Margie, don't. You're a beautiful woman."

"I feel bitter and old, and I know it shows on my face. Do you think we'll ever forget all this ugliness?"

"No. It's part of us now, but in time, the worst memories will fade." He took her hand. "Promise you won't forget me."

"How could I ever forget you? You'll be coming back to Michigan, won't you?"

"I don't know. It depends on where the *Tribune* sends me."

"Oh!" The thought of Wade not being there frightened her. For nearly three years he had been her protector and provider. "You'll write to me, won't you?"

"I had something more in mind than letters, Margie." He hesitated. "Would you consider marrying me? Can you love me that way?"

The proposal caught her by surprise. She cared deeply for Wade, but she'd never thought about marrying him. There were no sparks of first-love excitement that she and Abe had shared, or fires of passion like Royce had ignited.

"We can put all this behind us," he said. "Start our lives fresh, you and me together. I'll work at the newspaper, and you can stay home. You'll never have to work again if you're my wife."

She listened. What Wade offered sounded appealing—a carefree and stable life. She could be finished with nursing and put the horrors of war and this prison camp behind her. She would be free to have the babies she had promised her mother. It could be a good life, with a good man.

"We'll fill the house with babies," he said, as if reading her thoughts. "Margie, will you marry me?"

"I have no feelings at all right now. I'm empty inside."

"I'll help you heal."

Dear Wade, a writer, musician, and kind nurturer. He had seen her at her worst, emaciated, neurotic, and full of demons—demons they shared. No one would ever understand or know her the way Wade did, and he wanted her for his wife. Her gaze explored his longing face, and she saw the love in his eyes. Saying no would be a stab to his heart, and she couldn't bear hurting this compassionate man who'd been so loving and giving.

"Yes," she said. "I will marry you." The decision made, she felt giddy for a moment.

He twirled her around and kissed her, and then placed a wooden ring in her hand. "It's beautiful," she said, holding it up to see the deep mahogany grain swirling amid delicate carvings of tiny flowers. "Where did you get it?"

"I made it for you a while ago. We can have a double wedding with Gracie and Kenneth."

"Wait. You're going too fast."

"I already asked them, and they said it was okay."

"You already asked them? I don't know. A wedding today—it's too soon."

"Why?"

"I'm not ready." She walked a little way off.

"There's nothing to get ready," he said to her back. "Kenneth reserved the chapel and lined up the preacher. All of our friends will be there. There's even a party planned for afterward, like a real wedding. I don't want you leaving without getting this settled."

She slid the ring on her finger and held her hand up to admire it. "It is settled. I want to be married in my church at home, with my parents there, and your family, your sister Carol. I want to be married in a wedding dress."

Wade circled her with his arms. "Knowing you're right makes me love you all the more."

She pushed him back, unable to muster even a hint of desire.

"What's the matter, Margie?"

The matter was that she was bruised and torn from a vicious rape, emotionally dead, and worried she would never want to be touched in an intimate way again.

"Nothing's the matter, silly boy. I'm going to save myself for our wedding night. Isn't that what a good girl's supposed to do?"

CHAPTER 16

Santo Tomas / San Francisco, February 1945

Jubilation reigned. After thirty-one months in captivity, euphoric nurses piled into open-bed trucks and left Santo Tomas Internment Camp to rousing cheers and shouted promises of "See you in the States!"

Twin-engine C-47s waited on Dewey Boulevard, Manila's main thoroughfare. Hearing bombs in the distance and gunfire nearby, the women hastened to board. Over the roar of the engines, the pilot yelled, "Everyone up front! We're overloaded and need to lighten the tail." Sniper fire crackled as they taxied down the middle of the road. The pilot held the brakes while pushing the throttle forward, forcing the rear of the plane off the ground. They skimmed over the treetops, and the women cheered the captain's skill before taking their seats and settling in for the trip.

As the plane gained altitude, Margie gazed earthward, where she could see the full extent of the devastation of once-beautiful Manila. The curvilinear buildings in the business district and the geometric architecture of the theater district—gone. The parks, wide avenues, and palatial homes with tiled roofs and translucent shells for windows—also gone, replaced by piles of gray rubble that stretched for miles in all directions. Columns of black smoke marked areas where battles still raged. Leaning into the window, she saw Japanese artillery on the rooftops of buildings surrounding Santo Tomas, and the reality of the danger that still remained to those left behind burst her euphoric bubble. Shaken, she willed herself back into the safety of numbness.

They flew southeast to Leyte, another Philippine island. From her bird's-eye perspective, Margie saw an immense harbor crowded with hundreds of US ships. From an airstrip near the shoreline, bombers and fighter planes landed and took off, one after another.

Their C-47 landed smoothly amid the bustle. After disembarking, the nurses underwent evaluations at a nearby army hospital. The doctors recorded every detail of their depleted condition, admitting several of them for inpatient care.

Margie suffered from malnutrition and malaria. Because she had so little muscle tone and no fat left to support her internal organs, her abdomen was tender when palpated, and her bladder control weak. The doctor jotted notes about her achy joints and a few loose teeth. As the physical exam progressed, he noted bruising around her vagina and a tear in the perineum.

"What happened here?" he asked.

Knowing this question was sure to be asked, she had concocted a plausible answer. "I fell during the liberation. The ground was slippery and I lost my footing. I landed hard on a rock. It's better now. It doesn't burn anymore when I pee."

The doctor frowned. "The injuries are characteristic of—"

"Nothing like that happened. It was just a fall!"

He didn't press her further, but made more notes on her chart.

A Captain Riker interviewed her as part of his project to amass data for future war-crime tribunals. Stories came spewing out like a flood, one incident triggering the memory of another—hundreds of details. What a relief, to finally have the freedom to express her rage at Japanese cruelties and petty sadisms!

The captain nodded frequently and scribbled furiously. At the end of the hours-long interview, he said, "We're asking everyone coming out of the prison camps not to talk about any of this. I have a paper for you to sign saying you'll comply. You know how it is. Stories tend to grow; little things get magnified. It's best to keep silent. Just go about your life, get married, have your babies, be a pretty lady again." He shoved the paper and a pen toward her.

She read the title: *Publicity in Connections with Escaped, Liberated, or Repatriated Prisoners of War to Include Evaders of Capture in Enemy Occupied Territory and Internees in Neutral Countries.*

She couldn't comprehend it, and she was hungry again. Thinking about lunch, she signed the paper, certain she'd never want to talk about what she had been through.

After that initial outpouring of fury, Margie began to unwind. Housed in a quiet annex near the beach, she slept in a bed with a mattress and crisp sheets, and soaked in a bathtub, luxuries she had all but forgotten. She was offered more food than she could eat in a lifetime, and every meal seemed like a banquet. She sunbathed on Leyte's white-sand beaches and swam in the ocean, letting whitecaps wash over her. The base hosted beer parties, Ping-Pong tournaments, and poker games; Frank Sinatra songs played in the bars, and Fred Astaire movies ran at the theaters. Margie found herself obsessed with any news of home, whether from the radio, magazines, or newspapers. She learned about the rationing of food, shoes, and gasoline; of children placed in day care, and mothers working in jobs outside the home; and of other stateside oddities, like the once copper pennies being stamped out of steel.

She sent a wire to her parents. She loved them, she wrote. She would be home soon. She would phone as soon as she reached San Francisco.

The flight away from the Philippines continued across the Pacific, stopping to refuel on the island of Saipan. Margie brushed the wrinkles from her new uniform and put on her too-big hat. Glancing out the plane window, she saw a crowd on the tarmac. She nudged Ruth Ann. "Bigwigs must be flying in."

As the nurses emerged from the aircraft, the crowd gave a rousing cheer. Puzzled by the fuss, Margie forced a smile and waved shyly. She stood at attention as a band played "The Star-Spangled Banner."

A reception followed, with tables laden with food and favors. Margie ate a hamburger with mustard and onion, slurped down a Coke, and enjoyed a slice of a chocolate sheet cake, which was emblazoned with the message "Welcome Home to the Good Old USA." The few women stationed at this obscure airbase donated their own lotions and cosmetics for gift bags as a small tribute to the nurses. Rubbing lotion on her painfully dry hands, Margie said to a woman who worked there, "Much better. Thank you!"

Shortly, though, she started feeling ill from too much rich food, and the friendly commotion wearied her.

Unable to shake her dark mood, she wandered away from the crowd to stroll the fields where parked planes sat silently in long rows. She meandered in and around the aircraft, looking closely at wingspans, tires, and tail fins. Abe sprang to mind, how proud he had been of his shiny new pilot's wings, and how handsome he looked in his uniform. Now all she had left of him were the letters tucked away in a pocket of her duffel bag and the pilot's ring waiting for her at home. Her thoughts went out to his parents, who had lost their only son and a possible passel of redheaded grandchildren, had the war not intervened.

She peeked through an open warehouse door. The thousands, perhaps tens of thousands, of boxes of food and supplies stacked from floor to ceiling amazed her. What she wouldn't have given for one of those boxes just ten days ago! Hearing her name called, she spun around.

"Long time no see," Evelyn said, striding toward her with outstretched arms.

Margie shook her head in confusion, but she couldn't mistake those cornflower-blue eyes as belonging to anyone other than her old roommate. Crossing her arms protectively, Margie took a step back. "What are you doing here?"

Evelyn stopped short, dropping her arms to her sides. "I'm stationed here. I went back to school and retrained. I'm a flight nurse now." She touched the gold flight nurse's wings pinned to her uniform collar.

Margie stared in curiosity at Evelyn's wings. Flight nurse? She'd never heard of one.

"There's a small group of us. We fly out at daybreak and circle over the islands. When our fighters clear the sky of Jap planes, we land to pick up the wounded and bring them here to the base hospital."

Evelyn's shiny hair, clear skin, and trim figure testified to her good health. Margie hugged herself tighter, hiding her nonexistent bosom. "You're looking good, but that was always your strong suit, wasn't it?"

Evelyn swiped at tears. "Please don't be angry with me. You would have left Corregidor too if you could have. You know it. I did talk to your parents. I told them where you were and that it was hard to get mail out. They were relieved to hear you were okay."

"Thank you," Margie said.

"Did you see Max? I heard he was with the liberation forces."

Margie felt blood rush to her face. "What makes you think that? I didn't see him."

"Oh, well, you know rumors. I was just hoping. Our contact's been spotty. I heard about Royce. I'm so sorry. It must have torn you apart. I wish I could have been there for you."

"Why? We're at war. People die! Especially the good ones, like Royce and my friend Helen. She starved to death just before liberation. Have you ever seen anyone starve, Evelyn?" Margie's voice tightened. "First, she wasted away to nothing. Just before she died, her heart got too weak to function and her body swelled. Her lungs filled with fluid, and she gurgled when she breathed—"

"Stop it!" Shock registered on Evelyn's face. "I've seen my share of death! I'm sorry about Royce and your friend. I'm sorry you spent almost three years as a prisoner, but I'm not to blame!"

A deep aversion for this woman with an affinity for dangerous men welled up inside Margie. Her mouth twitched with suppressed emotion, and her fingers flexed as if preparing for attack. She stepped forward.

A look of fright crossed Evelyn's face, and she backed away.

A jeep drove up beside them. "All aboard," the driver called.

Margie climbed in, and the jeep sped away toward the waiting C-47. She felt strange, her head aching, her stomach sour, and her heart pounding.

Boarding the plane, she took a seat by the window and spread a blanket over her lap. A vision of Max licking her ear intruded into her thoughts. She remembered him saying, "When you see your little friend . . ." She remembered the rape, and when she and Gracie prayed over Helen's body while the church bells pealed . . . then, she remembered nothing until the arrival of the relief nurses from the States.

Still cold, she pulled the blanket over her shoulders. Her mind searched for a memory it couldn't retrieve. She lit a cigarette and inhaled deeply, feeling the nicotine calm her anxiety. She chain-smoked and focused on the journey home.

They left Saipan, bound for Hawaii. Before landing in Honolulu, Boots had the women up in the aisles learning the hula. "The hands tell the story," she said in a singsong voice. "Watch my hands. See the wave of the ocean and the rise of the sun? Okay, keep the hips going too. Come on. Think swivel hips. Think of those boys out there. No! No! Not bump and grind, girls! We're supposed to be beautiful. Think beautiful and graceful."

"Give it up, Boots," Gracie said with a giggle. "It's hopeless. I didn't know you were a dancer."

"Just a wannabe. I wanted to go into the theater, but my dad didn't think it was a proper thing for his little girl to do. If he only knew."

Seven hours after leaving Hawaii on February 24, 1945, the women arrived at Hamilton Field in San Francisco, California, the United States of America. They deplaned to a cheering crowd while a military brass band blared the national anthem. The nurses saluted the Stars and Stripes as it snapped in a brisk breeze. Some knelt and kissed the ground, and most cried freely flowing tears of joy. A brigadier general delivered a welcome-home speech, extolling their sacrifices and dubbing them the "Angels of Bataan and Corregidor." They all got promoted one grade and were awarded Presidential Unit Citations for heroism and Bronze Stars with two oak-leaf clusters for bravery. San Francisco's silver-haired mayor preened for the cameras, and pictures of the event made front-page news.

A horde of reporters surrounded Margie. A flashbulb popped, causing her vision to waver. One asked her if she could have her heart's desire, what would it be?

"A haircut," she replied without hesitation.

She got her haircut, as well as a manicure, a facial, and a large advance on the back pay the government owed her. Giddy from all the attention, she bought diamond teardrop earrings to complement her new hairdo, lacy underwear, stylish shoes, and a large bottle of Jergens hand lotion—because it smelled like her favorite candy. She purchased perfumes for her mother and Frank's wife, Irene, and a leather wallet for her dad. The gifts precipitated a tingle of anticipation that left her feeling vaguely anxious.

In her hotel room later, she hung up the phone on yet another reporter. She said to Ruth Ann, "It's like they think we're celebrities or something. He wanted to know my favorite lipstick color. Who could possibly care?"

Ruth Ann said, "Have you been asked *the* question yet?"

"What's that?"

"It comes disguised. One sleaze asked me to tell him my worst memory. I could have named a hundred, but none of them would have been what he wanted to hear."

"Like were we violated, ruined, molested, despoiled, raped, and disgraced?"

"They want all the details."

Margie called home. As she waited for the call to Little River to go through, she pictured the setting: Dad dressed in his favorite blue cable-knit sweater, smoking his pipe and reading the newspaper; Mama wrapped in one afghan and knitting another. At this time of night, the radio would be playing music. She heard a click, then a "Hello?" Her mother's voice.

The long-distance operator interrupted, first speaking to Margie's mother, then directly to Margie herself, saying, "You're connected. Go ahead."

She couldn't control the quaver in her voice. "Mama? It's Margie."

There was silence from the other end of the line.

"Can you hear me, Mama? It's me, Margie. I'm in San Francisco."

"Margie! Oh, my dear! Are you all right?"

"I'm fine. I'm on leave. I'll be home soon. It's good to hear your voice."

"Where are you?"

"I'm in San Francisco. Is Daddy there? Can you put him on too?"

The connection echoed, then buzzed and crackled.

". . . neighbors," Margie heard.

"I couldn't hear you. Is Daddy there? Can you put him on?"

"I'm sorry, dear. He's at a neighbor's. How are you?"

"I'm fine," she repeated. "I'm flying to Chicago tomorrow, then taking the train on Friday to Ann Arbor. I'll arrive there about six o'clock in the evening. Can Daddy pick me up?"

Mama hesitated. "Of course, dear."

Margie heard a screech. "Is that a baby crying?"

"Yes, that's Billy. Frank and Irene had a baby."

"Frank has a baby?"

"Yes. He's almost a year old. Would you like to say hello to Irene?"

So Margie talked to the sister-in-law she had yet to meet in person. Irene sounded young and hesitant. She said Billy had just started to walk and was cranky this evening because he was cutting teeth.

Margie commiserated. A silence stretched between them. She finally said, "Well, there's a line to use the phone here. Tell Daddy I love him and I'm sorry I missed him."

"Would you like to talk to your mother again? Wait, she went to the bathroom. I'm sorry. She's a little upset. It's been a hard time for us, you know."

Unsettled, Margie hung up the phone. The call was disjointed and confusing, and where was her dad? It had not gone as she expected.

CHAPTER 17

San Francisco / Little River, February 1945

While waiting for her flight to Chicago, Margie watched as soldiers and sailors jostled through San Francisco's airport. Thin and fit, the men conveyed a maturity in their faces that was beyond their obvious youth. Some swaggered past with an air of anticipation, carrying gift bags in addition to their duffels. They rushed to catch connecting flights, trains, buses, or taxis. Others walked more slowly, their expressions impassive; they were headed toward troopships anchored in the harbor and uncertain futures.

Waiting with Margie, Tildy kept busy by knitting a scarf. As her fingers flew and the needles clicked, she said, "Did we ever look like that?" She nodded at a woman wearing a tailored coat and veiled hat, with three equally well-dressed children trailing behind her. "Bet she's never pissed in a hole."

"Or missed a meal," Margie added as she eyed the handsome coat. "Can't believe I'm hungry again." She unwrapped a muffin

she'd bought earlier at the airport's café. "Don't look now, but . . ."
She inclined her head to the right.

A soldier and his young lady kissed without regard to others
watching, their eyes closed and bodies pressed together. The indul-
gent crowd parted to walk around them.

Tildy smiled. "Who's picking you up?"

"My dad. In Ann Arbor. How about you?"

"My brother. He got discharged after he lost his arm a couple
of years ago. He must be doing all right. Mom says he can drive.
That muffin smells good. I'm going to get one."

Tildy left for the café, and Margie continued people watching. A familiar voice caught her ear, deep and resonant with a
slow Texas drawl. Royce! Her body snapped to attention, her
head whipping left and right as she searched the milling crowd
for the face that went with that beloved voice. In an instant, she
felt herself bumping along in the back of a truck, feeling the concussive boom, boom, booms as demolition crews ignited stores of
ammunition. Eye-dazzling fireworks lit up the sky. In the distance,
Japanese bombs blasted. "Royce, I love you!" she shouted over the
din, watching him recede through blurry tears. She stretched out
her hand.

A few concerned passersby slowed to observe the wild-eyed
woman playing out a scene only she could see. Tildy hurried over
and talked Margie back to the present.

She was still shaky when they boarded their flight. "I could
smell the gunpowder, Tildy, and Royce was there, just like . . ."

She didn't finish—*just like our last minutes together.*

Margie spent the night in Chicago in a room on the twenty-third
floor of the Carlton Hotel. The bellhop opened the curtains before
he switched on the lights so she could see the majestic view of

Lake Michigan. He left her with a small bag of salted peanuts and a bucket of ice cubes.

Excited about seeing her parents tomorrow, Margie phoned home again.

Mama said, "Oh, my dear. It really is you, Margie. I was afraid I'd dreamed it."

"It's really me. Not a dream. I can't believe I'm home either. Can I speak with Daddy?"

"He's not here this minute." She hesitated. "He's at the feed store."

"Mama, is everything all right?"

"Yes. Don't worry. Hurry home. Please be careful."

Margie hung up the phone, feeling something was amiss, her hand lingering on the receiver.

Outside the window, a spectacular view of snow falling over the twinkling city below and the moonlit lake beyond dazzled her eyes. As she turned back to the room, it suddenly came to her that she was all alone. All by herself in this room with its double bed, crisp sheets, and feather pillows. And the bathroom, luxurious, clean, private.

She soaked in the bathtub, reveling in the sweet-smelling soap and tiny bottle of shampoo. Afterward, she dried off with the fluffy towels and wrapped herself in the terry robe provided. She ordered dinner and a bottle of chardonnay from room service to enjoy on her own. *Decadent,* she scolded herself as she drank the wine and fought off sleep, not wanting to miss a moment of this splendid, magnificent, glorious solitude.

Next morning's wake-up call came too early. Before she had pulled out of her wine-induced stupor, she found herself on a train, sitting next to a soldier.

"You're a nurse?" he said, seeing the insignia on her uniform. "Are you coming or going?"

"Coming. From the Philippines."

"I was at Guadalcanal. Then New Zealand for R and R and New Caledonia for retraining. They're sending me back to the Pacific. How about you?"

"Who knows? Our lives aren't our own, are they? Do you know where you're headed?"

"Just rumors. This trip has already taken up two days of my ten-day leave. I have to get home, because I'm getting married." He opened his wallet to show Margie a picture of a pretty girl wearing a striped bathing suit.

"Congratulations!"

"Thanks. We'll have five days together before I have to report back for duty. My goal this week," he said with a grin that started in his eyes and worked its way down his face, "is to get my bride pregnant."

Margie chuckled. "Good luck. Have lots of fun."

The conversation took her back to her years with Abe, when nurses in training and pilots in flight school couldn't be married. How cruel those restrictions were, and how many tears she had shed. She let herself dream about what life would have been like in Little River with a houseful of his children, all blue-eyed, blond, sensitive, and artistic. The musings made her smile, but then she blinked back tears.

The train chugged and hissed around the southern tip of Lake Michigan, making stops in Kalamazoo, Battle Creek, and Jackson. She read, slept, and chatted with the soldier. As they drew closer to Ann Arbor, she gazed out the window, searching the landscape for anything familiar. At the station, she said good-bye to her companion and went inside to look for her dad.

A young woman in a worn tweed coat approached. She had large eyes framed by wire-rimmed glasses, her light-brown hair soft and curly around her heart-shaped face. "Margie? I'm Irene, Frank's wife."

Frank's wife? She looked to be barely out of her teens. Detecting a sadness in her demeanor, Margie asked, "Is Frank all right?"

"Yes, as far as I know. I got a V-mail yesterday. I'm assuming so."

Margie hefted her duffel and said, "You'll have to catch me up. Is Dad waiting outside?"

"Um . . . no. Just me. It's best we go to the car, where it's quiet. I have something to tell you."

Margie followed Irene through the parking lot. "Something's wrong, isn't it? Is he sick? Was there an accident? Mama sounded so evasive when I talked to her." She took the passenger seat, and Irene started the engine.

Margie received the news of her father's death while sitting in the car he had restored for her as a present for graduating from nursing school. A year ago, he'd suffered a heart attack. Everyone thought he had recovered, but then another, bigger one hit four months ago, killing him almost instantly. Since then, Irene said, Mama hadn't been herself. Maybe having Margie home would help.

Irene switched on the car's heater and warm air blew on Margie's face. This couldn't be true, she thought. She'd survived to get home and safe. Her mama and daddy were supposed to be here, just as they always had been. Through a constricted throat, she said, "Tell me about Mama."

"She's not sleeping; I hear her pacing around. The doctor gave her sleeping pills, but she's not taking them. She won't leave the house. When friends visit she's . . . well, short with them. Some have stopped coming."

"That doesn't sound like her."

"I didn't think so either. The only thing keeping her going is Billy. She watches him while I'm at work. Sometimes she calls him Frankie. I'm glad you're home, Margie. She really needs you."

Unseeing, Margie stared out the window, not at all confident she could muster the strength to be needed.

Sleet slicked the roads between Ann Arbor and Little River, making driving hazardous and slow. The car sloshed through rivulets of slush, and the windshield wipers slap-slapped. Margie gawped at the changed landscape. Farmland once devoted to acres of corn and wheat now sprouted boxy apartment complexes, low-slung motels, crowded trailer parks, and restaurants. Garish neon lights illuminated miles of formerly unlit roadway.

Irene said, "The factories work three shifts. Before they built these apartments, rooming houses in town rented out rooms in shifts too. It was crazy." She slowed to negotiate a patch of ice. Once past the slippery spot, she said, "Mama's cooking your favorite meal. She jumped through hoops to get extra sugar for a dessert."

"She didn't have to do that," Margie said, not sure what her favorite meal had been.

They passed the diner where she and Abe had spent many date nights. It looked the same as before—red, white, and shiny chrome. In town, the windows of Mitchell's Department Store and Haley's Hardware displayed meager wares. Home Made Cafeteria, Nick's Pool Palace, and Brian's Irish Pub filled storefronts on Main Street. They were all new to her. They'd opened after she'd left for the war. The Strand Theater's marquee advertised *Spellbound* with Ingrid Bergman and Gregory Peck. A sign in front of her church read "Spaghetti Dinner. Every Thursday at 5:00 p.m. All Are Welcome." A bus chugged by, spewing exhaust. "What happened to the trolley?" she asked.

"They pulled up the tracks for salvage. Buses run through town and out to the factories now. It's how I get to work."

They caught up to a horse-drawn hay wagon bedecked in red, white, and blue and loaded with old tires. Teens riding on top shouted and whistled. A bass drum boomed, trumpets blared, and streamers whipped in the cold February air. Cheerleaders chanted, "We tell the story! We tell the whole story! This is Bulldog territory! Are you proud to be a Bulldog?" The other kids shouted back, "Yes! We! Are! Go, Bulldogs!"

"Basketball game?"

"Not tonight. The kids collect tires for salvage. There's a rivalry between them and Ypsilanti."

Margie smirked. "You keep the car in the barn, right?"

"With the door barred," Irene deadpanned.

Irene turned on North Bensch Road. The real countryside started beyond the high school. The last of the day's light painted the landscape purple and gray. Houses set back on acreage nestled among outbuildings and fences that corralled cows, horses, and chickens. Margie knew who lived at each place the car sped past: the Sheldens, with their seven children; the Browns, who'd had a new baby just before she had left; and the Robbinses, whose grandmother lived to be 101 years old. Just one more mile down the road, and Margie knew her mother would be watching out the window.

The house looked the same, with its wraparound porch and tall windows glowing with warm light. Margie saw a silhouette move from the window toward the front door and felt her heartbeat quicken. Before she got to the porch, Mama had the door open. "Come in! Come in! I was getting worried."

"The roads were bad," Irene said. Billy toddled to his mother and buried his head in her skirt.

Margie stepped forward with her arms outstretched. "Hello, Mama."

They hugged, Mama's grip tight. "Just let me hold you."

Margie snuggled into the warm, calming embrace she had dreamed about for three long years. The scent of her mother's sachet brought back little-girl memories. They stood in the hug a long time before Mama took a step back and studied her face. Margie stood uncomfortably, expecting to see revulsion in her mother's eyes at her beaten-down appearance.

Mama said, "I always knew this day would come, and I'd see your beautiful face again."

Margie smiled and tears sprang to her eyes. "It's good to be home. Are you doing all right, Mama?"

Mama stepped back. "A day at a time."

In the corner, Dad's chair still stood angled toward the fireplace, the cushion depressed, an afghan thrown over the arm as if he had just gotten up to go into the kitchen. However, his eyeglasses, smoldering pipe, and stack of books no longer cluttered the side table. A pile of folded diapers and a wooden toy truck had taken their place. Margie sniffed, hoping the odor of Dad's pipe still lingered, but even the air in the house had changed.

Irene lifted Billy up. "This is Aunt Margie. Can you say hello?"

He ducked his head into Irene's neck.

"Hello, Billy," Margie said. The child looked exactly like his mother, with the same heart-shaped face and softly curling light-brown hair.

He burrowed deeper into Irene's shoulder.

She laughed. "Give him a minute and he'll be all over you."

Mama had set the dining room table with her best china, silver, and damask linens. The meal *was* Margie's favorite, she remembered—chicken and gravy and Mama's special dumplings, big and soft as pillows, with green beans from last summer's garden put up in mason jars and stored in the cellar. Apple pie followed for dessert.

Though they all enjoyed the delicious food, conversation felt stilted, and Margie understood Irene's concern—Mama wasn't her usual vibrant self. Mama said she liked Margie's new haircut and asked about her trip from San Francisco. Margie told how decadent she felt ordering room service at the hotel last night, and about the soldier on the train rushing home to get married before shipping out again. The conversation stopped and Margie couldn't think of anything else to say.

Preoccupied with feeding Billy, Irene added little to the chitchat. "Why are you such an imp tonight?" she said in exasperation as she scraped food from the front of her blouse.

The three women turned their attention to the child. Wasn't he adorable with his rosy cheeks and curly hair? He looked so much like Irene, didn't he? Smart as a whip too—he already knew several words. Still, Margie found his refusal to eat and whining annoying.

Irene helped clear the table before taking Billy upstairs for his bath. While her mother filled the kitchen sink with soapy water, Margie put all the leftovers in covered bowls, including the chicken bones, half-eaten dumplings, and a few green beans from their plates. She drank the milk left in Billy's cup. Watching her daughter carefully preserve table scraps, Mama's brow furrowed as she plunged her hands into the dishwater.

Although it had been years since Margie worked in this kitchen, she knew where everything went in the cupboards, even guessing right about Billy's bowl and cup.

Turning to her mother, she said, "Tell me about Daddy."

Moving deliberately, Mama rinsed a big pot under hot water and put it in the dish drainer. "He had two heart attacks, you know. He slowed down after the first one, but he walked to the post office every day, no matter the weather, hoping for a letter from you or Frank. He didn't suffer, Margie. The last heart attack was massive. He was gone before the ambulance got here." She pursed her lips and sniffed. "He never gave up believing you'd come home."

"Did he know where I was, or even if I was alive?"

"No. We heard very little. Your friend Evelyn called and said that she had been with you on Corregidor, and that you were doing okay. I asked why you hadn't come home with her. She said something about her fiancé. Why couldn't he have helped you too?"

Margie bridled at hearing Evelyn's name, and her tone turned sour. "Getting out wasn't that easy, and he didn't have anything to do with it anyway. Evelyn had an uncle high up in the navy, and he kept close tabs on her. I suspect he got her out of the Philippines."

"We read in the newspaper that the Japanese had captured Corregidor," Mama said. "Not too long after, we got a telegram saying that you were missing in action, then . . . nothing. About a year ago, Myra heard through the Red Cross that a group of nurses were being held at a prison camp in Manila. She couldn't get names, but we had to believe you were there. It's all we had to hang on to."

"I'm sorry, Mama. I would have written if I could. I worried about you and Daddy too." She dried the big pot and put it away in the bottom cupboard behind the frying pan and an assortment of lids. She took a deep breath, searching for something positive to say. "I do have some good news. I met someone. We're going to be married." She told her mother all about Wade and the coincidence of them not bumping into each other until they met at Santo Tomas even though they grew up a few miles apart.

"Oh my! Oh dear! Wade Porter? I know who he is. I knew his mother, Barbara. She died young, and his dad remarried. I worried so, thinking you were on your own over there."

"I had friends. Good friends. Gracie and Kenneth, Ruth Ann, Tildy, Boots." She couldn't bring herself to say Helen's name yet. "We were like a family. We helped one another through it."

Mama hesitated. "Do you mind me asking, dear, what happened to Royce?"

"He was killed on Bataan. The Japanese shot him while he was helping a fallen soldier. I don't know much else."

Mama's hand went to her chest. "Oh! I knew it had to be bad. I'm so sorry."

"It happened three years ago. I've gotten past it," Margie said, even though she knew she hadn't.

The dishes washed and the kitchen straightened, she wandered from room to room, all of them smaller than she remembered and somehow faded to sepia. A mirror over the fireplace reflected the living room, and family pictures crowded the mantel. One, tinted by an artist's brush, showed a pretty young girl with curly red hair that fell onto the shoulders of a soft-green blouse. She had blue eyes, pink cheeks, and full lips.

Margie stared at her graduation picture, remembering it being taken in the studio downtown, an important event for high school seniors. Her gaze moved to her reflection in the mirror, where she saw an angular, gray face with creases around the mouth and on the forehead, and sunken and haunted eyes. She could not find one iota of resemblance to the smiling girl in the photograph.

Mama came into the room. "I hope you don't mind. We put Irene and Billy in your room. It was the only one large enough for a bed and a crib. You'll be in Frank's room. Is that okay?"

Margie pulled herself away from the picture. No, it wasn't okay. She wanted her own bed in her own room, with all her books and the bits and pieces she treasured, and to have her clothes hanging in the closet exactly as she had left them. What she said was, "Sure, anything's fine," visualizing Frank's dingy blue room cluttered with model airplanes.

She hefted her duffel and climbed the stairs. On the landing, portraits of all four grandparents hung on the wall. She paused to study their faces, seeing similarities between generations she hadn't noticed before.

When she stepped into Frank's room, it smelled of fresh paint and glowed a soft yellow. New sheers hung at the window, and a reupholstered chair was tucked into a corner. Her maternal grandmother's cherry four-poster bed took up much of the room, neatly made up with a new hand-stitched quilt and matching pillows.

She read the bottom corner square of the quilt: "Welcome Home, Margie. With love and gratitude from your friends at Little River Methodist Church."

How wonderful to be home surrounded by love. She felt her heart expand with joy. Yet, she tossed and turned in the big bed all night, her body still swaying with the rhythm of the train, and her ears tuned to detect sounds of an enemy approaching.

CHAPTER 18

Little River, spring 1945

March in Michigan is a mean month, the beauty of pristine snow a memory and the warmth of spring only a desire. Margie looked out at the brown and white landscape and complained, "I'm so cold. I don't think I'll ever feel warm again."

"You're skin and bones," Mama said, handing Margie an afghan to wrap up in before heading to the basement to stoke the coal furnace.

A fedora-topped reporter published her story in the local paper, and civic functions kept her busy. Little River organized a parade in her honor, with the Girl and Boy Scouts and veterans groups from the American Legion joining the other marchers. From a flag-draped dais, the mayor presented her with the key to the city, and the high school band belted out "The Star-Spangled Banner." The Rotary Club and the Little River Women's Club asked her to speak to their groups. When she obliged, everyone clamored to ask questions about her experiences.

She talked about Bataan's monkeys and toucans, the beautiful orchids high in the trees, and getting lost in Corregidor's amazing Malinta Tunnel. She stressed the importance of mail from home. She kept silent about her constant fear, being rife with disease, numb with despair, and living with death. She didn't mention the swarms of deadly mosquitoes, the snakes, the lizards . . . dirt raining from the rock ceiling, or blood filling her shoes . . . the weevils she ate . . . the too-short coffins . . .

The war dragged on as a weary public's interest waned. To incite outrage, the United States government released the Bataan Death March records, whipping the country into a frenzy. After reading accounts of bayoneted and beheaded prisoners of war strewn like trash along sixty miles of road between Manila and Camp O'Donnell, Mama turned off the radio and hid the newspapers from Margie.

Keeping Margie in the dark wasn't difficult, because all she wanted to do was sleep. She couldn't seem to get enough of it. Her appetite, which had returned, disappeared again, and she felt queasy most of the time. She smiled and laughed through welcome-home teas, luncheons, and visits from old friends and neighbors, but they were exhausting ordeals to get through. She missed her army friends who shared her torments and fears. She needed to talk with someone who understood about the images stuck in her head, and the dreams from which she woke up crying.

Rummaging through a closet one afternoon, she found the dress she'd made for her and Abe's wedding; it hung far in the back and was covered with a bedsheet. Removing the sheet, she held the dress close to her body and looked in the mirror, seeing a cloud of white chiffon over nylon—a lovely dress designed by and made for a young girl. She twirled around and watched the chiffon playfully poof in the air, a sad reminder of what might have been, but neither the playful girl nor her handsome fiancé existed anymore. She put it back on the hanger and covered it with the sheet, thinking about the young brides in town who would cherish the beautiful dress, and with a sigh of goodwill and regret she decided to donate it to the church's charity closet.

Later that day, she borrowed several recent issues of *Brides* magazine from the library to see the latest styles.

"Are you sure about this wedding, dear?" Mama asked. "This might not be the best time to make such a big decision."

"I'm capable of making my own decisions," Margie snapped, but she knew it wasn't true. She had trouble picking out what to wear each morning, or choosing between pancakes and cereal for breakfast. She concentrated on the details of her new wedding dress, drawing and redrawing sketches before designing the perfect one, when the agonizing over fabrics and accessories began.

Watching her work, Mama said, "It's going to be beautiful; you have such flair. Best we make it a little larger, though. You're bound to fill out some."

Margie scrutinized her scrawny figure in the mirror. Her eyes, still too big for her face, looked less haunted, and the ten pounds she had gained filled out her breasts a little, but her elbows, knees, and hip bones still protruded, knobby and Halloween-skeleton ugly. She wondered what Wade's parents would think when they met her.

Abe's mother telephoned. She was glad Margie had arrived home safely. She'd heard Margie was engaged to be married and wanted to extend her best wishes. She invited Margie to lunch; they could have a nice chat.

Margie knew this reunion would be a sad one and tucked a hankie in her pocket. She covered her hair with the silk scarf Abe had given her years ago and retrieved her bicycle from the barn.

Though she was wobbly at first, her body quickly remembered how to balance. With growing confidence, Margie rode through Little River's familiar streets to the Carson home. Their front yard blazed with daffodils and tulips, the lawn already thick and green. The mature sugar maple leafed out like it did every spring, just as if nothing had changed. A "Sons in Service" flag hung in the window, the blue star in its center replaced by a gold one, showing that Abe had been killed in action.

The front door opened, and Mr. Carson welcomed her in.

Abe's parents looked much older than Margie remembered, their expressions weary and tinged with sorrow, but their hugs told her they were genuinely glad she had come. They led her into the living room, where a picture of Abe, now forever young and handsome in his dress uniform, dominated the space over the mantel. Mrs. Carson offered Margie a chair and brought her a glass of lemonade. The lump in Margie's throat softened after a few sips, and she said, "I'm very sorry."

"Thank you, dear. It's a difficult time for us. I doubt if we'll ever fully recover. There's a group in town we belong to, the Gold Star Mothers. And wives. Families, really. We help one another." She stopped and sighed. "You've had a loss too, your daddy. He was a fine man. He loved you so much and was so proud of you. If you ever need to talk about him, or Abe, we're here."

Margie stammered out a thank-you.

Mr. Carson held out Abe's pilot's ring. "He wanted you to have this."

"I can't. You should keep it."

He placed the ring in Margie's hand and folded her fingers around it. "Those were Abe's instructions."

Margie admired the heavy sterling-silver ring with its blue stone and Abe's name engraved inside the band, and she blinked back tears.

"Tell us about you, Margie. What are your plans?"

She hesitated. How could she chatter about her wedding to Abe's grieving parents?

Mrs. Carson said, "It's all right, honey. We can talk about Wade. I knew his mother, Barbara. She would have been pleased he chose you for his wife."

Margie flashed Mrs. Carson a grateful smile. "I don't know when Wade will be home, so I can't set a date. I designed my dress, though, and it's almost sewn."

Mrs. Carson said, "I know it will be beautiful. I can hardly wait to see you in it."

"Thank you. It's ivory crepe. It has a high collar and long sleeves with some beading on them. I cut the skirt on the bias so it would drape gracefully."

On the coffee table was a box, and Mrs. Carson nudged it toward Margie. "This is what came home to us. I thought you might like to look through it. The letters you sent to Abe are in there. I haven't read them, Margie. Take them with you if you like."

Margie opened the box, remembering how personal her letters to Abe had been. "Are you sure?" she asked.

"Yes, dear. They belong to you."

Margie found the packet and put it in her purse. Then she carefully looked through the rest of the box's contents—flight manuals, schedules, test papers, and souvenirs from Abe's travels around the globe. Finding pictures of him posed in front of his airplane, Margie focused on the nose art. She made out her own face and a cascade of wild hair.

Mrs. Carson said, "Abe dated a few of the women pilots. They had a lot in common, flying and all, but he always asked about you, Margie."

On the way home, Margie rode her bike through Davis Park, thinking back to the night Abe had become her first lover. She chuckled as she remembered the confines of the car and the clumsiness of the escapade. "You still have a place in my heart," she whispered to the heavens.

Margie found mail from Wade waiting for her on the hall table. After leaving Santo Tomas, he had moved to a shack in the countryside, where he felt safer. His letter relayed news of the violence in Manila. The Japanese were firmly entrenched within the stone-walled buildings of Intramuros, and MacArthur had ordered the use of tanks and howitzers to root them out. For days, US artillery rammed through the stone walls, killing tens of thousands of Japanese soldiers and trapped Filipino civilians. Facing death or capture by Allied troops, and intent on eradicating Manila's whole population, the Japanese army lived up to their reputation by mutilating and raping Filipino men, women, and children.

> *My darling, the savagery and destruction I've seen here are beyond telling. It is far greater than anything I saw in Europe. I can't imagine that Manila will ever recover from this carnage. Its beauty has been obliterated, and its culture annihilated.*
>
> *I miss you. I love you, but sadly, as yet, I don't know when I'll be home. I pray sooner than later.*
> *Longing to be in your arms,*
> *Wade*

Margie put the letter in her bureau drawer, deciding not to share it with Mama and Irene. Its unblinking account of the barbarity of war was upsetting even to her. She sighed. Second thoughts had surfaced about marrying Wade, a decision made in haste and at the worst of times. Now at home, her outlook was changing, and Wade seemed a part of another life, one she had no desire to summon up. She feared his presence would rekindle feelings of despair and degradation she was trying so hard to tame. She hardly knew him, she felt. How could she possibly meet his expectations of her as his wife? She didn't know what to do.

Letters arrived from Frank sporadically and out of sequence. Mama left the microfilmed V-mails she received out for all to read, but Irene shared only parts of her missives, which were more intimate.

At twenty-three, Irene was four years Margie's junior. She worked as a bookkeeper at the Ford plant and, as mother to an active little boy, seldom got a full night's sleep. Patient and nurturing even after a long workday, she spent most of her free time with Billy, supervising his dinner, bathing him before bedtime, and lulling him to sleep with baby songs and softly told nursery rhymes. She watched over what he ate with an eagle eye, making oatmeal gruel like Margie's mother had taught her, and cooking and mashing his fruits and vegetables herself. She collected hand-me-down clothes from her sister and friends, washing and ironing them on Thursday nights. She coped with uncertainty, loneliness, and fear; just the sight of a Western Union boy delivering telegrams guaranteed her an attack of itchy hives.

"We have a code," Irene told Mama and Margie. "When Frank asks about the baby kicking, I know his unit's on the move. I cross-reference the date with newspaper accounts of troop movements and the maps in *Life* magazine showing the latest offensives. I can guess where he is, or rather, where he was." According to Irene's calculations, he'd traveled north through Italy into France. Mama looked up the locations of unfamiliar faraway cities in the atlas kept open on the coffee table.

In his letters, Frank complained about the food, the weather, the fatigue, the boredom, and the lack of mail. He revealed little about the other men in his unit, or the war itself, except to say it was hell.

Pensive after reading his latest, Irene asked Margie, "What was it like? You were there."

Flipping through a recent issue of *Life*, Margie studied the pictures of scruffy-faced and shirtless marines; they looked fit and strong standing beside their tanks and supply trucks. She thought of Wade as she last saw him, bone-skinny and hollow-eyed. Choosing her words carefully, she said, "Guess it depends on where you are. These guys in *Life* don't look any worse for wear." She knew better, but what else would she tell a young wife pining for her soldier-husband? *Think of hell, multiply it by a thousand, and you wouldn't even begin to get close to the savagery, the horror, and the images that burn into your brain.*

Margie looked her directly in the eye. "Frank will be all right. The medics go behind the troops and pick up the pieces. He's not in much danger." Then she ducked back behind the magazine and hoped her performance had been convincing.

CHAPTER 19

Miami, spring 1945

Margie's leave ended, and she received orders to report to the redistribution center in sunny Miami, Florida. She dressed in her uniform and assessed her image in the mirror. She had put on some weight, her face looked less drawn, and her hair shined as it hadn't in a long time. She wondered if her friends would recognize her.

She placed her makeup bag and toothbrush in her suitcase, then snapped it shut and carried it down the stairs. Her mother stood close to the radio. When she turned, Margie saw tears on her face.

"Mama? Mama, what's wrong?"

"I just heard President Roosevelt had a cerebral hemorrhage and died."

Stunned, Margie put down the suitcase and hurried to her mother's side. "I hadn't heard he'd been ill."

"They said it was sudden. Oh, Margie. What's the country going to do now?"

Margie didn't know. A four-term president, Roosevelt had just always been there in her recollection. To calm her mother, she said, "Our country's bigger than one man, even President Roosevelt."

Mama wrung her hands. "But we need him to win this war. Nobody can deal with Stalin and Churchill like he can. It's why I voted for him."

She didn't want to leave her mother on this sad note, but she couldn't miss her train. "I've got to go, Mama. I'll call you as soon as I can. Will you be all right?"

Mama nodded and gave Margie a hug. "Be safe."

Margie mulled over her mother's concern for the future as Irene drove her to the train station. General Eisenhower had demanded Germany's unconditional surrender, and she wondered, with the United States in both mourning and transition, if the Nazis would take advantage of the distraction and harden their position. Most of the world, like Mama, equated Roosevelt with America.

Irene stopped the car in front of the station, and they watched a workman lower the flag to half-staff, then take a rag from his pocket to wipe the tears off his face. Other men took off their hats, and both men and women shed tears.

Irene lamented, "I'm never going to get Frank home."

Margie would never give voice to it, but she worried that too. She could only nod to Irene, afraid her fears would come true.

The train from Detroit to Miami covered the fifteen hundred miles in thirty hours. Cozied up in her berth, Margie read the *Ann Arbor Tribune* articles about Vice President Harry S. Truman's swearing in as thirty-third president of the United States, and his promise to keep Roosevelt's cabinet intact. *At least there will be some continuity,* she thought. She read the plans to transport Franklin Roosevelt's body to his home in Hyde Park, New York, where he would be buried in the family rose garden. The print blurred before her eyes, and she turned out the light.

Arriving in Miami the next morning, she gathered her things and caught a taxi to the redistribution center. A familiar figure stood outside the center's door. Margie waved and hollered, "Hey! Boots!"

Boots trotted over. "Margie! You look great! Are you an old married lady yet?"

"Not yet. I can't get my other half home."

Boots laughed. "That's not all bad. Come to breakfast. Some of the old gang's here."

The center was crowded with soldiers, but not one was familiar to Margie. The men she had cared for on Bataan and Corregidor were still languishing in Japanese prison camps—if they were alive—or hiding in the mountains, fighting with the guerrillas that harassed the enemy. She heard her name called, and turned around and saw Larry, a medic she had trained with at Walter Reed. Glad to see him, she smiled. "You're a sight for sore eyes. Looks like your mama's feeding you well."

He limped over with the help of a cane. "Margie, I saw your picture in the newspaper. I'd recognize that wild hair anywhere."

"Where have you been?"

"Africa mostly. I was wounded there, and I'm staying stateside for the duration. There's a desk job for me in Texas."

"Join us for breakfast. I'm sorry about your leg. How's it doing?"

"It holds me up."

At the table, Gracie grabbed Margie's hand. "Guess what? Kenneth accepted an assistant professorship at U of M. I've requested to be assigned to the veterans hospital in Ann Arbor. You and I might be neighbors."

Margie thought that was wonderful news.

She sat with Boots, Gracie, Larry, and a few others for break-fast. She felt at ease with this group and able to let her guard down. Nobody looked at her askance when she said that her joints ached like an old lady's, or when she mentioned she woke up crying at night and couldn't remember why. She noticed that Gracie still favored her arm.

"My shoulder never healed right," Gracie said, demonstrating its limited range of motion. "The doctor says it won't get better without surgery."

Boots looked over a platter of pastries on the table and selected a blueberry muffin. "I heard Ruth Ann lost all her teeth. Wouldn't that be a kicker? Has anyone heard from Tildy?"

Margie had received a letter from Tildy a week ago. She had been in and out of the hospital several times with stomach pains and the doctors couldn't find the cause. "Last I heard she said she was coming. She's having problems with her stomach. She might be sick again. I have her address if you'd like to write to her."

"Well, I've got good news," Gracie announced. "I heard through the grapevine that Miss Kermit is getting married!"

Everyone at the table smiled at the news. "Who to?" Boots asked.

"Some old beau who she's known for decades."

An officer quieted the room by tapping his spoon against his water glass. He made several announcements and led a silent prayer for the late president.

Afterward, Larry said, "They may say he wasn't sick, but my buddy is an MP, and he saw Roosevelt close-up recently. He said he looked like death warmed over. Personally, I think he worked himself to an early grave."

"So, who knows anything about Truman?" Boots asked.

No one answered.

As the days passed, groups of soldiers cycled through the redistribution center, new ones arriving as others left. Temporarily housed in nearby hotels, they energized any area they occupied, monopolizing the local marinas and beaches by boating, fishing, swimming, and playing beach volleyball. At night, they overflowed restaurants that offered live entertainment from crooners to rousing dance bands. Still later, they crawled the bars and strip joints that stayed open into the wee hours of the morning.

Underneath the gaiety, however, dark rumors circulated. Soldiers huddled over beers to discuss what they had heard. An invasion of Japan's main island was a certainty, with protracted bloody battles expected. The soldiers serving in Europe could be reassigned to the Far East as soon as Germany surrendered.

Margie glanced around the bar filled with drinkers and dancers. She wondered who in this assembly of war-weary, seasoned fighters—wanting nothing but peace, tranquility, family, friends, and a life away from the battlefield with its dangers and atrocities—who would be asked to serve, yet again, on the most dangerous of turfs?

The army doctor who examined Margie asked how was she coping, and how she got along with her family. Had she resumed contact with friends and neighbors? Did she have any health concerns?

She told him how things at home had changed: her dad's death while she was in the Philippines, her mother's difficulties adjusting to his absence. She worried about her brother, a medic still posted in Europe. When she got home, she met the sister-in-law and nephew she hadn't known existed. Twirling the mahogany ring around her finger, she told him of her wedding plans, although her fiancé's return home was still uncertain.

"How are you sleeping?" the doctor asked.

"I sleep okay, but sometimes I dream about the soldiers I cared for—the ones who died. Sometimes when I'm awake, their faces flash in my memory. I'm anxious. It comes and goes. I'm fuzzy-minded too. I have trouble concentrating. I can't read. Is this normal? Given everything?"

The doctor jotted notes. "What you're describing is not normal per se, but it's not uncommon either. It's a nuisance, but not serious. Studies indicate that you nurses are more resilient, recovering from these symptoms better than the men do. We think it's because of your professional training. The anxiety, sleep disturbances, and what you call fuzziness will disappear with time. Keep yourself busy and try not to worry about it."

He glanced at his watch, then the lab results. He told her she tested anemic; he would prescribe an iron supplement. Then he gave her a quick physical exam. During the pelvic portion, he inquired about her menstrual history.

"My periods have been unpredictable. In the camp, I'd skip several months, and then have three or four in a row. I don't remember the last one. I haven't thought much about it since I got home."

"Are you having sexual relations?"

She felt warmth creeping up her neck. "No. I'm not married."

The physical over, he took out his prescription pad and order forms. "You're still underweight, and your uterus is slightly enlarged. I'm ordering additional tests. Go to the lab for another blood draw and leave a urine sample." He got up to leave, and halfway out the door, he said, "If I find a problem, you'll hear from me. Otherwise, your records will be sent on to Captain Hennessey."

Glad the exam was over, Margie dressed and left the examining room. She heard a commotion coming from outside and went to investigate. A rowdy herd thundered by, and Gracie grabbed her arm to pull her along.

"You won't believe this! Hitler's dead! Dead as a doornail! A double suicide. Him and his mistress! Come on! We're going out to celebrate!"

The doctor and his tests forgotten, Margie joined the noisy crowd to celebrate the head Nazi's self-termination. They drank rounds of beers and sang bawdy songs with the dead devil-despot and his hated mistress as the subjects.

When Margie reported to Captain Bert Hennessey for follow-up, she sat quietly while he read her file.

"Good morning, Miss Bauer." Clearing his throat, he said, "I wasn't aware of your condition."

She blinked rapidly in surprise. "What condition?"

"Surely you discussed it with the doctor."

"I'm sorry. I don't know what you're referring to."

Captain Hennessey picked up a paper from the top of her file. "Your pregnancy test came back positive."

"What? What pregnancy test?"

He passed the paper to her.

She looked at the incriminating document. It said, *Friedman test for pregnancy, Positive.* "This can't be," she objected. Her heart pounded and blood rushed to her face. "There must be a mix-up."

Captain Hennessey rummaged around in her file. "Hmm . . ." His brow furrowed. "This is the doctor's report from when you were first released from Santo Tomas. It says here there was bruising around the . . . um . . . vaginal and anal areas, and evidence of a tear in the perineum." Blushing, he peered over the top of his half-glasses. "Miss Bauer. Given the timing, was there ever an occasion—"

"No! I told the doctor it was an accident. I stepped backward. I stumbled over a rock and sat down hard on it."

Captain Hennessey persisted. "A Jap soldier. One of the guards?"

"I said no! It was nothing like that."

His stare bored through her before he lowered his gaze. "Very well. It's tricky with you women. Things aren't always clear. The doctor recommends that you be discharged. I'll send the paperwork through. It'll take a few days." He scribbled a note and closed her file. "Do you have a young man?"

Her mouth was so dry it was hard to answer. "My fiancé. He's still in the Philippines. I don't know when he'll be home."

"The fighting's bad over there. When he returns, he'll need help adjusting. Be patient with him. Give him lots of love and good meals, but don't hover. Men don't like women who hover." The captain courteously opened the door and patted her shoulder. "Good luck, my dear. I must say, you look like a girl who could bake a great apple pie."

Soon—after four years living under Uncle Sam's jurisdiction, and two months after leaving Santo Tomas—Margie could once again call herself a civilian. In a matter of days, she boarded the Detroit train traveling north. Her purse held a manila envelope containing her honorable discharge from the Army Nurse Corps of the United States Army Reserves, her medals for meritorious service, a copy of the *GI Bill of Rights*, and her full compensation with instructions on how to pay back taxes.

The pregnancy test results occupied her thoughts: no test was foolproof, she reasoned over and over. She had certainly seen enough false positives in her time as a nurse. In disarray from the stress and starvation that disrupted her delicately balanced cycles, her hormones would readjust once she resumed a regular schedule and a good diet. She dismissed the test results as erroneous.

Moving westward, she watched the landscape pass by, marveling at its far-reaching openness. A sense of freedom filled her; the realization of her personal liberty and the absence of fear made her giddy. She laughed aloud, her mouth wide open and her head flung back, delightedly savoring the feeling of well-being.

CHAPTER 20

Little River, summer 1945

Margie told the family the army discharged her because they con-sidered her underweight. Ecstatic to have her home for good and out of harm's way, Mama made it a project to fatten her up.

Margie had to admit she felt better than she had in years, her appetite and energy increasing daily. She spent long hours in the garden, as she had always done; but this year the soil seemed richer, the rain softer and sweeter, the plants greener, the fragrances more intense, and the yields more abundant.

That spring, the Allies accepted Germany's unconditional surrender, and the reign of terror that was Adolf Hitler's Third Reich ended. German troops all over Europe had orders to cease firing immediately. As President Truman declared May 8 Victory in Europe Day, parties erupted throughout the Allied world. However, festivities at the Bauer household were tempered when no word came that either Frank or Wade was coming home.

May bled imperceptibly into summer. With the harvest came the need to preserve it—canning vegetables; putting up jams, marmalades, jellies, and fruit butters; and bringing in honey from the hives out back. Mama and Margie stored all the jars either in the pantry off the kitchen or down in the cool cellar, along with bushel baskets of new potatoes, onions, and carrots. To Margie, the cellar smelled like heaven on earth. They hung bunches of herbs to dry from the rafters of the attic.

One day in early July, Billy toddled outside with Aunt Margie. She showed him how to pick green peppers off the bush and cucumbers from the vine, putting the vegetables into the little basket he carried. Steadier on his feet now, he'd started climbing everywhere—up the steps, on the furniture, into the bathtub. Margie even lifted him off the hood of her car once, wondering how his short legs had negotiated such height.

She heard her mother calling from the porch. Scooping Billy up into her arms, she hurried to the house. Waving an envelope, Mama said, "We got a letter from Frank." She carefully tore it open.

June 24, 1945

Dear Mama,

> *Just a note this time. The good news is since VE Day there is no more shooting. My unit is occupying a German village, and we are waiting for the units that manage conquered territories to arrive and take over. After that, I don't know for me, a reassignment to the Far East or mustering out. I should hear soon. In the meantime, I'm sleeping in a soft bed and even got to wash my clothes.*

> *Just wanted to say hi and that I'm all right.*
> *Your loving son,*
> *Frank*

Mama said, "They won't send him to Japan. They couldn't possibly. Would they?"

Margie shifted the baby on her hip. "We can only hope not."

Clingy and overtired that evening, Billy refused to go to sleep. Irene alternately cajoled and threatened, but he wouldn't settle down. Frazzled, she said, "I'm taking him for a walk." Margie watched as she put a pillow, his blanket, and a teddy bear in the wagon.

"Mind if I come?" she asked.

With the cranky toddler in tow, the sisters-in-law walked along the side of North Bensch Road, the steamy July heat causing sweat beads to form on their foreheads. Billy sat up for a while, pointing at horses in the fields and other sights along the way. Finally, he lay down in the cozy nest his mother had made for him and fell asleep, his thumb in his mouth and his blanket held against his cheek. Irene stopped to remove the thumb. "My little lamb. He can be a scamp. I wonder how Frank will be with him?"

"Frank's a big kid himself," Margie said, chuckling. "He'll love playing with Billy." Irene's pinched look told her she'd missed the mark. "He'll be a good father," she revised.

They resumed walking, the wagon rattling behind. Irene confided, "We'd only dated for six months before he got drafted; then we made this grand decision to get married. Don't get me wrong, Margie . . . I love your brother. He's sweet and caring, and he's fun. I just wish, well . . . things are complicated." They continued on awhile in silence before she elaborated. "The last picture he sent, the one taken in France, it's not him. I mean it's him, but it's not. Something's different. I don't feel like I know him."

"Well, I know him. I know him to be kind, smart, and responsible. He's a good guy."

Irene sounded hesitant. "You know what they say, that war changes a man."

By *they*, she meant women's magazines, purveyors of this anxiety. Their pages overflowed with advice on how to live with a husband hard-bitten by his barbarous life in the military—an existence a wife could never imagine. They cautioned that once he returned home, he may be restless and short-tempered, indifferent or self-absorbed, and suffer from nightmares. He may drink too much and want to prowl at night. Marital relations might not be the same, they warned; expect anything from none at all to strange cravings. Above all, the publications counseled, don't talk about war, don't press him for details, and don't try to hurry him through his readjustment to civilian life. Keep up your looks and stay cheerful.

"We talk at work," Irene said. "Rita's husband came home in a wheelchair, and she says they fight all the time. He's jealous, and she's like his prisoner. I can see Frank like that. He questions everything I do, even what I wear when I go out. Go out! That's a laugh."

"That doesn't sound like Frank."

"And that's my point. Do you worry about Wade?"

"It's different for us. We were together until a few months ago."

Although, she reflected, not really so different in a reverse sort of way. They went through the thick of it together. What would it be like to share good times? They never discussed what life might be like after Santo Tomas; that dream was fragile and seemed a world away at the time. Mostly, they'd talked about the old days, growing up in Little River. And, of course, food. How to grow it, preserve it, prepare it, and how much of it they could eat. They concocted a myriad of recipes, not one of which could she remember now.

Margie and Irene turned to go home when they reached the high school. "What're your plans when Wade comes home?" Irene asked.

"First off, the wedding." Margie chewed on her lower lip before adding, "Myra asked if I'd come back part-time at the Red Cross.

Wade will be at the *Tribune*. I haven't thought much beyond that. How about you?"

"I'd like to keep my job, if Mama doesn't mind watching Billy. It makes me feel worth something, and the money's good. I'd like Frank to finish school. He was pre-vet before he got drafted. Someday, I'd like Billy to have a brother or sister. Not right away."

As they neared the house, a staccato of pops crackled, followed by a boom. Margie jumped in fright and dropped to her knees to drape her body over Billy's. More pops came in quick succession, and then a sharp crack.

For a moment, Margie relived the horror of Japanese shells setting Santo Tomas on fire—the crackle of the tinder-dry shanties burning; the hot, thick smoke clouding her vision and burning her throat; and Gracie shouting, *Died on impact! Margie, come with me!*

Irene hugged Margie's shoulders. "It's only firecrackers. Tomorrow's the Fourth. The kids are getting an early start, that's all." She took Margie's arm, helping her to her feet. "Let's get you into the house."

Huddled together, they ran across the street, Irene carrying a wailing Billy and Margie pulling the wagon. Margie flew up the stairs to her room and slammed the door.

Mama hurried behind her, drying her hands on her apron. She knocked softly, then let herself in.

Margie sat on the bed trembling. Mama sat down beside her. "Honey, you heard firecrackers. There'll be a lot more tomorrow and fireworks too. It's the Fourth of July." She gathered her daughter in her arms. "Oh, my poor baby. What did they do to you over there?"

"I'm sorry, Mama," she said, relaxing into her mother's embrace but unable to control the quaver in her voice. "I'm just being silly."

Margie was back to her prewar weight, plus a little bit more. The lines of her face had softened, and her breasts were fuller than before. Sometimes she worried that her monthly periods hadn't resumed, though she occasionally had bouts of cramping. Lately, she'd experienced abdominal flutters she attributed to gas.

Wearing only her bra and panties, she combed through her closet for something to wear. Nothing seemed to fit anymore; she had been leaving the top button on her skirts and slacks open for a while now. As a wave crossed her stomach, she put both hands on it. An unwelcome realization dawned. She pressed in, feeling a firmness starting just below her navel. In the mirror, she saw a bulge she could no longer deny. She fought back rising panic.

With her shirttail hanging out over her too-tight skirt, she went downstairs to breakfast and dished up oatmeal from a pan on the stove, adding milk and a sliced peach.

Her mother looked at the untucked shirttail sharply. "You look a little pale."

"I didn't sleep well."

"Why don't you stay home today?"

"I can't. Myra needs me to be there." She had started working part-time at the Red Cross, organizing blood drives to meet the still-considerable need.

Her thoughts whirled as she drove to work. How would she tell Wade? What if he didn't want it, and she was left alone? The thought terrified her. Barely able to take care of herself, she wasn't ready to be a mother. Then a darker thought intruded—could it be Max's? Could she terminate the pregnancy without anyone knowing? Her mind flitted through the options.

That evening, a letter from Wade waited for her on the hall table. Margie took it up to her room to read. Fighting in the Philippines had slowed almost to a halt, with Japanese resistance compressed into small pockets on isolated islands.

August 1, 1945

My Dearest Love,

I have too much time on my hands, and being away from you makes it stretch on forever. I'm spending my days writing about those endless years in Santo Tomas. I can't get my thoughts down on paper fast enough. They tumble out of me with great sadness followed by a healthy sense of release. Then I have a few hours of calm, but the tension builds again, and I go through the cycle once more. Someday, I'll burn these cheerless pages and bury the ashes.

I'd like to write, Margie, but something different from bad memories or newspaper stories. I'd like to take a year off from the Tribune *and write a novel, pure escapism, a whodunit with sultry women, strong men, and a plot that twists and turns. I have an outline in my head. It will be set in Paris with all the intrigue that city has to offer. I have some money put away, and we can live cheaply in Grandpa's cabin on the shores of Lake Michigan. It's a fine place on a bluff overlooking the lake. I've dreamed of someday building a house there.*

I haven't heard anything official from the Tribune, *but I feel I'll be home to you soon, and I'm counting the days until we are together.*
My love forever,
Wade

Margie put the letter down. A year on a secluded beach far away from her family, no income, a child. She couldn't agree to that. She felt a flutter as the wee being rolled around. "What are we going to do, little one?"

CHAPTER 21

Little River, fall 1945

Three cuckoo clocks arrived at the Bauer house that Frank had sent from Germany's Black Forest to temper his bad news. He wrote that he was at Camp Lucky Strike, a redistribution station near Le Havre in France. He'd be there for a few weeks, and then he was being shipped to the Pacific.

Margie felt heartsick as she followed the news. The war continued to escalate, even though Allied forces continuously fire-bombed Japanese cities, airfields, and harbors, greatly reducing the numbers of enemy planes and ships. Word circulated that thirty million Japanese soldiers and civilian men, women, and children had declared their readiness to die for the emperor. Frank was scheduled to leave soon for that hellish inferno.

At risk of extermination, Margie grimly read, were an estimated 170,000 prisoners of war held by the Japanese. *Like cattle in a pen. Those cowardly Nip sons of bitches.* She threw down the newspaper and looked out the window to see Irene and Billy playing ring-around-the-rosy.

That evening, the women wound down their day together, doing needlework and listening to Rudy Vallee singing "Deep Night" in his soft, distinctive style on the radio. No one spoke, each lost in her own worries. An announcer interrupted the program.

"Good evening from the White House in Washington. Ladies and gentlemen, the president of the United States."

"Turn it up," Mama said. Margie reached over to adjust the volume. President Truman's Missouri accent filled the room.

My fellow Americans:

The British, Chinese, and United States governments have given the Japanese people adequate warning of what is in store for them. We have laid down the general terms on which they can surrender. Our warning went unheeded. Our terms were rejected.

The world will note that the first atomic bomb was dropped on Hiroshima, a military base. That was because we wished in the first attack to avoid, insofar as possible, the killing of civilians. But that attack is only a warning of things to come. If Japan does not surrender, bombs will have to be dropped on her war industries and unfortunately thousands of civilian lives will be lost. I urge Japanese civilians to leave industrial cities immediately and save themselves from destruction.

I realize the tragic significance of the atomic bomb. Its production and its use were not lightly undertaken by this government. But we knew that our enemies were on the search for it. We know now how close they were to finding it. And we knew the disaster which would come to this nation and to all peace-loving nations, to all civilizations, if they had found it first. That is why we felt compelled to undertake the long and uncertain and costly labor of discovery and production. We won the race of discovery against the Germans.

Having found the bomb, we have used it. We have used it against those who attacked us without warning at Pearl Harbor, against those who have starved and beaten and executed American prisoners of war, against those who have abandoned all pretense of obeying international laws of warfare. We have used it in order to shorten the agony of war; in order to save the lives of thousands and thousands of young Americans. We shall continue to use it until we completely destroy Japan's power to make war. Only a Japanese surrender will stop us.

The Bauer women stared at one another, stunned.

The world waited for Japan's response. When after three days the emperor refused to surrender, a second atomic bomb obliterated the port city of Nagasaki. Headlines across the world shouted, "IS TOKYO NEXT?"

His country facing total annihilation, Emperor Hirohito finally announced Japan's unconditional surrender. On Sunday, September 2, 1945, on the deck of the battleship *Missouri*, representatives from the Empire of Japan signed the Japanese Instrument of Surrender, officially ending World War II.

Mama insisted she watch Billy while Margie and Irene went out to celebrate downtown. Revelers jammed the streets, hugging and kissing, hallooing and whooping. Car horns tooted, bands blasted, a siren wailed from the firehouse, church bells chimed. Margie and Irene blew whistles as they joined a conga line snaking along sidewalks where newsboys peddled special "WAR'S OVER" editions.

Monday morning, churches held services of thanksgiving. Mama attended the one at Little River Methodist, celebrating in her own quiet way by giving thanks that her family would soon be reunited. Afterward, she put flowers and a flag on Dad's grave, now gone ten months, telling him the good news that both their children were safe, that she missed him and would love him dearly always.

A letter arrived from Frank, saying his orders had been canceled. He had never left France, and he was now on his way home. Preparing for Frank's homecoming sent Mama into a flurry of activity. She fretted that the front porch needed a fresh coat of paint, but settled for scrubbing it clean instead. She purchased a new flag to fly from the holder on one of the columns. She helped Irene move Billy's crib from the bedroom to an alcove off the stairs. The transition proved painful for everyone: Billy's heart-wrenching screams of protest lasted several nights.

The more Mama fussed, the more anxious Irene became. She retreated to her room in the evenings, claiming headaches. She sewed a new dress for herself and a romper for Billy. She had her hair styled at the salon in town and painted her nails red before reconsidering and changing the color of the polish. She ate very little and lost a few pounds.

The town spruced itself up for the returning soldiers. Flags hung from every lamppost and waved over the fire and police departments, the hospital, and city offices. Store windows displayed patriotic themes, and a banner reading "Welcome Home!" stretched across Main Street. Red, white, and blue bunting festooned most porches.

As Frank's train rumbled into the station, the high school band played "The Stars and Stripes Forever." The crowd cheered as soldiers hung out of the windows to whistle and wave at the girls waiting on the platform. The train hissed to a stop, and a flood of khaki poured out the doors. Cries of joy rose, increasing the chaos when families reunited. Billy began to scream, and Irene tucked his head into her neck, covering his ear with her hand. Margie scanned the swarm of humanity for a beloved face, a distinctive gait, an identifiable voice. Mama spotted him first—tall, lanky, carrying his duffel and a teddy bear. She waved frantically, yelling, "Frank! Frank!"

He pushed through the crowd, his pace quickening to a trot. In an instant, the family joined together in a joyous hug; their arms entangled, each wanted to touch Frank. Margie broke away first. Then Mama reluctantly let go, allowing Frank to kiss his wife and howling baby.

Irene calmed Billy with a giggle and sweet words, then held him out to Frank. "Can you say Dada?" she asked. She had been coaching him for this moment for over a month, but the overwhelmed baby buried his face in her hair.

Although Frank's laugh rang out as heartily as Margie remembered, when their gazes locked, her heart sank, for in his eyes she saw a jaded and depleted spirit—a world-weary soul.

With Frank home, the energy level in the household rose, his presence and happy banter lifting the mood. Over dinner, they reminisced about a rare 1932 summer vacation on Mackinac Island, when they'd rented bicycles and ate a picnic lunch on the boulder-strewn beach of Lake Huron's cold shore. To Irene's delight, Margie recounted the fallout when both of Frank's "steady" girlfriends attended the same pajama party.

As friends dropped by to welcome him home, he stood with his arm around Irene's waist and talked about his plans—the university allowed late admissions for returned veterans, and he would apply. He had already completed two years with a good grade-point average, and didn't anticipate any trouble being readmitted. He sidestepped all questions about the war, shifting the conversation to baseball. "Did you catch the Tigers last night? Dizzy Trout pitched a shutout. Trounced those Yankees 10–0." He would lower his voice: "I have five bucks on the World Series. You want in?"

Margie thought it wonderful to see Mama happy again. She sang along with the radio as she cooked large meals, washed extra loads of laundry, and ironed clothes. She seemed not to mind picking Frank's towels up off the floor, carrying the dishes he left on the table to the sink, or moving his shoes to where they couldn't be tripped over. His sloppy behavior irritated Margie, though. When she'd jabbed, "Were you raised in a barn?" he just laughed and called her Nurse Prissy.

Though exuberant during the day, his mood darkened as the sun set. He roamed the house like a caged cat, chain-smoking and peering out windows, his ear cocked for strange noises. He wasn't sleeping much, Irene confided to Margie; when he did manage to drop off, he tossed and turned, his legs windmilling under the covers, tears and sweat both pouring from him, soaking the sheets.

After an initial shyness, Billy warmed up to Frank, who played with him differently from the way Irene did, wrestling and teasing. Sometimes the roughhousing brought Billy to tears.

"Frank! Don't!" Irene scolded, whisking Billy away to give him a cookie.

"Stop with the cookies already. He's too fat."

"He's not either. Look at your baby pictures. You were a chub." When she put Billy down, he immediately ran crashing back into Frank's legs, and the wrestling and screeching started again.

Covering Billy's mouth to muffle the shrieking, Frank said to Irene, "Come bowling tonight. Sue will be there with Ed." Billy wriggled away. His cheeks were pink and his chin wet with spit. From the floor, Frank grabbed his leg and Billy squealed.

Irene covered her ears. "Can you stop that? You've got him all worked up."

Frank let Billy go, and he crawled away.

"Come on. We'll have a few beers."

"You know I can't. I have to work tomorrow."

Carrying a toy truck, Billy toddled back over to Frank. With a jump and a laugh, he flung the toy, which hit his father's upper lip. Immediate and violent, Frank's reaction sent Billy crashing against the nearby wall. "Get away from me, you little piece of shit."

Up in her room, Margie tried to write Wade, but the words wouldn't come. *There's something you need to know,* she began. No. She wadded the paper up and tossed it in the trash can. *I have a bit of a surprise for you.* That one got pitched too. *Have you ever thought about becoming a father?* As the trash can filled up, she decided that maybe she would wait until he came home to tell him. She might have had the baby by then. Which would cause the worse shock? She couldn't make up her mind.

One thing was certain—she would have to tell her mother soon. Maybe tonight, if Irene and Frank went out. Hiding her swelling tummy under her clothing was getting harder. Besides, preparations had to be made for this new arrival. Where would he sleep? He would need diapers, nightgowns, and bottles. Or should she nurse? She hadn't thought much about it and wondered what Irene had done. She really wanted to talk to Irene about having a baby but couldn't force herself to bring up the subject. She worried about the health of an infant conceived when she'd been so malnourished.

The sounds of Billy wailing and Irene shouting rose from the living room. Similar noisy incidents had erupted since Frank had come home. She heard thuds on the stairs and Irene's bedroom door slam.

Mama's voice filtered up. "What has gotten into you! Touch that child like that again and you can pack your bags and get out of here! Do you understand me?"

The front door banged open and shut, followed by Frank's truck speeding out of the driveway, its tires squealing. Running downstairs, Margie found Mama in the kitchen drying her tears on a dish towel, her whole body shaking. "I don't know what's happened to your brother. He's like a stranger."

"He's confused, Mama. He's been through a lot. He needs time to forget."

"He'd better forget real quick then! I won't put up with that behavior. Margie, I know Irene's frightened. Is there something you can say to help her?"

Mama wouldn't approve of anything she'd say to Irene—keep your job, be ready to run. Lights flashed through the window, and a vehicle stopped in the driveway. Margie peeked through the curtains and said, "That couldn't be Frank back already. Are you expecting someone, Mama?"

When she opened the door, a man who wasn't Frank stood on the porch. She stared at him uncomprehendingly for a minute before gasping out, "Wade! Is that you?"

CHAPTER 22

Little River, fall 1945

Wade stood at the door, looking young and sophisticated with stylish tortoiseshell glasses and a roguish mustache. He wore well-fitting slacks and a fine sweater. Margie gasped again. "What are you doing here?"

He laughed, his smile shining mischief, and handed her a bouquet of pink roses. "I got in this afternoon. I thought I'd surprise you. Maybe I should've phoned first."

"No," she said, regaining her composure, but warmth crept up her neck and her heart galloped. "Come in! You look wonderful." She admired the roses, then put them on the side table, shy and unsure what to do next.

Not shy at all, Wade gathered her in his arms and said a lover's hello, his mustache tickling underneath her nose.

Breathless, she ran her finger over the bristle. "I like it. It suits you."

His loving gaze searched her face. "You are even more beautiful than I remembered." He kissed her again, squeezing her tight against him.

"Who is it, Margie?" Mama asked, coming into the room.

Margie stepped back from Wade's embrace. "Mama, you remember Wade Porter?"

Mama's face lit up like a sunny day.

Wade was staying with his father and stepmother, who invited Margie to the family's celebration of his homecoming. His sister, Carol, hugged her and told her how glad she was that her little brother had finally decided to settle down. She introduced Margie to the many aunts, uncles, and cousins at the gathering. Margie found herself immediately considered part of Wade's warm extended family.

The following week, Wade's colleagues from the *Ann Arbor Tribune* held a party for all the correspondents recently returned from overseas. Margie discovered that, though a bit older than she, they were a fun and rowdy crowd—they bantered irreverently about current events and old-boy politicians.

More days passed, and Margie still hadn't told Wade the truth. Hiding her pregnancy proved an emotional burden that kept her awake at night and headachy during the day. At last, resigned, she vowed to end the torment and reveal her secret on Friday, during their dinner date.

In her room that evening, she dressed, then raised the window shade to watch for his car. She wandered from bed to door to window and back again, practicing what to say. Should she wait until after dinner or tell him the news immediately? Noticing she'd become breathless, she stopped pacing. When the doorbell rang, her hands flew protectively to the bulge hidden by her sweater. She gave herself a last once-over in the mirror and nervously reapplied her lipstick.

Hearing Mama welcome Wade into the house, Margie peeked over the stair railing. In a tizzy, she retreated to her room, knowing she could no longer put off this conversation. She steeled herself against whatever might happen and pasted on a big smile, then went downstairs.

"You two have a good time," Mama said. "Where are you going?"

"Luigi's for a pizza. I won't be late."

She found her jacket in the closet and slipped it over her shoulders, not trusting her fingers to button it properly. Wade opened the car door, and she slid into the passenger seat, swallowing hard, her mouth sticky-dry. Wade let himself in the other side and reached for the keys. She put her hand on his arm. Her voice sounding strange in her ears, she said, "Before we go . . ."

And she blurted out her news. "I'm pregnant."

His jaw dropped. "You're what?"

"I'm sorry. You don't have to marry me. I can live with my mother. She'll help me with the baby. I have my job at the Red Cross."

"What *are* you talking about?"

"Things have changed. You hardly know me."

"I know you to be strong and reliable. Charming. Smart. Talented. Even-tempered. I know that I love you. Are you saying you don't want to get married?"

"No, I'm saying I'm not going to hold you to a promise made in another life."

"For Pete's sake! What do you mean, 'a promise made in another life'?"

"You've made plans, that cottage on Lake Michigan, the book you want to write."

He ran his fingers through his hair. "That's a dream, Margie, not a plan. There's a difference. I wouldn't make any *plans* without talking to you first."

"With a baby, there'd be no way we could do that."

"Then the dream goes on hold. We'll get married, and I'll work at the newspaper."

"But it's not what you want."

"It's *you* I want! Just you." He held her chin and looked into her eyes. "Do you want me?"

She felt increasingly attracted to this handsome, kindhearted man, and her baby needed a good father. She whispered, "I do."

He pulled her to him in a warm, strong embrace. "Well then, that's settled. When's the baby due?"

"November."

"November already?" He broke out laughing. "What a wonderful homecoming present!"

Later, when Margie told her mother, she scolded her. "November! You should have told me sooner, Margie! Have you seen Dr. Middleton?"

"No. I'll make an appointment today. I'm sorry, Mama. I didn't believe it myself for a long time. I was going to tell you, but . . ." Tears came to her eyes.

Mama wrapped her in a hug. "It's all right. It's just, you may need extra care. What did Wade say?"

"He's happy about it. We're going to get married right away."

Plans for a late-September wedding fell quickly into place. Margie wanted to be married at the Little River Methodist Church, and Wade wished it to be a candlelight ceremony. Family and friends filled the church with gold and burgundy mums from their gardens.

Margie looked stunning in the ivory crepe dress that Mama had artfully altered to accommodate her tummy bulge. She carried a bouquet of mums and trailing ivy. Frank, dressed in a suit he'd borrowed for the occasion, walked Margie down the aisle. She smiled—radiantly, she hoped—but hidden behind her glowing face were thoughts of her father, and how much he had looked forward to this moment. Gracie, wearing a deep-rose suit-dress, stood beaming as her maid of honor, and Kenneth supported Wade as best man.

As Margie approached Wade at the altar, she saw abiding love in his eyes, and she felt protective of his feelings. In a silent vow as she stood facing him, she pledged to be a devoted and attentive wife to this gentle man who cared for her so dearly.

Everything had happened quickly, and a honeymoon hadn't been in Margie's plans. She was delighted when Wade surprised her with a getaway to a friend's cabin on Old Mission Peninsula, north of Traverse City.

Driving west through Michigan's farm country, they enjoyed their freedom and being alone together for the first time since those surreal days in Santo Tomas. Margie twirled the gold band encircling her ring finger, still unable to grasp the reality of the past few whirlwind weeks. *Mrs. Wade Francis Porter. Marjorie Olivia Bauer Porter. Margie Porter.*

"A penny for your thoughts," Wade said.

"You'll laugh."

"I promise never to laugh at you."

"I'm getting used to my new name. Mrs. Porter. It sounds like a schoolteacher, or somebody's mother."

Wade roared. "Whoops, sorry. I promised not to."

"What was your mother's full name?"

"Barbara Jean. Barbara Jean Wilson Porter."

"What was she like?"

"A lot like you. Pretty. Smart. Warm. She taught school before she had Carol. She liked Mark Twain's humor. She would quote him." Striking an attitude, he intoned, "'Familiarity breeds contempt—and children.'" He guffawed. "I was about thirteen when she first laid that one on me. It took a while before I understood it." As he removed his wallet from his back pocket, the car swerved a bit. "Here's her picture."

Margie admired the photograph of a young woman with dark hair, a distinctive nose, and a strong jaw. "You resemble her, except for your coloring."

"Yeah, her hair was almost black. I never saw a strand of gray in it. Her great-grandfather on her mother's side was a Cherokee warrior."

"No kidding. So that's where you get your profile. It's very striking, you know." Margie resisted the urge to rifle through the wallet, and handed it back to him.

"I've been thinking of names," Margie added. "How about, if it's a girl, Barbara Ann, after our mothers? And if it's a boy, Joshua Wade, after my dad and you?"

Wade grinned. "If I wasn't driving, I'd give you a big kiss."

As they turned north, the landscape changed from flat farmland to that of the Manistee National Forest, with its scrubby jack pines and tall white spruce, paper birch, aspens in their golden glory, and maples displaying a spectrum of color from yellow to deep scarlet. Farther along, they passed through the lake-dotted Traverse City area, stopping for dinner and groceries. They located the cabin down a narrow road on Old Mission Peninsula, extending out into Grand Traverse Bay.

Inside, the cabin smelled of cedar. Large windows overlooked the water, and a stone fireplace dominated the opposite wall. Wade tossed a match on the waiting pile of tinder and logs, and soon the small space felt cozy. On the trestle table, a basket filled with fruit, nuts, cheeses, crackers, wines, and chocolate contained a card that read, "Happy Honeymooning from your friends at the *Tribune*." Wade brought in their suitcases while Margie filled the refrigerator and cupboards with groceries and supplies.

After settling in, they snuggled together under a blanket on the settee on the screened porch; they sipped red wine and watched the sun set over the bay before retiring. The two renewed their acquaintance with each other's bodies—Wade explored the curves that hadn't been there before, and Margie delighted in the muscles under his taut skin.

The peninsula was almost deserted save for a few locals, and it didn't offer them much to do except enjoy nature at its most stunning. They strolled both the east and west shores of the bay, absorbed equally by the views and each other. They visited the lighthouse and the Old Mission Inn, played Scrabble and Monopoly, finished off the food they brought, and then resupplied at the Old Mission General Store. Wade chopped more wood for the fire, and Margie cooked stews and rice puddings.

They unwound, napped, made love, and slept. Margie glowed with contentment, and the lines on Wade's face softened.

One afternoon, he said, "Get comfortable. I'll give you a massage."

"Like in the hospital? I gave them to my patients."

"Oh, much better than that."

"Where did you learn . . . Much better?"

"Here and there. You have to get undressed."

"Okay. Now I see where this is going. What's that you're holding?"

"Olive oil."

"You plan on roasting me over the fire?"

"It's all I could find. We're not exactly in Paris. Tie your hair up. You'll like this."

She secured her hair with a clip, took off her shirt and bra, and straddled a chair in front of the crackling fire. Wade applied warm oil to her neck and shoulders with long strokes.

She murmured with pleasure. "Rough hands, like a loofah sponge. Give me a man who chops wood."

"That's me, all right. A regular Paul Bunyan." His hands moved in broad circles over her back and shoulders, along the sides of her neck and upper arms.

She said, "We only have one day left."

"Shh . . . Stay in the moment."

Margie tried to let her muscles go limp, but her mind raced ahead. "It's crowded at home. When the baby comes, it'll be worse."

He increased the pressure, working deep into the tissues of her neck. "I'll find us a place. You're tightening up."

She stretched her neck and shoulders. "I want to live near my mother. She needs help with Dad gone." She moaned in response to the force Wade applied to the back of her skull.

"Am I hurting you?"

"No, it feels wonderful. It'll be a bit of a drive for you to work. At least gas isn't rationed anymore. Is my car okay?"

"Shh . . . It'll do fine." He kneaded up and down the sides of her spine with his thumbs. Just as she felt her neck relaxing, the baby's foot lodged under her rib. She arched her back in order to draw a full breath.

Wade's warm, oily hands came around front, stopping to feel the movements inside her belly. "It doesn't hurt?"

"No. His foot's under my rib, is all. Put your hand right here. Feel that?"

"No."

"Give it a minute. Be real still. Feel it?"

Wade waited, concentrating. "Yeah, what is it?"

"A hiccup."

"What? You're kidding me, aren't you?"

"No. It's a hiccup. Maybe he didn't like what I had for dinner. What did we have?"

"Barbecue."

"That spicy sauce."

Wade moved his hands over her breasts, circling each one, then back to her neck and up into her hair, massaging her scalp.

"You're right," she sighed. "*Much* better."

Reluctant to begin the drive home, Margie and Wade walked arm in arm along the water's edge to enjoy, one more time, the crisp morning air, the colors of the rising sun, and the coos of the mourning doves. She said, "Frank's having a hard time adjusting. You'll have to be careful around him. I think he's jealous of you."

"Me?"

"Yes. You're older. You have a job waiting. He's drifting. He's belligerent. Irene says he cries easily and tries to hide it."

"I'll do what I can to help him."

"I'd appreciate it. He's going to be hard to live with. I feel sorry for Irene. She'll catch the brunt of it."

Wade moved into Margie's small bedroom. She liked having him sleeping beside her. He paid attention to her aching back and swollen feet and was awed by the waves of activity crossing her abdomen. She slept sounder and had fewer disturbing dreams than before.

Although a job at the *Tribune* waited for Wade, he didn't know exactly what beat he'd be covering. Helping him dress for an interview, Margie safety-pinned a tuck in the back of his too-big shirt.

"Don't take off your coat and these pins won't show. You need to go shopping."

Wade cinched in his belt to hold up his pants. "I tried. You can't buy a white shirt to save your soul in this town. Or shoes."

"The pants and sweater you've been wearing fit you good."

He hesitated a moment. "They belonged to Kodak's younger brother. Poor kid didn't make it home."

"You didn't tell me."

"It's not a happy story." He checked his pockets for handkerchief, wallet, and keys, then shrugged into his suit coat.

She smoothed a wrinkle off his front and tried not to smile at his baggy look. "Maybe you'll start a new style."

"That bad?"

"No, you look fine. Good luck." She kissed him. "Tell them no more globe-trotting."

After Wade left, Margie helped Mama with the laundry by hanging sheets and towels on the clothesline out back. Later, she chased Billy around the yard to wear him out, so he might sleep through the night. Since Frank's return, the tot frequently woke up crying for his pacifier, a habit they all thought he'd outgrown months ago.

Bringing Billy in for a snack, she found Frank sitting at the kitchen table, drinking a beer and smoking. He had taken to carousing at night, coming home in the wee hours of the morning, and then sleeping until midafternoon. His college plans had apparently vanished, like the smoke from his cigarettes.

"Welcome to the land of the living," Margie said as she sat Billy in his high chair and brought him a handful of Cheerios and a cup of milk.

Frank watched through bloodshot eyes. "Get me another beer, will you?"

"In your dreams. I'm not your wife."

Frank flicked the ash of his cigarette, missing the ashtray.

"For Pete's sake, Frank! Watch what you're doing." She threw a cleaning rag at him.

Working at the stove, Mama said, "That's enough, Margie."

"Mama! It's time he—"

"I said that's enough."

Just then the front door banged, and Wade walked in carrying a bouquet of yellow daisies. Margie fussed over the flowers. Finding a vase under the sink, she arranged them prettily and placed them on the table.

Frank scowled at the flowers.

Margie smiled at Wade. "You must have good news."

Frank snarled, "Yeah, big shot. Tell us the good news."

The kitchen became very still, everyone staring at Frank, whose face broke into a nasty grin. "Did you tell them you knocked up my sister?"

"Frank!" Mama said.

He smirked. "Or that you were 4-F because you're half blind?"

Wade's jaw clenched. "How many of those beers have you had, little guy?"

Frank knocked over the flowers. The vase shattered and water ran off the edge of the table. He leaped toward Wade, who met him with a slug to the chin. Frank lost his footing and fell to the floor.

Billy screamed.

"Stop it, this minute! Both of you!" Mama cried, scooping up the frightened baby.

Frank staggered to his feet, rubbing his chin. "Just you wait," he threatened, and ran out the door.

Wade shook an ache from his fingers. "I'm sorry," he said ruefully. "I shouldn't have provoked him. Please forgive me."

Mama hugged the crying baby. "Frank did all the provoking. He's not like that. I don't understand." Fighting back tears, she carried Billy upstairs.

"You didn't have to hit him," Margie said.

"I said I was sorry. I didn't think." He started to clean up the mess on the table, stacking the glass chunks from largest to smallest and carrying the dripping shards to the trash can.

She sopped up the water with a towel. Finding another vase, she filled it with water and rearranged the flowers. She said, "Never mind Frank. Tell me about today."

"I got offered an assistant editorship on the European desk. There'll be some travel, but not much." He managed a half grin. "The current editor plans to retire in two years. It's a good opportunity."

"Is it something you'd like?"

"Yes. It'll be a challenge. I'll have to brush up on economics and European politics. I'll be doing some writing, but mostly I'd work with the correspondents. It's good pay and benefits. We could afford a house of our own. What do you think?"

The prospect pleased her. "I think we've already made up our minds."

CHAPTER 23

Little River, fall 1945

Several days passed; Frank didn't come home. Tight-lipped, Irene picked at her meals. After dinner, she retired upstairs to spend time with Billy, who had become unruly. He lashed out at everyone, glowering and flailing his little arms. She held his struggling body close against her own, singing lullabies until he wore himself out and dropped off to sleep.

During the evenings, Mama helped Margie alter Wade's prewar shirts and suits, all too large and smelling of mothballs. She frequently stopped sewing to wander over to the window, where she stared out of the parted curtains, sighing deeply. "Where do you think he is, Margie?"

"I don't know. Not too far, I hope."

Although the sky threatened an early snow, Margie put on a coat and hat, then searched through the closet for gloves. "I need more thread. I'm going into town. If you make a list, I'll stop at the grocery store."

She drove slowly through the center of Little River, eyeing every man wearing army-issue pants and an olive-drab jacket. A group roughhousing in front of the pool hall whistled and gestured as she crept by, but Frank wasn't among them. Inside, she knew, the guys would be telling war stories. Wherever veterans congregated, they damned the military or the government, bemoaning lost years, lost health, lost wives, lost girlfriends.

Margie parked in front of Reba's Five and Dime and purchased the thread she needed. She chatted with the gray-haired clerk about the shortages. Incoming stock sold even before they had time to take it out of the boxes it shipped in, the woman told her.

"You wouldn't have any white shirts, would you?"

The clerk shook her head. "I haven't seen one in months, honey. We did get in a shipment of men's dress socks this morning. They're still in the back. I can sell you three pairs."

Stowing her packages in the car, Margie walked the block to the pool hall. Out front, she saw a high school classmate leaning on a cane, a cap half covering the scar on his forehead.

"Dale! Hi. Good to see you."

A smile emerged from behind a scruffy beard. "Margie! How you doing? I heard you got married."

"Yeah, to Wade Porter. You know him?"

"The name's familiar. He plays the guitar. Right?"

"That's him. Hey, you seen Frank around?"

"Yesterday he was at the bowling alley. Haven't seen him today. He said he has a kid."

"Yeah, Billy. What've you been up to?"

"Not much. Getting used to this new leg."

"I'm sorry to hear that."

"Could've been worse. If you see Frank, tell him he owes me five bucks."

Returning to her vehicle, Margie drove to the bowling alley. She walked from one end to the other of the crowded, smoky interior, chatting with men she knew. No one had seen Frank. Frustrated but not ready to give up, she circled the YMCA, where men rented rooms by the day, week, or month. Still no luck. On a whim, she drove to the park not far from the high school, where she found him slouched on a bench, his hands tucked into his armpits. He looked up when she tooted the horn but made no move to join her. She opened the car door, letting in a blast of cold air. "The car's warm!" she yelled in his direction.

He sauntered over and slid into the passenger seat. "What're you doing here?"

"Looking for you." She wrinkled her nose, waving her hand in front of it. "You smell like a barn floor. Where've you been sleeping?"

He shrugged. "I don't know. Wherever I land."

"We've all been worried sick about you."

He looked out the side window. "I don't give a shit." Shaking his head, he said, "Forget that. I say things I don't mean."

"You always were a smart mouth. Are you hungry?"

"I could use a meal."

She turned up the heat, cracked the window open to freshen the air inside the car, and drove to the diner in silence. She ran inside and stood at the counter, ordering two hamburgers, double fries, and coffee to go, then added an apple from a basket near the cash register. When the food was ready, she took the bag out to the car and handed it to Frank. He gobbled it all down, some color coming back into his cheeks. She waited until he finished, then turned awkwardly behind the steering wheel to face him. "Tell me what's going on."

He looked at the swell under her coat. "That guy you married. He's old as Methuselah. Where'd you find him, anyway?"

"This isn't about Wade. Give him a chance, for my sake, if for no other reason." She narrowed her eyes, watching for signs of the Frank she knew. "Talk to me. What's really going on?"

"Nothing much. I'm stuck in this Podunk town. It's like watching paint dry." He wiped his mouth on a napkin. "You should've seen me in France. I crawled on my belly through enemy fire to the guys who needed my help. They called me Doc. The villagers cheered us like we were heroes." He balled up the napkin and threw it to the floor. "Now it seems us vets are a threat to society."

"Where'd you hear that?"

"It's in the papers. How could you miss it?" His face screwed up, and he fought back tears. "Fuck 'em. They just don't know—" He gazed out the window, continuing in a monotone. "I found this kid in a ditch, covered with blood and shit. He was my age. God, we even had the same color hair. His guts were hanging out of his belly. I stuck him with morphine, dressed the wound, and held his hand while he talked. He said he had a sister named Margie. Would you believe that?" The tears that had threatened earlier now coursed down Frank's face. "I watched him die, and I thought it was me! I *fucking* couldn't sort . . . it . . . out!"

"It's all right, Frank."

He slammed his fist on the dashboard. "No, it's not all right! No one listens! No one wants to hear it. I got all this stuff going around in my head. Irene says I have nightmares, that I kick and cry. I don't remember them, but I wake up feeling like a fucking time bomb."

"It's not only you."

He smirked. "Don't I know that? The VA hospitals are full of us nutcases. We're very much in vogue."

"There are psychiatric services—"

"And make it official! Frank Bauer, nutcase! Two years of my life. I could have finished school. Be working at a job. Giving Irene and Billy what they deserve. Did you hear the GM plant went on strike? I'd kill for a job, and those assholes are picketing for higher wages."

"Then go back to school."

"Look at me. Can you see me sitting in a classroom?"

"You can draw GI benefits. It's what Irene wants."

He bit his lip almost to the point of bleeding. "How's Irene doing?"

"She needs you." Too late, Margie remembered her first weeks at home, too weak in mind and body to be needed. She tried again. "You need her. She's steady and smart. She's amazing with Billy. Don't blow it with her, Frank."

She thought she saw him soften a little.

Out on the street, screeching brakes preceded the sound of metal crumpling. Brother and sister both jumped, and Frank ducked down as far as he could in the seat. People from the diner rushed to the scene of the accident.

He fumbled for the car door handle. "I gotta get out of here!"

"Stay! I'll drive you home!"

He opened the door and leaped out.

"Here! Take this!" Margie said, holding out all the cash she could grab from her purse.

He shoved the money in his pocket and sprinted through the parking lot, away from the growing crowd.

Engrossed in her thoughts, Margie completely forgot about the groceries until she pulled into the driveway. She knew battle fatigue when she saw it: men who looked fine on the outside but churned with pain and paranoia internally, their behavior unpredictable, tempers quick to flare, and their coarse language hard on the ears.

She drove the car into the barn and sat alone in the half dark. She almost envied Frank. What would it feel like to spew venomous anger? To writhe with hate? To cry bitter tears? To truly love and feel loved in return? To care deeply and passionately about something or someone? Was she destined to live emotionally flat forever?

She closed the barn door and locked it. From inside the house, she heard Irene crying and Mama saying, "Things will work out. They always do."

"What's going on?" Margie asked as she shed her outerwear.

Irene sputtered in anger. "Ford's government contract expired and they're cutting personnel. I was laid off. Most of the women were."

"I'm so sorry," Margie said.

"They gave my job to a man who *has a family to support*! I've been asked to stay on for two weeks and train him! How am *I* supposed to live? I have Billy to support. Frank is gone heaven only knows where."

"He's here in town. I saw him today in the park. I bought him lunch, and we talked."

Irene snapped to attention. "Did he say when he's coming home?"

Margie debated how much to tell Irene. Aged in years and spirit, Frank was no longer the kid brother she remembered. She had no idea when he planned to return home, or even if he ever would. So she just said, "Give him time. He's working through some problems."

His job secure, Wade suggested they start looking for a house. On a Sunday afternoon in October, they drove to Ann Arbor to meet with a real estate agent. Arriving in town early, they stopped to visit Gracie and Kenneth.

After hugs all around, Gracie patted Margie's extended belly. "You're not so big. You're due, what, in about four weeks?"

"About. I feel as big as an elephant."

Gracie had a pot of coffee perking, and she put out a plate of pastries. They caught each other up on the latest news—Kenneth's job was going well and his mother was pressing them for a grandchild.

"Tell them what's going on with you," Kenneth prodded Gracie.

She shook her head. "I'd rather not talk about it."

"Tell them. They should know."

She shot Kenneth a blistering glance. "Seems I'm not considered stable."

Margie said, "What? You? You're joking, right?"

"I'm afraid not. It seems I am 'awkward' and have a 'funny look.'"

"That's awful! It's absolutely not true! Who says that?"

"My supervisor at the VA hospital. She has a lot of people whispering about me, and it's pretty uncomfortable. For the last two months, I've been pulling split shifts, and have been relegated to giving bed baths and delivering meal trays, the two things that hurt my shoulder the most. My tour of duty finished up last week. Yesterday I turned in my resignation. I think the little bitch is glad I'm gone."

"Oh, Gracie, I'm sorry. Could you have transferred to another department?"

"Probably, but I'm a little sour on the whole place right now. Maybe I just need a break." She passed the plate of pastries to Margie. "Here, help me drown my sorrows."

They discussed Gracie's options—she could go back to school for specialized training on the GI Bill, apply for a teaching position in the university's school of nursing, or maybe start a family and make Kenneth's mother happy.

Gracie said she didn't feel up to tackling any of those options.

As Margie and Wade got ready to leave, the foursome made a date to get together, soon—before the baby was born—for dinner and a movie.

The real estate office was a few blocks away. The agent, though friendly and exuberant, wasn't very helpful. He said that listings in the Ann Arbor area were practically nonexistent. Houses that came on the market sold before agents had time to advertise them. The shabbiness of the few properties available dismayed Margie, and the high asking prices shocked Wade. The drive home was quiet, as both felt the day had turned into a dismal one.

They looked for a house in Little River, but the situation there was no better. Families lived with relatives in attics, in basements, or in trailers parked in the yard. And those families were growing. Everywhere Margie went—the grocery store, the beauty parlor, the library—she heard women chatting about morning sickness, fatigue, and the cute maternity tops they made to cover their expanding figures.

Frustrated, Wade and Margie decided their best option would be to stay in the house with Mama, at least until after the baby arrived.

CHAPTER 24

Little River, fall 1945

By the end of October, Margie's blood pressure soared frighten-
ingly high, with accompanying headaches and bouts of dizziness.
Dr. Middleton prescribed medication and bed rest. After several
days of confinement, she waddled down the stairs at five o'clock in
the morning, placing her swollen feet carefully. Despite the early
hour, she found Mama sitting at the kitchen table. "Good morning,
Mama. How come you're sitting here in the dark?"

Mama startled in surprise. "I didn't hear you come in, honey.
You shouldn't be out of bed!"

"I know. I just need to sit up for a while."

Mama scooped oatmeal into a bowl, added cream and brown
sugar, and handed it to Margie. "When I was pregnant with you, I
sat at this same table in the early mornings when I couldn't sleep."

"Did you swell up like this?" Margie held up a puffy foot.

"No, but you were a big baby and sat high under my ribs, so I was always uncomfortable. I was ready to go through anything to get my body back."

"I'll never do this again."

"That's what we all say. You feel miserable right now, but you'll forget most of it. You'll be overcome with new feelings. Nothing compares to mother love."

Margie wouldn't admit it, but she didn't have any feelings for this baby, though she went through the motions, hoping they might arise. She sewed tiny nightgowns, stitching bunnies and flowers on the bodices and hems with colored threads and ribbons. She fussed over the pastel sweaters, hats, and booties her mother and Irene knitted and played all the silly games at the shower Wade's sister, Carol, threw. The baby would surely be a boy, her girlfriends had predicted after hanging Margie's wedding ring on a string over her belly and watching it swing in a circle.

"No, it's a girl," Carol had said. "She's carrying high and out front."

As the women traded their stories of their own good and bad birthing experiences, Margie's emotions had reeled from dread to anticipation.

But at this moment, sitting at the kitchen table and massaging her aching back, the only emotion she felt was fear.

"Were you afraid, Mama?"

"Of course. It's normal. You're facing an unknown. Dr. Middleton delivered you, and he's a good doctor. We'll all be there with you, just outside the door. You're going to be fine."

The words didn't comfort her. Given the undetermined paternity, her fear reached far beyond the birthing. She tried to eat a spoonful of oatmeal, but it sickened her stomach. Headachy and anxious, she lumbered back to bed.

Early that afternoon, Dr. Middleton climbed the stairs to Margie's bedroom. Puffing by the time he got to the top, he mopped sweat from his brow with a kerchief. He pulled a chair over by the bed and settled his hefty frame. "How are you feeling, my dear?"

"Fat and ugly."

"Oh, my, my. Don't say that. You're beautiful as ever." He retrieved a stethoscope from his black bag and listened for fetal sounds, estimated the baby's size, then checked Margie's blood pressure. "Not good, not good." He rubbed his chin while deliberating. "The baby's small. We might have miscalculated the due date. Still . . . well, I think we'd better induce labor and get you out of this situation. I can schedule it for first thing in the morning. Is Wade around? I'd like to talk to him."

"No, he's at work. Do you expect any problems?"

"With your blood pressure high and the baby small, we need to be prepared for additional risk. I've delivered hundreds of babies, Margie, and I know what to do. Your job is to rest. Don't eat anything after midnight. I'll call the hospital. I want you there at seven in the morning."

When Dr. Middleton left, she phoned Wade at work. "Guess what? I'm having the baby in the morning." Both were relieved the pregnancy would soon be over and frightened by the birthing still to face. Margie lay back on her pillow and wondered, *Joshua Wade or Barbara Ann?*

Mama helped her wash her hair, and Irene gave her a manicure, buffing Margie's nails to a shine. Margie asked, "What's giving birth really like?"

"I don't really remember much about it, except it took a long time. I remember being scared, but not the pain. Toward the end, they gave me something that knocked me out. When I woke up, there he was, all six pounds twelve ounces of him." She put down the buffer. "There, all groomed. You need help shaving your legs?"

Margie giggled. "Oh, would you?"

Wade came home from work early, stopping on the way to put gas in the car and air in the tires. He had meticulously attended to those chores these last weeks. After dinner, they packed a suitcase with nightgowns, a robe and slippers, personal items, and a book, then set up the cribbage board to pass the time. Neither could concentrate on the game, and the minutes ticked slowly by. Wade tried to hide his anxiety by whistling.

"Please stop it," Margie barked as a sharp pain ripped through her insides. She doubled over.

Wade jumped up. "What's wrong?"

She brushed the cards aside, lay back on her pillow, and assessed her condition. The pain had passed, but her heart still thumped wildly. She felt a shift. "He's moving around. I think he wants out."

"Should I call Dr. Middleton?"

"No. Not yet. It's too soon. I have a headache. I'd like to sleep." She shuffled to the bathroom, aware that something had changed. She thanked her lucky stars all this would be over by tomorrow afternoon.

Wade tucked her back into bed, then switched out the light and went downstairs to sit with Mama and Irene.

Margie immediately fell asleep. An hour later, her face began to twitch, and her respirations stopped. Her body went rigid, the muscles alternately contracting and relaxing in rapid sequence, causing her to bite down hard on her tongue. She woke up gasping for air, and yelled, "Wade! Mama!" Sinking into a coma-like state, she dreamed she was swimming in a warm pool.

From outside the house came the sounds of squealing brakes and a vehicle door slamming. Panting, Frank charged through the front door and into the living room. "Where's Irene? Is she all right?"

Ignoring Frank, Wade took the stairs two at a time and turned on the bedroom light. He froze for a second when he saw the pool of blood on the bed, then shouted for help.

Frank raced up the stairs, Mama and Irene right behind him.

Struggling to come to, Margie heard Frank's urgent voice. "For God's sake, call an ambulance!"

He took off his coat, pushed up his sleeves, and rolled her onto her side. He ordered Wade to support her back and told Irene to boil water and bring towels, string, and scissors. "Margie," he said, hovering just inches above her, "I want you to breathe in through your nose and out through your mouth like you're trying to whistle. Watch me." He demonstrated the technique. Margie followed his lead as a crushing pain in her head preceded another contraction, this one longer and harder. Something inside her wanted to tear her apart. Seizing again, she went rigid, then slipped into darkness, only to wake up with a towel clenched between her teeth and feeling a mass between her legs. The bedroom was full of strangers. As emergency personnel lifted her onto a gurney for the trip downstairs to the ambulance, her last memory was of Frank carrying a bundle wrapped in a towel, tears streaming down his face.

She regained consciousness in the hospital with a blood-pressure cuff strapped onto one arm and the other one immobilized on a board. Lines of tubing hooked her to bottles of blood and IV solutions hanging overhead. More tubing brought oxygen into her nose, and a catheter drained urine from her bladder. Her mouth felt dry, her tongue swollen and raw. The room seemed too bright, and the beep of the paging system hurt her ears.

A soft voice from near her head said, "Margie, I'm Donna, your nurse. You're in the hospital. You had a little girl."

"A girl," Margie repeated groggily. She drifted back to sleep, feeling the blood-pressure cuff expanding and squeezing her arm.

By late afternoon, she was well enough to sit up. Her head felt fuzzy, and the vision in one eye blurred. She heard Dr. Middleton out in the hall. He came into the room and pulled the curtain around the bed. "You gave us quite a scare, young lady. Do you know you were having seizures?"

"I don't remember much."

"We almost lost you. You're familiar with eclampsia?"

She had studied it in school—the high blood pressure, swelling, and headaches that could quickly progress to seizures, life-threatening for both mother and fetus. She said, "Is the baby all right?"

"It's too soon to tell. She's small to begin with, and when you seized, her oxygen was restricted. If she survives the next twenty-four hours, we'll know better. I've asked Dr. Crane to take over her care. He specializes in preemies."

"Can I see her?"

"Not yet. She's in isolation, and I don't want you out of bed. The medication in your IV controls the seizures, but it makes you sleepy. I've ordered a private-duty nurse for you." He stood. "Wade's outside. Would you like to see him?"

She hadn't even thought of what Wade must be going through. She nodded.

"All right. Ten minutes. No more."

Wade came to Margie's bedside, looking disheveled, apprehensive, and carrying a teddy bear. He kissed her, told her how beautiful she was and how much he loved her. She assured him she was all right and asked about the baby. He said he hadn't been able to see her. After a few more minutes, Donna insisted he leave. He gave Margie the teddy bear and promised to be back in the morning.

Alone, Margie held the teddy bear against her bosom and feared for her tiny daughter struggling to survive. If only her depleted body had been more nurturing. If only her heart had been more loving. If only she hadn't denied Barbara Ann's existence for so many months. She mumbled a prayer, asking forgiveness.

Every day was touch and go, as Barbara Ann clung to life by a thread. She remained in isolation and on around-the-clock surveillance. Restricted to her bed, Margie could only dream of her daughter.

During one of his many visits, Wade relayed the details of the night of the birth to her. How Frank had a premonition that he was needed at home, and how he had rushed in the door just as Margie called for help. He said, "Frank took complete charge. He was amazing. I'll never think of him as a kid again."

"You need to tell him that. He needs to hear it. Do you know where he is?"

"He's at home with Irene and Billy."

After several days, the threat of seizures passed, and Dr. Middleton allowed Margie out of bed. Wade walked with her to the nursery. For the first time, Margie beheld Barbara Ann, a scrawny little being with a bush of silky dark hair.

Wade said, "She's certainly distinctive. She looks like my mother."

Dark and distinctive—like his mother. Margie hoped Wade was right, but she didn't feel so sure.

Her hospital stay dragged on for three more weeks. As her strength returned, she took frequent walks to the nursery to watch Barbara Ann sleep, naked except for the tiniest diaper. Her daughter grew stronger every day. When the nurse positioned the incubator by the window, Margie baby-talked and tapped on the glass, hoping to generate a response from the baby or feel some sort of connection in herself. Neither happened, making her feel inadequate and sad.

Margie got home in time for Thanksgiving Day, but with Dad gone a year now and Barbara Ann still in the hospital, the family felt incomplete. Frank claimed his dad's place at the head of the table to say the blessing and carve the turkey. He kept up a steady banter. "What side of the turkey has the most feathers?"

Irene smirked.

"Come on, take a guess. Margie, what side of the turkey has the most feathers?"

"The outside?"

"Aw. You heard it before."

"You've been telling that joke since you were six. Can't you come up with a new one?"

"Not anything for mixed company."

They feasted on turkey stuffed with Mama's sage-and-raisin dressing, potatoes, gravy, green beans, and beets. Later, they played Parcheesi and ate pumpkin pie with homemade ice cream. Margie luxuriated in being back home, where Wade doted and Mama fussed. Frank seemed more settled in his mind, though Irene still eyed him warily. Billy patted Margie's tummy and asked, "Where's the baby?"

Margie stepped out to the back porch to join Frank in an after-meal cigarette. They both stared up at the sky. He said, "I don't do well in small spaces. I spent too many nights spooning with my buddies. You ever been that cold?"

"I was in the Philippines. We prayed for a breeze." She blew out smoke. "When did you learn how to deliver babies?"

"I never did, but I know a lot about pain and seizures. Good thing I was there. Your husband was useless."

"He loves you too, little brother." She shivered in the brisk air. "He's grateful for what you did. He admires you. Your ability in an emergency. He said you were amazing."

"He did?"

"Yes. What was that about a premonition?"

"You never get them? My gut told me something bad was happening. I thought it was Irene or Billy. They mean a lot to me. I know that now."

"I'm glad you're home. Are you doing better?"

"I'm trying. Out there . . . I reacted . . . you know. There wasn't time to think. I can't turn it off. And I have these awful images. I never know when they're gonna hit. Irene won't leave me alone with Billy, and I don't blame her."

"She said you're seeing a doctor, a psychiatrist."

"Yeah, she made me. Dr. Garber. He works with vets."

"Is he helping?"

"I don't know."

Margie hugged her brother. "I'm so proud of you."

Barbara Ann continued to gain weight and her breathing stabilized. The neurological tests Dr. Crane performed didn't reveal any immediate deficiencies. Pleased with her progress, he moved her from the incubator to a bassinet on the first of December. He wrote in her chart that Margie could hold her, and the nurse phoned her with the good news.

"I envy you," Wade said while getting dressed for work and straightening his tie. "What time are you going in?"

"Noon. I'll be giving her a bottle."

"Give her a kiss for me and tell her I love her." He kissed Margie good-bye.

At the hospital, the nurse gave her a gown to wear over her clothes, then left her alone in a small room off the nursery that contained a rocking chair and table. Posters on the walls gave how-to instructions for feeding, diapering, and swaddling an infant. Margie dressed in the gown, read the information on the posters, and then sat in the rocker. Nervous, she smoothed the wrinkles from her gown and drummed her fingers while watching the door.

At last, the nurse wheeled in Barbara Ann's bassinet. Swaddled in a pink blanket, she wore a wee knitted cap on her head. Her eyes were closed and fringed with dark lashes. At six weeks old, she was still tiny, but her cheeks showed signs of chubbiness. Her rosebud mouth suckled.

The nurse put her in Margie's arms and handed her a bottle. "She's a sleepy one. You'll have to jiggle her a bit. She'll eat well enough once you get her started."

Margie was in awe, holding her child in her arms for the first time. She jostled her awake only to be rewarded with a frown. "Goodness! What a pouty face!" She placed the nipple to the baby's lips. Barbara Ann ignored it. Margie laughed. "I guess this is going to take a while."

"Keep trying. She should be hungry. There's a call bell on the table if you need me."

The nurse left Margie alone with her daughter. She'd fed newborns as a nursing student, and she knew how to tickle a fuzzy cheek and stroke under a tiny chin. Barbara Ann started to take the nourishment while Margie studied her face for clues to her heritage. *I won't let it matter.* After two ounces of formula were gone, she lifted the infant to her shoulder and patted her back, feeling her weight and warmth. Barbara Ann burped as robustly as any man, and Margie laughed again.

She greedily finished the bottle. Margie made a lap and placed her there, removing the cap and unfolding the swaddling blanket. Barbara Ann lay curled, tight-fisted, bowlegged, a perfect miracle, her silky newborn hair plentiful and black, her skin tones dusky. A petite dimple decorated the tiny chin. A foreboding stirred in Margie. She stroked a downy-soft cheek. *I won't let it matter.* Unable to quell the need to know, she traced the baby's hairline with her fingertip and found the hint of a widow's peak. Barbara

Ann opened her dark eyes wide, and Margie found the gaze familiar and mesmerizing.

She felt like she had been punched in the chest. This wasn't Wade's child. A wicked, violent man spawned her. *It doesn't matter! She's my baby too!*

CHAPTER 25

Little River, 1946

Margie felt the walls closing in around her. She quickly placed Barbara Ann back in the bassinet, tore off the gown, and grabbed her coat. With no nurses in sight at the station, she hurried from the nursery to her car—something was not feeling right in her head. Wavy lines crossed her field of vision, so she needed several tries to get the key in the ignition. When the engine turned over, she slammed the transmission into gear and raced out of the parking lot. The miles flew by as she stepped hard on the accelerator, but she couldn't outrun the disturbing memory trying to surface.

Blinding images struck like bolts of lightning—she heard shells blasting, felt fires raging, experienced again the smell of the dead and the moans of the dying. Unable to see, she drove off the side of the road, her front right wheel angled into a ditch.

Bent over the steering wheel, she relived the terror as if it were happening this minute—Max grabbing her throat, her knee ramming his crotch, his convulsing, her collapsing onto him, the

syringe of morphine plunging into his neck, his lifeless eyes staring accusingly at her. Every muscle in her body shuddered.

"Oh God! Oh God!" she whimpered.

Leaving her purse on the seat and the keys in the ignition,
she stumbled out of the car. She turned her collar up and shoved
her hands in her pockets and started to walk. Unaware of either
her surroundings or destination, she plodded down the side of
the road, one foot automatically moving ahead of the other, her
thoughts a jumble of horror and self-loathing. When passing cars
slowed to offer help, she waved them away, not wanting anyone to
see the real her, the evil core of her.

Time passed, as did the miles. The landscape gradually
changed from rural to commercial, neon signs glowing in the
darkening sky. The temperature dropped, and snowflakes swirled
around her head, landing on her nose and chin. Hunger made her
stomach rumble, and a sore spot on her toe caused her pain with
each step—a just punishment, she thought, welcoming each stab.

A horn honked, and a car came to a screeching halt in front of
her. The passenger door flew open and Gracie scrambled out, trot-
ting over just before Margie collapsed in a heap by the side of the
road. Right behind Gracie, Kenneth took Margie's arm; together
they steered her into the backseat of the car. Gracie made a quick
assessment of her condition.

"Everyone's looking for you, honey. What are you doing out
here?"

Margie's parched throat wouldn't allow her to respond. Feeling
light-headed, she lay down on the seat, curling into a ball.

Gracie removed her own coat and tucked it under Margie's
head. "Let's get her home," she said to Kenneth. "I don't think she's
totally with us."

Their apartment was only a short drive away. Once inside,
Gracie settled Margie on the couch with a pillow and blanket, a

shot of whiskey, and a glass of water. Brushing the hair away from Margie's eyes, she looked deeply into them.

"Can you hear me?"

Margie nodded, not entirely sure where she was.

"Kenneth talked to your mother. Wade is out looking for you. He'll be here as soon as he can. Are you hungry?"

Margie nodded again. "I need the bathroom."

Gracie pointed down a short hallway.

What she saw in the mirror frightened her—the skin of her face all splotchy, eyes overly bright and ringed by dark circles. The blister on her foot burned, and her fingers and toes ached from the cold. She splashed water on her face and tried to fluff up her matted hair. She had only the vaguest recollection of how she came to be in Ann Arbor.

Back in the kitchen with Gracie and Kenneth, she sipped some water and tried to eat the soup and crackers Gracie heated up for her.

"How did I get here?"

"It seems you walked," Kenneth said. "The police found your car in a ditch just outside Little River. They contacted Wade and started searching for you down there. No one thought to look here. It's fifteen miles from the accident."

As the events of the recent past came back to her, Margie's hands began to tremble so hard she dropped her spoon. Focusing her gaze on Gracie, she moaned, "Oh, Gracie. No! No!"

Gracie motioned to Kenneth to leave them alone. He nodded and left the room.

Keeping her voice low, Gracie asked, "What happened? Can you talk about it?"

Margie's voice sounded strangled. "I was holding the baby. She's not Wade's. Did you know?"

"I knew there was a chance."

Desperate for reassurance, she grabbed Gracie's arm. "You won't tell anyone, will you? Not even Kenneth?"

"I promise. I won't say a word. How much do you remember?"

"I don't know." A sob escaped her, making her reply barely intelligible.

"I killed Max, didn't I?" Her eyes grew large, and her hand covered her mouth. "Oh God! Oh God!"

"Margie, Max died from a blow to his head and there's nobody on this earth who can say any different."

"I know what I did! And now there's this baby! She looks just like him. It's like he's reaching out to me from the grave."

Gracie leaned in closer. "You've got to tell Wade about the rape. It's all he needs to know. I'll back up whatever you say."

"It'll tear him apart."

"You have to. You can't keep this baby. It's unthinkable. I'll help you find a home for her. Do it now. The longer you wait, the harder it will be."

"I can't. Wade has fallen in love with her. He thinks she looks like his mother!"

Just then, the telephone rang. Gracie answered it and spoke for a moment.

"That was Wade. He's on his way."

Margie buried her face in her hands.

When home, she couldn't stop crying. She woke up every morning feeling exhausted. Bathing and dressing used the whole day's energy; combing her hair was out of the question, as her arms felt so heavy she could barely lift them. The smell of food sickened her, so she ate almost nothing.

Wade pleaded with her to tell him what had happened, but she couldn't explain. She said only that she felt she'd fallen to the bottom of a well and couldn't climb out. He phoned Dr. Middleton, who paid a house call.

The doctor perched on a chair beside her bed. "My dear. What's going on with you?"

She said, "I'm so tired. I just want to sleep."

He took her temperature and blood pressure, then checked her from head to toe. "Are you having any pain or cramping? Any burning when you pee?"

"No. Nothing like that."

"I'm not finding anything physical." He took out his prescription pad and scribbled a note, then handed it to her. "Take one of these vitamins each morning. I'm going to tell your mama to make your favorite dishes, and I want you to eat. You need to get your strength back. Every day, I want you outside walking, no matter how hard it seems. Start with fifteen minutes and increase the time every couple of days. Take someone with you until you're stronger. Will you do that?"

She nodded, but wondered if she could, when getting from the bed to the bathroom seemed a monumental task.

He said, "You had a hard time giving birth. Even in the best circumstances, some new mothers go through periods of sadness. It's both physical and psychological. Your hormones are all over the place. Your body is changing. Your life has changed too, and you're going through a period of adjustment. When the baby comes home, caring for her will lift your spirits." He packed his instruments in his bag. "I looked in on her today. She's a cutie. She has quite a head of hair."

Margie tried to smile and said, "Wade says she looks like his mother." She turned her face toward the wall. *If only it were true.*

In the middle of December, Margie and Wade brought Barbara Ann home from the hospital. The house took on a new-baby aura, with everyone's senses on high alert for the slightest flutter of her lashes or her tiniest gurgle. Mama and Irene took turns feeding and diapering. Excited by his new cousin's presence, Billy climbed on the edge of the bassinet to see her, almost tipping it over. Wade carried his daughter on his shoulder when she cried and in the crook of his arm when she slept, gazing into her face as if trying to memorize it. Margie watched him nervously, waiting for the moment he guessed her horrible secret.

The holidays rolled around again. Frank stuffed Billy into his snowsuit, and the excited little boy hopped all the way from the house to the truck. Wade retrieved a saw from the barn, and the men of the family left to find the perfect Christmas tree. Irene rearranged the living room furniture to make space for it, and Margie hauled boxes of decorations down from the attic.

Most of the ornaments dated from Margie's childhood. She picked up one of her favorites, a delicate blown-glass angel, and felt tears welling. She wanted to delight in the holiday preparations denied her for so many years, but this year they brought no joy. She quickly dried her eyes so no one would see her crying again.

Irene patiently replaced each bulb on a long string of lights, searching for the burned-out one that kept the others from illuminating. She said, "Next year we'll have our own tree, though I swear, I don't know where we'll put it."

Irene and Frank had plans to move out soon after the holidays. He'd gotten readmitted to the university's preveterinary program, and they would rent a small silver trailer in university housing beginning January first. It had a banquette that collapsed into a double bed, and a couch that folded down for Billy. The kitchen was minuscule, and behind an accordion door a tiny space housed a toilet and sink. They would shower and do laundry in the community facility.

"I think it's great he's going back to school," Margie said. "Is he looking forward to it?"

"Yes and no," Irene responded. He thinks he's too old. He's worried about money. I'm licensed to do income taxes, but that's another whole issue—me working."

"He seems more settled," Mama said.

"Yeah. But he's still impulsive, and has trouble sleeping. Then there're those terrible nightmares. I wish I could do more to help him. His attitude's changing, though. He's not so negative. I think talking to Dr. Garber helps." She replaced a bad bulb and the whole string lit up.

"Yay!" the women chorused.

Irene looked at the tangle of lights still on the floor. "One down, six to go," she said, putting the repaired string to one side. "Margie, why don't you go see Dr. Garber? It couldn't hurt."

Both Frank and Irene had urged her to make an appointment with Frank's psychiatrist. She resisted the idea, believing she would regain her footing on her own, given enough time. She answered, as always, "I'll think about it."

Snow fell in earnest a few days before Christmas, blanketing the brown and gray countryside with a thick layer of unspoiled brightness. Margie thought of the days in the Philippines when she yearned for snow, to hear the squeak of it under her boots, to feel the sting of a snowball on her frozen fingers, to catch falling flakes on the end of her outstretched tongue. She watched from the kitchen window as Frank, Irene, and bundled-up Billy played tag, leaving trails of footprints in three different sizes.

"Why don't you go out and play?" Mama suggested. "It would do you good."

She had heard that line and its myriad variations hundreds of times as a child, Mama shooing her out of the house into the fresh air. It *would* do her good, she decided. She put on her warmest coat, dug out her snow boots from the back of the closet, and then joined the others, helping build a family of snowmen. Mama supplied carrots for noses and old hats for their icy heads.

Feeling a thud on her back, Margie spun around to see Frank with an armload of snowballs. The fight began, three against one. Margie, Irene, and Billy pelted Frank relentlessly; in the end, he had to beg for mercy.

When Wade returned home from work, they were all still pink-cheeked, bright-eyed, and ravenous for bowls of Mama's hearty beef stew, served with thick slices of bread still warm from the oven.

Margie hadn't played like that in years, and it exhilarated her for a while. Even in that storybook setting, though, surrounded by love and laughter, the black cloud of her depression returned, leaving her feeling detached and alone. She laughed at Frank's silly jokes and watched Irene roll her eyes but wondered if her smile looked as fake as she knew it to be. Ugly thoughts scrolled through her discontented mind. *I don't belong here. I don't deserve to be happy.*

CHAPTER 26

Little River, 1946

Moving Frank, Irene, and Billy into their new home didn't turn out to be much of a job; they had little to take with them, and no space to put even that. After waving good-bye from the front porch, Wade and Margie went back upstairs to begin their transfer to the larger bedroom. Pointing to the longest wall, Wade said, "If we put the bed there, you won't have to climb over me in the morning—not that I mind." So they dragged the four-poster bed there and manhandled the highboy to the space by the door.

Margie paused to evaluate the results. She had enough room left to put her cedar chest under the large window and for a comfortable chair in the corner by the smaller one—a sunny place all her own, a luxury she hadn't enjoyed since 1941.

"While I'm in London—" Wade said, interrupting her reverie.

"I wish you didn't have to go."

"It's only five days. Mama will be here. Will you be okay?"

She didn't know. A constant anxiety kept her jumpy and unsure. She wanted the stability Wade represented close to her. Besides, who would rock Barbara Ann to sleep?

"While I'm gone, you can fix up Barbara Ann's room, you know—curtains and things. Make it girly. She can be up here with us. We'll be like a real family." He lifted Margie's hand to his lips.

Inexplicably, the gesture brought on a wave of nausea. In the bathroom, she sat on the edge of the tub and laid her head on the sink, the porcelain cool against her cheek. When the sick feeling passed, she returned to help Wade make up the bed. Together they transferred their clothes to their new, more spacious closet.

Margie felt best when she kept busy; while Wade traveled to London for work, she sewed a coverlet for the crib in a bunny print and matching cushions for the rocking chair. She replaced sheer panel curtains at the window with ruffled priscillas. While Mama hung pictures, Margie filled a bookcase with her childhood books and Barbara Ann's baby toys.

At the end of the week, they stood back to admire their work. "Wade's going to love this," Margie said.

They finished their chores while listening to soap operas on the radio. Later, Margie fed the baby as Mama made dinner. Ladling leftover stew into bowls, Mama said, "Tonight's my quilting guild. Why don't you come with me?"

"I don't know. The baby . . ."

"She'll be fine. My friends would love to see her."

Barbara Ann kicked her legs as if excited by the prospect.

"You want to go bye-bye, sweetheart?" Mama cooed, kissing her tiny fingers. "Look how bright she is. It's almost like she knows what I'm saying."

Margie sometimes got that feeling too, that Barbara Ann knew what she was thinking, especially when the baby's expressive dark eyes locked onto her face. She hefted Barbara Ann to her shoulder and held her there as she poured glasses of milk and put crackers and bread on the table. "You go and have a good time, Mama. I'd just be a wet blanket."

Mama spread a napkin on her lap. "I don't like leaving you alone. I know you're unhappy. Can't you tell me what's wrong? I don't mean to interfere, but is it you and Wade?"

"No, Wade and I are fine. Dr. Middleton says it's just the baby blues, and it's not unusual. He says I'll perk up soon. I'll try not to be such a sad sack."

Mama said, "I don't know, Margie. It seems more than that to me."

At seven o'clock, Mama left with her arms full of sewing supplies, and the house fell quiet. Margie wheeled the bassinet into the kitchen and placed Barbara Ann into it, hoping she would be content watching her new butterfly mobile, a hand-me-down gift from Billy. Giving it a spin to set it in motion, Margie turned to folding the diapers that had dried on a line in the basement. That task finished, she took the stack to the hall table. Returning to the kitchen, she sterilized baby bottles in boiling water and cooked oatmeal gruel. The pots, pans, spoons, bottles, nipples, caps, funnels, and the cheesecloth used to strain the mush cluttered up Mama's usually neat kitchen.

Barbara Ann began to fuss. Margie changed her diaper and dressed her in a nightgown; she was struck anew by how much she resembled Max at three months. Her plentiful dark hair had not fallen out, as the maternity nurses predicted. To Margie's eyes, the nascent widow's peak and the dimple in her chin grew more prominent daily. Mentally shaking herself, Margie kissed her daughter's perfect foot.

"You look just like your grandma Porter. Your daddy says so, and he ought to know," she said aloud.

She felt her heart rate increase, her attempt at self-persuasion unconvincing. She felt heat rising from her chest to the roots of her hair, and within minutes her body was drenched in a cold sweat. She gave Barbara Ann her pacifier and replaced her in the bassinet, then lit a cigarette to slow the tide of anxiety—the feeling of imminent doom, the racing heart, the ragged breaths—that threatened to break down her carefully cultivated defenses.

Barbara Ann spat out the pacifier and began to cry. Margie jiggled the bassinet, telling the baby, "In a minute! In a minute!" She took a bottle of formula from the refrigerator and placed it in a pan of water to heat up. Barbara Ann's protests and Margie's anxiety level escalated. Without taking the time to test the liquid's temperature on her wrist, she offered the bottle to the fussing child. In her haste, however, she neglected to tighten the cap: the heated milk cascaded onto Barbara Ann's face. She sputtered, then howled, her little arms and legs alternately stiffening and flailing.

In tears herself, Margie picked up the drenched and furious baby and paced the kitchen with Barbara Ann on her shoulder, agitatedly patting her back. "Mommy's sorry! Mommy's sorry! Please don't cry. I can't stand it when you cry."

She stopped long enough to remove the sodden nightgown and wrap Barbara Ann in a blanket. After warming another bottle— and testing the cap—Margie placed the baby on the couch in the living room and propped the bottle on a pillow. Sucking greedily at the nipple, Barbara Ann quieted, but kept her eyes open. Margie took a step sideways. Barbara Ann's condemning gaze followed. Fighting the persistent wave of panic she knew would reduce her to jelly, Margie snatched a diaper off the pile on the hall table and draped it over the infant's face.

Her hands still shaking, she looked around for something to do to calm herself. She opened the newspaper to the crossword puzzle, scrabbling for a pencil in Mama's stationery drawer. Tucked at the back she found a packet of letters in her own handwriting postmarked "Manila, the Philippines, 1941," those golden days of golf in the early morning, pool parties, and dressing for dinner. Curious, she opened the one on top.

Manila, Philippines
December 8, 1941

Dear Mama and Daddy,
It is early morning, my favorite time of day. If I sit real still, I can feel a breeze coming through my shutters, and it's refreshing. I received your last letter and will watch for your Christmas package. I sent one to you too, and it should arrive soon.
Enclosed is a picture taken a week ago at a holiday dinner dance. It was at the Manila Hotel, and as Evelyn said, mucho swanky. Royce wore his dress uniform. Isn't he handsome? We looked spectacular together. I can't wait for you to meet him. He's very special to me.
Evelyn's doing fine. She loves her job at the navy base. The other man is her fiancé, Max Renaldo. Mama, I despise that man. I know it's unchristian to feel that way, but the man is just evil. I think she is making a huge mistake, and I don't know how to tell her.

The picture was still in the envelope, two couples toasting the camera—Royce's arm draped over Margie's shoulder, and Evelyn cuddled up to Max. She stared for a long time at Royce's face and in her mind she heard his voice say, *I love you. I love us.* Her tears flowed freely as she grieved over all the tragedy, so many young lives lost.

Her gaze shifted to Max and his mesmerizing eyes. When she touched the scar on her ear left by his bite, a shudder started in her chin and spread downward until her whole body trembled. With a shaking hand, she grabbed a pencil. "Rot in hell!" she hissed from

between clenched teeth, stabbing at his image until she obliterated it. Hyperventilating, she staggered to the kitchen to find her
cigarettes. Sitting on the floor with her knees tight to her chest,
rocking back and forth and chain-smoking as she sobbed, Margie
was shattered from reliving her worst nightmare. She wondered if
she was losing her mind.

That evening, Wade returned home from his trip a day early.
Letting himself into the eerily silent house, he found Barbara Ann
left alone, asleep on the couch, milk dried around her mouth and
a diaper covering her head. An empty bottle lay on the carpet. He
whipped the diaper off her face, then touched her lips, relief filling
his heart when she suckled. He found another blanket to tuck her
in with, then went to find Margie. He noticed a packet of letters on
the dining room table; on the floor, a pencil lay beside a picture
with one man's face stabbed beyond all recognition.

He located Margie. She was still rocking back and forth on the
kitchen floor, hugging her knees to her chest, her face mottled and
tearstained, her dress damp and smelling sour. Whimpering, she
lit another cigarette from the ash of the one she'd just finished. The
ashtray near her feet overflowed with butts.

He glowered down at her. "What the hell is going on here?"

CHAPTER 27

Little River, 1946–1947

The next morning, Wade scheduled an emergency appointment for Margie and himself with Dr. Garber, the psychiatrist. Adamant about keeping it, he told her he couldn't trust her alone with Barbara Ann anymore. Margie cried, swearing she would never hurt her daughter.

They arrived at the doctor's office just as the previous patient came out, a flat-faced and shuffling old man presenting symptoms of Parkinson's disease. Wade held the door for the man's slim, white-haired wife as she steered him through it. The couple looked vaguely familiar, Margie thought.

Waiting in the reception area, Wade tapped his foot while Margie paced until Dr. Garber opened the office door.

A tall man, he filled the doorway. He wore a well-tailored suit, a starched shirt, and a paisley tie. His plentiful dark hair had grayed gracefully at the temples. He indicated he would like to speak with Margie alone first; Wade could join them later.

His office contained an antique oak partners desk, the requisite couch, a round table with four tub chairs, and two matching wingback chairs upholstered in a heavy floral-print fabric. The doctor directed Margie to the table, which held a file folder with her name on it. While he flipped through her medical history and Dr. Middleton's report, she sat primly with her hands in her lap, surreptitiously picking at her thumbnail. He peered over half-glasses perched on the end of an aquiline nose. "You were a nurse in the Philippines?"

"Yes." The word came out as a squeak. She tried to swallow, but her rhythm was off, so she clamped her teeth shut and tried to look nonchalant.

He handed her a cup of water from a dispenser in the corner. "My nephew, Vince Robb, was stationed at Camp John Hay."

She remembered Dr. Robb. After the Japanese invaded, he and Helen had tried to escape to the mountains with the enemy right behind them. Both had been captured, and Helen eventually was sent to Santo Tomas.

"I met him once," Margie said. "What happened to him?"

"He survived the Bataan Death March. He was shrewd enough to fill his gas mask with C rations and rice and pick up canteens of water off the dead. He spent three years at Cabanatuan working as camp doctor and living on fish heads and rice."

"*Lugao*," Margie said. "The watery fish soup. They made it in huge cauldrons. He told you about it?"

"He's writing a book about his experience. It's gruesome."

"He's okay now? Going on with his life?"

"No one gets off that easy. The human body determined to survive is a hard thing to kill. The mind, though . . . it's more fragile."

"Can't you help him?"

"He's coming along. Progress is slow."

"Do you think you can help me?"

"I can't promise that. I've worked with many veterans, and I'm a World War I veteran myself. One thing I've learned in my practice is whatever progress you make is entirely up to you. I can guide you, but I can't bring you to wholeness unless you're willing to work. You'll have to be truthful. Sometimes it will be painful. You're going to have to face things you may not want to." His well-modulated voice was calming, and he appeared relaxed, sitting back in his chair with his long legs comfortably crossed. He balanced a leather notebook on one knee and held a gold pen in his right hand, poised to jot notes. "This is a safe place to talk, and I want you to say whatever comes to your mind. Start by telling me why you think you're here."

"I—I," she stammered. She swallowed and tried again. "I'm having bouts of intense fear . . . anxiety. I try to control them, but I can't. They started after Barbara Ann was born, and they're getting worse." She blinked rapidly. "My family doctor, Dr. Middleton, says it's postpartum depression."

"And you don't agree?"

She felt herself flush. "I didn't say that. How can you tell?"

"It's not hard if you know what to look for. Little things give a person away—facial expressions, body position, hand signals, even voice inflections. Right now, I know you're very uncomfortable."

She held herself stiffly erect, hands folded, her face blank. "Yes, I am. You said this is a safe place to talk. How safe is it?"

"Our sessions are confidential. Without your consent, I can't release any of your records, not to your husband, parents, or children—not even to law enforcement, nor would I. Before you leave today, I'll discuss my confidentiality policy with your husband. Do you have any other concerns?"

"There's this . . ." She took a sip of water. "I signed a pledge before I was discharged that said I couldn't talk about what happened while I was in the Philippines." She plucked at a hangnail. "And there are other things I don't want anybody to know."

The doctor nodded. "Most of my patients carry the burden of secrets they can't disclose for one reason or another. I'm bound by law and professional ethics to honor your privacy. This pledge"— he strode to the file cabinet and pulled out a document, then handed it to her—"is this it?"

She read the first line: *Restricted. Subject: Publicity in Connection with Liberated Prisoners of War.*

"Yes, this is what I signed. I was sick at the time. The language was hard to understand. The doctor told me to sign it and keep quiet, and I have."

"It's a standard form the military requires all prisoners of war to sign upon release. Technically, it's to safeguard sensitive information. The paragraph pertaining to you is right here, number 2a. It says persons released from liberated areas may relate their experiences, but only after clearance by the public relations officer of the War Department. Then it lists a number of things they cannot talk about under any circumstances, like the names of organizations or persons who helped prisoners escape."

He threw the document on the table. "I understand the intent, but I'm angered by what I hear about how it's presented. The POWs have to sign it at a time when they can barely think beyond their next meal. Most of them hear only one thing—keep quiet or face punishment. So they internalize all the horrible things that happened and it eats away at them." He took a long breath. "My policy is that you tell me as much as you are comfortable revealing, and, in time, I hope to earn your trust. Before I bring Wade in, I'd like to teach you a technique you can practice at home to help you relax."

He asked her to lean back and close her eyes and then led her through a series of mind-clearing and deep-breathing exercises. His voice flowed over her, smooth and slow. "In this meditative state, your mind is more receptive to suggestions . . . Let yourself sink deeper into the relaxation . . . deeper . . . and deeper."

A pleasant feeling came over Margie as she sank into a deep relaxation. Her breathing became slow and regular and her body felt light, like it could float. Her hearing focused on Dr. Garber's voice, which seemed to come from far away. He stated that though anxiety was uncomfortable, she was not in danger. She could control the symptoms by learning to evoke the relaxed state. He repeated the message and it became part of her thinking. *Anxiety is uncomfortable . . .*

She lay there enjoying a feeling of well-being until Dr. Garber's voice intruded to wake her up. She opened her eyes and stretched.

"How do you feel?"

"Wonderful. Serene. Telling myself I'm not in danger will work?"

"Yes, it will. Anxiety is self-fulfilling, and you can counteract it. Later, when you are in the meditative state, I'd like you to think positive thoughts: I'm calm, I'm loved, I'm loving, I feel pleasure. You can pick your own words. Practice this technique at home every day. The relaxed state will get easier to evoke the more often you do it. If you agree, I'd like to see you twice a week for a while. We have a lot to talk about."

While at home, Margie deliberated on how much to tell Dr. Garber. He knew about the ravages of war, and how they could alter a person's mind. Gruesome, he had called his nephew's memoir. He assured her nothing she said would go beyond his office. That he was recommended by Frank, who seemed to be stabilizing, encouraged her. She desperately needed a release from the crippling guilt she felt. And she needed to protect Barbara Ann and regain Wade's trust.

During her next session with Dr. Garber, Margie chattered nervously about her reasons for agreeing to continue therapy and the need for his strict confidence.

He reaffirmed his privacy policy.

She took a deep breath and said, "Before you can help me, there are some things you should know. During the liberation of the prison camp, I was raped by a doctor I knew in Manila."

In a gush, a long moan spewed from her, and tears coursed down her face. Choked with emotion, she could hardly breathe and she doubled over to bury her face in her hands. The convulsing sobs seemed to go on forever.

Dr. Garber offered her tissues, then sat quietly while the episode ran its course. Afterward, she freshened her ravaged face in the washroom. Returning and still shaky, she said, "I'm sorry. That was totally unexpected."

"How do you feel now?"

"Foolish." In truth, she had a terrific headache.

"You shouldn't. It was a visceral response to a horrendous degradation. If it makes you feel better, you should cry, kick, and scream. I bet you haven't, have you?"

"No. What would be the sense of it? I'd be a raving fool. There's more to this sordid story that has brought me to your office a withering mess." She lit a cigarette and laid it out emotionlessly.

"Wade and I were having intercourse while we were in the prison camp, one of our only pleasures. When I discovered I was pregnant, I had no way of knowing the father. After Barbara Ann was born, it was obvious to me that the doctor was her biological father. I haven't told Wade, and I don't intend to."

"Might the doctor come back into the picture?"

"No. He died a few days after the rape. The Japanese shelled Santo Tomas and a wall fell. The medics brought him to my field station with a head injury." She felt such a strong need to wash her hands that she balled them into fists. "I relived that day. How is that possible? One minute I was driving my car and the next the flash of exploding shells blinded me. I steered into a ditch. Everything seemed as real to me as the day it happened. I even felt his blood on my hands."

"There's a medical term for what you're describing—*hypnagogic regression*, the reliving of a traumatic experience. It's common among veterans who saw combat and POWs who suffered years of abuse. Not much is known about it. Right now, it carries a stigma, so it's not often talked about openly."

"I thought I was going crazy."

"You're not going crazy." He rat-a-tapped his pen on the notebook. "You felt his blood on your hands?"

"Yes." She wiped wrinkles from her skirt. "He was injured and covered with blood. Because of what he had done to me, I wanted him to suffer, so I threatened him with a syringe full of morphine. We struggled, and he grabbed my throat. I fell forward onto him, and stabbed the syringe into his neck." She lowered her voice. "I killed my daughter's father, and every day she reminds me of how evil I am. What can anyone possibly do to help me?" She studied Dr. Garber's face, seeing that it showed no horror, rejection, or even surprise.

"I can give you something to hold on to," he said.

Over the next few sessions, Margie couldn't stop talking. She told Dr. Garber in great detail about the deprivations and humiliations suffered by Santo Tomas's internees, and their elation when the American soldiers arrived. For the first time since her encounter with Evelyn on Saipan, she talked about Helen. The memory of her death from starvation and of praying with Gracie at her bedside while church bells pealed gaily brought tears of pain. "I was on my way to get plasma for Helen when . . ." She choked back a sob. "If Max hadn't . . ."

Dr. Garber nudged a box of tissues forward and waited for her to regain her composure. He said, "Your life turned into a nightmare in the worst sense of the word. Listen to me carefully now: this is vital for you to understand. When you live in a nightmare, you react as if in a nightmare. I've seen it a hundred times—soldiers broken down, then beating themselves up later over things that happened in the heat of battle. Frames of reference change. Horrors occur. What you did can't be undone, but I can help you understand why it happened, and change your reaction to the memory of it. You are guilt-ridden and anxious, and, believe it or not, that's a good sign."

Margie startled. "What I'm feeling is good?"

"Yes. I'd be far more disturbed if you showed no reaction at all. We can work with it. At home, when you are relaxing, I'd like you to reflect on this statement: *An abnormal reaction to an abnormal situation is normal behavior.* Think about what it means and how it applies to you."

Margie repeated the statement in her head: *An abnormal reaction to an abnormal situation is normal behavior.* She didn't comprehend it.

"You've been making good progress," the doctor said. "Many of my patients take months to get to where you are after only a few weeks."

When at home, she didn't feel like she had made any progress at all. The relief she hoped would come by confessing the rape and Max's murder didn't materialize. She couldn't evoke the relaxed state she'd experienced in the doctor's office, and anxiety still overwhelmed her, sending her scurrying to the bedroom with her cigarettes until the worst of the episode passed. She obsessed about Abe, Royce, and Helen, feeling an overwhelming desire to connect with them; because she couldn't, guilt brought on crying jags. One afternoon, while Barbara Ann napped, she crept up the stairs to the attic to look for her army duffel bag, which she found tucked under the eaves.

Unfastening the hook from the grommets released smells that brought back memories of the months on Bataan, and the thousands of injured and dying soldiers lying under the trees. *Was it a bad dream?* She took out a pile of wrinkled uniforms, unearthing a packet of letters and some snapshots Evelyn took during those early, untroubled weeks in Manila. She thumbed through the pictures. *We had some good times.*

A small box contained a few pieces of jewelry. Abe's silver pilot's ring had tarnished; she polished the blue stone thoughtfully on the sleeve of her shirt. *What if . . . ?* She put the ring down gently, those dreams dashed long ago.

She clipped on the string of pearls Royce had given her and admired herself in a dusty mirror. She tried to bring back the sound of his voice, the feel of his hands on her skin. *You're more beautiful than I ever dreamed possible.*

Wade came into the attic. Involved in her memories, she jumped at his entry.

He surveyed the contents of the duffel strewn on the floor. "What's all this?"

"I'm sorting through it. Some of these things shouldn't be in the attic. Like this." She held up the mahogany ring he'd carved for her while a prisoner of war.

"You kept it?"

"Of course I did. It's a work of art." She slipped it on her ring finger, wondering what to do with it. She loved the source, but not the association.

She held up a fountain pen and read the inscription aloud: "*To Helen, Happy Birthday. Love, Mabel.* We should have sent this back to Mabel months ago. Do you think it's too late?"

Worry lines creased Wade's forehead. "Are you sure you should be doing this?"

"I'll be okay." She opened the four small leather cases holding her medals: the Philippine Defense Medal for protecting the islands against the Japanese; the Presidential Unit Citation for extraordinary heroism against an armed enemy; the American Pacific Campaign Medal with a Foreign Service clasp; and the Bronze Star with two oak-leaf clusters. She picked up the latter, the fourth-highest combat medal awarded by the military, and read the inscription on the back—*Heroic or Meritorious Achievement, Marjorie Olivia Bauer.*

Looking over her shoulder, Wade said, "We should have these mounted and framed."

"No, I was no hero."

She stuffed the uniforms into the now-empty duffel and gave it to him. "You can throw these out."

"The duffel too?"

"Yes. It smells moldy, like a dirty tent."

She found a pretty hatbox, its surface printed with spring flowers. Removing the hat, she replaced it with her medals, letters, and mementos of her friends, then carried it to her bedroom, where she added the stacks of letters she and Mama had saved.

Wade held out a large envelope.

"What's this?" she asked.

"Pictures of the war Kodak sent me. Do you want to see them?"

"Of the war? Not yet. Maybe some other day."

He lifted the lid of the hatbox and dropped them inside.

Searching through her drawer, she found a blue ribbon to tie the hatbox shut, then put it in the cedar chest and closed the lid, feeling like she had completed an important task.

Her sense of accomplishment was short-lived, however. That night, Dr. Garber appeared in her dream, saying, "You may have to face some things you don't want to." She woke up in a sweat.

Margie got out of bed quietly and padded downstairs. In the kitchen, she poured a glass of wine and sat in the dark, contemplating what the psychiatrist had told her: *An abnormal reaction to an abnormal situation is normal behavior.* She mulled over the years of hunger and fear, the surreal aura of the liberation, the physical pain of the rape, and its mental devastation—*when you live in a nightmare, you react as if in a nightmare.*

She envisioned Max covered with blood and begging for mercy, and Reverend Markel's sermons based on a verse from the Gospel of Matthew came to mind. *But I say unto you, Love your enemies, bless them that curse you, do good to them that hate you, and pray for them which despitefully use you, and persecute you.*

Muddled in mind and drained of spirit, she struggled to reconcile her rational mind with her religious conscience. She prayed, *Please, Lord, accept my love, and forgive my sins. Help me understand what has happened to me and lead me to the path to become whole again.*

One afternoon, Mama thumbed through *Good Housekeeping* magazine, concentrating on appliance advertisements. Her oven hadn't heated evenly for several months. "Have you seen this, Margie? The new Frigidaire stove has a burner that recesses for slow-cooking soups and stews. What will they think of next?"

Margie looked at the ad. "It's electric. I didn't think you liked electric stoves."

"I wouldn't know. I've never cooked on one." She looked up at the ceiling. "I think I hear Barbara Ann."

Margie climbed the stairs to the nursery, where Barbara Ann lay on her back in the crib, playing with her toes. Margie cooed, "How long have you been awake? It's past your lunchtime. You must be hungry." She changed the baby's diaper while Barbara

Ann's little legs kicked wildly, making an unpleasant job extra difficult.

Barbara Ann seldom cried anymore. Margie often found her awake in her crib, entertaining herself for long stretches with her toys or her toes. "She's a different sort of child," Mama said. Where Margie had been a happy baby, and Frank stubborn and impatient, Barbara Ann displayed a serious temperament.

Margie ran a finger under the baby's double chin. "Can you smile for me? Come on, you can do it." *Or not,* she thought. As Barbara Ann stared unblinkingly at her, Margie had to look away.

Dr. Garber continued to reinforce the message that a person beaten down by hunger and fear did not function normally, and that that, in itself, was normal behavior.

"I understand, but all my life I've been taught to love my enemies."

"It's a tall order. We mortals are a fallible bunch even in the best of times. God gave us prayer. Have you prayed for forgiveness?"

"Every night."

"Then find it in your heart to forgive your weakened self . . . as you would a burdened friend."

Margie nodded, seeing a glimmer of light.

"Today, if you don't mind, let's reflect on your years in the Philippines. Did anything good come from it?"

"I guess, in retrospect, I'm not totally sorry for the experience. I served my country proudly. I helped hundreds of soldiers when they needed it, lying cut up and shot up in the jungle and in those horrible tunnels. I don't think I did anything to deserve those medals they awarded me, just my duty and what I had to do to survive. Some good things did come from it. I met some brave, selfless people, like Helen. She was at Camp John Hay. Did your nephew mention her? Helen Doyle? She hated it there. She wanted to go to Europe so she could serve closer to the front. And Gracie. She got shot in the shoulder when we evacuated to Corregidor from Bataan. They gave her two chances to leave, but she wouldn't go. She said she was in for the duration. There were others, lots of others—like Royce, a doctor I fell in love with, and Wade."

She went to the office window and watched people coming and going on the street for a while. "Truthfully, I mostly think about being so hungry my stomach felt like it was eating itself. I try to push it out of my mind, but it always comes back."

"Don't fight it," Dr. Garber said. "It's important you not bury your sufferings. And you did suffer, terribly, but now it's as much a part of your history as your accomplishments. Turning misfortune into triumph is a way to conquer it."

"I can't begin to imagine how I would do that."

"It's a problem you'll have to solve at some point. You're a young woman with years and years still ahead of you. I want you to think about what you'd like to do with your life. What would bring meaning to it? When contemplating that, consider your sufferings as well as your accomplishments. Both are a part of who you are and what you have to offer."

During the summer of 1947, Margie and Mama harvested bushels of sweet corn, cucumbers, beans, beets, squash, peas, and cantaloupe. Sweet potatoes and the second crop of broccoli and cabbage had yet to mature. They canned and preserved everything they could, filling the pantry with mason jars of tomatoes, peaches, and applesauce. The cellar began to overflow with bags and baskets of produce.

Margie had been seeing Dr. Garber for over a year, her appointments only once a month now. She felt his message had become repetitive, and against Wade's advice, she decided to discontinue therapy.

She arrived at the psychiatrist's office feeling jumpy, wishing she'd taken the coward's way out and just telephoned. He didn't greet her immediately, as he usually did. She waited in a huff, pacing the reception area while checking her watch—thirty minutes, sixty minutes. Just as she'd made up her mind to leave, the office door opened. Out stepped the elderly woman she had seen on her first visit, the one with the shaky husband. Dr. Garber helped the woman into a waiting cab and paid the driver.

Striding back into the office, he said, "Come in, Margie. I'm sorry to have kept you waiting. Mrs. Bender's husband died last night. A lovely couple. They were together for sixty-two years."

She settled in the easy chair, feeling contrite. "I'm sorry. What's going to happen to her?"

"She has a son in town and many friends. Mr. Bender owned the drugstore on Main Street years ago. You may remember him."

"Mr. Bender. Of course I do. He gave me lollipops when I was a kid."

Dr. Garber opened her file. "Now, how about you?"

She told him about wanting to discontinue therapy—the feelings of anxiety and depression rare now, and she was able to calm herself with the techniques he had taught her. She thanked him for helping to put the horrors of her past into perspective. She was no longer burdened with guilt.

Tenting his fingers, he sat back in his chair. "You've come a long way, Margie, but you still carry around a lot of tension. In itself, it is not a bad thing, if directed toward a worthy objective. Have you given that any more thought?"

"I don't have time to do anything more. I work part-time at the Red Cross and have a large garden that always needs tending. Barbara Ann keeps me busy too."

"Of course she does. How old is she now?"

"She's almost two."

"Lots of hugs and raspberries on her tummy?"

"She doesn't go without."

"From you?"

Margie nervously fidgeted with the clasp on her purse. He was close to the truth that she avoided the daily care of her daughter. Just recently her mother had sat her down for a talk. "The child is craving your love, but you turn your head, or your back, or you push her aside. Don't you see the hurt in her eyes? Do you even know you're doing it? Why can't you embrace her?" Mama had been in tears.

She said to Dr. Garber, "I cuddle Barbara Ann on my lap when she's tired. She loves to be read to, so that's what I do." She felt her eyes blink rapidly.

"These are the years to build strong bonds," he said. "As she grows older, especially when she enters her teen years, she may take on characteristics of her father. It could be a crisis time for both of you. It's better to head it off by preparing for it."

Margie opened her purse to fish out her keys and sunglasses. Things at home had stabilized. Physically healthy and precociously curious, Barbara Ann was a happy child, according to Mama and Wade, who both doted on her. And Margie had promised her mother she would be warmer and more loving to her daughter. She said, "We are okay for now, and I don't foresee any problems."

He shut her file. "Come in and chat with me next year at this time. Will you do that?"

She nodded but didn't commit.

"What are your plans for the future?"

She told him how busy she was with the garden's harvest.

"And beyond that?"

She hadn't really thought about her future, and she left his office feeling distraught. Dr. Garber's therapy had taught her how to calm her anxiety and rationalize her tremendous guilt, but not how to stop the vivid memories of Barbara Ann's conception and its evil aftermath. *Was there no help for her?* Sitting in her car, she wept inconsolably.

CHAPTER 28

Little River, 1947–1948

Margie couldn't get Mrs. Bender off her mind. In the weekly newspaper, she read her husband's obituary: Richard, pharmacist, married to Marla for sixty-two years; a son, Michael; a daughter, Marcy, died in infancy; and a grandson, John, killed in Europe. Margie looked up the address in the telephone directory, then waited a couple weeks before driving across town to visit.

The house sat back from the road, a huge maple tree dominating the front yard. A stone path edged with a flurry of fall flowers led to the porch, where a two-person swing hung invitingly at one end. Margie lifted Barbara Ann from the car seat and automatically removed the thumb from her mouth: outraged, she stiffened and screamed. Margie sighed, not wanting a scene in Mrs. Bender's front yard.

Entranced by the new surroundings, Barbara Ann quieted down after a second. With the toddler on one hip and a bag of fresh produce on the other, Margie kicked the wooden screen door with the toe of her shoe, hoping it sounded like a knock. She watched the elderly lady slowly approach across her living room. Through the screen, she called, "Mrs. Bender. I'm Marjorie Porter. I saw your husband's obituary in the paper. I remember him from when I was a child. I just wanted to say I'm sorry for your loss, and I brought you some strawberry preserves and vegetables from my garden."

Mrs. Bender's face creased into a smile. She opened the door and stood back so Margie could enter. "My dear, how kind of you. What a sweet baby. What's her name?"

"Barbara Ann."

"That's a pretty name. Here, let me help you." She took the bag of produce, and Margie followed her to the kitchen. "This looks wonderful! And there's so much here! I hope you don't mind if I share with my neighbor. She's struggling a bit."

"I don't mind. I can bring more, if she could use it."

"Could you? She'd be so appreciative. She's just a girl herself, with two children. She lost her job at the Ford plant, and her husband up and left her. They ought to hang him by his toes. I do what I can, but I know some nights those young ones go to bed hungry. Come in and sit down." She gestured toward the living room. The house was small and the furniture well worn but immaculate. Family pictures crowded the mantel and many of the occasional tables.

"I can't stay," Margie demurred.

"Please do. I get tired of talking to myself. I'm afraid I'm not very good company."

Margie found just the opposite to be true, and the two women spent a delightful hour chatting. Despite her recent loss, Mrs. Bender's upbeat personality shone through. She had known Richard for as long as she could remember, she told Margie—their mothers had been best friends. A kind and good husband, he had financed the start-up of her resale shop after their son went off to elementary school. She closed the shop ten years ago; now with Richard gone, she found time hanging heavily on her hands.

"You ran Marla's Resale on Second and Lenox?" Margie asked.

"Yes. You know it?"

"I bought my first purse there, black patent leather with a gold chain. I still have it. I loved your shop. My mother donated all my outgrown dresses."

"We certainly appreciated our donors. Marla's proceeds helped support our church's soup kitchen. We fed hundreds of families during the Great Depression. Raising my son and running that shop—those were happy, busy days."

Mrs. Bender's reaching out to help her neighbor, even in her own time of sorrow, touched Margie's heart. Thoughts went to the well-stocked pantry on North Bensch Road, and the still-overflowing garden. She recalled her own pain from hunger and the distress of deprivation. The following morning, she packed a box with vegetables and a jar of peach preserves and left it on the doorstep of Mrs. Bender's young neighbor.

When her position at the Red Cross was eliminated, Margie found herself at loose ends. She didn't enjoy spending long days at home but had no desire to look for work in her profession. Since the end of the war, too many former military nurses vied for too few civilian positions. Her first love, fashion design, was out of reach to women with husbands and children. She started doing alterations and simple sewing for the ladies in Little River to fill the hours. Although jobs poured in, she found most of them tedious and unfulfilling.

One September Saturday, she was feeling especially blue. Trying to help, Wade said, "It might be a good time to have another baby."

She dismissed that idea right away. "No. I'm not ready for that."

"How about a new house then?" He handed her a colorful brochure. "It's a new community going up just this side of Ann Arbor. They have model homes we can go through." He bent to pick up Barbara Ann, who clung to his pant leg. "Want to go for a ride, sweetheart?"

So they all piled into their new car, Wade driving and Margie holding Barbara Ann on her lap, leaving Little River to head toward Ann Arbor. Wade turned right at a billboard that read "Welcome to Shady Acres, the Community of the Future."

Hundreds of houses stood in various stages of completion. Trucks delivering lumber, roofing, windows, Bendix washing machines, and General Electric kitchen appliances congested freshly paved streets. The sound of hammering filled the air, and workmen bustled all over the site. Not a single tree had been left standing.

"Shady Acres?" Margie scoffed. "Is that a joke?"

Inside the sales office, a salesman pointed to a large wall map depicting the community's layout: three thousand homes on forty-by-eighty-foot lots that lined winding streets. Glancing at Barbara Ann, he added that the master plan included several playgrounds for the kiddies, and sidewalks that would lead to the development's own school. The community, he assured them, had been planned right down to the last brick, board, tree, and flower garden.

Countless families milled through the houses. Although identical in size, the models differed in exterior color and roofline configuration. The cozy, if similar, floor plans featured a living room, two bedrooms, a bathroom, and a large, fully equipped kitchen—in all, eight hundred square feet of privacy and comfort. Lucky buyers could own a piece of Shady Acres for ninety dollars down and fifty-eight dollars per month.

They were selling like hotcakes.

Standing on the front porch of one of the models and looking out at the view, Wade asked, "What do you think?"

"They're cute enough, but it will feel like living in an anthill."

"Barbara Ann would have playmates. She could walk to school."

Margie nodded noncommittally.

On the way home, she laid the sleeping baby on the seat and covered her with a sweater. Turning to Wade, she said, "Would you consider staying where we are?"

"I thought you wanted something new."

"I'm having second thoughts about leaving Mama. The house is too big for her to manage all alone. I doubt if she would ever move or give up the land."

"The place is run-down, Margie. It needs a lot of work—new windows and a roof, for starters. And I saw a crack in the foundation when I was mowing the grass last weekend."

"If Mama agrees, we could sell off a few back acres and use the money to fix up the house. I'd like to convert the porch off her bedroom to a sitting room with her own bathroom, so she could have some privacy."

"Have you talked to her already?"

"No, but I've been thinking about it."

She *had* been thinking about it because she wanted—no, needed—her mother's help with Barbara Ann. No one suspected the anguish the child evoked when a certain expression crossed her face, or the uncomfortable chill Margie felt when their eyes met and held. She learned things went better if she kept a distance between them, a decision that brought with it sadness and guilt. She vowed to herself to carry the burden silently. That was a sort of love. Wasn't it?

Autumn edged toward winter, the days growing shorter. Most of the garden had died off, but the cool-weather crops—cabbages, spinach, Swiss chard, and a large patch of pumpkins—still produced.

Margie continued to deliver boxes of food to Mrs. Bender's neighbor, plus a few other families the elderly lady told her were struggling because of abandonment, joblessness, or illness.

Some parishioners at Margie's church heard about her mission through the grapevine and asked to be included: they too had more food growing or preserved than they could use. Reverend Markel got into the act, supplying names of even more families in need. When the supply of fresh food dwindled with the arrival of killing frosts, the pastor appealed to the congregation to donate what they could from their cellars and pantries. One of the prayer groups baked bread to help fill Margie's boxes. She began soliciting at grocery stores and restaurants for food past its prime.

By the time spring rolled around again, she had commandeered a storage room in the church basement for supplies and assembled a dedicated cadre of volunteers, who inventoried the donated food and regularly delivered boxes to a dozen area families. As her enterprise continued to grow, Margie found she needed a refrigerator, but she didn't have the money to buy one. She talked to Reverend Markel about it, and he suggested she apply for grant money.

One evening, she sat at the kitchen table, swearing under her breath, papers strewn in front of her.

Wade laughed to see her when he came in from work. "It can't be that bad," he teased.

She waggled her hands in frustration. "I think I'm in over my head. Reverend Markel suggested I apply for grants, and he gave me this list of organizations and what I need to submit to qualify for funds. Look at this! They say I have to have a board of directors and a mission statement. What's that?"

"Just a sentence stating your purpose. Let me see."

Together they read through the requirements for obtaining money from charities, churches, businesses, and the government. "They're all similar," Wade pointed out. "All you need is a cover letter, the application, and a list of executives. Who do you want on your board of directors?"

"What do they do?"

"It's an oversight group. They help you make executive decisions."

"Executive? Do I need to wear a suit?"

"You'd look cute in a suit."

"I don't see that *looking cute* is a requirement for anything here."

"You're not being serious. Who do you want on your board?"

As Margie worked step-by-step through the application process, her organization got a name: Abundant Harvest Food Pantry. A board of directors: Reverend Markel, Mrs. Bender, and Tom Lewis, a new attorney in town. A president: her. A budget director: also her. And a staff of volunteers. She and the board developed a mission statement: "To provide food to needy families who are dealing with difficult life circumstances." She conducted a needs assessment and set program goals and objectives. She completed all the groundwork by late May, then wrote cover letters and executive summaries and filled out a dozen grant applications. By the first of June, she hauled a dozen packages to the post office to mail. All summer long, rejection letters dribbled back, thanking her for her submission, but they received many applications and, though her project was noble and well designed, it couldn't be funded at the present time. Please try again next year.

Margie resisted the urge to tear them up and filed them instead.

Too busy to stew over the rejections, Margie lost herself in tending to the garden and administering her growing food pantry. Wade started updating the kitchen, causing Mama to fret—she had peaches to can, and she didn't like her new electric stove. Barbara

Ann grew an inch a month, it seemed, looking more and more like a little girl than a baby. At age three, she drew many admiring comments about her dark hair and skin that tanned beautifully. She pointed to words in her books, trying to read, and could even pick out tunes on the piano. Delighted by her budding musical talent, Wade bought her a violin and spent many patient hours teaching her to play it.

One morning in late August, two letters addressed to Margie came in the mail. More rejections, she believed, so she put them aside. She forgot about them until after dinner, when she found them on the hall table. Tired and feeling a little blue, she opened the one from the Circle of Women's Charities, which contained a check large enough to purchase a refrigerator for the food pantry. Wearing a broad grin, she trotted into the living room, waving the check in the air before passing it around for Wade and Mama to see. When she opened the second envelope, she couldn't believe what she saw. The congregation of the Ann Arbor Methodist Church had selected Abundant Harvest Food Pantry as their preferred charity project. They would provide a monthly stipend to cover operating costs, renewable on a yearly basis. Wade picked up Barbara Ann and the four of them danced in a circle, Margie and Mama laughing, Wade whooping, and Barbara Ann clapping her hands.

Thoughts of how to allocate the new revenue kept Margie awake that night. Storage and transportation of food had the potential to become costly, and she would need help with record keeping as the pantry added new clients. Wade had suggested she join Little River's chamber of commerce for community contact and support.

Margie woke up the next morning feeling woozy and attributed it to her restless night, but when early-morning nausea continued through the week, she knew it was more than temporary jitters.

Standing over the sink with a cold washcloth on her face, trying to force back a bilious wave, she cursed herself for being careless for having misplaced her diaphragm. How does anyone in their right mind lose a diaphragm? She had found it in the wash the following Monday, but by then, too late.

She laid her head on the coolness of the porcelain sink.

Wade found her like that. "Are you sick, Margie?"

"I think I may be pregnant."

He responded at first with a grin, but then a frown acknowledging her immediate discomfort. "Are you okay with it?"

"Right now's not a good time to ask." She burped. "Sorry."

"It will be different this time. You're healthy going into it. There's a doctor in Ann Arbor the women at the *Tribune* go to. I can find out his name if you want. He's a specialist, an obstetrician. I think you should see him just to be on the safe side."

Margie groaned. Even the thought of doctor visits, embarrassing exams, months of discomfort, worry, and knowing there was no turning back brought another wave of nausea. She hung her head over the toilet. When the wave passed, she said, "How am I going to run the food—" The mention of food turned her stomach over again.

"Oh God," she sighed.

The next two months were the worst of it. She sailed through the rest of her pregnancy with nary a twinge of discomfort. Gary was born fat and happy, and Barbara Ann adopted him as her own live baby doll.

CHAPTER 29

Little River, 1960

Margie combed her short hair with her fingers, letting it curl naturally around her face. She'd given up any hope of wearing the ratted and smoothed styles other women wore. Looking closely in the mirror, she identified two gray hairs and plucked them out. She'd seen tiny wrinkles at the corners of her eyes too, but there was nothing she could do except pretend they gave her an air of sophistication.

She dressed in a gray suit and ivory blouse, adding a string of pearls and matching earrings. This morning she had an appointment with the school board to discuss their annual food drive to support Abundant Harvest Food Pantry. Much had changed since she'd started the food pantry ten years ago. It had moved from the church basement to a building of its own, and though they still delivered food to homebound clients, most customers came to the pantry to pick out what they needed. She had a paid staff of five and a large workforce of volunteers. Money was always critical, and she spent much of her time acquiring it through writing grants and organizing community fund-raisers.

Wade searched the top of the dresser. "Margie? Have you seen my watch? I put it right here last night."

Margie helped him search. Seeing it peeking out from under his shirtsleeve, she said, "Have you checked your wrist?"

"Am I losing my mind?"

"You've just got too many things going on. We both do."

Gary poked his head in the bedroom door. "Mom, have you seen my shoes?"

"Have you checked your feet?" Margie said, and she and Wade laughed. Gary walked away shaking his head.

"I guess that wasn't fair," Margie said, still snickering.

Life had turned hectic with the growth of the food pantry and Wade's increasing responsibility at the *Tribune*. He often worked late, and to wind down, he played his guitar and sang at the clubs around Ann Arbor. He had a large following and had even cut a few records that got airtime on the local radio stations. It was always a pleasant surprise to suddenly hear his voice coming over the air.

Dressed and groomed for another day, they went downstairs to the kitchen, where Mama was serving Barbara and Gary a breakfast of oatmeal and sliced strawberries.

"You found your shoes?" she asked Gary.

"Yeah," he said, his head hanging low over his breakfast bowl.

"Sit up straight," she instructed as she poked his back. He was a good-sized kid for ten. Strong and coordinated, he excelled in gym class and recess. Now, Margie thought, if he would only get serious about math and history.

"Barbara Ann," Margie said, about to congratulate her daughter, again, on her performance last night at the high school's talent contest. She'd won first place, playing the guitar and singing "Frankie and Johnny" in her husky voice. It was a joy to watch as she bantered with the audience and stomped her feet for rhythm like Wade did, but midperformance she'd added a riff that had brought the audience to its feet.

Wade had gushed as they got ready for bed. "I had no idea she could do that. The intricacy, the timing—it was pure genius."

There were times Margie noticed Wade looking at his daughter as if wondering where this beautiful genius had come from. That look on his face always brought her unease, and she wondered if he suspected anything. On the occasions of Wade's doubt, Margie made a point to reinforce his paternity. "She inherited your talents, Wade."

Barbara Ann gulped the last of her milk and slung her bulging book bag over her shoulder. As she left, she said, "Don't call me Barbara Ann. I'm not a baby. I'll answer to Barb."

Margie dropped the idea of congratulating her daughter, thinking, *barb, how appropriate.*

Wade scowled. "There's no call for that. Apologize to your mother!"

"Sorry," Barb said with a smirk, and let the door slam behind her.

Margie had time for a second cup of coffee, and with the family gone, she and Mama shared a few minutes together.

Margie said, "What's happening to my little girl?" She'd seen Barbara's change in attitude coming on this past year: school, once a joy, was now a bore; the rolling eyes and sighs; the longer hours in her room playing the radio.

"Fourteen-year-olds are all attitude. You were a bit of a snip yourself at that age."

Payback, Margie thought—but no, with her genetic makeup Barbara's bad attitude had the potential to be more than that. As Dr. Garber had predicted, she was taking on Max's mannerisms and the haughty, better-than-thou attitude that Margie had despised. Physically too, she was growing into his image, her body lithe, and the streak of white in the front lock of hair beginning to show.

Margie finished her coffee and put her cup in the sink, her mind on this afternoon's work. The tomato and pepper seedlings she had started several weeks ago in the greenhouse were ready to be transplanted. "You look pale this morning, Mama. Why don't you leave the planting to me? I'll be home around noon."

Margie was worried about her mother. Working in the garden was becoming more difficult, with her taking frequent breaks to "catch her breath," as she would say.

"I'll be fine. I'm just a little tired. I didn't sleep well last night. I had a dream about your dad."

"Oh? What was it about?"

"I don't even remember. I just felt his presence."

"Should I call Dr. Middleton, Mama? It's been a while since you've had a checkup."

"Heaven's no. You better get going or you'll be late to your meeting."

Margie hugged her mother and decided she would make an appointment regardless of her mother's objection.

Margie didn't care much for sitting in meetings or for going over financial reports, but both were a necessary part of her life now. She spent the morning listening to others' business discussions before she got her ten-minute allotted time on the agenda. Driving home, her mind drifted to her mother's dream of her dad. Sometimes she dreamed about him too: sitting in his chair by the fireplace, wearing the blue cable-knit sweater Mama had knitted, reading Wild West fiction—Zane Grey a favorite author—his glasses perched on the end of his nose, his pipe smoldering in the ashtray. One time a dream seemed so real she woke up with her eyes stinging from tobacco smoke.

Mama wasn't in the house when Margie arrived home. She was probably in the garden, which wasn't unusual. Margie changed into an old pair of slacks, a long-sleeved shirt, and a ratty cardigan sweater. She ate a bologna sandwich and drank a glass of milk before going outside. She slipped on her garden boots kept on the back porch and grabbed her trowel and gloves. She didn't see her mother anywhere. She checked the greenhouse and the shed, but both were empty. She called, "Mama! Are you out here?" There was no response. The only obstructed view was the rows of blackberry bushes that had just begun to show signs of new growth. She walked out there, expecting to see her mother pruning dead vines.

The third row back, she found Mama sprawled on the ground, her mouth slack, eyes open, and her hand gripping the front of her dress. Margie fell to her knees and gently jiggled her shoulder. "Mama! Mama!" Feeling her mother already cold, she laid her head on her mother's silent chest and sobbed.

The first wave of tears past, she closed her mother's eyes and arranged her hair softly around her face before covering her snugly with her sweater, tucking it under her chin and firmly around her arms. *I shouldn't have left her alone.* Stumbling to the house, she called Wade and told him to pick up the children from school. After she called the ambulance, she hurried back to the field to stay with her mother until it arrived and took her away.

Family and friends gathered to lay Mama to rest next to Dad. Standing at the graveside, the coffin hovering over that deep hole in the ground, Margie remembered her mother's dream of Dad being beside her, and she drew comfort from it. *Is that why she told me?*

Sad and drained, the family returned to the house that felt too big, and the next several days were lost in a blur of mourning. But then, Wade and Margie returned to work, and Barbara and Gary went back to school. Gary's baseball team played a game, and the family attended to cheer the team on—as usual. They gradually absorbed the chores Mama had just assumed to be hers. However, it was weeks before Margie could water the flowers her mother had planted or wear a sweater she had knit without a tear coming to her eye. Time passed and her intense sadness began to dim.

However, Barbara wasn't healing. Instead she became withdrawn, spending long hours in her room. If allowed, she'd sleep all day, then roam the house at night. She avoided her friends and declined to participate in family activities. She lost interest in school and her grades dropped, and when Wade questioned her about it, she said her grades wouldn't matter anyway. Margie noticed on some days the clothes she wore were dirty and her hair needed washing.

Wade tried to interest Barbara in her music again and invited her to play with him at the Delta Ray. Margie hoped it would be a breakthrough, but Barbara declined the invitation; instead she stayed in her room and played sad Patsy Cline songs over and over on her record player.

Margie worried about Barbara's sadness, remembering herself when she was depressed and not having the will to pull out of it. "She needs to open up to someone," she said to Wade. "I'd like to call Dr. Garber and see if he'd talk to her."

Wade agreed, and Margie called his office, but the doctor was out of town until the end of June.

The month of July arrived blazingly hot and humid. Inside, even with circulating fans blowing on high, the sodden air barely moved. A fly buzzed irritatingly around Margie's face while she prepared a dinner of roast beef with fresh-picked broccoli and cauliflower, the cooking of vegetables giving the house a musty smell. From outside came the grinding sounds of heavy trucks paving the road. Dirt whirled up and the air reeked of fuel.

Wade and Gary had left a couple hours earlier to attend first a baseball tournament at the park and then a carnival the town brought in for Fourth of July celebrations. Barbara wasn't interested in the carnival, instead saying she'd rather go for a walk, and Margie saw her heading toward the pond at the back of their property, where she liked to sit under a tree and read.

Margie had detected an improvement in Barbara's demeanor these past few weeks. Though Barbara still spent many hours in her room, Margie could hear her playing her guitar, and sometimes she came out and chatted awhile with whomever was around. She was growing this summer and stood taller than Margie now.

The teakettle began to whistle and it didn't stop even after Margie took it off the burner. The shrill noise hurt her ears, and a fly wouldn't stay away from her face. A drop of sweat rolled into her eye, causing it to burn, and another dripped down her cheek and she brushed it away with the back of her hand. She felt woozy in the oppressive heat and sour smell of the kitchen.

She heard a crack, a buzz, and several loud pops. She jumped with a start, all her senses acute, her breathing short and heart thumping. She whirled around and saw a dark figure standing in the kitchen door, thin and pale with a white lock of hair falling over his forehead. Max Renaldo! Her throat constricted and her vision dimmed. "Get out of here! Get out! Get out!" She grabbed an iron skillet and leaped toward the figure, swinging it with all her might, chasing Barbara off the stoop. The child ran into the barn.

When Wade returned, he found smoke rolling from the kitchen, the roast beef and vegetables burned to a crisp on the stove, and Barbara wide-eyed and trembling in the barn, hiding behind the tractor.

Margie lay curled, fetal, in her bed, glassy-eyed and wondering what she would have done with that iron skillet had she caught her daughter.

Barbara sequestered herself in her room, refusing to come out even for meals.

Margie, teary and shaky, talked to her through the door: "I'm sorry, Barbara. You startled me. The light was behind you. When I saw you at the door, I couldn't tell it was you. I thought you were an intruder. I'm sorry. Please come down to dinner."

Wade tried to coax her out. "There's an open mic at the club tonight. Come with me. We'll play a few duets."

She said she didn't feel like going.

She let Gary into her room with a plate of food. He reported back that Barbara said she didn't want to live at home anymore. She hated it here without her grandma, and now she didn't feel safe.

Margie called Dr. Garber's office and felt relieved that he could see her the next day. She didn't tell Wade about the appointment. She'd stuck to her story about the intruder, but she wanted to tell Dr. Garber the truth.

She arrived at his office worried that he would admonish her for not taking his advice. Years ago he had suggested she continue with counseling to head off a crisis in Barbara's teen years. His office looked a little worn, and his hair had gone to gray, but his easygoing manner was the same. Her file lay open on his desk.

He said he'd been following her children's school careers as they were reported in the local newspaper: Barbara an honor student and accomplished musician, and Gary a budding sports star. He asked about Wade and the Abundant Harvest Food Pantry. He offered his condolence for her mother's recent death. The catching up aside, he said, "Tell me what brings you in today."

"It's my daughter. Like you predicted years ago, she has grown into the image of Max Renaldo. She's even taken on some of his mannerisms." She told him the latest incident, her eyes batting and mouth going dry—saying it out loud magnified the horror of it. "I'm not so sure I wouldn't have hit her with that iron skillet."

"Did you feel you relived the moment you killed Max?"

"No! Oh God, I hope not. But the rage I felt seeing him standing at my door!" She closed her eyes and felt a shiver go down her back. "Barbara's been depressed about her grandmother's death. Now she's scared of me. We've never had a warm relationship, and I'm afraid what I did will break it completely . . . both of us scared of each other."

"Does she know who Max Renaldo is?"

"No. I've never told anyone. There's no reason to. She and Wade share a special bond. I don't want that bond damaged."

"And as long as your mother was there to act as a buffer between you and Barbara, everything seemed fine."

"It was fine. Both of the children thrived."

"Besides this vision of Max, have you had other images or vivid recollections of traumatic events that happened when you were in the Philippines? It's common, we're finding. In the literature, it's called a *flashback* now."

"Nothing as vivid as this. Occasionally, I'll have a nightmare. I don't remember them, but I'll wake up crying or in a cold sweat. Sudden loud noises still startle me. The Fourth of July week is always the worst. When I feel jumpy, I use the techniques you taught me to get through it. Sometimes it helps."

"Except for this recent episode, have you noticed an increased nervousness in yourself—say, over the last year?"

Margie thought back to last summer and the year leading up to her mother's death. "Wade told me a few times I was being irritable and short with the children. I thought I was overtired, and you know how kids are . . . they *can* be irritating. I had a checkup with Dr. Middleton, who didn't find anything wrong. He prescribed Valium and told me to get some extra sleep."

Dr. Garber jotted notes. "I suspect this crisis has been a while in coming, and it was precipitated by your mother's death. I'd like to speak to the whole family together, and with Barbara alone, and then with the three of you. How much have you told the children about your past?"

"They know that Wade was a journalist during the war. He's told them some stories about when he was in Europe. They know I was a nurse and worked for the Red Cross. Neither one of us has ever mentioned the Philippines. When you talk to the children, I'd rather you not mention it. They don't need to know about those horrors."

Dr. Garber met with Barbara twice that week, and Margie watched her daughter for clues of what they might be discussing. The image of her wielding an iron skillet at her daughter wouldn't leave her thoughts.

She said to Wade, "Every time she thinks about me, it's what she'll remember."

"Margie, it was a natural response. You thought she was an intruder."

"But why wouldn't I recognize my own daughter?"

In her mind, she worried it would happen again, and she agonized—was she a danger to her daughter? Should she have given Barbara up while she was still a newborn and before Wade had a chance to fall in love with her, as Gracie had suggested? She quickly dismissed that thought. Despite the harsh images Barbara's presence had the potential to evoke, Margie loved her, and would do whatever was needed to protect her.

Wade canceled his weekend commitment at the Delta Ray. He left for work later in the morning and came home earlier in the evening. Even Gary hung out around the house more instead of playing with his friends out in the fields. Barbara stayed in her room most of the time. Margie saw her reading a catalog, but her daughter didn't tell her what it was about.

Dr. Garber called Barbara, Margie, and Wade in for a group session. They gathered at the same round table where Margie had sat years ago while trying to come to terms with her own depression. Barbara, looking afraid, kept glancing at her parents, and Wade kept folding and unfolding his hands, while Margie tried not to think about those conversations from the past. The catalog Barbara had been reading sat in front of Dr. Garber.

He surveyed the group. "Why all the glum faces? No one is on the way to the gallows. We've all done some good work here."

Margie felt her shoulders relax, and Wade's hands quieted.

"I've consolidated my notes, and with your permission, Wade, I got copies of Barbara's school records. As I'm sure you know, her IQ is right up there. She's accomplished in everything she does. It's my opinion that the high school program here in Little River is not going to be enough of a challenge for her. There's a private school in East Lansing that's affiliated with Michigan State. The name is Lake Charles Academy. I think she may benefit greatly from their program. They're selective about who they admit, and the academics are rigorous. Almost a hundred percent of their graduates are accepted at the top-tier universities."

Margie saw the color drain from Wade's face. He said, "Send her away to school?" He turned to Barbara. "What do you think, honey?"

"Well." Her voice sounded tiny. "I've read through the catalog. Some of the students do research in the university's biology labs, Dad. That would be so cool. They have a good music department too. Maybe I could learn to play the harp. I've always wanted to try it. The campus is on a lake, and there are canoes."

He said to Dr. Garber, "Isn't there anything else we can do? She's only fourteen."

"According to the tests I've given her, she's a mature fourteen, and she'll be fifteen in November. As an alternative, you can keep her home and supplement her academics with classes at U of M. She needs to be challenged academically. It's your decision to make, but my recommendation is to consider the private school."

Margie was hearing what Wade was not, that for the mother-daughter relationship to work, there needed to be some distance between them. A private school only an hour away seemed like a solution, but she wondered if Barbara would feel pushed out. She asked, "Would you be okay living away from home, Barbara?"

"I think so. I'd like to see the campus."

"I don't know," Wade resisted. "Maybe next year."

Dr. Garber sat back in his chair. "Give it some thought. I can make an appointment for a campus tour and a meeting with the headmistress. I know her personally. She's a wonderful woman—a Ukrainian and a survivor of the Holocaust."

A flicker of realization came into Wade's eyes, and Margie felt another level of relief. A woman who'd survived a prison camp knew the struggles of former internees and their families.

After two weeks of tours, testing, and interviews, and the family debating the pros and cons, and upon Dr. Garber's recommendation, Barbara was accepted to start the fall semester at Lake Charles Academy. Margie felt heartened by Barbara's interest and excitement as they bought clothing and assembled supplies.

There were tears in Wade's eyes when he hugged her good-bye. Margie felt sad too, and on the drive home she tried to soothe their gloom. "It's only an hour's drive. She'll be home every time we turn around." However, in reality the emotion she felt most was relief, a release from the daily reminder that deep down she had a dark core, an evil side that could be triggered, given the right circumstance.

CHAPTER 30

Little River, 1996

In Memory of Wade Francis Porter, Margie read on the small card to be given out at today's service. She had known this day was coming. Wade was eighty-five, and his heart had been weak for a few years, but foreknowledge didn't make the day any easier to face. She heard Gary's car in the driveway and got up to unlock the door. Catching her reflection, she saw a pouf of cotton-white hair, a stark contrast to her black dress—one attached to so many sad memories.

Gary, at forty-six, still moved with the grace of an athlete. He taught mathematics and coached football and basketball at Little River's new high school. On this cold November morning, ice crystals glittered on the shoulders of his charcoal topcoat. A blue plaid scarf circled his neck, and leather gloves covered his hands. The look on his face reflected the sadness she felt.

"You're late," she said.

"The roads are bad."

"Is Barbara here yet?"

"No. Her flight was canceled. She got on another one and should be here soon." Gary brought Margie's coat from the closet. "Mom, we've got to go." He held out her coat.

A sudden wave of weariness swept over her, and she couldn't make her feet move. "Promise you won't leave me alone?"

"Not for a second. Please, put this on."

He helped her shrug into the long, heavy garment. She arranged a silk scarf inside the collar, then grappled with the buttons, her fingers stiff and moving slowly. She wavered on her feet.

Gary gathered her into his arms and held her close. She buried her face in the rough fabric of his coat and wept. They stood clutched together, mother and son, wishing away the hours ahead and longing for a rewind of the clock.

With Gary on one arm and his wife, Liz, on the other, Margie entered the church's vestibule, which was crowded with sad-faced people brushing sleet from their dark coats and out of their hair, mumbling softly to her: *I'm sorry for your loss. He had a good, long life. I loved his music. I didn't know he was a war correspondent until I read his obit. You probably don't remember me—Wade called me Kodak.* Margie drew a sharp breath, and her eyes searched this man's face, remembering their meeting in Wade's shack in Santo Tomas.

She fell into the arms of Barbara's daughter, Jillian, a pediatrician, newly pregnant, and married to Shane, who stood beside her. They had driven from Kalamazoo, where they had both recently joined a practice of young physicians. "Mom should be here soon, Grandma. Her flight was supposed to land half an hour ago. Did she tell you Dad's in Beijing? He's sorry he can't make the funeral. He sends you his love."

The smell of flowers was intense and the music a lament. Gary guided Margie up the aisle and placed her in the first pew, where the family congregated. In front of the altar stood Wade's casket, handsome and substantial. The service started, but there was still no sign of Barbara.

The black-robed minister described Wade as a faithful husband, a loving father and grandfather, a brave war correspondent, a talented editor, and a mentor of young musicians. Margie nodded her agreement, and then added in her own mind—*a provider of food in the face of starvation, of comfort in those years of deprivation, and of support in the war's long aftermath. He was a good man.*

A hymn interrupted her reverie, and the congregation filed out. The family gathered around the casket to say their last good-byes. Gary slipped his arm around her waist, and feeling light-headed, she leaned against him. She wanted to go home; she wanted to sleep, but she dutifully and numbly attended the graveside service and then brunch at the Riverside restaurant.

The day blurred. She remembered talking to her brother, Frank. He had sold his veterinary practice to his son, Billy, a decade ago, and he and Irene were world travelers, having sailed into almost every cruise port. Gracie was there. Kenneth had died a few years ago, and she had recently moved to a condo in Ann Arbor. Margie clung to her friend, and they both murmured they didn't see each other often enough. Margie looked around for the man called Kodak, but he wasn't there. Nor was Barbara. Jillian said her plane had been diverted to Chicago, and she had rented a car to drive the four hours to Little River.

Windshield wipers slapped at the drizzle as Gary's car sloshed through the streets. Liz turned to Margie in the backseat. "Can't I talk you into coming home with us, Mom? The twins are there.

They will be going back to college in the morning. I fixed up the guest room for you."

Margie didn't want to be anybody's guest today, and as much as she loved Seth and Eric, she wanted to be alone with her memories. "Thank you, but I'd like to go home."

Gary walked her to her door and helped her over the threshold. "Are you sure you're okay? I don't like leaving you alone."

She patted his arm. "I know you're concerned, but I'm very tired. I want to lie down."

His face was puffy, his eyes weary and indecisive. "All right. I'll stop by later."

She hung her damp coat on a hook in the kitchen to dry and changed into warm pull-on sweats. She took her wedding picture off the mantel and studied it, Wade radiant and she seven months pregnant, but barely showing. Exhausted, she lay on the bed, covered up with a quilt, and hugged the picture to her heart.

What was Wade thinking the last time he closed his eyes? About his parents and sister Carol, who had preceded him in death? The honky-tonk tunes he strummed on his guitar, or the Brahms's sonatas he played on the piano? Did he regret he had never written the novel he had planned to, or built his dream house on his grandfather's land on the shores of Lake Michigan?

Neither sleep nor rest came, and her memories continued to churn. She wanted to look through her photo album to see the pictures of him as a young man, and to read the letters he'd written that were stored upstairs in a hatbox. Her grip tight on the handrail, she climbed the steep stairs, taking a long time to get to the top.

The central hall opened to three bedrooms and a bathroom. The floors were hardwood smoothed from use, and the walls wavy from layers of paint. A leak in the roof left a stain on the ceiling, and a few months ago Gary had warned her about the upcoming expense. She and Wade would be better off in a condo, he had urged. A new development was opening near his house.

In the front bedroom, an old flowered rug, still rich in color and soft underfoot, covered a section of floor, damping its squeaks. Her grandmother's cherry highboy and four-poster bed had gracefully aged to a satin patina, and a white chenille spread covered the mattress. Sheer curtains framed tall windows, and roll-down shades provided privacy.

Breathless from the climb, she sat on the bed. This room had been Wade's and hers since early in their marriage until after Mama died and they moved to the bedroom downstairs. Her cedar chest sat under the window. The lid felt heavier than she remembered and she dug through layers of wool sweaters and blankets until she found the hatbox. She placed it on the bed along with the photo album from the bottom drawer of the highboy. Turning on the lights and peeling back the chenille bedspread, she made herself a nest of pillows and quilts and crawled into bed. She heard the cuckoo bird in the clock that hung on the wall by the kitchen chirp four times as she lifted the hatbox lid.

Her four military medals sat on top of a pile of letters, photos, and military papers. She opened each small leather box and inspected the medal inside, remembering how faint with fatigue she had been when they were presented. Fifty years ago, she had chucked the medals rudely into the hatbox, but seeing them now, she felt a reverence for them and the service they represented. She put them aside and continued to search.

The string of pearls from Royce had dulled, as had her memory of him, and Abe's pilot's ring had tarnished. She didn't want these brave young men who had died serving their country to be forgotten. It shouldn't be so. She picked up a fountain pen and read the inscription: *To Helen. Happy Birthday. Love, Mabel.* Tears sprang to her eyes. Maybe this wasn't such a good idea.

She slid the mahogany ring Wade had made for her while at Santo Tomas over the knobby knuckle of her little finger. The finish had aged to a sheen that added depth to the intricate carving. How many hours had he worked on it, hungry, and hunched in his bamboo hut, in love and dreaming of marrying her, while she held back?

The ink had faded on the letters he had written while they were engaged, while he was still in the Philippines. She leaned closer to the lamp to read his loving words. She'd had doubts then and wondered, now, if he had sensed her uncertainty. Self-reproach stabbed her, and she wished she could have returned his feelings during those times when they had nothing else.

Her passion for him came later. After Gary's birth, feelings ignited that surprised and exhilarated both of them. Days filled with warm embraces, knowing smiles, and a desire to be closer preceded passion-filled nights. In time, their love mellowed and deepened. Happy memories of those good years swirled in her head, and she dozed.

Sometime later she heard a voice, a one-sided conversation—Barbara talking on a telephone. Margie opened her eyes, not sure where she was at first, then recognized her upstairs bedroom. Letters were strewn around her, and the photo album lay open on the end of the bed. Sitting up, she quickly tried to stuff her things back in the hatbox.

Barbara came into the bedroom looking travel weary, her dove-gray slacks and coral silk blouse deeply creased and her chin-length hair tucked behind her ears, the front mostly silver-white now. She had flown in from Los Angeles, where she was a professor of neuroscience at the University of Southern California.

"I'm sorry, Mom. Did I wake you? I was talking to Gary. He asked how you were. I told him you were asleep."

Margie welcomed her with a warm embrace. "I was worried about you. You must be exhausted. Are you hungry?"

"No. I got a hamburger on the road. Are you okay?"

"I am now that you are here. It's so good to see you, Barbara."

"I'm glad to be home. I'm sorry I missed Dad's funeral. I feel awful about it. Gary said he died in his sleep."

"He did." Margie had thought over Wade's last night alive, wondering if she had missed any indication of his impending death. Slowly he had been getting weaker, but there were no overt clues. "He just didn't wake up."

They both dried tears, and Barbara helped her mother repack the hatbox with the letters and pictures. She picked up the military medals and curiously examined them. "What are these?"

"Just some of my things. They're not important." Not wanting to open the door to that part of her life, Margie tried to close the cases, but Barbara held on to the Bronze Star, admiring its weight and luster.

Turning it over, she read the inscription aloud: "Heroic or Meritorious Achievement, Marjorie Olivia Bauer." With puzzlement, she asked, "This is yours?"

Resigned that her past, at least in part, was going to come to light, Margie replied, "Yes. There are some things that happened long ago that Dad and I never talked about."

Barbara carried the hatbox and the photo album downstairs. She placed them on the kitchen table, then brewed a pot of herbal tea.

Margie contemplated how much of her life in the Philippines to reveal as she sliced apples and uncovered a plate of shortbread a neighbor had brought over. She removed the four medals from the hatbox and placed them on the table.

Over a cup of hot tea, she told Barbara about being an army nurse in the Philippines, working in the field hospitals on Bataan and in the tunnels on Corregidor. Barbara watched her face as if she were a stranger, but then, maybe in many ways she was.

After listening intently, Barbara asked, "Why did you keep it a secret?"

"Because, we were told not to talk about it. Not that I wanted to, anyway. It was a bad time. We were under constant fire with little food and few medicines. I scrimped, scratched, and fought with one goal in mind—to keep my patients and myself alive."

The experience had left its mark. Even now, half a century later, the faces of the men she cared for sometimes floated through her dreams, and, occasionally, a blast from a bomb would jerk her breathless out of sleep. On those nights, Wade would hold her until she calmed. How much she was going to miss him!

Barbara held up the Philippine Defense Medal, and the American Pacific Campaign Medal. "What did you go through to be awarded these?" She put them down and picked up the Presidential Unit Citation. "That time when I was fourteen, Mom—could you have been having a flashback?"

Margie had not anticipated that question. Surprised, she snapped, "I told you then how much you frightened me. I thought you were an intruder. Don't go reading more into it. What could you possibly know about flashbacks?"

"A lot. In grad school, I researched post-traumatic stress disorder. I learned flashbacks are immensely more powerful than a simple remembrance. There's a neurological basis for them, an adrenalin surge and an oversecretion of stress hormones—a double whammy. I was curious, because of you, and what I'd seen—your nightmares, sleeplessness, hypersensitivity, and how sometimes you seemed to be in another world. You fit the profile of a person with PTSD, and I suspected some sort of trauma in your past." Barbara gestured at the medals. "But not this. I never guessed this. I thought I had something to do with your nervousness, the way you pushed me away when I lived at home."

"That's poppycock," Margie said, her heart racing. "So I had nightmares. If you had seen what I had seen, you would have had nightmares too. If you thought I avoided you, it was all in your imagination." Margie felt her jaw clench. Why couldn't she tell Barbara the truth and end this charade? She blurted out, "From the minute I first held you, I loved you more than I was able to show. I've always found it hard to say those words. I can't help it." Bursting into tears, she ran to the bathroom.

Barbara followed and knocked on the door. "Mom, I'm sorry. I didn't mean to make you cry. The day is sad enough without this. Is there something I can do to make you feel better?"

Margie struggled to compose herself; her usually tightly held emotions were close to the surface today. She took a few deep breaths before opening the door. "No. It's me, not you. I know I hold back my feelings, but I've tried to be a good mother."

"You are. You've always been supportive. You talked me through some bad times of my own. Remember when my old fiancé broke off our engagement? I was devastated. You were there when I needed you." Barbara put her arm around her mother's shoulder. "Come back to the kitchen. We can look through your photo album. I saw a picture of Uncle Frank and Dad hanging diapers on a clothesline. Were they mine or Billy's?"

Slowly turning the pages of the old album, they poured over grainy gray pictures and reminisced about long-ago Christmases, birthdays, and vacations they'd taken on the shores of Lake Michigan. Margie found the activity soothing, and she said, "Wade loved his grandpa's cabin. He was always relaxed there. It was where he wrote some of his best love songs."

Barbara said, "I remember falling asleep in the bunk bed in the back bedroom, listening to the waves of Lake Michigan pounding the shore, and Dad composing his music. I've got his songs on CDs. They take me back."

Coming to the end of the album, Barbara reached into the hat-box for more pictures. The conversation reverted back to Margie's early days in the Philippines. She told Barbara about her high school sweetheart, Abe, and his heroic death. And then about Royce and her best friend, Evelyn, and the good times they'd had in prewar Manila. "It was a beautiful city. They called it the Pearl of the Orient, but after the bombs, there wasn't much beauty left. Our lives got dangerous then."

Barbara's look grew pensive. "How did you handle the fear of being so close to the fighting?"

"Oh, Barbara. There was no time for fear. We lived in the moment. The wounded didn't ever stop coming. We just took care of what was in front of us."

"Was Dad there too? Is that where you met him?"

Margie blew across the surface of her tea while contemplating how veiled she could be. "No, we met later. He was transferred from London to Manila just before the Japanese attacked the Philippines. He was living on a university campus when we met. I spent a little time there. I was lonesome, and he was from Little River. It didn't take long for us to become good friends."

Barbara's eyebrows shot up in surprise. "Please tell me it wasn't the University of Santo Tomas!"

Margie's breath caught. "How do you know about Santo Tomas?"

"When I was researching post-traumatic stress, I read several case studies of men and women held in prison camps during World War II. Santo Tomas was a camp in Manila for civilians rounded up by the Japanese. I interviewed one of the internees. I know a group of nurses were held there. Tell me it wasn't you."

Margie said softly, "Well, there you go. Now you know."

"Oh my lord! You and Dad!"

Margie saw Barbara's distress and reached across the table to squeeze her hand. "It wasn't as bad as the camps where the Japanese imprisoned the soldiers."

"Don't make it sound less horrible than it was, Mom. I know it was an ugly, dirty place, and the internees died of disease and starvation. This answers so many questions—why all the jitteriness, and the fear of loud noises, why all those acres of gardens, all the canning and preserving, and neither one of you ever throwing out a morsel of anything edible." Barbara sat back in the chair and sighed. "It's why you founded the Abundant Harvest Food Pantry, isn't it? I always wondered why you worked so hard for so little in return."

Margie studied her clueless daughter's face. "Little in return? You're so wrong. I worked hard because I had a hunger inside me that no amount of food could satisfy. I found relief from it by feeding others. I got more out of the food pantry than I ever put into it."

There were tears in Barbara's eyes. "Why didn't you tell me?"

"Because you wouldn't have listened. Nobody did. When we came home, nobody wanted to hear what we nurses had been through. We were expected to carry on from where we left off— get married, have our babies, support our husbands' careers. That's what I tried to do, but I had a bad time for a while." She began picking up the papers strewn around.

Barbara gathered up the pictures, and finding two stuck together, she carefully peeled them apart. She scanned them quickly, but then studied one more closely. She pointed to the man standing next to Evelyn. "Who is this?"

Margie glanced at the picture and felt her skin grow clammy. She thought she had destroyed all the pictures of Max. "He was a friend of Evelyn's. I don't remember his name." She tried to take the picture from Barbara, but she wouldn't let it go.

Barbara stared at the picture while running her fingers through the silver streak in her hair. She turned it over and read aloud,

"Evelyn and Max before our wild ride in a *banca*. Sierra Madre, 1941." She sat back, frowning and chewing on her lower lip.

Knowing her sharp-minded daughter would soon deduce her secret, Margie swallowed dryly and steeled herself for a torrent of questions.

Barbara held the picture up to the light. "That silver streak in his hair, those hypnotic eyes—even that haughty expression. He could be my brother . . . or given the timing, my father?" She reeled around to face Margie.

She cringed under her daughter's accusing gaze. "I have no idea what you're talking about. Wade is your father, and don't you ever forget that!"

Barbara held the picture closer to Margie's face. "Look at this and tell me I'm not a dead ringer for this guy." She got up to pace around the kitchen, and Margie could almost see the wheels turning in her head.

Coming back to the table, Barbara said gently, "No one would blame you under the circumstances. It would be natural to seek a little pleasure—"

"Pleasure!" Margie blurted out. "There was nothing pleasurable or consensual—" Her hand flew to cover her mouth.

Barbara blanched, and she quickly came to Margie's side.

Margie pushed her away with a slap of her hand. "Don't touch me!"

Barbara stepped back. "I'm sorry. Please forgive me. I didn't know—not for sure."

Margie felt like every nerve in her body was firing, and she ached for the comfort of Wade's arms. Barbara approached her again, and Margie allowed her embrace.

Barbara's voice quavered. "I've suspected for a long time that you had been badly hurt—I didn't know how or when. I'm the result of a rape by this man, aren't I?"

Voiceless, Margie nodded.

"Did Dad know?"

"I never told him." Margie's heart went out to her daughter, whose life had just turned upside down. "I never meant for you to know either."

Barbara's voice turned hard. "It's a good thing you didn't tell me earlier. I might have found a gun and shot the son of a bitch."

Margie's head jerked at the venom she heard in Barbara's voice. "No—no. You have to live with yourself, Barbara. No matter how evil the situation, no matter how beaten down you are, no matter how justifiable an action might seem, you lose precious years trying to reconcile what you did."

Barbara's gaze was long and appraising. Margie shrank back, anticipating her next question.

Barbara asked, "What happened to him?"

Margie felt her fingers curl into fists. "He died. The Japanese were lobbing shells into the camp. A wall fell, and one side of his head was crushed."

Barbara's face crumbled again with emotion, and Margie reached for her daughter's hand. "Don't mourn him, Barbara. The worst of him is gone, and the best of him lived on in you for Wade to nurture into the wonderful person you are. Celebrate the beauty that blossomed from that dark deed."

Barbara dried her eyes. "Is that even possible?"

"Yes. I'm telling the truth as I see it now."

For Margie, the horrors of all that had happened inside the barbed wire and brick confines of Santo Tomas Internment Camp had faded to a shadow in the light of the resulting goodness—Barbara, brilliant and beautiful; Jillian, equally stunning and nurturing the next generation; and her passion and saving grace, the Abundant Harvest Food Pantry, still feeding hundreds of hungry people.

The back door opened, and Gary entered the kitchen, his snow-covered boots leaving tracks on the floor. He dropped his coat on the back of a chair. "I've been trying to call, but the lines are down." He kissed Margie's cheek and hugged Barbara hello. "How are you two holding up?"

Barbara said, her voice husky with emotion, "We're okay. We've just been reminiscing about Dad."

Margie went to the stove to brew another pot of tea. She knew over the next few days Barbara would pepper her with questions. Could she change her old ways and be honest and open? Could she love Barbara without fear and hesitation? She wondered if she could foster the mother-daughter closeness she had been denied for so many decades. Would Barbara even reciprocate? She handed Gary a mug of tea and nudged a plate of shortbread toward him.

He said, "Dad and I had a heart-to-heart a couple weeks ago. He said then he felt the end was near. He was worried about you, Mom. I reassured him that you would never be left alone. He seemed at peace with that. He was so weak and tired. I think he was ready to let go."

The three sat quietly, listening to the tick of the clock.

Gary's focus went to the medals lying on the table. He picked up the Bronze Star and admired it. "This is the fourth-highest combat medal awarded, you know. Is this Uncle Frank's? I knew he was a medic. I didn't know he was decorated." His eyes widened when he read the inscription on the back. *Heroic or Meritorious Achievement, Marjorie Olivia Bauer.* "This is yours?"

Barbara's and Margie's eyes locked. Out of habit, she quickly looked away; then she forced herself to glimpse up and hold the gaze. The look on Barbara's face was warm and inviting. So, it wasn't too late to change old ways. Keeping Gary in suspense, they both smiled.

"Mom?" Gary said again.

She blinked and glanced at Gary, seeing a quizzical look on his face.

"Yes, it's mine. There are a few things I need to tell you."

ACKNOWLEDGMENTS

A sincere thank-you to those who offered their help and encouragement: to my daughter, Emily, who read multiple drafts, and whose delusions of grandeur kept me writing; and to my family, neighbors, and book-club friends, who read early drafts and weren't afraid to tell me what they didn't like. A special thank-you to my husband, who kept me fed and watered during my long sessions at the computer. A grateful shout-out to the editors and designers who supported me through my long journey to publication, each adding their magic touch to my story: Kathy Fitzgerald, Claudia Fulshaw, Linda Hobson, Carin Siegfried, and Susan Warren. A special thanks to Phyllis Wilson for lending me her father's World War II journal. And of course, I'm indebted to the talented and hardworking editors from Lake Union Publishing, Terry Goodman and Melody Guy. And to copyeditor Michael Trudeau.

A NOTE FROM THE AUTHOR

The characters in *A Pledge of Silence* are fictitious, but the incidents they experienced were taken from historical records, oral descriptions, and written accounts of the nurses who served in the Philippines during World War II. I purposely blurred some facts, however, to keep the story from becoming convoluted. For instance, the army nurses and navy nurses were two distinct groups with their own chains of command, though I didn't make a clear division between them. Additionally, there were two field hospitals on Luzon, not one, and two main prison camps that interned the nurses, Santo Tomas and Los Baños.

Of the real-world nurses, ninety-nine were evacuated from Manila to the Bataan Peninsula. Twenty-four escaped from Corregidor on submarines or small aircraft that slipped through the Japanese blockades, and the remaining seventy-five became prisoners of war. The average age of those interned at the beginning of the war was thirty-one years old. The average weight loss during captivity was thirty-two pounds. Though some of the nurses were wounded during the bombing and shelling raids, none died from their wounds, or from malnutrition or mistreatment while in the prison camps.

For those readers who are intrigued by my fictional story and would like an in-depth nonfictional account of the POW nurses, I suggest reading *We Band of Angels* by Elizabeth M. Norman, *All This Hell* by Evelyn M. Monahan and Rosemary Neidel-Greenlee, and *Pure Grit* by Mary Cronk Farrell, written for young adults. All three books include interviews with the nurses and extracts from their diaries, journals, and letters. In 1995 at age 81, Dorothy Still Danner, a World War II navy nurse, published *What a Way to Spend a War*, a fine memoir of her years in the Philippines and her dramatic rescue in February 1945 from Los Banos prison camp.

The war didn't stop at liberation, or VE Day, or VJ Day for the nurses who spent years as prisoners of war. Many lived their entire lives with the aftereffects of starvation, deprivation, and fear. But, they were women and nurses, and they were expected to be silent about what they had seen—or done—and to carry on as if nothing had happened. Some did, but many struggled like my heroine, Margie.

For more information, and a look through Margie's scrapbook documenting her years in the Philippines, visit my website, www.apledgeofsilence.com.

ABOUT THE AUTHOR

Flora J. Solomon and her husband relocated in 2004 from Michigan's winter wonderland to the beautiful North Carolina coast. Besides reading and writing, she enjoys dinners out with her husband, visits with her children and grandchildren, a hard-won tennis match, and an occasional round of golf.

DISCUSSION QUESTIONS

1. Margie thought of herself not as a hero, but as a survivor, doing only what had to be done. Frank saw his actions as a medic heroic. Do you agree with their self-assessments? What is the difference between a survivor and a hero?

2. Both Margie and Frank came home from the war physically exhausted and psychologically damaged. How did their homecomings differ? How did society's expectations for their futures differ?

3. Dr. Garber counseled Margie to consider her sufferings as well as her accomplishments when deciding what to do with her life. He said turning her misfortunes into triumphs was a way to conquer them. How was Margie able to do this?

4. Do you think Margie was ever able to forgive herself for her pivotal and malevolent deed during the Japanese shelling of Santo Tomas? How would one rationalize such an act?

5. Which nurse—Margie, Evelyn, or Gracie—do you think displayed the greatest strength of character? Why did you choose her?

6. The experiences of the POW nurses was generally unknown until the mid-1980s. Why do you think their story remained obscure for so many decades? What was happening in the 1980s that brought their story to light?

7. How would women's roles in the military today be different if the valor of the women who served during World War Two had been recognized and valued?

8. While hundreds of Santo Tomas internees died during internment, all of the real-world nurses returned home. What factors might have played a role in their 100 percent survival rate?

9. The opportunities for women expanded during World War II but were suppressed again in the 1950s. This is often cited as one root of the second wave of the women's liberation movement. How would that be so? Where are we now in this cycle? What might provide the next push for women's equality?

10. Upon repatriation, military POWs were required to sign a document stating they would keep silent about their experience in the camps. What was the purpose of it? Did the purpose justify the psychic havoc it caused?